Praise for
The Carrick Hall N

"Sarah Arthur creates a world that embeds bot
which will captivate readers both young and o.

—LEAH PORTER, 2021–22 Michigan Teacher of the Year

"*Once a Queen* is reminiscent of beautiful books of magic written in the past, but it's also a fresh, delightful new tale for our wonder-hungry era. With a rich sense of place, vivid characters, a page-turning plot, and a redemptive theme about the healing of generational wounds, Sarah Arthur has created a story that lingers in the memory and shapes the soul long after reading the last page."

—MITALI PERKINS, National Book Award nominee

"Readers of Lewis and L'Engle, prepare to be enchanted. This is a captivating novel that will make you want to revisit the fantasy stories of your childhood."

—SARAH MACKENZIE, author of *The Read-Aloud Family*

"As soon as I started reading Sarah Arthur's book *Once a Queen,* I felt like a little kid again and I simply didn't want to stop reading. The detailed setting, the memorable characters, the mysterious storyline—everything comes together to create a generational book."

—SHAWN SMUCKER, author of *The Day the Angels Fell*

"*Once a Queen* is written in sumptuous language that makes this poet's heart sing. The magic here is palpable as Arthur deftly ferries readers from one world to another and back again with a wave of her pen. Best of all is the tenacity of hope woven throughout this tantalizing coming-of-age tale of a young girl bravely exploring her family's painful secret past in search of healing for them all in the present. This may be a fantasy, but it many ways it is all too real."

—NIKKI GRIMES, *New York Times* bestselling author

"*Once A Queen* is Sarah Arthur's love letter to great children's literature. Throughout this book, beginning with the title, one sees her great love for classic writers such as C. S. Lewis, J.R.R. Tolkien, and E. Nesbit. However, this book is no simplistic homage. Within these pages, Sarah Arthur tells her own unique tale, full of intrigue and wonder, which is sure to enchant the imagination of a new generation of young adults."

—DAVID BATES, co-host of the C. S. Lewis–themed podcast *Pints with Jack*

The Carrick Hall Novels

Once a Queen
Once a Castle

Once a
Castle

Once a Castle

 A CARRICK HALL NOVEL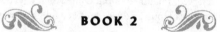

BOOK 2

SARAH ARTHUR

WATERBROOK

Trade Paperback ISBN 978-0-593-19448-5
Ebook ISBN 978-0-593-19449-2

The Library of Congress catalog record is available at
https://lccn.loc.gov/2024950784.

Printed in the United States of America on acid-free paper

waterbrookmultnomah.com

1st Printing

Interior art credit: lyotta © Adobe Stock Photos

Book design by Sara Bereta

For Abbie, the Elspeth to my Tilly:
Thanks for being my only sister.
Always. For keeps.

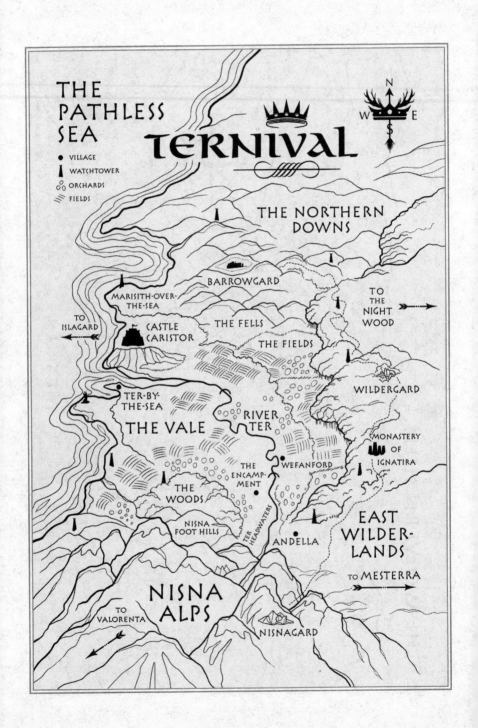

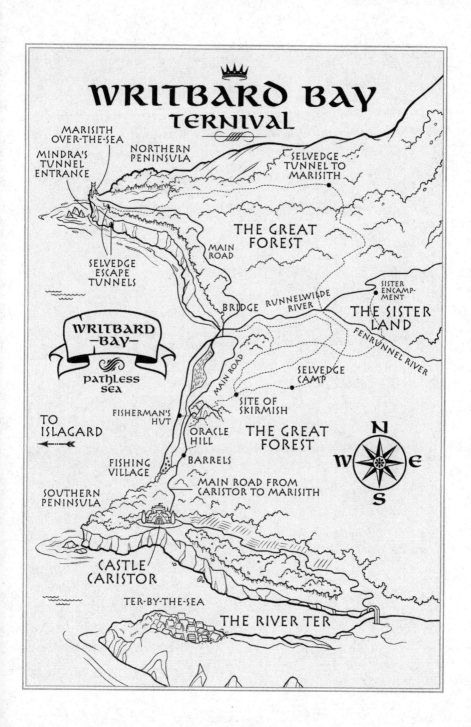

Cast of Characters

From Tellus (Earth)

THE ADDISON FAMILY

Frankie   oldest of five siblings; postgraduate student at Cambridge

Tilly (Matilde)   second-oldest sibling; works at Mrs. Rastegar's tea shop

Jack   middle sibling

Elspeth   second-youngest sibling

Georgie   youngest sibling

Holly (née Stokes)   Mum; housekeeper at Carrick Hall

Jim   Dad; head gardener at Carrick Hall

THE RASTEGAR/TABARI FAMILY

Professor Rastegar   owner, New Warren's bookshop; previously Iran's foremost expert on Shakespeare

Mrs. Rastegar   owner, Much Ado About Cream Puffs tea shop; maker of world-famous pastries

Arash Tabari   the Rastegars' grandson

Mahsa Tabari (née Rastegar)   the Rastegars' daughter; Arash's mum; expert weaver

THE JOYCE FAMILY

Eva Joyce   American graduate student; heiress to Carrick Hall

Gwendolyn Joyce (née Torstane)   Eva's mum; owner of Carrick Hall; archivist at Whitby College in Chicago

Robert Joyce   Eva's American dad; professor at Whitby College

AT CARRICK HALL

Ivy Fealston   retired housekeeper

Paxton   handyman and former chauffeur

THE HEAPWORTH FAMILY

Lord Edward   old family friend of the Torstanes; expert on medieval tapestries; father to Edward IV (Eddie), Charles, and Aurora

Charles   middle sibling; star cricket bowler

Aurora   youngest sibling; Elspeth Addison's best friend

From Ternival and Beyond

KEY CHARACTERS

The Fisherman   lives in a hut on Writbard Bay between Marisith and Caristor

Zahra the fisherman's granddaughter; only child of his late daughter

Goodwife (Goody) Pearblossom seller of vegetables and herbs from the village of Ter-by-the-Sea

Bem Goody Pearblossom's daughter

Goldleaf dryad; guide and mentor

THE SELVEDGE ARMY

Lord Bayard Chief Sentry of Ternival

Starwise centaur; counselor to the Chief Sentry

Fangard captain of the royal hounds; protector of Caristor

Vahrberg dwarf chieftain of Nisnagard

Hotosho, Leonora, Rushyon wolfhound scouts

Lepp young sentry; wounded in the attack on Caristor

Smithfield older sentry

Barkwhistler feisty groundhog with a unique vocabulary; sometimes called a whistle-pig

FROM TERNIVALI LEGEND AND HISTORY

Magister the World-Weaver; creator of Tellus, Mesterra, and countless other worlds

The Great Stag powerful being who watches over Mesterra and all its realms, especially its sovereigns

The Engela spirit beings who inhabit Inspiria, Magister's realm/palace beyond all worlds

Children of Tellus humans from Earth

First Queen of Mesterra former gardener at Carrick Hall and aunt to Stokes; summoned by Magister to steward Mesterra at its creation

The Wood-Carver husband to the First Queen

Mindra the Enchantress ancient enemy to all Children of Tellus; seeks the crown and gems of the First Queen; takes the form of a human

Stonefist one of Mindra's giants

The Three Queens Children of Tellus (Florence, Claire, and Annabeth) who restored the crown and gems and defeated Mindra. Their disappearance years later—together with the crown—has been a source of Ternivali speculation ever since.

FROM VALAN

The Weaver tapestry maker; stumbled through a portal into Valan with his wife and son

The Weaver's Son first sovereign of Valan

The Sentinel Valani prince in disguise; eventually king of Valan

Eryliessa refugee princess from Tarani; married the sentinel

Mirza great-grandson of Eryliessa and the sentinel-prince; aided Tarani in its war against a witch-queen; eventually king of Valan

Ziba wife to Mirza

Pejman oldest son of Mirza and Ziba

Navid middle son

Shahin youngest son

PART ONE

The sense that in this universe we are treated as strangers, the longing to be acknowledged, to meet with some response, to bridge some chasm that yawns between us and reality, is part of our inconsolable secret.

—"The Weight of Glory" by C. S. Lewis, 1941

And you? When will you begin that long journey into yourself?

—Attributed to Rūmī, thirteenth century

Chapter

1

The castle had appeared out of nowhere.

Jack Addison had hunted for geodes in this valley before, at least a hundred times. Normally the place contained only some scrubby underbrush and one small lake fed by a burbling stream, all encircled by stony bluffs. But today, at the far end of the lake, stood a castle.

And not just any castle. Boxy and unadorned, with sheer stone walls rising to high battlements, it had the same twelfth-century features as a fortress he'd visited on a class trip last term.

But this was no ruin. It was fully intact. In fact, it seemed to be inhabited. A wisp of smoke spiraled lazily from the highest battlement. A strange rumble echoed across the water, like someone rolling a cart across a stone courtyard. Back and forth, back and forth.

Jack began to edge around the lake toward the castle, following what looked like the familiar path. He felt slightly dizzy, like maybe he'd cracked his head harder while rock climbing yesterday than he'd realized. This couldn't be the same valley. He'd taken a wrong turn somewhere.

But no. There was the scree of fallen rocks where he'd found that simply spectacular geode last summer. There was the boulder where he'd eaten leftover fish-and-chips on Sunday. He'd chucked the newspaper into the shrubs, he remembered now. If it was the same valley, wouldn't it still be there?

It was. After a brief scramble, he found the newspaper balled up nearby. Another wave of dizziness swept over him. He glanced back and forth between the smoke curling from the battlement and the paper in his palm.

Same newspaper. Same valley. But castles didn't just grow from the ground.

One lone arrow slit toward the topmost battlement seemed to stare at him like an unblinking reptilian eye. It made him feel small and vulnerable, which he didn't often feel these days—a mighty growth spurt after his thirteenth birthday had taken care of that. But now he felt tiny as an insect, easily crushed.

The rumble grew louder for a moment, paused, then resumed, a little deeper now. Jack stayed put, watching warily, until curiosity drove him forward again.

Now he was in the castle's very shadow, its grim exterior rising to an impossible height. As he drew nearer, a nauseating smell hit him: an organic sourness that reminded him of wet dog and sweaty PE clothes, but worse. The rumble shook the ground beneath him, with more pauses filled by a strange whooshing, like enormous bellows.

For about ten seconds he considered retreating up the path that had brought him here. He'd climb back to the ridgeline that connected the high summit of Giant's Beacon to Table Mount and descend from there to Carrick Hall, his parents' workplace. He'd enter the normal chaos of the estate's kitchen, study his maps at the table, and regain his bearings over tea and scones.

But the castle wall was almost within reach now. Just a few more steps and he could confirm whether or not it was real. Plus, he was beyond range of the arrow slit, which gave him a sudden boldness. He reached out.

Real. He could feel the grit under his fingers, the clammy coolness. He could feel the rumble, too, vibrating through the rock, and smell the stench. The sound, at least, was coming from somewhere on the other side of the castle.

Jack stepped gingerly through the rubble at the base of the wall and made his way around the building, deep in shadow from the bluffs. As he turned the corner, he expected to find a portcullis or some other entrance, but instead, the route was blocked by what looked like massive lumpy earthworks, or like a section of bluff had crashed down against the castle wall. He could see no way around it either. The shadowed mound extended all the way to the bluff. He'd have to climb over it or take the long way around.

He decided to climb. But as he approached the mound, the stench grew so strong that he nearly retched. The rumble increased, like the earth itself was moving.

And then it was.

Right before his eyes, the top of the mound rose like an inflating zeppelin, with a thunderous rumble, and fell with a mighty whoosh. Then up and down again, up and down. For all the world as if the ground was snoring.

Jack froze. Heart racing, he scanned the mound from one end to the other. It couldn't be.

But it was.

Stretched out full-length on the valley floor, next to a castle that had appeared out of nowhere, lay a sleeping giant.

Arash would've warned the kid if he could.

From behind a large boulder, Arash had been watching the sleeping demon for at least ten minutes before the other kid had appeared. It was Jack Addison, from school. The stocky redheaded loner who was too cool for everyone. The outdoorsman who Arash had often seen wandering the Wolverns, like himself, except without a metal detector.

Clearly, the kid had no idea what was lying there.

Arash watched, horrified, as Jack walked right up to the gigantic demon. As if he meant to climb over it. *Stop. Run.* But the words wouldn't come. Not in English. Nor Farsi. Nor any other language he knew.

Plus, yelling would awaken the demon—and then what?

Jack suddenly backed away, realization dawning on his freckled face.

And that was when the demon stirred.

"Fee, fi, fo . . ." it mumbled, its voice like rocks tumbling over and over. "I smell . . ." The voice tapered off into a huge snore. Then the demon rolled over.

The entire valley shook. Boulders the size of postboxes careened down the cliffside. Dust filled the air, leaving a film on Arash's glasses. Then a great section of scree slid past his hiding place near the crevasse and roared to the valley floor. The noise rumbled across the Wolverns like a thunderstorm, leaving a silence broken only by an extended snore. The demon slept on.

But Jack—where was he? Crushed, surely. The demon had rolled away from the kid, but the falling scree had filled the passage from the cliffside to the castle wall. If Jack had even survived, his path was now blocked.

Arash wiped his glasses and looked again. Still no sign of Jack.

Trembling, Arash propped his metal detector against a nearby rock, adjusted his backpack, and made his way downward along a dry streambed toward the valley floor. It was slow going. The treacherous scree offered almost no solid footing. But before he'd gone more than a dozen steps, he heard muffled coughing. To Arash's relief, Jack staggered out from behind a pile of rocks, covered from head to toe in fine dust. He looked like the walking dead.

Jack stopped short at the sight of Arash. As they stared at each other, Arash pointed back over his own shoulder, toward the crevasse, then turned and began retracing his steps. Jack followed. When Arash reached the opening of the crevasse and began scrambling up into the narrow cleft, he looked back.

Jack had paused. His breath was coming fast, in shallow gasps. Arash motioned him to keep going. Jack gaped at him hollowly, then shook his head.

Puzzled, Arash looked up. Was there a snake or something? All he could see was the narrow slash in the rocks with perfectly spaced boulders for climbing, as if some ancient inhabitant had carved it for just this purpose. Hundreds of feet above them, a ribbon of blue sky shimmered.

Arash beckoned again. The kid shook his head—belligerently, this time—then turned and began picking his way back down the scree. Back toward the castle and the sleeping demon.

"Stop at once!"

They were the very words Arash wanted to yell. But they hadn't come from him. They'd come from another voice, cold and furious and female, somewhere high in the tower.

Both boys froze.

"Awake, worthless pile of filth!" bellowed the voice.

The huge demon stopped in mid-snore and rolled over again,

grunting. The ground trembled, and more rocks clattered down the cliffside, whizzing past Arash's head. Jack pitched forward to his knees, arms flailing.

"Smell that?" the enraged voice continued. "Children of Tellus, I'd wager my throne."

Jack stared at Arash, panic in his eyes. Then he clambered to his feet and half ran, half stumbled toward the crevasse.

Chapter

2

"Giants again," said Tilly's little brother Georgie. He sat contentedly at the breakfast table in the Addisons' cottage, slurping chocolate milk through a straw. Loudly. As only a nine-year-old can do. "That's what thunder is, you know. When giants play at ninepins."

"No, silly. That wasn't thunder." Tilly play-swatted the back of his head as she walked past his chair. "Just the crews getting ready down at the green. How much chocolate powder did you put in there, anyway?" She stood in front of the mirror and twisted her long dark hair into a messy topknot. She could just picture her sugar-hyped little brother terrorizing the village of Upper Wolvern while she was at work—on midsummer festival weekend, no less.

"It was, too, thunder," said Georgie, scowling. "Giant thunder."

"Your bow is all crooked," said their middle sister, Elspeth. The twelve-year-old came up behind Tilly and untied her apron strings with fastidious fingers.

"Wh—stop!" Tilly said, pulling away. "I'm fine."

"No, the bow was lopsided. You know how Mrs. Rastegar is. She'll want it to be just right." There were times when Elspeth's perfectionism was helpful—say, when cleaning Carrick Hall with their mum. But now was not one of those times.

"Well, hurry up, then," Tilly snapped. She stood, arms out, as Elspeth smoothed the strings and began a carefully executed bow.

"There'd better not be storms today. I need Eva's flight to be on time." Frankie, their oldest brother, strode into the kitchen. Tall, lean, and almost painfully nerdy, he wore his red bow tie and best blazer, with his fancy leather briefcase slung over one shoulder. Eva, his girl-friend, had given him the briefcase upon his acceptance into the doctoral program in theology at Cambridge. Elegant lettering, stamped across the front, read *Franklin J. Addison.*

He snatched a piece of toast from Georgie's plate and then stood next to Tilly at the mirror, straightening his bow tie with the other hand.

"That was mine!" Georgie protested.

Frankie took a huge bite. "There's more."

"The stag is watching, you . . . you *toast troll.*" Georgie stabbed a finger toward the framed sketch that hung over the kitchen sideboard. A leafy dryad and bright stag ran through a tangled forest toward the safety of a castle. Frankie himself had drawn it for his siblings as a Christmas gift several years before. To most people, it was just a fairy tale scene. But to the Addison siblings, it was part of a larger story—one that had come crashing into the real world. Many times, actually. And it could crash through again.

Frankie clutched his chest as if he'd been mortally wounded, then tossed the toast back onto his brother's plate. Georgie scowled and took an extra loud slurp of milk.

"Gah—Georgie! That's so annoying." Elspeth yanked Tilly's bow with frustration.

Tilly pulled away. "Stop. It's *fine,*" she snarled. The two sisters glared at each other. Elspeth tossed her dark hair—as long as Tilly's, if not longer—and plopped down at the table, arms crossed, face turned away.

Tilly sighed. When had they stopped getting along? They'd always been close, the only two sisters of the five siblings. From the time Elspeth could walk, she'd been Tilly's little companion, following her around like a smaller version of herself. But right around Elspeth's twelfth birthday, something had changed. She seemed determined to argue with Tilly about *everything*. But there was no time to fix whatever weirdness was going on right now.

"Where's Jack, anyway?" Frankie said.

"Up in the hills," Tilly replied. "He left early, I think."

"Playing at ninepins with giants," Georgie added with another slurp. "That's why it's so rumbly up there."

"Will you *stop* with the *slurping*?" hissed Elspeth.

"Well, I'm off," Frankie announced. "Train for London leaves in twenty minutes. Say goodbye to Jack for me."

"And say hi to Eva!" Tilly said.

"You can tell her yourself, remember?" Frankie smiled at her. "We'll be back later tonight. After we meet with the publisher for lunch, we'll wander a bit, have an early supper on our own somewhere. And then catch the six-fifty from Paddington Station. Eva wants to see Mrs. Fealston, of course."

"Oh, right . . ."

Mrs. Fealston, the ancient retired housekeeper of Carrick Hall, wasn't doing well these days. Not at all. Nobody wanted to admit it, but if Eva Joyce, heiress of the estate, didn't visit the manor house before returning to America, she might never see the beloved old woman alive again.

"I wish this was Eva's home already," Georgie said wistfully. "Do you think, this time, you'll pop the question?"

Frankie's neck turned crimson.

"Georgie!" Tilly admonished.

"What?" Georgie protested. "She'll say yes."

There was a brief pause. "Well, I'm off," Frankie repeated in a strangled sort of voice, then dashed out the door.

"What if she says no?" Elspeth looked at Tilly, wide-eyed.

"She won't," Tilly reassured her.

"But how does Frankie know? How does anyone know?"

"Maybe you just do."

"Oh, like you and Charles?" Just like that, Elspeth's tone had shifted to sarcasm.

Now it was Tilly's turn to blush. Heat raced from her neck to the tips of her ears. "Of course not. Nothing like that."

"I wager ten pounds Charles turns up at the tea shop this morning."

"To drop off his sister for weaving lessons," Tilly retorted. "And to pick up his dad's usual weekend order of pastries."

"So why doesn't Lord Edward do that himself?"

"What's gotten into you?" Tilly exclaimed. "Are you replacing Jack now as Smart-Aleck-in-Residence?"

Elspeth crossed her arms again and looked away.

"Right. I'm off too," Tilly said. "Georgie, behave yourself. No more chocolate milk. And if Jack isn't back before Elspeth's lesson, you'll have to come with her." Then to Elspeth: "See you at the shop."

As Tilly opened the door, a faint rumble rolled down the valley from the hills.

"I told you it was giants," Georgie said with a satisfied smirk.

He bent his head toward his straw—but quick as a flash, Elspeth snatched the glass away.

Chapter

3

When the giants came, it wasn't from the north, as expected. Sentries had been standing guard along the northern downs for years, waiting for the familiar rumble of massive feet. Yet the fells and fens had remained quiet.

No. This time, the giants came from the Pathless Sea. At night. By the light of a half-moon.

First it was just a whisper of unrest, out over the dark water. Zahra, the fisherman's granddaughter, sat up straight in the rickety boat and peered due west. This close to midsummer, sunrise over the mainland behind them would arrive early, in just a few hours, but the western sky was still dark. And yet something moved against the horizon. Something massive, obliterating the stars.

"Grandad," Zahra said.

He dozed at the oars. "Mm," he grunted.

"Something's in the west, over the sea. Coming this way."

"Ay." The old man shook himself awake. "Clouds, no doubt. This fine weather couldn't hold."

"Nay, Grandad. Something's out there, moving. Do you hear it?"

They sat perfectly still, ears trained from long practice to notice the least change in the air, the waves. There it was again, a strange rumble like breakers rolling over a sandbar. Otherwise, dead calm on every side.

The darkness against the western stars grew. It drew closer. First in a mass, now three distinct sections, like mountains or towers.

Suddenly the fisherman's body went rigid. "Haul in the nets, lass," he hissed. "Now!"

Zahra sprang to the side of the boat. They didn't often go night fishing anymore—not since Grandad's recent bouts of weakness, anyway. But it was a quiet night, and Zahra was nearly full-grown, able to haul in the nets and take her grandad's place at the oars when needed. Now she scrambled to bring in their catch—a good catch on an ordinary night—while the fisherman set the oars.

"But what is it, Grandad?" Zahra asked, her heart thundering. "Not a storm, surely? Nor ships, by the size of them."

"Hsst, lass! Not a sound. To shore with us, and quickly."

Zahra had barely dragged the nets above the waves before her grandad turned the boat and began long, sure strokes, skimming across Writbard Bay. It was all she could do to bring in the fish without the usual whacks and wallops of a good haul.

Over her shoulder, she could make out the three masses drawing steadily toward shore. It couldn't be a kind of creature or pod of creatures, could it? There was an intention in their movements, almost like striding. Purposeful. And by Zahra's reckoning, they were headed not for the lonely shingle where the fisherman's hut hugged the shore of the bay but rather for the southern peninsula. Where Castle Caristor stood.

Against the stars, one of the towering masses paused. Zahra wasn't certain, but a glowering malevolence seemed to turn in the boat's direction.

"Garn," came a mighty voice over the calm, calm waters. "D'ye hear that? Oars, methinks." A loud snort followed. "Fishermen, by the smell of 'em. And right close."

Zahra's throat squeezed tight. Grandad pulled the oars ever harder, silent and strong.

"Steady on, Stonefist," came a different voice. "No time for a snack. We've espied the castle. Why nibble when ye can feast?"

"But me belly's a-shrinkin'," whined the first voice.

There came a smack like a clap of thunder and a smothered roar of rage. "That'll learn ye to follow yer belly," growled a third, even fiercer, voice. "Steady on, and keep it quiet."

The three figures pressed on toward the tip of the southern peninsula while the fisherman powered the boat to shore. Within minutes, the weathered little craft scraped against the shingle, and grandfather and granddaughter leaped out. The fisherman took five steps, then sank to his knees.

"Grandad!" Zahra cried, grabbing him by the shoulders.

"Listen, child," gasped the old man. "Fly to Lord Starwise, as fast as ever you can. He'll be atop Oracle Hill on a night like this—already guesses that trouble's afoot, no doubt. Tell him he must warn the castle."

"But is it . . . Are they . . ."

"Ay, lass. *Giants are upon us.*"

Neither boy ever forgot that race up the crevasse.

Arash never forgot, because halfway up he realized he'd left behind his metal detector. His brand-new Garrett Infinium LS. One of the first-ever models that worked underwater. It'd been a surprise birthday gift from his mum and grandparents, who'd probably scrimped and saved for more than a year. According to the catalog, it was worth more than his grandfather's car. Guilt and shame might've overwhelmed Arash in this moment, if it weren't for the sheer terror of trying to survive.

So, he launched himself upward. He reached the top in under five minutes and collapsed near a shelf of rock, out of sight from the valley.

Jack, too, never forgot that race. It beat any recurring nightmare he'd ever had about getting stuck in an elevator or dragged underwater or swept along in the crowded London Underground. Normally he loved bouldering in the free air—just not in tight spaces. Never in caves or tunnels. And especially not in crevasses like this, which might close on him, pin him under a hundred ton of rock, crush the life from his lungs.

But he couldn't go back. The unthinkable waited down there. So somehow Jack kept climbing. Right hand up, grasp the ledge, then left knee up, and pull. Left hand up . . .

At one point, the crevasse became so narrow that the sides brushed against his shoulders. He closed his eyes. *Blue sky. Table Mount in high summer. The open fields near Carrick Hall. Swallows winging overhead, free and beautiful.* He deliberately dragged each breath in and forced it out, counting to twenty. Then thirty.

Eventually his breathing slowed. The rumbling below had stopped. The raging voice was now out of earshot, and the other kid had vanished over the clifftop. For all Jack knew, the kid was halfway to Upper Wolvern by now. Good. The last thing Jack needed was an eyewitness to his crippling claustrophobia. No doubt, the story would be all over the village by suppertime anyway.

Or no. The kid wouldn't tell. Jack had recognized him immediately: Arash Tabari, a classmate at Wolvern and grandson of the older couple who owned some shops in the village. Until a month or so ago, he'd played cricket for Wolvern, but otherwise Jack knew little about him. Arash kept his head down and his mouth shut. Come to think of it, Jack had never heard him speak a word—ever.

Plus, no one would believe a story like this.

Then again, Elspeth might. Even at twelve, she still accepted fairy tales as historical fact—including the stories that Frankie (Frankie— the grown-up!) told them about adventures in other worlds. And little Georgie, of course, believed everything. Then there was sixteen-year-old Tilly, Jack's oldest sister, who was so completely guileless that once, when they were small, Jack had convinced her to hide in the Hall's larder for hours because giants were on the loose.

No. It was Jack himself, the middle child, who normally wouldn't believe a story like this. Not unless he saw it with his own eyes.

Well, he'd seen it now.

He resumed climbing. Higher, higher, one ledge at a time, till he pulled himself over the top and collapsed in the open air.

He heard rustling. There was Arash, eyes wide, seated against a shelf of rock next to one of the many cairns that dotted the Wolverns. Neither of them spoke. They sat, chests heaving, staring into the sky.

But then, far below—from the valley that shouldn't have contained a castle and a giant—came another rumble.

They leaped to their feet and ran.

Chapter

4

"Hail, milord!"

Zahra attempted a curtsy, fighting a stitch in her side. She'd scrambled up the bluff and into the forest in less time than it took to clean a fish, but now she could barely move.

Lord Starwise—half man, half horse, majestic in strength and matchless in knowledge—was exactly where her grandad had guessed he'd be. He could often be found here, atop Oracle Hill, reading the pattern of the skies. But especially as midsummer drew near, when the veil between worlds was said to be thinner.

"Trouble from the west," said the centaur, his voice deep and wild. "That much the stars have spoken. But thou hast further news. Speak."

"Giants, milord. From the sea." Zahra tried to steady her voice. "Three of them, at least, wading against the tide. Grandad and I saw them ourselves as we were fishing the bay. They make for Caristor. He says to sound the alarm."

"From the sea, thou sayest." The centaur's usually calm face creased into a frown. "The oracle foretold the coming of the Children of Tellus, at which the hearts of mine grandsires rejoiced. And the Three Queens appeared, and the reign of peace began—which continues

still, despite the absence of a sovereign in Ternival these sixty years."
He paced forward and stood before Zahra like a towering giant him-
self, grim in the starlight. "Yet I knew it could not last. But this . . .
'Tis worse than I feared."

The centaur lowered his forelegs to the ground.

"Though many might think thee unworthy of such an honor,
Fisher Lass, and many a queen would envy thy chance, ride thou
must. For the sentries must know what thou hast seen, before the
hour is past. Quickly!"

Zahra scrambled onto the centaur's broad back. There'd be no
cantering in dignity like a fine lady: Her experience on horseback
was precisely nothing. She pressed against the centaur's torso and
clung tightly.

The centaur sighed. "Well, if that is thy best, at least thou shalt not
die. Ready thyself, Fisher Lass. For now, we *fly*."

Zahra never was certain how she survived that ride.

Starwise's hooves, it seemed, barely touched the ground. Now he
leaped from rock to rock, or careened across a clearing, or wove
through the darkened forest speckled with moonlight, untroubled by
tangled roots and vines. On and on he raced, cutting across the base
of the southern peninsula till he reached an open clifftop.

Ahead rose Castle Caristor, towering over the mouth of the River
Ter. Zahra had never been this close. Normally she and Grandad kept
to their isolated hut on Writbard Bay, away from public spaces. They
never even went to market. Instead, they entrusted their fish to a
neighbor who took it to Ter-by-the-Sea and returned with any meager supplies they could afford. But it had been her mother's dream to
one day visit the ancient seat of Ternival's sovereigns. To see its tapestries for herself. To bring, with her own hands, one of the beautiful
weavings she and Zahra had crafted by firelight, before fever had stolen her away.

It would never happen now.

To Zahra's right, rocky headlands jutted out into the Pathless. And rounding the farthest point were three dark figures, tall as mountains.

The centaur broke into a full gallop. Zahra no longer tried to keep her head up but pressed her face against his back and prayed not every bone in her body would break when she fell. But somehow she didn't fall. The trees flashed by in the moonlight. *I shall never forget this night as long as I live. If I live.*

Before them loomed the castle wall with its ornamented gates. As Starwise skidded to a halt, a mastiff rose in the torchlight.

"Lord Starwise," said the dog in a deep voice, bowing. "A great honor, sir."

"No time, Fangard. I must speak with the Chief Sentry at once. Rouse the castle! We are under threat from the sea."

"At once, milord!" The mastiff sent up such a baying as Zahra had never heard in her life. Every hair on her arms stood on end.

Soon they were through the gates and galloping across the shadowed courtyard as Fangard raced ahead. Starwise's hooves rang like drumbeats. Around them, sentries spilled from doorways, hoisting spears and lighting torches. "Raise the alarm!" Fangard barked. "The castle is under attack!"

Bells in the high towers began clanging, and a pair of large doors crashed open in front of them. Starwise took a set of steps four at a time into a great hall hung with shields. He cantered to a stop, sides heaving.

A stocky, grim-faced warrior rose from a chair by the open fire. He was dressed in the leathern armor of the Chief Sentry, the steward of Ternival, with the great stag of Andella engraved upon the chest piece. Fangard circled restlessly, panting.

"Hail, Lord Bayard," said the centaur.

"Hail, Lord Starwise," the Chief Sentry replied. "Fell news?"

The centaur lowered his forelegs again, and Zahra all but tumbled to the flagstones. It wasn't quite a dismount, but somehow she landed on her feet and dipped a wobbly curtsy. Lord Bayard barely glanced at her.

"Fell news indeed," Starwise said. "A threat from the sea."

Fangard growled. "Ships?"

"Nay. Worse, I fear. The girl saw it with her own eyes. Speak, Fisher Lass."

Zahra attempted another curtsy, her mouth dry. "Three of them, milord," she croaked. "Tall as mountains."

"Three of *what*, lass?" said Lord Bayard. "Speak plainly."

"Giants!" Zahra cried. "Giants are upon us."

Silence fell over the hall. Zahra could hear the hissing of the torches, the swinging of the bell ropes, the distant breakers.

"Friendly, perchance?" asked Bayard after a moment. "Perhaps to parley?"

"N-nay, milord," Zahra stammered. "We overheard their plans. They come to feast on our bones."

The horrified pause that followed was broken by a renewed clanging of bells.

"But from where?" said Bayard, as if to himself. "Not from the north, or I'd have known. Surely not from Islagard, abandoned all these years? But no time to waste on wondering. Alert the archers, Fangard! And tell the rest to ready the catapults. By sunrise, those foul creatures will wish they'd never set foot in our waters."

Arash ran.

He didn't know whether the demon was following them. But he wouldn't wait to find out.

With every step, he felt the absence of the Infinium, a reminder of the real reason he'd gotten up so early to hike the hills. To find more. More of what he'd discovered three days ago. Not a hoard, but a treasure nonetheless.

Just one artifact. It hadn't been buried so much as stashed, tucked into a niche in the rocks below Table Mount. As soon as he pulled the stones away and saw the object glimmering there, he knew. It was a huge find, the kind of archeological triumph that makes the news.

Which was why he hadn't told anyone.

Technically, legally, he had fourteen days in which to turn it over to the proper authorities. But he hadn't yet. He wanted to enjoy it first, for just one more day. Maybe two.

Behind him, Jack was crashing through the gorse. Arash could hear his painful gasps as he tore along, heavy boots thumping. If Arash was hoping to escape the giant undetected, Jack's presence didn't help.

Arash jumped over a boulder and took a hard right onto a path leading downward, toward Upper Wolvern. He caught a glimpse of one of the many rock cairns he'd built that summer, which marked the spots where the Infinium had acted weird. Nothing had ever turned up in those places, but he'd marked them anyway, intrigued by the near-perfect line they made along the ridge. Occasionally his little stacks would get kicked over by livestock or hikers, and he'd carefully rebuild them.

But it was the outliers, the ones that didn't follow the ridgeline, that really fascinated him. There was the line he'd traced down toward Carrick Hall, for instance, which had led to his spectacular find. And then the line that followed the narrow crevasse to the lake, where he'd been hoping to test the Infinium's underwater capabilities. In the valley where a castle now stood. Where a giant demon had been sleeping. Where a bellowing voice had awakened the demon and, for all Arash knew, sent it in hot pursuit.

He heard Jack make the turn and stumble down the hillside behind him. They plunged on. The straps of Arash's backpack began to cut into his shoulders—and he wasn't even carrying the artifact, which he'd wrapped in an old T-shirt and stashed under his bed. His mother and grandparents would be mortified if they knew about it. What if he got fined? Or even arrested? It could sink the family businesses, just when things had never been better. And right now, his grandfather's bookshop, New Warren's, and his grandmother's tea shop, Much Ado About Cream Puffs, were gearing up for the biggest weekend of the year.

So he'd kept his mouth shut. Which wasn't hard, because he always kept his mouth shut. In fact, he hadn't spoken to anyone outside of family since he and his mother had arrived in the Wolverns four years ago. Not to his classmates. Not to his teachers. No one.

But someone needed to warn the village. Someone needed to sound the alarm about what he and Jack had seen.

Because, in a few hours, the hills would be crawling with tourists, and the boys wouldn't be the only people running for their lives.

Chapter

5

The tea shop was humming with activity by the time Tilly arrived. Two tour coaches were already parked on High Street, taking up half the drivable space in Upper Wolvern. Sure, it was the morning of the midsummer festival, so the village was bound to be crowded. But in addition to the festivities, Mrs. Rastegar's traditional Persian pastries were world-famous.

Tilly took her spot behind the register next to Mahsa Tabari, the Rastegars' daughter. She was a striking dark-haired woman whose usual hospitality seemed strained, like she was trying very, very hard not to smash a saffron cake into someone's face.

"Oh, thank heaven!" Mahsa murmured to Tilly. "They're all yours." Then Mahsa frowned. "When Arash finally turns up, send him to me, will you? I can't imagine why that son of mine is not back yet from tromping about the hills . . ."

"Neither is Jack, Mrs. Tabari," said Tilly. "He left freakishly early, as usual."

Mahsa tapped her temple. "Brilliant, those two. They know how to make themselves scarce just when they're needed most. Anyway, I need to help Maman in the kitchen, or we'll run out of ranginak and there'll be a riot."

It was the calm before the storm. Over the next few hours, crowds of tourists would swell the region's population to record numbers. The Wolverns weren't quite Stonehenge, but supposedly they were the next best spot for experiencing midsummer the way the ancient druids did, if you were into that sort of thing. Especially atop Table Mount, the highest peak, at sunrise, surrounded by tilting boulders of questionable powers.

"Ley lines, now," one of the tourists was saying as he and a friend studied the pastries in the glass case. "Like great strands of electromagnetic power, connecting ancient landmarks and structures, across the whole of Britain. Especially strong here, in the Wolverns." With his flat cap and professorial tweed blazer, he looked like someone's respectable older uncle.

"Across the whole *planet*," his younger companion corrected him as Tilly rang up two pistachio cookies and a coffee. This second guy definitely seemed on the weirder side. More of a Stonehenge type, with his hooded brown anorak that looked vaguely druidic and a pin that read *I want to believe*. And was that a staff he carried instead of a walking stick? Yes, definitely a staff. As if he was some kind of wizard. He probably thought he was.

The older gentleman ignored his friend. "The Wolvern ridge is one great ley line from north to south, of course. All eleven miles. Have you read Watkins? He mapped the whole thing."

"Landing strips for aliens, mate. I'm telling you," the younger guy said. "And those energies are strongest right now."

Mahsa had returned, loaded down with a tray of Persian baklava. "Who comes up with such crazy theories?" she whispered to Tilly. "Ley lines. Aliens. So-called Earth mysteries. Next, they'll be saying the earth is flat."

Tilly snorted.

"It's why metal-detecting is so unreliable up there." Oblivious, the young tourist droned on. "Have you tried? Impossible. Probably a hundred Saxon hoards in the Wolverns, but you'll never find them. You can't get an accurate read."

The older gentleman sniffed. "It's cheating anyway," he declared. "A hoard should be pursued with a divining rod, by the light of a full moon. Might we have a half dozen cream puffs, please?"

"They've got normal appetites, anyway," Mahsa murmured to Tilly. "Thank goodness." She tromped off to the kitchen.

"Have you visited New Warren's?" Tilly asked the two men as she rang up their order. "It's the bookshop next door. Loads about the Wolverns there. And the owner, Professor Rastegar, is an expert on . . ." She paused, trying to pinpoint some sort of connection between divining rods and the shopkeeper, who'd previously been Iran's foremost expert on Shakespeare. "Old stuff," she finished lamely. "Really old stuff."

The older man looked at her like she'd sprouted an extra nose. "And what would a foreigner know about that?" he said. He took his cream puffs and marched away to an empty table.

Tilly blinked at his retreating back.

The younger guy coughed to get her attention. "Ah, he-he, don't mind Fitzhugh. He's a bore." He leaned his elbow on the counter. "So . . . er . . . there's a bunch of us gathering at the beacon later, you know, for a watch fire and all that . . ." The next customer in line harrumphed irritably.

Tilly refrained from rolling her eyes. It wasn't the first time a customer had attempted to flirt. Something about the sculpted cheekbones, Frankie would say, teasing. And the straight dark hair, like she was some kind of Celtic shield-maiden. Not that she felt particularly alluring, most of the time. More like painfully self-conscious, especially in a frilly apron and messy topknot.

Thankfully, the next customer edged the guy out of the way and began to order. But as Tilly reached for the powdered sugar on top of the pastry case, she noticed a folded slip of paper tucked between the sugar and a jar of chocolates. Her heart sank. Not another one. And today, of all days. How could people be so cruel? She grabbed the slip and opened it, but she already knew what it would contain. Another anonymous note, like the ones she and Mahsa had been finding all summer, half-hidden around the shop. Beastly, threatening. *TERRORISTS. MURDERERS. GO BACK HOME.*

At that moment, the bell at the front door jangled above the noise. She stuffed the note into her apron pocket and glanced over long enough to spot a blond-haired guy making his way toward the counter. Deliberately, she turned her face away. As if she was much too busy to care. As if her heart hadn't just started pounding. As if Wolvern's star cricketer, the middle son of Lord Edward Heapworth, hadn't just entered the shop like he owned it, owned the whole world, but was gorgeous enough to get away with it. Which he was.

"A bunch of us . . . watch fire . . . beacon . . ." The anorak guy was babbling now.

"Oi, there, Merlin." Charles's smooth voice cut in from behind the line of customers. "Seen Galahad anywhere? Arthur's looking for him."

The tourist whipped around angrily. After sizing Charles up, he sniffed and stalked off to his friend's table.

Charles winked at her.

"Hullo, Tilly!" It was Charles's sister, Aurora—Elspeth's best friend. Solid and sturdy, she bounced toward the counter as if this was the most exciting day of her life. Her thick braided hair was so blond it was nearly white, and per usual, her wardrobe choices were . . . unexpected. Today: a tattered orange pullover and crumpled pink shorts, as if she'd found both in a ditch. How Aurora could be related to the ever-glamorous Lord Edward—much less to his fashionable son—Tilly had no idea.

Elspeth, meanwhile, trailed petulantly behind her friend, Georgie in tow. Skinny, brooding Elspeth couldn't have been more Aurora's opposite if she'd tried. "Ten pounds," Elspeth mouthed at Tilly, holding up both hands and waggling her fingers. She tilted her head triumphantly in Charles's direction. Tilly made a face.

Georgie, his eyes round as cricket balls, pressed his nose against the pastry case.

"Not a chance," Tilly warned before he could start begging.

"Do you know where Mrs. Tabari is?" Aurora asked. She glanced around the crowded shop. "Although, honestly, I'm not sure why we scheduled to weave with her on festival day. This is bonkers!"

"I wouldn't count on a lesson this morning, that's for certain," Tilly agreed. "She's in the kitchen, helping her mum."

"Maybe we could help too!" Aurora suggested. Tilly opened her mouth to protest. It was a terrible idea, actually. She couldn't think of anyone who was more oblivious, more inattentive to detail, than Lord Edward's youngest child. Case in point: Aurora's fashion sense. Tilly could just imagine Mahsa's reaction if Aurora got ahold of, say, the rose water syrup.

"Don't be an idiot, Roar," Charles interjected. He always used Aurora's childhood nickname—the one she hated. "It's much too crowded in here. Go away and weave your little pot holders or whatever you do."

"Tapestries, Charlie," Aurora snapped, eyes flashing. "We're weaving tapestries. And don't call me Roar."

"Don't call me Charlie."

"Okay, Charlie."

"Okay, Roar."

She stuck out her tongue and skulked away with Elspeth.

Tilly continued to ring up orders, trying to ignore how Charles's light blue polo set off his phenomenal eyes. She could tell he was staring at her. *He's just bored. Not much else to do in this small village except flirt with one of the few local girls his own age.* But could it be more than that?

"So, Jack never turned up?" she asked Georgie.

Georgie shook his head, still focused on cream puffs. "That one," he said, pointing.

"No," Tilly said.

"Yes," Charles intervened. He cut deftly in front of a tourist and winked again. "Add it to Dad's usual order."

"You're insufferable," Tilly dared to say, hiding a smile.

He laughed. "I know." Then he leaned one elbow on the counter in a perfect imitation of the wizard wannabe. "So . . . tonight there's this watch fire up on the beacon and all that," he quipped. "I don't suppose you'd like to run in the opposite direction, would you?" he asked, lowering his voice so only Tilly could hear. "Take a ride with me instead? With school called off today, there's no cricket practice either. And Dad's out of town, hunting for antiques and all that. So I've got the keys to the Rolls-Royce. What do you say, Guinevere?"

The shop bell rang again, and in dashed two teenage boys who looked for all the world as if a monster was chasing them.

"Arash Tabari!" Mahsa glowered from the kitchen doorway. "Where have you been? Your grandmother needs you. Now."

Arash looked like he'd just witnessed a murder. His glasses were askew, and he seemed on the verge of shouting some kind of warning, but words escaped him. Jack, who was incredibly filthy, halted and bent forward, hands on his knees, huffing.

"Jack," Tilly called, "take Georgie home. *Please,* for the love of . . . everything. And shower, would you?" She reached behind the counter, pulled out Lord Edward's weekly pastry order, and handed the box to Charles. "Sounds good, Lancelot," she told him. She was surprised at how coy she sounded.

Charles grinned broadly. "After the shops close—say, five-thirty? At the roundabout. Oh, and mum's the word." Tilly grinned back.

"My cream puff," Georgie insisted. Tilly groaned, reached into the glass case, and handed him the smallest one she could find.

Meanwhile, the Rastegars' grandson was sidling through the crowd.

"Son of mine!" Mahsa called again. "Where is your metal detector?"

"Oh, *that's* right, Tabari," Charles chimed in, grinning sardonically at Arash. "Heard you gave up cricket for detecting. How's that treating you?"

"Detecting, eh?" The younger tourist swiveled around to address Arash, whose expression had grown even more panicky. "Best be careful up in the hills, you know. Much too dangerous right now. Ley lines are far too strong. All that energy . . . You never know what might happen."

"Cool!" Georgie exclaimed.

Arash blinked at the tourist with dismay.

"And anyway"—said the one named Fitzhugh, sniffing with disapproval—"it won't work. A divining rod is what you want. By moonlight. Much more reliable."

"But keep an eye out for giants!" Georgie added.

And that was when Jack fainted.

Chapter

6

"So, that was . . . not great," Elspeth said. She licked the tip of some scarlet yarn and attempted to thread her tapestry needle.

"What—Jack fainting?" Aurora said dryly. "Or Tilly kicking all of us out?"

"Everything." Elspeth peered at the needle's eye and aimed. The lighting in her family's cottage was so much worse than at the tea shop. But she and Aurora didn't have a choice.

After Jack's unfortunate moment, Tilly had banished her siblings from the tea shop. She'd even summoned the boldness to shoo away Aurora and Charles—albeit in a teasing, flirtatious tone that made Elspeth cringe. So, once Jack revived, Aurora and Elspeth had bundled up their weaving supplies and trekked back down High Street to the Addisons' cottage, Jack and Georgie trailing behind.

Now poor Jack lay on his bed upstairs while Georgie chattered away next to him—ostensibly to keep him company. As if that was something Jack wanted, ever. The girls could hear Georgie enumerating all the amazing pastries he would've eaten if Jack hadn't passed out and ruined everything.

"Will Jack be okay?" Aurora asked. Somehow she'd gotten ahold of a long fluff of raw wool and was looping it by hand through the warp of her frame loom.

Elspeth waved a hand. "He'll be fine. Faints all the time. He hates crowds and confined spaces."

"The boys looked like they'd run all the way from Great Wolvern." Aurora paused, musing. "I wonder why Arash never talks?"

"I'm sure he does, just not to us."

Elspeth pinched the yarn and tried threading the needle again. Nope.

"Do you think Charles actually likes my sister?" she ventured.

Aurora shrugged. "Maybe? I don't know. He's hard to read." She pulled the wool through the last of the warp threads, leaving its tail dangling.

Elspeth frowned. She couldn't put it into words, but she didn't trust the guy. Not one bit. He was . . . *too* good-looking. And Tilly was so famously gullible. That moment last spring, when Elspeth caught her putting on lipstick in the bathroom mirror, something had twisted in Elspeth's heart. It'd always been just the two of them, together. And now there was this . . . this . . . third *thing*.

Finally Elspeth managed to thread the needle. She poked it through the warp threads where she'd left off last time. All she'd accomplished in two weeks of weaving was one square inch, part of the small tapestry pillow she was making for Eva. But it was a darn good square inch. Nearly perfect. The problem was, at this rate she wouldn't finish till Eva was as old as Mrs. Fealston.

Aurora, by contrast, seemed to thrive on messes. Her project was entirely experimental, full of found objects—twigs, leaves, ornamental grasses—in no particular order. She'd weave all the way up one side of the frame loom while leaving huge gaps in the rest, then tear everything out and start over, just for fun. Elspeth secretly found Aurora's approach stressful.

As did Mahsa, their instructor. Except not so secretly. *Weaving is an ancient Persian art,* she'd admonish. *Without a pattern, it's just chaos.* She'd point to the intricate tapestry that hung in her tiny studio off the back of the tea shop—one of the oldest, most interesting weavings Elspeth had ever seen. At first glance, it seemed patternless: all gold swirls and calligraphic letters, in some other language, against a striking blue background. But when studied closely, it revealed a clever repetition of circling birds with curving necks and elegant wings, from which the calligraphy emerged as if by magic.

"What do the letters say, Mrs. Tabari?" Elspeth had asked one morning.

The weaver shrugged. "It's a kind of prayer. For salvation, deliverance."

"Can you translate it?"

"No," Mahsa replied shortly. "Now, back to weaving."

For a few weeks, Aurora had dutifully copied one of the basic patterns Mahsa had given them. But then one morning, on the way to lessons, Aurora had found a tall bulrush with a particularly puffy head. And that was that. Now Elspeth watched as Aurora rifled through the designer bag she used for her weaving supplies—a Louis Vuitton, no less—and pulled out a wad of feathers, which she began spearing haphazardly into the wool.

"What's that supposed to be, anyway?" Elspeth finally asked.

"Not sure. A wall hanging, maybe. Or a table runner."

"You should give it to your dad, say you found it at an antique shop." Elspeth pretended to peer at Aurora's loom with a magnifying glass. "Fifteenth century, at least, I'd wager my Rolls," she said in that languid aristocratic manner Lord Edward had perfected. He was basically Charles, only older. "Highland wool, of course. And whatever drake donated the feathers should be knighted."

Aurora giggled. "I'll take it," she said airily, mimicking one of her father's clients. "I shan't be outbid this time." Lord Edward Heap-worth was an expert on medieval tapestries, regularly summoned to attend auctions and advise wealthy collectors from all over the world. He was presently in London, in fact, tracking down something or other—which was why Aurora was hanging out with Elspeth for the day. The Heapworth estate of Wolvern Court was full of such art. By far the most prominent was a large showpiece that had once hung in the dining room at Carrick Hall: the framed tapestry of a hunting scene featuring a majestic stag chased by hounds. The same stag as in Frankie's sketch above the sideboard here in the Addisons' cottage.

"So . . ." Elspeth began slowly. They didn't discuss the topic very often. But when they did, it was in hushed tones, like they'd entered a church. "Do you think he's gone for good? The stag, I mean."

Both girls paused and studied Frankie's sketch. The dryad was just transforming from an elegant beech tree into a human—or vice versa—and she seemed in mid-flight, chased by some unknown evil. Behind her, the glimmering stag emerged from the dark trees. And above the trees, near the top of the frame, castle towers rose like a beacon. The usual wave of longing washed over Elspeth, the feeling that if the dryad could only reach the stag, everything would be all right.

Because the stag was real.

He'd appeared on the grounds of Carrick Hall summers ago, when Frankie and Eva were teenagers. In fact, Eva claimed to have followed the stag and found herself in another world—a story that still gave Elspeth goosebumps. But prior to that, the stag had appeared, on and off, at the Hall for decades. As if the framed tapestry couldn't hold him.

At some point, though, Lord Edward had purchased the tapestry and removed it to Wolvern Court. And no one had seen the stag in the real world since. He remained a mere image in a work of art, immobile.

"I don't know," Aurora whispered. "Early this morning, I thought I saw him, in the hills. There was something up there, anyway, wandering amongst the rocks." She shook her head. "But there are all sorts of hikers up there right now, people camping illegally. Who knows?"

Elspeth sighed. "Maybe moving the tapestry to Wolvern Court broke some kind of spell."

The girls studied the sketch again, gazing at the intricate carvings on the frame. Elspeth's late grandfather—who'd served as head gardener at Carrick Hall for fifty years—had often told of how, long ago, his aunt and uncle had stumbled into another world called Mesterra, where his aunt had become its First Queen. She'd reigned for years and years. But then, for reasons no one ever learned, she and her husband had returned to this world. They'd brought with them cuttings of pear trees, which they'd planted at Carrick Hall. And when the trees matured, Grandad's uncle had carved beautiful things from the wood. Including this frame.

Delicate notches ornamented the top and bottom edges, along with swirls of leaves and branches. In one corner, the wood-carver's signature could be seen: a crown encircling a pear tree. According to Frankie, the signature appeared on every object the carver had created from the Hall's pear trees.

The house phone rang. Elspeth jumped up to answer it.

"Oh, hey, Ellie," came a young woman's voice.

"Hullo, Eva!" Elspeth was always a little startled by Eva's flat American accent, especially if they hadn't seen each other in a while. The young woman seemed so entwined with life in Upper Wolvern that it was easy to forget she wasn't actually from here. This morning, however, she sounded tired and stressed—but after an overnight flight from the States, anyone would sound like that.

"I've just arrived at Paddington from Heathrow," Eva continued. "Everyone okay there?"

"We're fine. Did you have a good flight?"

"Yeah, mostly . . ." Eva's voice definitely sounded strained. "But I can't seem to find Frankie. We're supposed to meet the publisher for lunch in about fifteen minutes, but he's not here yet. Do you know if he caught his train on time?"

Elspeth frowned. "That's odd. He left earlier this morning. Should be at Paddington by now."

Aurora lifted her head with a quizzical look.

"Frankie's not there yet," Elspeth mouthed.

"Odd," Eva agreed distractedly. "I can't imagine what's happened. I guess I'll just . . . Oh, wait." Elspeth could hear Eva speaking to someone over the sound of a platform announcement. "A pub?" she said to whoever it was. "Well, that's kind of you—thank you." Then to Elspeth: "So, there's this nice lady who says she chatted with Frankie on the train—you know how he's got that briefcase I gave him, with his name on it? She says she saw him enter a pub once they alighted. She's offered to walk with me."

"Well, that's generous of her," Elspeth said. "Hopefully you can find him. Keep us posted, will you?"

"Will do," Eva said. "Talk to you soon."

Elspeth sat back down.

Maybe it was just a simple mistake. But it wasn't like Frankie to get mixed up—although maybe it was travel-weary Eva who'd gotten muddled instead. Even so, it was odd.

Very odd.

Chapter

7

As soon as Lord Bayard issued his commands for the defense of Caristor, Starwise turned to Zahra. "Since thou canst not wield a sword nor nock a bow, run thee to the east side of the castle, lass, away from the sea. And stay well hid."

"But my grand—" Zahra began.

"Fly!" Starwise commanded.

So she flew. She stumbled through the chaos toward the castle's eastern gate. But before she could find a place to hide, one of the towers exploded and debris rained down.

The next thing she knew, someone was dragging her onto a wagon full of barrels. The sun was barely peeking over the horizon. Her head throbbed.

"Hurry, Bem!" said a woman's voice from the wagon seat.

Around them was pure mayhem. Dust and smoke filled the air. Rocks flew. Sentries fled. Entire sections of the castle were gone, as if they'd never been.

"Retreat! To the northern peninsula!" the voice of Lord Bayard bellowed over the din. "To Marisith-over-the-Sea!"

The wagon lurched forward, sending the barrels rolling.

"Are ye tryin' to kill us, Mum?" someone shouted from the wagon bed.

"The last of those giants is aimin' to, that's for certain!" shouted the driver. "*I'm* tryin' to save ye!"

As the wagon clattered through the eastern gate, away from the castle, Zahra sat up, head swimming. Beside her, a girl her own age was clinging to the wagon rail. It was Bem, the scrappy redheaded daughter of Goodwife Pearblossom from the village of Ter-by-the-Sea. And the driver was Goody herself. During Mother's illness, the woman had kindly assisted Grandad by bringing herbal remedies and poultices—and recently Goody had stopped by the hut with jars of mulberry juice for Grandad's bouts of weakness. Her daughter, meanwhile, had cheerfully attempted to befriend Zahra several times. But Zahra's shyness had proven insurmountable.

The wagon now bumped and jolted along the wooded road that ran from Caristor to the stronghold of Marisith, pulled by an ancient mare that was either deaf or unflappable or both. Sentries raced by on horseback, others on foot. Creatures of all kinds passed them, hinds and hounds and hares, bounding among the trees. Boulders continued to whizz through the canopy, occasionally answered by a flaming arrow from a Ternivali archer. But the giant couldn't traverse the dense woods. Those who fled there were safe—for now.

A mighty boom sounded behind them. Above the trees, the last remaining tower of Caristor listed perilously. Then slowly, almost gracefully, it fell with an echoing crash.

"The coward!" Bem cried. "Attack us in broad daylight, ye great sack of dung!" Angry tears streaked her dust-caked face.

"But what happened?" Zahra finally managed to ask. "Where are the other giants? And is the castle lost? I must've gotten bumped on the head."

Bem rubbed away her tears with both fists. "Ye did. We saw ye fall, in fact—Mum and me—right as we pulled up with a delivery for the sentries. So, we dragged ye into the shelter of the gateway." She then went on to narrate all that had happened since that moment.

The sentries, under Lord Bayard's command, had fought valiantly. They'd battered the giants with huge stones from the catapults, felling one monster into the sea. The creature never rose again. Then they'd set a second giant afire with blazing arrows—and when he tried to douse himself by swimming into deeper water, he drowned. Finally Ternivali hawks had descended, screaming, to tear at the remaining giant's face. But nothing could withstand a monster that size. He'd swatted them, one by one, to their watery deaths.

Then he'd pressed forward steadily, like the tide. He'd caught the rocks that came flying and hurled them back. He'd reached into the shallows, grasped boulders the size of shacks, and flung them with wickedly accurate aim, demolishing first one tower and then another. A particularly well-thrown rock breached the westernmost wall before the giant was even within range of the archers. Finally he lumbered ashore and scaled the cliff.

By sunrise, the castle was lost.

Bem's voice faded to silence. As the mare plodded on, Zahra stared numbly into the forest.

It didn't seem possible. Castle Caristor had stood on the southern peninsula for hundreds of years. Even during the reign of Mindra the Enchantress, who'd partially demolished it, the central walls had remained intact. And then the Three Queens from Tellus had come, from beyond the walls of that world, and Mindra had been overthrown, banished deep into the Wilderlands. And Caristor had been reestablished, stone by stone.

There it had stood in glory for the past sixty years, even after the

Three Queens had vanished. Chief Sentries like Bayard had been its caretakers ever since, keeping it in readiness for the next true sovereign, whoever that might be.

Zahra's eyes blurred with tears. Caristor gone. Mother would've been devastated.

"Halt!" commanded a familiar voice. The wagon lurched to a stop.

Zahra peered over the wagon rail. Ahead on the road, Lord Bayard himself sat astride a stunning chestnut warhorse that tossed its head as if itching for battle.

"The barrels—leave them," Bayard told Goody Pearblossom. "You can return for them later. Transport these wounded instead." He pointed toward a small group of sentries who carried several men on stretchers.

"Ay, milord," said Goody. She leaped into the wagon bed as two of the sentries climbed aboard to help. "Come, Bem. People are more important than pickled beans."

Bayard flicked a glance at Zahra. "Well done, Fisher Lass. We should all be corpses under the rubble were it not for you." He turned his horse and galloped back the way they'd come. She could hear him shouting encouragement to the stragglers at the end of the retreating line.

The wagon was swiftly emptied and the wounded loaded, together with the two sentries. One of them, a great boar of a man with a bristly beard, wordlessly climbed into the driver's seat and took the reins.

"Oi! What are ye—" Bem began, but her mother shushed her.

The sentry flicked the reins. The mare didn't budge.

He tried again. Nothing.

"Giyyup," he commanded, but the horse refused. He slapped the reins down, hard, on the mare's back. The old horse took a step and stopped. "Move, ye bag of bones!" he roared, then stood to slap the reins even harder. But before he could do so, Goody Pearblossom leaped lightly onto the seat in such a way that if he'd swung, he would've hit Goody instead. He halted in mid-strike.

"Not to worry, sir," she said in a fake cheerful voice. "Poor thing is deaf as a stone." Before the man knew what was happening, Goody had grasped the reins and flicked them. The mare lurched forward, the sentry fell back into the wagon bed, legs in the air, and Bem's mother eased into the driver's seat as if it was just another market day.

Bem glanced at Zahra, eyes dancing. Zahra bit her lip to keep from smiling. Even the other sentry, a youngish fellow with a black eye nearly swollen shut, stifled a guffaw.

The bearded sentry—who'd narrowly missed landing on the wounded—rolled to his side, red-faced and grumbling, and attempted to sit up. Which, given the wagon's jolts, took a few tries. He scowled at the goodwife, muttering, then glanced around the wagon as if daring the rest of them to laugh. His gaze fell on Zahra, and his scowl deepened.

"And what's *she* doin' here?" he snarled. He looked Zahra up and down, from her long dark braids and olive skin to her colorful woven sash and sandaled feet.

"Savin' yer hide, is what," Bem snarled back. "Didn't ye hear Lord Bayard?"

The younger sentry sat up straighter and peered at Zahra with his one good eye. "So it was *ye* who warned the castle," he said with awe. His voice cracked on the word *ye*. He was even younger than he looked.

"Shut it, Lepp. And how'd she know they were a-comin'?" the bearded sentry sneered. "The Valorentians are on *their* side, I tell ye. These foreigners are spies, the lot of 'em."

Zahra's face grew hot, then cold. She didn't often hear comments about her family's obvious heritage as people from the land that the

Ternivali called Valorenta. Visits by Valorentians—usually merchants who'd traveled many months over deserts and mountains to trade in the market squares—were so rare that many Ternivali had never met one. But even if they had, no one had ever made such awful insinuations about her family's loyalty before.

"Oh yes. *I* know," Bem said sarcastically. "Before me enemies get destroyed, I'll warn 'em that me mates are a-comin'. Because that's smart."

"Ye never know," the sentry shot back, glowering. He turned his face away as if the conversation was beneath him.

The younger sentry, the one named Lepp, glanced at Zahra uncertainly, then also turned away.

"Cowards," Bem said under her breath.

Zahra felt nauseated, like she'd just been punched in the stomach. Even the kindest people always assumed they knew the whole story. They thought her grandad had come to Ternival because it was supposedly better than the land of his birth. But his love for his homeland didn't make him a traitor here. They knew nothing. There was no one more loyal to Ternival than Grandad. No one.

The wagon jerked to a stop.

Zahra peeked over the side again. A ragtag ensemble of robed and hooded citizens—humans and animals alike—emerged onto the road via the steep footpath that climbed upward from Writbard Bay. They were fisherfolk from the small village south of where Zahra and her grandad lived. And they were armed to the teeth with pikes and rods and knives.

"'Tis true?" one of them called. "Has the castle fallen?"

"Alas, 'tis true," Goody replied. "We are to retreat to the watchtower."

"Then we shall do the same," said another. "We'll fight, every one of us. To the last."

"Climb ye aboard, then."

"Nay, let 'em walk," the bearded sentry protested. "We've got wounded here, and it's crowded enough already."

Goody ignored him and instead climbed out, strode to the back of the wagon, and lowered the tailboard. As the fisherfolk scrambled up, she looked at the sentry boldly. "If 'tis so very crowded, then a great strapping warrior such as yerself can walk, now, can't he?"

His face grew so red with fury that Zahra thought he might strike. He stood up slowly, gave Bem's mother one scorching look, and began helping people aboard.

But as he reached out his hand to the last hooded citizen, he suddenly pulled back. "Away, old man!" he bellowed. "We don't need another Valorentian spy here." He shoved the fellow, whose hood slipped back from his face.

"Grandad!" Zahra cried.

Chapter

8

Jack peered through the bow window into the bookshop. The place was crawling with tourists, which made his lungs feel tight again. Not panicky, but not comfortable either. Even so, he'd risk it.

Until about ten minutes ago, he'd been hiding in his bedroom, mortified that Aurora and the rest of the tea shop had witnessed his spectacular swoon. Thankfully, there'd been no more rumbling from the hills, no sign that the giant had spotted the boys or followed them out of the valley. So hopefully that meant the village was safe—for now. But Jack had been on edge for hours, listening.

Finally he'd decided to head back to the shops and look for Arash. What, if anything, did the kid know about the events of that morning? And if Arash wasn't around, maybe Jack could track down information about giants. Specifically, how to get rid of them.

"How now, good sir?" Professor Rastegar, the shopkeeper, waved from the front counter as Jack entered. He was a stooped, balding man of slight build, with keen eyes behind thick spectacles. "What news?"

Jack hesitated. Did the professor know something? Had Arash

confided in him? But no. Maybe Professor Rastegar meant Frankie and Eva. After all, he'd been keeping tabs on the manuscript they were presenting to the London publisher today, so perhaps he simply wanted an update.

"None, my lord," Jack quipped dutifully, "but that the world's grown honest."

Professor Rastegar beamed. Whenever someone responded with the correct Shakespearian line, he was over the moon. Especially if it was *Hamlet*. That was his specialty. "Then is doomsday near?" the shopkeeper continued.

This was a little too close to the mark. "Something like that," Jack muttered.

A customer approached the counter, as if he wanted to chime in. Good. The tourists would keep the professor occupied while Jack poked around. He began to edge away.

"Such strange rumblings up in the hills this morning," the guy said, riffling through a set of maps.

Jack's knees felt suddenly mushy.

"Ah yes." Professor Rastegar nodded. "From the quarry, most likely."

"And have you heard about the stock that's missing in the hills?" a second customer said. "A farmer mentioned it at the post office just now. Half a dozen sheep, gone. He checks them every morning."

With studied nonchalance, Jack slipped out of sight into the nearest aisle and steadied himself against a bookcase.

"Indeed?" Professor Rastegar's voice sounded troubled. "Danger deviseth shifts," he murmured, as if to himself. "Wit waits on fear."

"Beg your pardon?"

"Nothing, nothing." The shopkeeper seemed to recover his composure. "Now, if it is a map you seek, here we have a fine selection . . ."

There was no sign of Arash, which meant he was probably still next door at the tea shop. But Jack felt queasy just thinking about the place. He'd wander around the books here instead, in case Arash eventually turned up.

The bookshop's inventory—which the Rastegars had relocated from an older shop they'd owned in Cambridge—was famously esoteric. Each section had been labeled in longhand: *Fifteenth-Century Persian Tapestries* stood adjacent to *Raptors of the West Midlands,* while *Ley Lines Versus Fault Lines: Debates in Modern Seismography* took up a good portion of six shelves. Customers often felt like they'd fallen into a rabbit warren—hence the name Warren's, or New Warren's, as it was now called. If he found anything about giants, it'd be accidental.

He turned down the middle aisle and paused at a section called *Ogres and Related Species.* That sounded promising. But the first book he pulled from the shelf wasn't the right thing at all. He replaced it and pulled out another. Ah yes. Here were the English fairy tales he remembered. Those ones always featured Jack the Giant Killer, who bested one monster after another with apparent ease—by luring them into pits concealed by branches, for instance, or lassoing them around the neck from atop castle gateways.

The problem was how those tales tended to conclude with some variation on "No sooner had this occurred than the whole castle vanished away in a cloud of smoke, and from that moment giants vanished also from the land." As if giants were a thing of the past.

But Jack knew better.

"What do you read, my lord?" The voice made him nearly jump out of his skin. But it was merely the professor, standing at the end of the aisle and smiling kindly. Quoting *Hamlet* again, of course.

"Words, words, words," Jack managed to respond.

The professor's smile broadened. Then the old man glanced at the section where Jack was browsing. His face grew still. For a moment, Jack worried he was having a stroke. Then he looked at Jack sharply.

"Interested in old fairy tales, now, are you?" Professor Rastegar asked. "I thought geology was more your line."

Jack shrugged.

The old man stepped to the bookcase where Jack had found the English tales, reached up to a high shelf, and pulled down a slim soft-cover volume that he handed to Jack with deliberate care. Across the cover was typewritten, in all caps, *THE PRINCESS AND THE DJINN,* with the subtitle *Selected Tales of Valan.* There was no author listed, no accompanying illustrations.

Jack flipped through it. A collection of stories, apparently, none of which seemed to feature giants—although there was the occasional ogre. Plus, lots of djinns, whatever those were.

"My gift to you," Professor Rastegar said. Then his expression became stern. "There are more things in heaven and earth, Horatio," he said in a low voice, "than are dreamt of in your philosophy."

Jack gulped. "Er, right. Thanks, professor." He wasn't sure what else to say.

He nodded awkwardly, then left.

Arash waited till the bookshop was empty before he emerged from the back room. The place had cleared out at lunchtime, but the tourists would return afterward. In force.

His grandfather looked up as he approached. The old man always seemed to know when something was wrong, and today was no exception. "*My boy?*" he said in his native tongue.

Normally Arash loved speaking what Grandfather called the language of their hearts. It was what their family spoke when no one else was around. To Arash, it sounded like music. Like water bubbling

from a spring. Like a grandparent gently shushing a child to sleep.
Speaking it was one of Arash's favorite things in the whole world.

But not right now. Once he started talking, he wouldn't stop. He'd
tell Grandfather everything.

"*You are troubled,*" the old man pressed. "*Tell me.*"

Arash shrugged. "It's nothing, sir." For some reason, it was easier
to lie in English.

"It is not nothing that makes those lines on your forehead." Grandfather gestured to the space between his eyebrows. "You have seen
something. Or heard something. *Tell me.*"

"It's truly nothing," Arash repeated.

"You are a terrible liar," the old man teased. "Just like your mother.
But no matter. You will tell me eventually. *Because a secret like that will
eat your insides like a demon—*"

That did it. "*But there is a demon!*" Arash burst out. "*Up in the hills,
near the lake. It's big as a house, bigger than two houses. Next to a castle
that's never been there before. I've seen it myself. And so has Jack Addison.
We each found it separately, while it was sleeping.*" He gulped down a
great sob that had been building in his lungs for hours. "*We heard a
voice yelling. A woman, from the top of the castle. She seemed to know we
were there somehow—could smell us but couldn't see us—and she was angry
that the demon just kept sleeping and sleeping. Then the demon woke up, and
we ran, and I . . . lost my . . . the . . .*" Arash swallowed. "*Baba, who are
the Children of Tellus?*"

His grandfather stared at him. Slowly he put the back of his hand
to Arash's forehead.

"Fever," said the old man gruffly in English. "That's what ails you.
Go lie down."

Then Arash's grandfather turned away, opened the till, and began
counting money.

Chapter

9

ahra jumped from the wagon and threw her arms around Grandad. They held each other for a long moment.

"Leave 'em!" bellowed the sentry to Goody Pearblossom, who stood near Zahra. He towered over everyone, blocking the tailboard.

Goody didn't reply. "There's room with me," she said in a low voice, leaning toward Zahra. "Come." Quickly they followed her around to the front and scrambled up to join her on the seat. She flicked the reins, the wagon rumbled forward, and the sentry had no choice but to sit down and keep his peace.

It was a tight squeeze, but Zahra didn't care. They were together. Safe. Her head still throbbed, but it no longer made her vision swim. And the sentry was trapped in the back of the crowded wagon, where he couldn't reach them.

Grandad peered into her face. "I nearly sent you to your death, lass," he whispered. "Are you hurt?"

"Just a bump." She patted the sore spot on her head. "But are *you* well? I hated to leave you alone in such a state—"

He waved a dismissive hand. "I'm fine, fine. So, you made it to Lord Starwise."

"Aye, and he let me ride with him to the castle."

He stared at her in surprise. "Did he, now?"

"We were in time to sound the alarm, but not to save it."

Grandad's face seemed to crumple. "*I never thought I should live to see this day,*" he said in his mother tongue. It was a language they spoke so rarely that sometimes Zahra wondered if she'd forget what it sounded like. "*I wanted nothing but peace for my daughter's daughter. But I have been foolish.*" He said no more.

The woods had grown quiet. Their wagonload seemed to be the last of the stragglers fleeing toward Marisith-over-the-Sea. As they drew closer to the northern peninsula, an uneasy silence fell over the company.

Like Caristor, Marisith had stood for centuries as a castle stronghold. But its history made Zahra's skin crawl. Mindra the Enchantress had lived there—and from it had ruled all of Ternival. Zahra had always hated the sight of its boxy tower rising from the clifftop at the end of the peninsula, its battlements like a set of giant's teeth, its arrow slits like cruel eyes. Under the tower, it was said, tunnels ran down to caves along the shore. Anything could be living there.

Zahra shuddered. Couldn't the company flee deeper into the woods instead? Wouldn't that be safer, where the trees grew too thick for the giant to give chase? But no, Lord Bayard had issued his command. Retreat to the watchtower. Perhaps the tunnels could save them.

The wagon descended to the bridge that crossed the Runnelwilde, near where the river emptied into Writbard Bay, then began to ascend toward Marisith. As the wagon drew closer, Zahra's dread increased. The woods were too quiet. No seabirds cried along the bluffs. No woodland animals stirred. Nothing. Something wasn't right.

The others in the wagon seemed to sense it too. They sat in taut silence, eyeing the trees. The sentries and fisherfolk kept their hands on their weapons. Goody Pearblossom gripped the reins as if ready to send the mare into a gallop. Only the horse seemed unbothered.

"If only the Children of Tellus would appear again," one of the fisherfolk said in hushed tones. "They would save us, as they did before."

"But what can mere children do?" the bearded sentry scoffed. "Nothin' but get in the way. Like these two." Zahra glanced over her shoulder to see him gesture at Bem and herself.

"Well, if *that* 'child' hadn't gotten in the giants' way," Bem retorted, pointing to Zahra, "ye'd be dead for sure."

The man growled but didn't answer. Next to him, the younger sentry named Lepp stole a glance at Zahra, clearly embarrassed by his companion's behavior. But once again, he looked away. Lepp truly was a coward. She faced forward again.

Goody patted Zahra's knee. "Not that yer a child, a'course. Nor is Bem, for that matter. We don't need the Children of Tellus if we've got the two of ye."

Zahra smiled weakly, fighting sudden tears. The woman's kindness made her miss her own mother with a sharpness that stabbed her heart.

Eventually they reached the battered stone walls that enclosed Marisith. The portcullis had been raised, leaving the way open to the courtyard beyond. There was no one to be seen.

Goody Pearblossom pulled in the reins.

"Where is everyone?" Bem whispered. "The sentries, the horses, the creatures? Where's Lord Bayard?"

"'Tis a trap," said the bearded sentry, glaring again at Zahra and her grandad. "'Tis what they planned all along—"

"List!" said one of the fisherfolk. "Hark ye?"

Zahra held her breath. Yes, she heard it. From somewhere inside the castle came the sound of muffled cries. At first, she thought it was people, trying to call out. But no, it was more like a crowd of animals, braying and croaking and roaring, a veritable menagerie.

"What in—" the sentry began, but the mare lunged forward. Ears alert, she dragged the wagon through the archway. Goody hauled hard on the reins to stop her, but to no avail. The mare didn't halt till the wagon had passed under the portcullis into the courtyard, which was full of jumbled supplies: carts, barrels, woodpiles, crates, all in scattered heaps. Finally the mare paused, trembling, next to a closed postern door at the base of the central tower, and whinnied loudly, as if answering the animals' cries. Apparently, she wasn't deaf after all.

A sliding crash behind them made Zahra jump. The portcullis had slammed to the ground, sending a spray of dust into the air. Grandad grabbed Zahra's arm.

"Here thou art, at last," said a cold female voice. "I wondered if thou hadst abandoned thy neighbors. Like the traitor thou art."

Out of the shadows strode a tall, beautiful woman in a crimson cloak. Zahra had never seen anyone so striking. Her skin was pale, her hair dark as Zahra's own, if not darker.

"Mindra!" Grandad whispered.

Zahra's heart nearly stopped. The enchantress? Alive, still? But—

With a shriek, the mare reared, then broke into a gallop, away from the enchantress, cutting a haphazard arc through the courtyard as the wagon's passengers tumbled and screamed.

Grandad grasped Zahra by the shoulders. "*Listen, child!*" he said urgently, again in his mother tongue. "*Jump as soon as you can. Hide yourself somewhere—anywhere. Do not let Mindra find you.*"

"*But, Grandad—*"

"*Zahra, my heart, look at me.*" She fixed her eyes on his face while the wagon tore around a woodpile. "*Whatever befalls, say nothing of the tapestry. Not to her, not to anyone. Do you hear me, child? Not one word.*"

"*I-I—*"

"*Swear to me on the soul of your sweet mother.*"

"*I swear—*"

"*Jump!*"

As the wagon pitched around another turn like a boat in high seas, Zahra swung herself over the rail and clung there, where Mindra couldn't see her. In the chaos, none of the other passengers seemed to notice.

Ahead stood several stacks of crates. As the mare swerved again, Zahra jumped.

She landed with a tumbling roll into the shadows. Stunned, she lay there for a moment—hard-packed dirt was much less forgiving than the Pathless.

She rolled to her belly, ears ringing, head pounding, and crawled deeper into the shadows behind the crates. Then she carefully sat up and peered through a slit between the stacks.

Mindra must've grabbed the mare's harness and yanked the wagon to a standstill. As the mare attempted to rear again, the edge of Mindra's crimson cloak fell back to reveal a muscular arm so white it looked like marble—like she was only pretending to be human. Her grip on the mare was as unmoving as stone.

"Down, traitor!" cried the enchantress. "Get thee down from that wagon and look me in the eye."

"Who're ye callin' a traitor?" From the back of the wagon, the bearded sentry stood. He pulled a long knife from a strap on his thigh while the other passengers cried out in alarm.

Grandad also stood and held up a cautionary hand. "Peace, good sir," he said in a commanding tone, more forcefully than Zahra had ever heard him speak. "Her quarrel is not with you."

"So, ye know her, do ye, old man?" snarled the sentry. "Family friend of yers?"

Mindra laughed, high-pitched and cruel. "In a manner of speaking," she said. Zahra went cold all over. There was nothing beautiful about this woman now.

"I knew 'twas a trap!" the sentry roared. He leaped down from the wagon and then paused, glancing back and forth between the enchantress and the old man, as if trying to decide which one was worse. Finally he ran full tilt at the enchantress.

In a flash, Mindra raised her free hand as though blocking a blow. The sentry kept coming. But he stooped suddenly, as if gripped by a stomach cramp. With every step, his shoulders hunched more and his neck seemed to thicken. Then, before Zahra could grasp what was happening, his leathern jerkin split clear down his back to reveal a coat of short bristles. His nose grew into a kind of snout, his bottom teeth shot up like tusks, and his legs and arms shrank.

Just before he reached the enchantress, he dropped to all fours and ran off, squealing, like the boar he'd become.

Chapter

10

"Has anyone heard from Frankie?"

Elspeth's mother stood at the massive range in the Hall's kitchen, stirring a pot of soup. It was their tradition to eat a late lunch together on weekends and school holidays, whenever possible. So, since school had been called off for festival preparations, the Addison siblings—plus Aurora—had been wandering in for the past half hour.

"He hasn't rung the cottage," Elspeth said. She and Aurora stood at the silverware drawer, counting spoons. "And Eva didn't ring again either."

"Odd," Tilly said. She removed her work apron, which she'd forgotten to leave at the shop, and slung it over one of the kitchen chairs. "You'd think Eva would've let us know whether Frankie turned up."

Elspeth didn't voice her real concern. That maybe the publisher had turned down the book altogether. That the demand for fairy tales had come and gone. That all of Eva and Frankie's hard work on revising and illustrating *The Writ of Queens* would come to nothing. Maybe the couple just didn't want to tell anyone.

"They're busy," Georgie announced, wiping his nose on the back of his grubby fist. He reached for the spoons in Elspeth's hand. "Let *me* set the table."

Elspeth snatched them out of reach. "Not before you scrub. Here, Jack. You're not busy. *You* set the silverware."

"I *am* busy," Jack said from the end of the table. He'd finally showered and was now snacking on plain toast and poring over a book he'd gotten at New Warren's. As if there was nothing to be done at the moment, in a busy kitchen, while lunch was being prepared for a large family.

"Clearly," Elspeth muttered.

"Still, they should've rung us," Mum said, an anxious frown on her already-anxious face. "To let us know which train they'll take home, at least."

"I'm sure they're fine," Elspeth tried to reassure her—which was harder to do lately. As the elderly Mrs. Fealston's health declined, Mum's job had gotten more and more stressful.

"But I don't understand why Frankie didn't meet Eva on time to begin with," Mum continued. "His train wasn't delayed, was it?"

Jack finally looked up from his book. "You know what? *You* lot are much too worried about"—he waved a hand vaguely—"everybody else. Let them live their life. And anyway, the publisher probably hated the book, or hated Frankie's illustrations, or doesn't care about fairy tales. And Frankie and Eva don't want to tell us. That's all. People just want to be left *alone*."

There was a pause.

"Well, aren't you just a cup of sunshine?" Elspeth finally quipped.

"So are you," Tilly shot back.

Elspeth glared at her. "At least I've got my head on straight." She began singing in sappy tones, "'You need someone older and wiser . . .'"

Tilly's ears turned bright pink. It was a low blow, and Elspeth knew it. Their family had always teased Tilly for watching *The Sound of Music* so obsessively as a kid that the video player broke. And Tilly *did* have a hard time making decisions. She was famously uncertain. It was her most frustrating quality—to herself and everyone else.

But Elspeth was feeling petty. "'I-I'll take ca-are of you,'" she crooned.

The door to the kitchen garden swung open, and in tromped Elspeth's dad. He plopped down on a bench by the door and slowly drew off his gardening boots. He looked tired but happy. Prior to becoming head gardener at Carrick Hall, he'd driven lorries all over Britain, sometimes gone for days at a time. But dirt was his love language. He was far happier in his current job than Mum had ever been in hers.

"Soup's ready," Mum said without looking up. "Someone call Paxton."

"I will!" Georgie shouted. "I think he's in the scullery."

As Elspeth passed the chair onto which Tilly had draped her work apron, she noticed a folded slip of paper on the floor. She bent down, picked it up, and swiftly opened it. Her heart started to race. It was one of those awful anonymous notes Tilly had told her about, which Mrs. Tabari and Tilly had been finding hidden around the tea shop all summer. Like someone's twisted idea of an Easter egg hunt.

"Give me that," Tilly whispered, coming up behind her.

"Isn't it the third note this week?" Elspeth whispered back, handing it to Tilly.

"Fourth," Tilly replied.

"I just wish Mrs. Tabari wouldn't throw them away. She should take them to the police!"

Nearby, Jack looked up from his book, then looked back down again.

"Still no idea who's been writing them?" Elspeth continued.

"No, and I haven't told her about this one either," Tilly replied. "But I'll show it to her after festival weekend. Maybe she'll be convinced to report it this time." She stuffed the note into the back pocket of her jeans as Georgie returned with Carrick Hall's handyman.

"Paxton was fixing the dumbwaiter!" Georgie announced, breathless with excitement. "Isn't that brilliant?"

Brilliant wasn't exactly the vibe Elspeth was getting—not from Paxton's dour expression, anyway. More like irritated. Like he hated dumbwaiters. And children. And interruptions. The glum old man had been, at various times, valet, butler, and chauffeur at Carrick Hall. But after the death of Eva's grandmother a few years ago, he'd taken to doing whatever was needed. Elspeth had always wondered if Paxton wanted to quit. Maybe he did. Maybe he was too old to imagine working anywhere else. Or maybe his face just looked that way. Perhaps, deep down, Paxton was fiercely attached to the Hall, for reasons of his own.

Everyone arranged themselves on mismatched chairs down the long rustic table and bowed their heads for grace.

As her father prayed, Elspeth glanced to where her mum sat, eyes open, staring into the middle distance. Mum's thin fingers tapped a restless, unconscious rhythm on her water glass.

Maybe Jack was right. Maybe it was better for everyone if they just stopped worrying and left people alone to do their own thing. But what if something really *had* happened to Frankie and Eva? What then?

Arash pulled a chair over to the window of his attic bedroom. From this vantage point, above the bookshop, he could see all the way up High Street to the roundabout and the village church. Beyond the church was the entrance to the drive that led to Carrick Hall, and beyond that, the narrow shortcut to the hills down which he and Jack had come at top speed. The path was hidden in the trees, but he knew it was there. And rising above the tree line, the Wolverns ranged from north to south, covered with specks like ants.

But the specks weren't ants. They were people. Lots of them. Some probably camping up there in the gorse illegally. With no idea of the doom that awaited.

What could Arash do? Nothing. His mother had sent him upstairs as soon as she heard about his supposed fever. No more wandering. No more tromping about the hills like those "lunatic tourists." Arash couldn't even help his grandmother in the tea shop kitchen. Instead, his mum had shooed him away to his room with a liter of carrot juice, which he hated, and shut the door.

Meanwhile, his grandfather hadn't said two words to him since the episode in the bookshop. Their usual ritual, ever since Arash was a boy, was for the old man to join him after supper and talk till late, telling stories in their secret language. Fairy tales, mostly. About the humble weaver, for instance, who could spin gold into thread from his hut on the shores of the Caspian Sea. And about the evil djinn who tried to trick the weaver into selling his finest tapestry—which failed, of course. When the djinn flew into a rage, the weaver rolled up the tapestry and fled with his wife and son into a nearby cave. But it was no ordinary cave. It was a doorway to another world.

As Arash had grown into a teenager, he and Grandfather had retained their storytelling ritual. It was the best part of the day.

But Arash had a feeling there'd be no storytelling tonight.

He reached under his bed and pulled out the treasure, still wrapped in his old T-shirt. He uncovered it and stared, mesmerized. It glowed softly on his lap. Even in the dim light of his attic bedroom, it was the most stunning object he'd ever seen. No one had found anything remotely *close* to this beauty before, not in the Wolverns. Not anywhere. He was certain.

Ever since his birthday, Arash had spent most of his free time in the hills with the Infinium, searching, searching for the perfect hoard. Gold coins, ancient tools, Saxon weapons—anything. Until three days ago, all he'd found were a few bottle caps, a cheap heart pendant, and modern coins totaling sixty pence—which he'd used to buy a soda. He kept trying. And his family had indulged these absences. Most of the time.

But lately Grandfather had started admonishing him. Whenever Arash returned home, the old man would rest a hand on his shoulder and declare, "Whatever you seek, it is worth nothing. You, my grandson, are part of a very great story already. A story that no one can take from you. Never forget this. Understand?" And then he'd close with some quote from Shakespeare: "Give every man thine ear, but few thy voice," for instance. The old man loved *Hamlet*—especially Polonius's famous farewell speech to his son, Laertes, which Arash could recite in his sleep.

Well, Grandfather didn't have to worry anymore. The Infinium was probably gone for good.

Arash gazed at the treasure on his lap. He wanted to show it to the old man. *See?* Arash would say. *They'll take us seriously now. After this, they won't dismiss us or tease us or pretend we don't exist. They'll stop sending horrible notes. And they won't laugh when we speak. Ever again.*

Grandfather hadn't checked on him since their talk in the bookshop. Arash tried to tell himself it was because no one wanted the shopkeeper to catch a fever, right when they needed him most.

But Arash wasn't sick. He knew it.

And his grandfather knew it too.

Chapter

11

As the boar that had been the bearded sentry fled from the enchantress, horrified silence filled the courtyard.

Then pandemonium.

The wagon emptied in a heartbeat. Its passengers scattered—all except Bem and her mother, who threw themselves protectively over the wounded. But to no avail. Mindra lifted her hand, over and over, as if swatting flies. And each time, one human after another became some kind of animal. A squirrel. An antelope. A marten. Meanwhile, those fisherfolk from the bay who were *already* animals—sea otters, a gannet, a gull—seemed to be struck witless. All dashing around in panic.

Zahra watched, aghast, as Goody Pearblossom and the wounded became a flock of hens and roosters, cackling in the wagon bed. But somehow Bem escaped from being transformed with them. She leaped from the wagon and charged at Mindra, carroty curls bouncing. But before Bem had taken five steps, the enchantress flicked a hand, and the girl shrank, down and down, till she was nothing but a ginger cat, streaking across the courtyard. She managed to sink her teeth into Mindra's ankle, though, before the enchantress shrieked with annoyance and kicked her away.

At some point in the mayhem, Grandad had dismounted from the wagon and was now flitting among the shadows along the courtyard wall, keeping well out of sight. But he wasn't running from Mindra. He was chasing down creatures and touching them. And every creature he touched seemed to calm instantly and regain its wits. A pair of pheasants flew up and out of the courtyard. The squirrel scaled the walls and vanished over them. Other animals hid among the supplies or slid deeper into the shadows.

"I know thy tricks," Mindra called. "But I have more." She released the mare, reached into the folds of her cloak, and pulled out a large seashell. It was dark and spiny, the former home of something poisonous. She put it to her lips and blew a blast, high and eerie. The sound echoed off the tower walls, over the trees, and out to sea.

From down the coast, near the smoking ruins of Caristor, came an answering boom. And another. And another. Drawing ever nearer. With each boom, the earth shook. Zahra stifled a cry. Giant footfalls, traversing the shallows of the bay. Coming toward Marisith.

Whatever calm had descended on the creatures now vanished. By the time a great shadow fell over the courtyard and a huge, hideous face peered above the wall, the animals were running amok again.

"Stonefist!" Mindra called up to the giant, a wicked smile spreading across her face. "Thou hast done good work today. Caristor is fallen. Time to feast!"

Grinning foolishly, the giant reached its enormous hairy arm down into the courtyard. A nauseating stench followed. Then the giant caught the boar by the tail and let the creature dangle, squealing, as Mindra laughed.

"Peace!" Grandad stepped from the shadows toward the enchantress. "If it is myself you seek, then here I am. Leave the others alone."

It was all Zahra could do not to scream. She wanted to run toward him, shield his old body from whatever blow might come. But she'd promised.

"Shall I smash 'im for ye, milady?" asked the giant. It dropped the boar, which limped away, and reached toward Grandad. Again, Zahra stifled a scream.

"Stay thy hand, Stonefist," Mindra commanded. She was no longer smiling. "The coward is mine."

Grandad walked slowly toward her, arms open, palms upward. "You have lost already, Mindra of Old. Come, now. To the winning side. Before 'tis too late."

"'Tis already too late, old man," she hissed.

"Perhaps." He continued to advance. "But even so. You have no true power here."

"Nay, fool. I have more power than ever."

From around her neck Mindra pulled a glistening chain. On it hung a gem so bright that it seemed to dim the sun. As faint music wafted like fairy bells on the air, Zahra gasped. She'd never seen or heard anything so beautiful. But a look of agony passed across Mindra's fine face, and the enchantress held the gem away from her as if it burned like fire.

Grandad halted. "It shall forever harm you," he said quietly. "The stag did not lie. Find all the gems—even the crown itself—and you will suffer in torment till nothing remains of your strength or sanity."

"The stag did lie," Mindra said, lifting her chin. She tucked the chain back against her chest, flinching. "As thou liest, even now. I am stronger than his trinkets. I know where the rest are hid. And the crown besides. After so many long years its voice is no longer muted— dost thou not hear it? 'Tis calling to the gems once again. Calling, calling, down the Warp of Time. I shall have them all, ere long. And I shall overmaster them."

"Can I smush 'im yet?" called the giant.

"Silence!" Mindra raised both arms and flicked her wrists.

Grandad seemed to brace himself, resisting. But then he rose into the air, growing smaller by the second till nothing remained of him except a pied kingfisher, fluttering overhead.

Before Zahra could open her mouth to scream, a fluffy ball of ginger fur collided with her face. It was Bem, clinging to her shoulders as she struggled to rise. The cat nipped her ear in warning, and Zahra sank back down, silently sobbing.

Quick as a flash, Mindra snatched the kingfisher from the air and thrust him into the folds of her cloak.

"Now, Stonefist," she called. "Round up the prisoners. 'Tis time."

"But what about me snack?" the great fellow whined. "Ye promised."

"Do as I tell thee! Or I shall turn thee into a great heap of earth. Thou shalt feast later."

Grumbling, the giant stepped over the courtyard wall, his footfalls shaking the ground. As animals scattered in all directions, Mindra stalked to the postern door at the tower's base, yanked it open, and disappeared inside.

Stonefist lumbered around the courtyard, shooing animals toward the open door, his ugly face towering over everything. Suddenly Zahra realized just how much danger she was in. Any moment, he might look down and spy her.

Bem must've realized the same thing, for she dropped from Zahra's shoulders and began slinking along the shadows toward the postern. She glanced back as if to say, *C'mon! Mum's in there, and so is yer grandad. It's our best chance of saving 'em.*

Zahra took a shaky breath and followed.

One by one, animals scurried past them toward the safety of the door, dodging the giant's feet. The trek seemed to last forever. Every time the monster turned his back, Bem and Zahra sneaked to the next pile of supplies. But as they reached an overturned cart near the door, they came face-to-face with a trembling dog whose right eye was swollen shut.

Bem hissed. The dog backed away. It was the younger sentry, of course. Lepp, from the wagon, who'd failed to stand up to the bearded fellow. Zahra was tempted to ignore him and keep going. But then she remembered Grandad standing before Mindra, arms out, palms up, advancing steadily.

"Peace, Bem," Zahra whispered. Then she looked the dog in his good eye. "Come, now," she said. "To the winning side. Before 'tis too late."

Lepp trembled. He glanced to where the giant was shooing the antelope toward the door. In a few more steps, the monster would be on top of their hiding place. Then Lepp looked back at Zahra, wagged his tail, and shot out from behind the crates, barking madly, toward the other side of the courtyard.

Stonefist swiveled his head. "Oi! Come back here, ye mangy cur!"

Lepp circled, snapped at the giant's ankles, then skittered off again, away from the postern door. Cursing, the monster followed.

Bem took advantage of the moment and bounded toward the doorway. She glanced inside, as if checking to make sure the enchantress was nowhere in sight, before turning back to Zahra. "Neow!" she mewed.

Zahra staggered forward and launched herself through.

Chapter

12

"All that thunder this morning," said Jack's dad between bites of bread and soup. "I thought it would storm."

"Giants," said Georgie smugly.

Jack felt a jolt in his stomach, like he'd been kicked. The kid was joking, of course. But still. Jack glanced at Aurora, who was demolishing her meal with gusto, oblivious.

Elspeth elbowed Georgie as he attempted a long slurp of soup. "Dad," she whined. "Make him *stop*."

"'Twasn't thunder," Paxton said in that morose tone of his. He gave Jack a sidelong glance.

"Might've been lorries," Dad conceded. "Up at the quarry." Grown men had a way of ignoring interruptions—especially from children—that made Jack mildly jealous.

"Doubt it," Paxton said. "Livestock's gone missing, too, they say."

Jack choked. He'd inhaled so fast, his soup had gone down the wrong pipe. Georgie cheerfully thumped him on the back as he coughed and spluttered.

"It's okay, mate," Georgie said in what he probably thought were comforting tones. "Go ahead and puke if you need to." He turned to the grown-ups. "Jack almost puked *everywhere* at the tea shop this morning. But he fainted instead."

"Shut it, Georgie," Jack hissed. He glanced at Aurora again, who was slathering butter on another slice of bread. "The tea shop was crowded. I don't like crowds. I'm fine. *Fine.*" To prove it, he picked up his book from New Warren's and pretended to read it. But he could tell Paxton was watching.

Jack's mum plopped a tray of food next to him. "Since you're in such *very* fine health, could you take this to Mrs. Fealston, please? If you're not too *busy,* that is."

Elspeth snorted. Jack rose reluctantly, tucked his book under one arm, and picked up the tray.

"She might be sleeping," Mum warned. She tapped on the door to the housekeeper's quarters off the kitchen. "But it's okay to wake her. Gently." Mum opened the door for him, and he stepped inside, balancing the tray. She closed the door behind him.

Mrs. Fealston's rooms were dim and quiet, a state of perpetual twilight. Her sitting room hadn't changed in what looked like half a century. But it was neat and clean, with bright pots of pink geraniums on the long windowsill overlooking the herb garden. Beyond this was her bedroom, where a hospital bed had replaced her antique one. The head of the bed was positioned so the tiny old woman could sit up and look out the open windows, which was what she was doing now.

As Jack entered the bedroom, she turned and gave him a cheery smile. "Hullo there," she said as if she'd never seen him before. Her eyes were rheumy, unfocused, like she was looking at him from a great distance.

"Hullo, Mrs. Fealston." Jack placed the tray on the overbed table and wheeled it forward till it rested just above her lap. Then—figuring he should probably make sure she didn't choke on the food or something—he hovered awkwardly.

"Pull up a chair, young man." She pointed toward an antique rocker.

"It's Jack, Mrs. Fealston." He set his book on the edge of the bed, pulled up the rocker, and settled into it with resignation. This could be a very long afternoon.

Mrs. Fealston immediately noticed the book. She drew it toward herself with a gnarled hand and ran her fingers along the cover. Then her eyes traveled over the title. They widened and seemed to clear, as if clouds had shifted and the sun had come out. She looked at him shrewdly.

"So, young Jack," she said, "I suppose you think you've found your calling."

Startled, he stared back at her.

"The rumblings in the hills," she continued. "The missing livestock. Do you think I haven't noticed? I can smell him on the wind, through those very windows." Even though her voice quavered with age, it was still authoritative, commanding, more like the housekeeper he remembered from childhood than the shriveled elderly person in front of him.

He opened his mouth and shut it again.

Mrs. Fealston continued to study him. "You've seen him, haven't you." It wasn't a question.

"I . . . well . . . er . . ." Jack mumbled.

"And I'm sure he's not alone." Mrs. Fealston shifted her gaze to the windows. "I suppose it was only a matter of time before she appeared again. But she's smarter now, no doubt. This time, she's staying well out of sight—making sure her great oaf stays hidden, too—until she feels the time is right." Her gaze slid back to his face. "But she doesn't know everything. Remember that. She doesn't know."

A wild shriek rose inside him. Were *all* the old people around here clairvoyant? How was it even possible? How was anything that had happened today possible?

"But I thought . . . all the giants in England vanished long ago." He stammered the only coherent thing that came to mind. "That's what the fairy tales say."

"Fairy tales don't always get it right," Mrs. Fealston said dismissively. "You don't really believe, do you, that evil simply vanishes—poof!—just like that? No, my dear. Evil merely goes underground. It bides its time and waits. Then it resurfaces, with every generation, in some new form." She leaned forward. "Don't be a fool. The most outrageous part about those fairy tales isn't the magic but the notion that one rash fellow can vanquish the enemy, all by himself."

"Oh, er, thank you, Mrs. Fealston," he managed to say. He rose, mumbled something about needing to help with the dishes, and fled from the room.

And anyway—he thought later as he walked back to the village with Elspeth, Aurora, and Georgie—the old lady was wrong.

He *would* figure out a way to kill the giant.

By himself.

Chapter

13

Zahra found herself in some kind of foyer, where dim torch-light flickered against thick stone walls. Mindra was nowhere to be seen.

Across the foyer, a spiral staircase wound up into the tower. Floating down from its dark heights came a cacophony of animal sounds: screeching and braying and whinnying and howling. Somewhere up there was Grandad.

With a clatter, the terrified antelope burst through the doorway behind her, followed by the dog. The antelope streaked past her up the stairs, but Lepp slid to a stop by her side, panting. "That's all of 'em, milady!" Stonefist's voice bellowed from outside. Then the postern door swung shut with a resounding boom.

"Silence, beasts!" Mindra's angry voice came floating down the stairs. "Or these cages shall be thy tombs." Instantly the racket ceased.

And that was when despair set in. It threatened to smother Zahra like a heavy blanket, and she wanted to curl up in a corner of the foyer and weep and weep.

All these years, so many years, Grandad had tried to protect her. And now she couldn't protect him. He was up there somewhere, in the clutches of their ancient enemy. Zahra herself was in danger. Even if she were to find him and release him without getting caught, how would his humanity be restored? Mother would've known what to do. Zahra missed her so fiercely she could hardly breathe.

A soft, warm body brushed against her shins. Then Bem took off across the foyer and disappeared up the stairwell. Bem was right. This was no time to wallow. It was now or never.

Zahra crept to the stairs, Lepp at her heels. Then she began to climb.

The stairwell wound up and up, past several landings with heavy wooden doors that were bolted shut. She kept going. And somehow the higher she climbed, the lighter she felt. The despair lifted. Maybe that was the key. Just take one step, then another and another.

She came to an arrow slit and paused, surprised at how high up she was, how beautiful and bright was the world beyond the castle walls. From here she could see south, down the coastline, where morning sunlight glinted off the blue Pathless and the bluffs shimmered with the play of light and shadow. Except for dark smoke rising from the distant ruins of Caristor, Ternival looked like a realm at peace.

Zahra gripped the narrow sill. *That* was the real world, out there. Ternival in midsummer. Clouds drifting across the hazy sky. Peace upon the land, its peoples, its children. Whereas this foul castle was a hideous dream, invented by the mind of a cruel and ruthless enemy. But like all dreams, it couldn't last. It had no real power. The sunlight would outlast it. The sea would outlast it. Even the peace—especially the peace.

Zahra glanced up the stairwell, then down at Lepp. He waited, blinking up at her with his one good eye. She brushed a hand across his scruffy head.

"Whatever happens," she whispered, "we chose rightly, you and I. As did Bem. Are you ready?"

But before the dog could so much as flick his tail, mighty footfalls outside shook the tower. A shadow blocked the sun.

"Oi, milady?" boomed the voice of Stonefist. "Is it time?"

"Indeed." Mindra's voice came from somewhere close—shockingly close, like she'd been standing on the landing right above them the whole time. Zahra recoiled so quickly, she nearly lost her footing on the stairs. "Hold fast to the castle, Stonefist," the enchantress commanded. "It shall be a treacherous journey. But whither we now go, there shall be feasts aplenty."

Then the tower began to shake. It shook so hard, Zahra had to brace her back against one wall and her feet against the other to keep from tumbling down the stairwell. She clutched the scruff of Lepp's neck as his paws slipped. It felt as though the entire building was spinning and shooting upward, like a boat climbing an unending wave. This went on for several seconds before the tower seemed to drop just as suddenly, down and down and down, till it landed with a tremendous crash.

In the stunned silence that followed, Zahra could hear the building settling around her, feel the grit of dust on her skin, smell the odor of unwashed dog. Then the shadow moved away from the arrow slit, light returned, and Stonefist was coughing and gagging.

"Back at last!" Mindra's triumphant voice rang from the landing above. "Back to claim what is forfeit."

Back? Back where? Zahra pushed Lepp aside and raised her head to peer out of the arrow slit. Her heart nearly stopped.

Outside was no longer Ternival.

It was a grim valley, ringed with stone cliffs. Somewhere strange. Somewhere beyond the realm of Ternival entirely.

Somewhere in another world.

PART TWO

Those friends thou hast, and their adoption tried,
  Grapple them to thy soul with hoops of steel.
    —Polonius, in *Hamlet* by WILLIAM SHAKESPEARE, c. 1600

Where there is ruin, there is hope for a treasure.
              —Attributed to RŪMĪ, thirteenth century

Chapter

14

"Just as long as you're home by dark," Mum had told Tilly.

After lunch, Mum had remained at the kitchen table, staring blankly at the phone on the wall. The landline had been silent while the kids cleaned up the kitchen. It'd been silent while Tilly's siblings left for the cottage with Aurora—and while Dad resumed trimming topiaries and Paxton returned to the scullery to finish fixing the dumbwaiter.

Then Tilly had needed to leave, too, for her afternoon shift at the tea shop. As she'd tied her apron back on, she'd told Mum that she planned to hang out with friends after work, which was mostly true. But Tilly wasn't sure what her mother would say about her *real* plans.

Was Mum okay? None of the calls they'd made to Eva's mobile had gone through, just straight to voicemail. And Mum hesitated to call Eva's parents, in the States, this early in their workday—not till it felt truly necessary, anyway. Meanwhile, Frankie didn't even have a mobile, which annoyed everybody. He claimed to prefer written correspondence: postcards, letters, the occasional email. Eva always rolled her eyes at this. "Writing is so *twelfth century*," she'd tease him, ruffling his hair. It was sweet and, honestly, a bit startling. Tilly couldn't get used to the fact that anyone found her oldest brother appealing. But she was smitten by their smitten-ness.

"I'm sure they'll call soon," Tilly had told her mother before heading out the door. But Mum had given no response.

Now the workday was finally over. The shops were closed, and everyone was making their way down to the green for the festival. As Tilly ambled toward the roundabout from the tea shop, she calculated what "home by dark" meant. This close to the solstice, the sun wouldn't set for another four hours. And on a cloudless evening, darkness wouldn't fall for another hour after that. Which meant she had something like five hours with Charles before Mum would shift from worrying about Frankie to worrying about her.

Five blissful hours.

Tilly could picture Charles in his dad's vintage Rolls-Royce—a 1969 Silver Shadow, according to Georgie—all the windows down, his blond hair windblown. She could picture his eyes, those amazingly blue eyes, gazing at her from the driver's seat, one hand lightly on the wheel and the other casually on the leather armrest between them, close enough to touch her hand . . .

Her face grew warm just thinking about it. *Don't be ridiculous.* How many girls had he driven around in that Rolls? Loads, probably. Tilly was just one more. But even so, she picked up her pace.

She strode past the pub, watching a pair of swallows swoop over the thatched roof. Perhaps Jack was right. The Addisons just needed to leave Frankie and Eva alone to be themselves. Maybe the two of them merely wanted the same thing Tilly did. Time alone with someone special. In fact, what if this was Frankie's plan all along—to whisk Eva away somewhere fancy for a romantic dinner? What if this was the moment when he'd finally pop the question?

And Eva would say yes, of course.

The alternative was simply unthinkable. But then again, Eva Joyce was her own person. She was the heiress to her family's estate and could do as she pleased. What if she didn't want to get married? What if she was planning to sell Carrick Hall instead—even though she'd talked her own mum out of doing so when her grandmother died? What if, after all the heartache her family had endured, Eva wanted to wash her hands of the Wolverns and start fresh somewhere else?

But Eva wouldn't. Would she?

The lanes were quiet as Tilly approached the roundabout. Good. That meant fewer prying eyes to witness the rendezvous. Fewer people to pass along gossip that might make its way to her parents. She was forced to share so many things with her family already: a room with Elspeth, the only loo with everyone, a family schedule that generally involved her supervising one or more siblings. This was the *one thing*—just one—that she wanted for herself.

Just Charles.

Tilly reached the roundabout and crossed into the center, which was anchored by a massive boulder. It'd been here for hundreds of years as a kind of marker for travelers—although it was almost impossible to imagine how medieval farmers could've unearthed something this huge, much less moved it to the main road between Upper and Lower Wolvern. No doubt that was why the legend persisted of how a giant had thrown the rock from somewhere up in the hills and this was where it had landed.

Whatever the case, the boulder was a traditional meetup spot. It even had what looked like natural steps up one side to the top, which was flat enough to sit on. And it commanded a fine view of all four routes as they converged.

She heard the Rolls before she saw it.

A luxurious purr, like a sleek cat. And then the glint of its shiny body as it approached from High Street. Tilly flicked a strand of hair out of her eyes and smoothed her eyebrows. Then she climbed down from the boulder and waited.

The Rolls entered the roundabout and cruised by her, windows down. Charles was at the wheel, of course, a teasing smile on his tanned face. She stood awkwardly, flustered, as he passed her and continued around the circle. Then he drew near and passed slowly again, still smiling with his perfect white teeth. As he circled again, she began to laugh. It was one of the things she liked about this boy: his outrageous self-confidence. It took her breath away.

Finally he pulled up next to her, one arm resting on the sill, car engine purring. His hair was every bit as mussed as she'd anticipated. Through the open window she could smell his aftershave—or maybe it was cologne—a combination of citrus and pine and something else she couldn't place, something like sage. It made her feel all melty.

"Sorry about that," he said, still grinning. "The car wanted to show off for you, I think."

She laughed again. "It worked. I'm impressed."

He laughed, too, appraising her hair, which she'd let down and brushed vigorously after finishing at the tea shop. "So am I," he said.

She felt all melty again. And, to her surprise, powerful. The second son of Lord Edward Heapworth of Wolvern Court, whose family had once owned all the land they could see—including the Addisons' cottage—was looking at her like *that*. He'd dressed this nicely, taken out such an amazing car, for *her*. Matilde Addison.

Her frustrations with her family vanished. This was *her* time. Hers.

"Ready, Guinevere?" he said with another grin.

"Of course, Lancelot."

Or no—she didn't mean Lancelot, did she? Hadn't that relationship ended disastrously? As she climbed into the Rolls, Tilly tried to think of a way to backtrack, to call Charles by the name Arthur instead. But nothing came to mind.

And anyway, it was time to stop second-guessing herself.

Chapter

15

Zahra couldn't move.

From her vantage point at the arrow slit, the desolate valley looked like a nightmare. Or a prison. Stony cliffs rose before her. The valley floor contained little vegetation, just some scruffy shrubs. Nothing moved; nothing lived. What dreadful world was this?

But there was no time to wonder. Footsteps descended the stairwell. "Not a sound from any of you!" came Mindra's cold, commanding voice. The faint animal noises from above ceased.

Once again, terrible despair swallowed Zahra. There was no escape. Why try? She slid to the floor, her limbs heavy. Bem gave her a sharp nip and then slunk toward a dark alcove under the stairs that Zahra hadn't noticed before. Lepp nudged her, too, till she started crawling toward it. By the time Mindra reached the arrow slit, Zahra had crammed herself into the shadows with Bem on her shoulders and Lepp on her lap. She dared not breathe.

The enchantress must've paused to look out. "Tellus, at last," she said triumphantly. "Stonefist! Where hast thou gone, thou great lump of earth?"

"Here, milady," came the giant's voice from outside. He sounded shaken. "What manner of magic was that? Nearly killed me, it did."

"'Tis none of thy concern," Mindra snapped.

"But what is this place? Ye promised food," Stonefist whined, "and I see naught but rocks."

"Silence, wretch! Stay and guard the tower. I shall depart for the village anon, but there is much to make ready." The enchantress laughed—a cold, lifeless sound. "For I have a train to catch," she sang to herself, then climbed back up the stairs.

Zahra was too terrified to wonder what Mindra meant. For the next half hour or more, she remained crammed in the alcove with Lepp and Bem, while Mindra's footsteps crossed back and forth, back and forth, somewhere above. None of the animal prisoners up there made so much as a whimper. Outside, the giant seemed to have fallen asleep—whooshing snores rose and fell like waves on a shore. The earth occasionally trembled as he stirred.

Eventually Bem grew restless. She scrambled from Zahra's shoulders to peek up the stairs. Then, with a glance back at Zahra, she vanished.

"Bem!" Zahra whispered. But soon the cat was back, skittering frantically into the alcove and onto Zahra's shoulders as Mindra's footsteps once again rang on the stairs.

The enchantress paused at the arrow slit. Then she sucked in her breath. "Stop at once!" she roared. "Awake, worthless pile of filth!"

Stonefist stirred. The earth shook.

"Smell that?" Mindra screeched. "Children of Tellus, I'd wager my throne."

Spluttering with rage, the enchantress plunged down the stairwell, passing Zahra's hiding spot without a glance.

Zahra's limbs unclenched. She wanted to weep with relief—even though the enchantress could return at any moment. But what had

Mindra meant by "Children of Tellus"? She couldn't mean the humans from Ternivali legend, could she? Here, in this valley?

The earth shook again, and Zahra could hear the giant moving about outside. Mindra must've reached the postern door, for it slammed with a crash, and now she was berating the giant in strident tones. Insults like "useless" and "oaf" and "base spawn of slag" wafted up from below.

Zahra pushed Bem and Lepp off her body and stiffly unfolded herself from the alcove so she could peer out the arrow slit. The giant slouched near the cliffside, arms limp, face belligerent. The enchantress stood beneath him—or at least, Zahra guessed it was the enchantress. For Mindra now looked entirely different. She'd exchanged her crimson cloak for the strangest clothes: trousers, by the look of them, and some sort of jerkin and gloves. Her hair fell back from her face in glossy waves, and she carried a large embroidered bag over one shoulder.

"I shall be abroad for the rest of the day," Mindra announced. "Thou shalt stay and guard the castle. But make no noise at all. Mark thou? None whatever. Do not let thyself be seen."

"Aye, milady," Stonefist muttered.

"And I'd best not find thee sleeping upon my return. Or it shall be the worse for thee."

Mindra spun around and stalked down a path that wove away from the tower. Quietly Zahra climbed down the stairs to the next landing, where another arrow slit faced a different direction, and watched as the enchantress skirted a small lake and departed the valley by a path at the far end.

Gone. The enchantress was gone.

Zahra nearly collapsed with relief. She would've knelt on the steps right then and there if Bem hadn't shot up the stairwell out of sight.

Grandad.

He was up there somewhere.

Now was her chance.

Zahra and Lepp dashed up the steps after Bem. They didn't have far to go. After one last landing with a locked door, the stairwell turned and opened onto a huge vaulted room with high windows. The top of the tower.

As Zahra's eyes adjusted, she realized the room was packed with cages. Cages upon cages of all sizes, stacked from floor to ceiling, lining the walls, hanging from the rafters. And, imprisoned within, hundreds of creatures. Minxes and lizards, brush wolves and geese, rabbits and mountain goats—plus larger animals like deer and horses, packed into pens.

At the sight of Zahra, the animals stirred. A faint honk, a low whinny of happiness, fluttering, and stamping. But they mustn't make a ruckus.

"Hush," she whispered frantically, "or the giant will hear you!" They quieted at once, but the very air crackled with hope.

From a corner of the room came a soft meow. It was Bem, climbing excitedly toward a set of enclosures that contained a flock of hens—toward her mother, of course. But where was Grandad?

Zahra began exploring. There was the antelope that had leaped into Marisith behind her. There was Bem's own mare, Bayard's chestnut steed, and a warhorse that might've been Bayard himself. She peered into cage after cage, growing more and more worried. Had the enchantress harmed the old man?

Bem meowed again, louder.

"I know, I know!" Zahra said. "In a moment!"

Then she spotted him, high overhead. A black-and-white pied kingfisher, trapped in one of the birdcages that swung from the ceiling.

Delirious with joy, she climbed higher and higher, over the cages of the agitated creatures, who whimpered and rattled their enclosures. But just as she reached the highest spot, from which she could touch her grandad's swinging prison, the kingfisher cocked his head and gave her a look so stern, so disapproving, that her heart sank.

He was right, of course. She should've tried to help Bem and the others first. It was what he would've done—and her mother too.

"I understand, Grandad," she whispered. "I shall return shortly."

Reluctantly, she scrambled down to where Bem was attempting to bite through the hinges of the hens' coop. Zahra tried the lock, but it wouldn't budge. She tried to bend the bars. No good. She tried to unstack the coop from the others around it, but nothing worked.

Desperate, Zahra tried another cage and another. One by one, to no avail. Finally she climbed again to where Grandad hovered, his expression mournful. And that was when she knew.

The cages weren't merely locked. They were enchanted.

At this, she began to weep the tears she'd been holding in all day.

"*I'm so sorry, Grandad,*" she whispered in his mother tongue. "*I tried.*"

He chirped softly.

"*I know not what to do,*" she continued, the words bubbling up from that secret place where she treasured the language of their hearts. "*How I wish Mother were here! How I wish the giants had never come. How I wish . . .*"

But no words in any language could express her turmoil. She descended to the cold stone floor and collapsed in a heap.

She didn't care if Mindra returned and found her. She didn't care if the giant smashed them all to bits. She was powerless to do any good at all. Nothing remained but grief.

Zahra lay there, Lepp at her feet and Bem at her chest, until she cried herself to sleep.

Chapter

16

Charles cranked the wheel in another turn.

"Are you certain this is the way?" Tilly asked.

She could read the road sign clearly. Three miles to WOLVERN-UNDER-LIZARD. But the tiny village, which was at the base of the hilltop known as Lizard Beacon, was *south* of Upper Wolvern. They needed to go north. Couldn't Charles see the sign?

She peered at him timidly. He sat with both hands on the wheel, jaw clenched. After a delightful drive to the village of Little Wolvern, where they'd gotten milkshakes and *almost* held hands on the quaint bridge, they'd headed back toward Upper Wolvern, driving slowly, taking all the country roads. But then, at one rural intersection, Charles had turned left instead of right.

At the time, Tilly opened her mouth to say something but didn't, thinking maybe he had some romantic view in mind. But no, they'd been driving now, in what felt like circles, for at least thirty minutes.

"Um, Charles?"

"What?" He didn't exactly snap at her, but it was close.

She felt stung. "Nothing."

They drove in silence for another ten minutes. And at each intersection, Charles turned the exact opposite way they should be heading. Sure, he'd only lived in the Wolverns part-time for most of his life, so he probably didn't know the countryside all that well. And it was easy to lose your sense of direction on the narrow, winding roads. Should she say something? She began biting a hangnail on her thumb. Everything had been so brilliant. And now it wasn't.

At yet another intersection, Tilly quietly read the road sign aloud, as if to herself. "Lower Wolvern, four miles." This one had an arrow pointing right.

Without speaking, Charles turned right at last.

It was the loud booms that woke Zahra. The floor beneath her trembled as huge footfalls shook the ground outside.

"Stay and guard the castle, says she," came a disgruntled voice from beneath the high windows. "Nothing about me supper. And the six sheep I ate for breakfast weren't near enough to fill me belly."

Suddenly two enormous fingers poked through one of the windows. The prisoners began to squawk and squeal and squeak with terror, but the giant couldn't reach any of the cages. Stonefist grumbled, and the fingers finally retreated.

"No tellin' when she'll be back," he muttered to himself. "So I'll just have to do me own huntin' again, curse her. She'll learn not to cheat ole Stonefist after this, that's fer certain."

Then his footsteps moved away from the building, farther and farther. They splashed through the small lake, then grew more muffled until Zahra could no longer hear them.

Silence. Was it a trick? Was he waiting somewhere, ready to pounce?

But the longer Zahra waited, the more certain she was that the giant really and truly was gone. She stood, legs wobbly, and crept to one of the windows. Bem and Lepp padded along beside her.

A breeze had sprung up. The air was fresh and clean. Zahra breathed deeply, filling her lungs. The giant couldn't be heard or smelled. Which meant she was free—at least for now.

As she turned from the window, her legs nearly gave out. When was the last time she'd eaten? Not since . . . supper, back at the hut the previous evening. Before she and Grandad had gone night fishing. Before the giants had come, before the fall of Caristor, before she'd landed in this strange world. A lifetime ago. If she was going to be of any use—to her grandad or anyone else—she needed to find food.

Zahra looked around at the caged animals, who were stirring restlessly. They needed some reassurance, some word of courage. "Dear ones," she announced in a trembling voice, "I do not know where we have landed. But the enchantress is gone, and so is the giant. And there's no telling when they'll return. But I need victuals. And I wager you do too. Come, Bem. Come, Lepp. Let us see what we can find."

The three of them slipped down the stairs. But they searched in vain. Not a single door on a single landing would open, in all that great tower. Finally Zahra dragged herself back to the top of the tower and scaled the cages to where her grandad's birdcage swung from the ceiling.

At the sight of him, her heart nearly stopped. His avian eyelids were closed, his beaked head lolling. He opened one groggy eye as she approached, then closed it again. His breast looked almost concave, and he was breathing shallowly. Even as a bird, apparently, he was prone to bouts of weakness. The sooner she could find food, the better.

Sobs threatened to overwhelm her again, but she gulped them

down. "The enchantress said something about a village," she said, hoping he could hear her, "though I can't see what could possibly be found in this desolate waste. But that's where I'm bound. If you have any peace to spare your granddaughter . . ."

She reached two fingers through the bars and brushed them against the bird's silky feathers. Instantly her breath slowed. Her body unclenched. The tears abated. Even though he was sleeping fitfully, the kingfisher's warmth flowed through her like a strengthening potion, and she felt as though she could face anything—anything at all. Reluctantly, she withdrew her hand, waved a brief farewell, then wound back down the stairs.

It was early evening by the time she emerged through the postern door into the lonely valley. By now, Lepp was a constant presence, her little shadow, while Bem scampered ahead, leading the way along the path that skirted the lake. But before the path climbed upward, Zahra turned and knelt beside the dog.

"Can you stay near the valley, Lepp?" she asked gently. "Keep an eye on things? We'll be back soon with nourishment. I promise."

Lepp whined in protest, but he seemed to understand. He sat, watching her with his good eye, as she followed Bem out of the valley.

"Look out!" Tilly cried.

A ginger cat dashed in front of the Rolls as if trying to attack it.

Charles slammed on the brakes. The car spun, tires squealing, in a full three-sixty. But just before it halted, it struck a figure that had appeared in the swale on the side of the road.

Tilly screamed. The figure went flying into the tall grasses beyond the front bumper.

"Was that a *person*?" Charles squawked in disbelief. "Did we just hit a *person*?"

"Oh no, no, no . . ." Tilly opened the passenger door. She dashed around the front of the car and began to hunt along the swale. Sure enough, a human figure lay crumpled and whimpering at the base of the hedgerow. A girl maybe Jack's age, with long dark braids and strange, almost-druidic clothes. Oh, great. A tourist.

Tilly knelt beside her. "Are you all right?"

The girl groaned and tried to sit up. She smelled faintly of woodsmoke. She was thin, almost fairylike, her dark eyes large in her anxious face.

"Whoa, wait a sec," Tilly cautioned. "You might be hurt."

But the girl was determined. Tilly offered her a hand, and she took it gingerly, trying to take stock of her surroundings. "Bem?" the girl said in a soft voice.

"Bem?" Tilly echoed, bewildered.

"The cat," said the girl. She had an unfamiliar accent. "Is she . . ."

"Oh," Tilly said. "We didn't hit her, if that's what you mean. Are you sure you're okay?"

The girl looked warily at the Rolls. "What *is* that fell thing?"

Tilly stifled a giggle. The girl had probably bumped her head. Or maybe she was yet another tourist who took the druid thing just a bit too far. "It's a Silver Shadow," Tilly said.

But the girl didn't seem to hear her. "I need to find Bem." She attempted to stand, but when Tilly reached for her other hand, she crumpled back onto the grass with a cry. "'Tis my wrist. Twisted, I fear. Or broken . . ." She winced.

"Can we give you a lift somewhere?" Tilly asked. "Or maybe call someone for you?"

"Nay!" the girl said sharply. "Do not call out. She might find us."

"The cat?"

"Nay." The girl tried to rise again, without success.

What was Charles doing? Just sitting there, in the car? "Oi, Charles!" Tilly called. "Give us a hand, would you?"

"Dad's going to kill me." His voice wafted to her from the driver's side window.

If he'd been Jack, or Georgie, or even Frankie, Tilly would've fired back with a sarcastic rebuttal. Something about how maybe, just *maybe*, a hurt person was more important than a stupid car. "Um . . . she's hurt?" she said instead.

Slowly the driver's door opened, and Charles climbed out. He walked around the car, peering at the bodywork.

"A scratch on the bonnet," he said in a flat tone. "I'm so dead. Dead, dead, dead."

Tilly, fighting irritation, ignored him. "She's in a lot of pain. The best thing will be to take her to hospital in Great Wolvern, get her checked out."

"I can't take her to Great Wolvern!" Charles suddenly yelled. "Dad doesn't even know I've got the car out with you right now. Way too many miles on it already, so he's bound to find out. Not to mention the damage. Plus, she's probably covered in mud . . ."

Tilly stared at him. Was he serious? Charles had taken her on a drive without his dad's permission? And now, after all the miles he'd racked up by driving in circles, he wouldn't drive just a *little* bit farther to help a person *he'd* hit with the car?

"To the Hall, then," Tilly conceded, attempting to mask her annoyance. Then to the girl: "It's where my parents work. You can make a phone call there, at least."

"A what?" the girl asked faintly.

"The Hall, Great Wolvern—what's the difference?" Charles had stopped yelling, but his voice remained high, strained. "I don't even know where we are!"

"A mile from Upper Wolvern, more or less," Tilly finally snapped, pointing to the nearest road sign. Carrick Hall wasn't quite a half mile beyond that. "See? It's on your way home."

"What about Bem?" the girl asked.

"Oh, right . . ." Tilly walked across the road toward where they'd last seen the cat. "Bem?" she called. "Bem! Here, kitty, kitty."

"She won't respond if you say it that way," the girl said from the swale. "She's not actually a cat."

Tilly suppressed a snort. She continued to call for Bem but eventually gave up.

"Sorry about that," Tilly said. "But maybe we can come back later, see if we can find her. For now, let's get you in the car."

Charles reluctantly came over to lend a hand but then recoiled. "Not another one!"

Seriously? Tourists were the reason Tilly had a job—and why her parents did, too, for that matter. Sure, the girl was muddy. And far too thin. But helping her was the right thing to do. Tilly pressed her lips together and assisted the girl to the back seat before climbing into the front passenger's side.

Charles finally got behind the wheel and backed the car around till it was facing north. He paused, staring stiffly ahead, as if waiting for Tilly's instructions.

"Straight," she said in a low voice. "Then take the next right."

Wordlessly, he did as she said.

Chapter

17

The bookshop door opened and closed.

Arash went to the window. The sun was slanting over the hills. Shadows had begun to lengthen. Villagers and tourists alike were probably all down at the green. But below, on the cobblestones, his grandfather was trekking up High Street.

The old man wore a light jacket over his usual attire, a satchel over one shoulder, and in his right hand he carried a walking stick. His stride was purposeful, determined. But his head was bowed, as if he was deeply troubled.

Arash threw on a hooded pullover, grabbed his backpack with his metal-detecting accessories, stuffed the treasure inside so his mother wouldn't find it, and raced downstairs. By the time he exited the building, Grandfather had already reached the roundabout.

Keeping close but not too close, Arash jogged behind. The old man continued up the lane with his walking stick, past the church, and through the archway that led to Carrick Hall, then turned toward the wooded hillside. Without a glance behind him, he entered the path to the hills.

Arash followed. Soon the trees thinned, and he emerged onto the open foothills that led toward the ridge, dotted with his own cairns. Ahead of him, his grandfather was climbing up and up, barely pausing for breath. No tourists were around, thank goodness.

When Grandfather drew near the ridge, he turned south, toward the valley. He appeared to be following Arash's cairns, in fact, aiming straight for the crevasse that Arash and Jack had climbed that morning. Was it only that morning? Well, brilliant. Arash might as well have set up neon signs pointing the way to the last place he wanted his grandfather to go.

Arash put on a burst of speed. By the time he drew near the ridge himself, his grandfather was already approaching the cliff's edge. The old man paused, glanced into the crevasse, then dropped in.

Panic sucked the air from Arash's lungs. It was almost as if Grandfather knew exactly what he was doing, exactly what was down there. But how?

Arash reached the edge. The descent was torturous. He tried not to disturb the scree and start another mini landslide, which could alert the demon—or, worse, bury his own grandfather. But finally he reached the bottom.

Ahead rose the castle, grim and forbidding. There was no sign of the demon, and none of the old man either. Was the woman with the angry voice—whoever she was—still around? But the valley seemed abandoned. And yet Arash could hear something. Muffled yipping, snorting, bleating, squawking—all coming from *inside* the castle. He crouched behind a boulder, where he could see without being seen.

Then footsteps. From behind a mound of scree, his grandfather emerged, apparently oblivious to Arash's presence. The old man glanced around warily, hefting the walking stick in both hands like a pikestaff.

Except it was no longer the walking stick.

It was the Infinium. He'd found it where Arash had left it.

"Not one more step, old man. Or I shall destroy them all." The woman. But now her tone was calm and heartless and dangerously near.

Jack had moped around the cottage after lunch, listening for any hint of disturbance in the hills. Nothing, to his relief. But it'd given him hours and hours to hatch a plan.

Now he tiptoed to the front door. Elspeth, Aurora, and Georgie were chatting away in the kitchen over a cold supper, and he didn't want to alert them—especially Georgie, who was the last person he wanted around, asking questions. Quietly Jack grabbed his backpack, which earlier he'd filled with a bag of crisps, a water bottle, a torch, and a length of strong rope that he'd found in his dad's toolshed. Then he left.

The village was quiet. Everyone had gone down to the green. As the sun slid toward the ridgeline of the Wolverns, the shadows lengthened—but of course, it wouldn't be dark for hours yet.

Jack's feet hurt. His heavy hiking boots had rubbed blisters on both heels during his mad dash that morning. But he kept trudging, past the roundabout and the church, under the archway toward the Hall, then up the path into the hills.

There was no sign of the giant. No trampled gorse, no massive footprints, no sheep bones. Even the occasional cairns, which Jack often found up this way, were intact. There weren't any tourists around, either—although he could make out a few tents farther north, near the beacon of Table Mount. Along the ridgeline ahead, a dog was chasing a small flock of sheep. If it was a sheepdog, it was a very badly trained one. Its owner wasn't anywhere about.

Had it all been a dream? The castle. The monster. The flight with Arash. But the ache in his feet told a different story.

Before long, he was descending into the valley from his preferred path at the far end. Not from the crevasse. He would never *ever* climb that thing again. Yes, there was the castle. Otherwise, the valley seemed abandoned. No slumbering monster, no smoke rising from the battlements. No stench either. Just cool evening air, calm and fresh. But right as Jack reached the path near the lake's edge, a furry figure dashed out from behind a cairn.

A stray dog, by the look of it. Skinny and scruffy, with one eye swollen shut, it stood awkwardly between him and the path to the castle, panting hard. It might be the same dog he'd seen near the ridge, chasing sheep. The stray wasn't exactly blocking Jack's way, but it wasn't being very friendly either. It was attempting—or so it seemed—to look fierce.

Jack remembered the bag of crisps in his backpack. He pulled it out, opened it, and tossed some pieces to the stray, who snarfed them up like it was half-starved. Jack tossed another few crisps, this time away from the path, and the dog sprang after them, tail wagging.

It worked for a while. Jack hurried down the path, putting as much distance between himself and the stray as he could. But soon the patter of paws followed him. Of course. Now the dog was trailing him, hoping for more. Just great.

Jack swiveled around. "You keep quiet, understand?" he commanded. "Not a peep."

The dog looked at him reproachfully but thumped its tail.

They kept going. As Jack drew near to the castle, he began to hear voices. One cruel and sinister, the other low and calm. But no sign of the giant. He paused.

Instead of picking his way along the base of the castle, as he had last time, Jack now headed toward the shelter of the cliffside and sneaked behind some of the boulders the giant had dislodged earlier that day. Crouching, Jack crept from boulder to boulder, hoping to find a spot where he could observe the castle without being seen.

And that was where he ran into Arash.

Chapter

18

Z ahra sat at the kitchen table of the vast house, wondering how to make a gracious exit.

She'd climbed out of the grim valley roughly an hour ago—where, to her surprise, the path had opened onto beautiful rolling hills, all waving grasses and pleasant shrubs tinged with yellow. An undulating ridge ranged behind her, along which several bare peaks rose in the distance. Ahead, a vast plain of what looked like farmland stretched all the way to the horizon. Sure enough, houses and roads and villages dotted the landscape. And people, most likely. People with food.

Bem had mewed insistently, already partway down a path into some woods, heading toward the inhabited plain. Zahra had followed.

They'd almost reached the woods when two human figures emerged. The first, a youngish fellow wearing a hooded brown cloak; the second, an older man wearing a strange sort of flat cap. She'd frozen. Everything in her had screamed to run. Men, at dusk, in an unfamiliar world. And herself, all alone. But her legs wouldn't move.

The man in the brown cloak had spotted her first. He'd given a crooked smile and waved.

"Camping here, too, are you?" he'd called. "Find a good spot?"

Zahra's throat had squeezed tight. They'd seemed in no particular hurry, simply on a jaunt through the hills. She'd stepped off the path out of their way, trying not to visibly tremble.

"We're camping over there, near Giant's Beacon," the younger man had continued, waving toward one of the bald peaks. Then he'd looked her up and down. "Cool costume, by the way."

The older man, by contrast, had studied her with a disapproving scowl.

"We're having a watch fire tonight—" the young man had gone on, but his companion had given him a nudge to keep moving. "Later, then!"

"Why must foreigners flock to rural Britain?" the older man had said as they climbed up the path behind her. "Ruins the authenticity."

But by then, her legs had become unstuck. She'd fled into the woods—where, thankfully, Bem was waiting. It had taken a good hour for Zahra to stop shaking.

After that, they'd wandered along a maze of paths, looping round and round till Zahra lost all sense of direction. Finally they'd stumbled onto a road.

And that was where she'd encountered the storm wagon.

First, a distant roar, like thunder—except it never ceased, just grew louder and louder. And then a sleek, gleaming body, powering toward her. Terrified, she'd flung herself against a hedgerow. But Bem—fierce, foolish Bem—had run at it, howling. And that was how Zahra had met the young woman who'd brought her here.

After being hit by the storm wagon, Zahra had been transported in the thing at breathtaking speed, as if drawn by six of Starwise's cousins, all invisible. Eventually they'd pulled up in front of a large house that looked like some kind of castle. Its grim walls rose into the evening sky, spiked by a central tower. There the young man had left them, muttering something about a bonnet, while the young woman—Tilly, her name was—had helped her inside.

"Mum must've stepped out to help Dad for a bit," Tilly had said. "He sets up barriers along the paths behind the Hall, to keep tourists from wandering about. We woke up one year to a whole village of caravanners out by the pavilion."

They'd entered what Tilly called the kitchen, although it was the strangest place Zahra had ever seen. Shiny contraptions of all kinds lined the walls, shinier than the most perfectly polished shields in Caristor. Tilly had settled Zahra into a chair at a long table and brought over a soft cushion to prop her wrist. Then Tilly had gone over to one of the contraptions—a tall, wardrobe-like thing—and opened its hinged door.

"How does leftover soup sound?" Tilly had said. "I can heat it up for you."

"Soup," Zahra had replied faintly. At last a word she recognized. "Thank you, best of hostesses."

Tilly had given her a bemused smile. She'd ladled a thick, creamy broth into a bowl and placed the bowl inside a small box, also with a hinged door, that sat on a long ledge. Then she'd closed the door and pushed several circles on the box's face. It had made a number of high, bird-like chirps before it began purring like a cat. When it chirped again, Tilly had opened the door, cautiously pulled out the bowl, and set it in front of Zahra.

"Careful," Tilly had warned, handing her a spoon so shiny, Zahra had hesitated to touch it. "Soup's hot."

Baffled, Zahra had watched the steam rise. How was this possible? The young woman had struck no flint, used no kindling, built no fire. But here was hot soup, and Zahra had been starving.

It was the most flavorful food she'd ever tasted. She'd eaten three bowlfuls, plus some sort of fluffy bread that required almost no chewing, and drunk two mugs of tea. All the while she'd murmured her thanks, overcome by amazement.

Now Zahra sat alone at the table, restlessly sipping tea. Tilly had stepped outside to find her parents, leaving Zahra with the instructions to "take it easy"—whatever that meant. But she couldn't help thinking about Grandad and the others at the castle, who were probably frightened and hungry and worried. She had to figure out a way to get back to the valley—not that she had any idea where it was from here . . .

At the same time, she wasn't much good to anyone in her current condition. Her wrist felt worse, if possible. She wasn't sure how much longer she could manage without help.

Just then, a faint voice reached her ears. Someone was calling from a nearby room. She shuffled over to a closed door. Yes, the voice was coming from behind it. Tentatively, she turned the knob with her good hand and peeked in.

"Tilly, dear, is that you?" an old, quavering voice said.

Zahra entered a long, low room. It had a lovely set of furnishings and a bank of windows overrun with some kind of pink flowers. Beyond this room was another. It contained a sort of divan from which a very old woman was staring at her with rheumy eyes.

"You are not Tilly," the old woman said. She didn't seem upset, merely curious.

Zahra drew near. "My apologies, venerable mother," she said in the formal way she'd been taught. "I'm Zahra. I know not where Tilly has gone."

The old woman continued to stare—kindly but intently. "I see," she said after a moment. "I was hoping she might open my window that I might hear the sounds outside. Birds, beasts, other creatures."

Zahra looked at the window. It appeared to be open already. She could see the gardens clearly. But as she stepped closer, she realized that the window was made of flawless glass. She attempted to open it one-handed, but the whole contraption baffled her.

"The clasp," the old woman said, pointing. "Lift that first. Good girl. Now, push the glass gently outward."

Zahra did as she was told. The woman settled back onto her pillows with a sigh. "Much better. I didn't want to miss anything that might transpire this evening." She peered at Zahra again. "You've come a long way, I see."

"Yes." Zahra had to be careful. She didn't want to say too little and risk offending her hostess, but neither did she want to say too much.

The woman continued to study her. "From Valorenta, I expect, by the look of you. Or no . . . your accent is Ternivali. Raised there, were you? But your people were from over the mountains."

Zahra blinked.

The old woman gave her a wise smile. "You'll keep your own counsel, no doubt. Just as you were told. As you should. But you're among friends here."

Zahra couldn't help it. "If I may ask, honorable hostess, Where *am* I, exactly?"

"Don't you know?" said the old woman. "You're in Tellus, of course. At Carrick Hall. And I'm Mrs. Fealston, attendant to the late High Queen."

Chapter

19

The stone cottage was chilly, but Elspeth could tell this was one of those warm, peaceful summer evenings. Which meant hordes of people down at the green. Thousands. Villagers as well as tourists. Enjoying live music and getting properly sloshed, no doubt. And then the hordes would hike up to the beacons for the sunset and the all-night watch fires.

"I don't see a soul out there right now," Aurora said. She, Elspeth, and Georgie had raided the fridge for a cold supper of ham and hard-boiled eggs—with toast, of course—while Jack had stayed holed up in the room he was forced to share with Georgie. Reading, probably. Wanting to be left alone. The door remained firmly shut, anyway.

"Just before sunset, it'll feel like we're hosting the World Cup," Elspeth said wryly. "We used to go up to Table Mount for the watch fires every year, but then one time we lost Georgie in the crowd, when he was maybe four or five. Dad found him about an hour later, eating a tub of ice cream with a group of students from Portugal. They'd adopted him as their mascot. Remember that, Georgie?"

But Georgie wasn't listening. He was standing stock-still, staring at the wall above the sideboard. He put his finger to his lips.

"Shh!" he said. "D'you see that? They're moving!"

Elspeth followed his gaze to Frankie's framed sketch. Did he mean the *characters* were moving? But the dryad and stag looked as they always did. Like a drawing.

"Georgie, what—"

He shushed them again and stared for another few seconds. Then his shoulders drooped. "I guess it was nothing."

"More toast?" Elspeth asked, half kidding. Then she sucked in her breath, because now she saw it too. "Oh! The dryad just—"

"I told you!" Georgie yelled.

The three of them stood in front of the sideboard. And then, sure enough, the dryad moved. She took a few steps, and one bare foot became visible under her leafy gown. And now the stag was moving, too, leaping away toward the castle.

And then . . . nothing. The movement stopped. But the action had frozen where it'd left off. The sketch was different now. It wasn't the same picture Frankie had drawn. Elspeth felt slightly dizzy, like she'd just looked up at the night sky to find a completely new set of constellations.

"What do you think it means?" Aurora gasped.

"Mrs. Fealston will know!" Georgie rushed forward to grab the picture. "Let's take it to Carrick Hall!"

Elspeth shouldered him out of the way. "Stop. You can't carry this yourself. It's far too heavy with the glass in there. But you're right. Mrs. Fealston will know. Aurora and I will carry it between us."

The girls maneuvered the picture from the wall and across the room while Georgie held open the cottage door. After they emerged onto High Street, he kept up a constant stream of commentary, like a sportscaster, eyes locked on the sketch in case the characters moved again. It was a good thing the streets were empty. The last thing they needed was a curious villager in the mix, eavesdropping.

"Dryad, still in position," Georgie announced. "No movement from the stag." His voice bounced off the shop fronts and echoed down the street.

"Honestly, Georgie," Elspeth said through gritted teeth. "Can you shut it?"

But they didn't see another soul. Not until the roundabout, anyway, when a vehicle motored up behind them. The driver tapped the horn. They stepped aside, and Charles swept by in the Rolls, waving with a smirk.

"Thanks for the lift, Charlie," Aurora yelled.

He gave a languid salute without looking back. "No problem, Roar." His voice drifted from the open windows.

Elspeth scowled at the retreating car. Seriously? He couldn't have stopped? Not even for his own sister? True, it would've been almost impossible for them to explain what they were doing. But neither had Charles bothered to ask. It was as if people were just flocks of sheep, mere nuisances. The only person he had any use for was Tilly.

Elspeth watched as the Rolls glided under the archway toward Carrick Hall.

What would happen when Tilly was no longer useful? What then?

Jack followed Arash's gaze beyond the boulder. Something big was going down. Really big. And it wasn't good.

Two figures faced off in front of the castle. One appeared to be a woman, an ethereal beauty with marble-white skin, a trim black suit jacket and trousers, and black gloves like some kind of assassin. She carried a large embroidered bag over one shoulder and a leather briefcase over the other.

The second figure, to Jack's astonishment, was Professor Rastegar.

"'Tis all mine," the woman was saying. There was something familiar about her voice. Her fine face twitched with rage. She was either a really unhinged tourist or a desperate solicitor with *serious* designs for this particular corner of the Wolverns.

Professor Rastegar, for some reason, was holding what looked like a metal detector. Arash's, perhaps? The one his mum had asked about this morning? Maybe this was a showdown over an Elizabethan burial ground or something. Jack imagined the professor hefting a skull in the air, like Hamlet. *Alas, poor Yorick!*

Instead, the professor set down the metal detector and straightened to his full height. "Begone from here." His voice rang with authority. "This world, which was lost, has already been won. But not by thee, Mindra of Old."

Jack did a doubletake. Mindra? Surely not. Surely the professor didn't mean the enchantress from Frankie's fairy tales—the stories that every Addison sibling believed except Jack. Right?

"Nay, old fool." The woman's eyes glinted with malice. "Dost thou hear it? 'Tis calling, louder than ever. Never have I heard it so clearly—not since that usurping child stole it. Which means 'tis near, near as thy heartbeat." A hungry, haunted look distorted her otherwise-striking face.

"Near or no, 'tis nothing without the gems," the old man replied.

Mindra laughed. Fierce and high and cruel. Jack glanced at Arash, who looked paralyzed with horror.

With gloved fingers, Mindra lifted a slim, glittering chain that hung around her neck. Something swung from it, something bright, almost terrible in its beauty.

The professor paused. "'Tis only one."

Mindra laughed again. She released the chain and grabbed the briefcase at her hip, flipping it around so the front was visible. Stamped across the leather face was a familiar name: *Franklin J. Addison.*

Jack nearly yelped. Frankie's briefcase! But wouldn't he have taken it with him to London?

Mindra unclasped the briefcase and pulled out an object. Jack recognized this too. It was an elaborately carved wooden box about the size of a biscuit tin. He'd discovered it once, when scavenging in Frankie's briefcase for candy. He'd thought it was just a locked pencil box in which Frankie kept art supplies, but now the enchantress displayed it like she'd found the Holy Grail.

"Nay, fool. 'Tis not merely one. 'Tis *all*."

"What hast thou done?" The professor's voice faltered. "Where is the youth?"

Mindra's laughter wasn't mirth. It was something else, something monstrous. She returned the box to the briefcase and then reached into her bag, from which she extracted what looked like a mesh snare. Jack could make out at least two small creatures inside it, wriggling and squirming.

The stray dog, who'd been cowering between Jack and Arash, now pressed its trembling body against Jack's leg, whimpering almost soundlessly. Arash gave a start and glanced down. The kid hadn't noticed the dog earlier, apparently.

"The youth?" Mindra echoed with a sneer. "Dost thou mean the foolish young man who trusted a beautiful stranger at the railway station? Him?" She reached into the snare and lifted one of the animals by its blunt tail. Even from a distance, Jack could see the velvety brown fur, the long-fingered front paws, the pale nose. It was a terrified mole.

But . . . but . . . this couldn't be possible. She was playing, of course. People didn't just get turned into animals. Jack's logical brain knew this. But then again, giants didn't just appear in valleys either. Frankie. His brother. A mole. No.

Mindra dropped the first creature back into the snare and pulled out the second, a reddish-brown mouse. It squeaked and trembled as it swung by the tail. "Or dost thou mean her?" Mindra said with unveiled contempt. "The usurper's heir?"

"The maiden . . ." The professor's voice was barely audible now.

"Oh yes. Both of them." The woman plopped the mouse back into the snare and stuffed the animals into her bag. "And there are others. Dost thou not hear their cries inside my great fastness? For this is Marisith, of course. Swept here by my powers. For I came not only for what was stolen but for all the thieves and usurpers under these faithless stars. Including thee."

She lowered the bag and briefcase to the ground, her eyes never leaving the professor's face. Then she raised her gloved hands.

"Look upon the sky of Tellus one last time, old man. For thou shalt never see it again."

Then two things happened at once.

Arash chucked a handful of scree, which struck the bluff about twenty feet from where they were hiding. And the stray dog, which Jack had all but forgotten, charged.

As Mindra's gaze snapped toward the bluff, the stray came streaking at her like a skinny, furry locomotive. It slammed into her, knocking her backward onto the ground. But the dog, bless its scrawny soul, was no match for the enchantress. She threw it aside so forcefully that it bounced against the castle's foundation and lay there, unmoving.

In a heartbeat, Mindra was back on her feet. This time, she didn't wait, didn't speak, but flung her arms up and out, toward the professor, as if throwing a snare over his head. To Jack's astonishment, the old man began to shrink. He seemed to curl in on himself, like a bird tucking its head under its wing. And all the while, the professor's body seemed to be molting, shedding its clothes and skin for what looked like banded feathers.

Then, no bigger than a falcon, he extended two wings and shot into the air.

For indeed, a falcon was what he'd become.

Chapter

20

Zahra stared at the old woman. It couldn't be true, could it? This couldn't be Carrick Hall, that fabled waypoint between worlds? And this ancient woman . . . she'd known the High Queen?

"Yes, my dear," Mrs. Fealston asserted, as if reading her mind. "This was where three maidens fell through the framed tapestry of dryads that once hung here and found themselves in Ternival, where they became the Three Queens. But after they disappeared from your world, do you know what befell them?" She gazed at Zahra expectantly.

Zahra tilted her head in bewilderment. According to Grandad, back when he was a child, the Three Queens had simply vanished one day into the East Wilderlands, never to return. "I do not know, good mother. No one does."

Mrs. Fealston's wrinkled face broke into a smile. "Oh, but some *do*. The girls came back here, of course." She pointed toward the door that led to the kitchen. "I saw them, with my own eyes, walk through that very door. Indeed, the High Queen herself made Carrick Hall her home. Here she raised her only daughter and lived to the end of her days."

"The High Queen . . ." Zahra could barely form the words.

"Gone, now. Died of illness a few years ago." Mrs. Fealston's eyes had grown misty. "But she isn't the only royalty to come from Carrick Hall. Even longer ago than all that—before the High Queen was born—this was also home to the First Queen and King of Mesterra. After they died, their nephew worked these grounds as the gardener, for years and years. His descendants run the place now. Tilly, for instance, who's about your age, maybe older."

"Oh!" Zahra said. "Yes, we've met."

"She's the second eldest of five," Mrs. Fealston continued. "But Frankie's the first. You haven't come across him, by the way, in your travels? Tall, dark-haired, too conscientious, much too confident? Accompanied by Eva. Willowy, fashionable. Granddaughter of the High Queen. Both went missing earlier today." The old woman frowned.

Zahra grew more and more amazed at everything her hostess said. "I fear that I have not seen them."

Just then, the door from the kitchen opened and Tilly peered in. "Hullo, Mrs. Fealston." She caught sight of Zahra and smiled. "Oh, there you are! I was worried you'd wandered off. How's the wrist?"

Zahra shook her head. "Not much better, alas."

"Tilly, dear," Mrs. Fealston interjected, "you mustn't pester her. She's come all the way from Ternival."

Tilly's eyes widened, but then the door opened farther, and a thin, dark-haired woman entered. She looked like Tilly except older, with deep lines of concern etched into her forehead.

"Zahra, this is my mum," Tilly said, "Mrs. Addison."

Tilly's mother looked Zahra up and down. Her demeanor wasn't unkind, exactly. More matter-of-fact. "Hurt your wrist, did you?" she asked. "Best have Paxton take you to hospital."

Zahra had no idea what the woman meant.

"If it's no trouble?" Tilly said to an unseen person beyond the doorframe.

"None at all," came the gruff voice of an old man.

For one wild moment, Zahra thought it was Grandad, borne here by some wind of mercy and restored to human form. But the dour fellow who now entered the room couldn't have been more unlike him—in demeanor, at least. This man looked as if he hadn't laughed in decades. He took in her straggly braids, her rumpled kurta, her dusty sandals, then glanced at her face. His eyebrows shot up.

"This is Paxton," Mrs. Addison said to Zahra. "You might call him our man-of-all-work here at the Hall."

"And this is Zahra," Tilly told Paxton.

"I thought you said she was a tourist!" the old man blurted, still staring.

"Nonsense," Mrs. Fealston said from the divan. "Zahra is from Valorenta, of course. By way of Ternival."

Mrs. Addison huffed, as if humoring the old housekeeper took all her self-control. "Well, wherever she's from, she needs a doctor."

"A doctor!" Zahra exclaimed. She pictured one of those robed and bespectacled scholars she'd occasionally seen on the main road to Caristor, the ones who advised the royal sentries. What could a bookish man do for a wounded wrist?

"My sentiments exactly," Mrs. Addison said grimly. "But don't fret. If those fellows at Great Wolvern won't see you right away, let me know and I'll alert Lord Edward. He has a way of sorting things out. Now, Paxton will bring around the Bentley, and you'll be on your way."

With one last glance at Zahra, Paxton nodded and left. Utterly bewildered, she allowed herself to be led toward the kitchen.

"You can trust Paxton, my dear," the old woman called from the divan. "He knows a great deal more than he lets on. More than the rest of us, I suspect. Come back soon!"

Zahra followed Tilly and her mother into the kitchen.

"Tilly, I need you at home, keeping an eye on your siblings." Mrs. Addison continued to give instructions like she was the Chief Sentry. "You never know what shenanigans they'll manage with Lord Edward's daughter in the mix—especially on festival night. Plus, I want you listening for the phone, in case Frankie rings the cottage."

Tilly sighed, clearly disappointed. She began twisting her hair up into a loose bun on the top of her head, as if preparing for an evening of endless work.

"And don't wait on Paxton to give you a lift either," her mother went on. "I'll make sure this young lady eats a bit more first. Plus, I imagine Paxton will want to take the motorway, in case the county lanes are clogged."

Tilly nodded and turned to Zahra. "It was really nice meeting you," she said ruefully. "But I'm afraid Mum needs my help tonight. Give us a ring once it's all settled, will you?"

A ring? What strange customs they had here in Tellus. "I—I don't have a ring," Zahra said.

Tilly laughed. "No, no—I mean, send us a message. Paxton will know what to do. Cheers!"

In short order, Zahra was plied with more food, bidden farewell by Mrs. Addison, and then bundled into the back seat of another storm wagon—this time, driven by Paxton. The old man barely said a word as she got in but instead gazed straight ahead, his face somber under some sort of cap.

As the storm wagon swept around a circular lane bordered by spectacular flower beds and sculpted hedges, she twisted in her seat and looked behind her. Framed by the darkening hills, the mighty house of Carrick Hall rose like a winged steed. Had she really just taken supper there, in the home of the great queens?

They continued down the long road. Suddenly a rumble from the hills on their right made Zahra jump. She peered anxiously through the window. Was the valley up that way somewhere, closer than she realized? Then came a louder rumble. Paxton was lifting the brim of his cap and peering forward, craning his neck. His expression had gone from somber to worried.

Then, as they passed a long hedgerow, Zahra glimpsed a flash of ginger fur.

"*Stop!*" she cried.

The wagon screeched to a halt. Zahra fumbled desperately with the door handle.

"*Wait,*" said Paxton. "Let me help you."

But she managed to open the door anyway and practically fell onto the road.

"No, child!" Paxton called.

But Zahra didn't heed him. She fled toward the hedgerow where she'd last seen Bem and pushed through the branches one-handed. Behind her, the driver's door opened and Paxton's quick footsteps followed. She pressed on. Soon she could no longer see the road.

And that was when realization struck.

The word she'd shouted to the old man just now . . .

She'd meant "stop," of course. But that wasn't the word she'd used. Instead, she'd spoken in Grandad's mother tongue. Her favorite language.

Which she'd never heard anyone, other than family, speak.

Until today.

Until just now.

When Paxton had said "*Wait.*"

Chapter

21

Blind rage—like fire, like boiling water, like an earthquake—
swallowed Arash's brain. As soon as his grandfather was transformed, Arash's whole body became one taut weapon:
muscles clenched, fists like missiles, legs powering forward as if by
some primal command. But then a pair of arms closed around him
like a vice.

Locked in struggle, Arash watched as the terrible woman snatched
the falcon from the air by his feet. The raptor put up a fight, beating
his wings against her face, but eventually Mindra wrestled him into
her bag with the others.

Arash resisted. The arms held on. He pushed forward. "She'll take
us down, mate." Jack's panicked voice hissed in his ear. "Just like the
others. My brother. Your grandfather. We'd be no good to them
then."

Jack's words sank in. This would be their fate if they dared con-
front Mindra in the open. Transformed into creatures. Imprisoned.
Helpless.

Arash sagged. Jack released his grip.

Mindra picked up her bag—that seemingly bottomless reservoir of wickedness—and withdrew what looked like a large, spiny seashell. She lifted it to her lips as if it was a horn and took a great breath. But then she paused.

"Nay," she said aloud to herself. "I shall not summon Stonefist this time. The wretch abandoned his watch, after all. And Ternival shall be mine by morning, with or without the brute." An awful smile spread across her face. "Rather, he shall be mine especial gift to this traitorous world."

She returned the shell to the bag and then picked up Frankie's briefcase. From it she pulled out the wooden box and opened it gingerly, as if it contained live explosives. Instead, a lovely sound—like fairy music or distant bells—wafted on the air. But to Mindra, apparently, the sound was agonizing. Her features twisted. Her gloved hands shook. Gasping, she removed the chain with its glittering gem from around her neck and stuffed it into the box. Then she slammed the lid and locked it.

The music stopped. Mindra's face relaxed. She closed her eyes and inhaled slowly, triumphantly, like she'd just ingested a pill that burns like poison but imparts the strength of a thousand men. Her fine features still twitched, but she seemed to stand taller, the muscles in her neck and arms corded like whips. Arash had the feeling that if a boxer struck her, every bone in the athlete's hand would shatter.

Mindra snapped the briefcase shut and stuffed the wooden box into her embroidered bag. Then she bent and lifted one last thing from the ground: the Infinium.

Arash took a step, but Jack's hand grasped his elbow.

Mindra approached the castle wall, yanked open the postern door, entered swiftly, and slammed the door behind her.

And then—as if enough unthinkable things hadn't happened already—the entire castle lifted from the ground like a rocket, swirled upward, and vanished.

Someone was yelling.

Loudly, practically in Jack's ear. But it wasn't Arash, who stood next to him, staring up at the empty space in the sky where the castle had gone. No, it was Jack himself. Howling. Just one incoherent note, like a frightened animal.

The fairy tales never talked about this part: the utter shock that impossible, horrible things were actually happening, right in front of you, to real people. The characters in those stories always seemed to take it in stride that—of *course*, duh—enchantresses not only exist but can also change people like your brother and his girlfriend and a local shopkeeper into small animals. And steal magical things from your family. Because—of *course*—your family has magical things. Oh, and enchantresses can make castles appear and disappear out of nowhere.

Jack stopped howling and took a shuddering breath.

And that was when he could smell it.

The giant.

Massive, earth-shaking footfalls began to descend into the far end of the valley. To Jack's horror, Arash bolted from behind the boulder where they'd been hiding and ran out into the open. He scooped up the unconscious dog in both arms, then staggered into the crevasse.

Stonefist appeared at the other end of the lake. Slung across his shoulders were three dead animals—two sheep and a cow. At the sight of the empty valley, he halted.

"Wh—" His gaze scanned the bluffs, then settled back on the spot where the castle should've been. Confusion swept across his hideous face. "She didna leave old Stonefist, now, did she?" He trudged along the lake, each footfall dislodging more rocks and scree. With every step, the stench grew stronger.

The giant looked up at the sky, his face mottled with anger. Jack's stomach dropped. An angry giant was not a good thing. Not good at all.

But then Stonefist did the last thing Jack expected. He burst into tears.

The oaf stomped his feet. He flung the livestock to the ground with a sickening thump. He picked up rocks and chucked them. He railed and cursed and seethed. If it hadn't been so terrifying, it would've been hilarious. The biggest living creature Jack had ever seen was throwing a full-blown toddler tantrum.

But a childish giant, apparently, was just as dangerous as an angry one. At any moment, either boy could be crushed.

As Jack squatted behind the boulder—the straps of his backpack cutting into his shoulders, the blisters on his heels raw—he felt the sudden outrage of a person who's been through a freakish amount of stress and now has to face something worse. It wasn't fair.

At the same time, this was what he'd come for. This, right here. To face the giant. And kill him, if he could.

Eventually Stonefist plopped down and bawled his eyes out—terrifyingly close to the crevasse where Arash was hiding. Then, just as suddenly, the giant stopped. He began to sniff. Turning his head this way and that, he sniffed and sniffed.

"Fee, fi, fo, fum," Stonefist growled. "I smell the blood of . . ." He paused, sniffing again. "The blood of . . ." The great fellow lumbered to his feet and scratched his head. "She was right, curse her," he muttered. "They're somewhere about." Then he stomped toward the crevasse.

Jack's limbs felt like they were made of peanut butter. What would Jack the Giant Killer do? But his mind was blank. Finally he did the only thing he could think of. He grabbed a handful of scree, just like Arash had done, and flung it at the bluff beyond them.

And then, like a terrified mouse, he ran.

Chapter

22

There it was again, just like this morning. The strange rumbling from the hills.

Tilly had been hearing it, on and off, ever since she'd set off down the drive toward the village. But it was louder than before, and closer. Unnerving, in fact. Even the birds had grown quiet, as if awaiting a storm.

A car came into view, heading her way. Was it . . . She hesitated, feeling panicky. Yes, the Rolls. She stepped to the side, hoping it was Lord Edward instead of Charles—and then hoping it wasn't, because his lordship might be on his way to inform her parents about the joyride and demand some sort of compensation for the damage to his beloved car. But that was ridiculous. He was the kindest man in five counties. And anyway, the damage wasn't even remotely her fault. So why the panic?

As the Rolls drew near, sure enough—there was the scratch on the bonnet. But it wasn't Lord Edward at the wheel.

The car pulled up. All the windows were down.

"Hullo," said Charles. He looked—was it possible?—a bit rumpled. But his gaze was direct and kind as he regarded her with concern.

"Hullo," Tilly replied. It was unfair, really, how some people could look so outrageously beautiful while disheveled. And yet it wasn't his looks, this time, that made her heart all fluttery. It was his demeanor. Intentional, apologetic—sheepish, even. He'd returned because she mattered.

"Where are you headed?" he asked.

"Home, to the cottage," she replied. "So my siblings don't mortify our family in front of Aurora."

"Doubtful," he said wryly. "If anything, it'll be vice versa. She's already leading them, like the Pied Piper, straight out of the village."

Tilly laughed.

Charles's gaze grew serious again. "Earlier—" he began.

She waved a hand. "It's fine. It'd been a long day of work. We were tired. The girl—I mean, how random, right?" She attempted a breezy tone. "Honestly, Charles. Don't worry about it."

He studied her for another long moment. Then his face broke into a grin. "Get in," he said. "I'll take you home."

"Whatever they're doing at the quarry, I wish they'd stop," Aurora said.

The girls had begun to sweat, lugging the upright frame with its heavy glass between them. Once they'd passed under the archway that led toward the Hall, the air had grown still and close. Elspeth walked this route a dozen times a week, but it'd never felt so long.

"Here, switch sides with me," she said to Aurora.

"It's my turn," Georgie whined. "I can carry it. I promise."

The girls ignored him. They switched sides clumsily, then resumed their trek.

Another boom, closer this time. Then another. Flocks of startled birds rose in the air. The racket sounded like it was just ahead. Coming from the wooded hillside, closer and closer, like huge footfalls.

"Is it just me," asked Aurora, "or are those trees moving?"

Tilly climbed into the Rolls. But as Charles made a U-turn and headed toward the village, a tremendous boom rumbled down the nearby hillside. Then a second. And a third.

"Terrible timing," he said. "They shouldn't be detonating at the quarry on festival day."

As Charles drove on, the concussions grew stronger, closer. Then Tilly spotted two figures on the right, sprinting down one of the steep paths from the hills toward the drive.

She realized, as the car swept past them, that it was Jack and . . . Was that Arash? But what was he carrying? The boys were running full tilt, obviously terrified.

"Charles!" she yelped.

But the earth was shaking repeatedly now, as if a jet plane had crashed into the hillside and was rolling down, down, down.

Tilly swiveled in her seat. Another car was barreling toward them from the direction of Carrick Hall. The Bentley. With Paxton at the wheel. But where was Zahra? Just as the boys burst from the path onto the drive, he pulled up alongside them and seemed to be yelling through the open back door. He slowed enough for them to jump in, then floored it.

And that was when she saw it. A huge figure, impossibly huge, an actual giant, blasting down the wooded hillside toward the drive. Trees rocked and swayed around it. The great hideous face took one look at the retreating Bentley, then pounded after it.

Tilly couldn't even scream. This wasn't real, right? She must've fallen asleep or something, back at the Hall, and this was the weird dream that resulted from way too much excitement for one day. But no. Apparently, Charles saw it too.

"What the—" He was staring in horror at the wing mirror. Then he slammed his foot on the gas.

The Rolls took off at top speed, the Bentley close behind, the giant on their heels.

Jack held on. From the back seat of the Bentley, he could see Paxton's death grip on the wheel. Where had the old man come from, anyway? Gravity had driven the giant downhill faster than Jack and Arash could run—and neither of them would've made it if the Bentley hadn't come roaring up, its back door already open, just in the nick of time.

Ahead of them, another car was racing away toward Upper Wolvern. Lord Edward's Silver Shadow. His lordship wasn't at the wheel, though. It was Charles, with someone in the passenger seat. Jack recognized the topknot. Tilly!

Next to Jack, Arash clutched the dog in his lap, his backpack still strapped to his shoulders. He stared ahead blankly, as if willing this whole situation to vanish like the castle.

Jack leaned forward. "What do we do now?" he hollered to Paxton. "How do we get rid of it? We can't just lead a giant into Upper Wolvern!"

But Paxton wasn't listening. He was craning his neck to peer at something ahead, in front of the Rolls. Jack followed his gaze.

People. Walking toward them from the village.

Elspeth, Aurora, and Georgie.

And the Rolls was headed straight for them.

Elspeth heard the cars before she saw them. Coming their way. Fast.

Suddenly Lord Edward's Silver Shadow shot into view.

"What on earth is Charlie *doing*?" Aurora cried.

Elspeth stared, aghast. "Wait—and is that *Tilly*?"

Behind the Rolls, another car followed at top speed.

"Oi, there's Paxton!" Georgie squeaked. "In the Bentley—with Jack and Arash! Look at him go!"

And then an enormous figure—larger than life, larger than houses, with a huge ugly face—came pounding after the Bentley. Its footfalls shook the ground. Elspeth could feel its angry bellows in her rib cage. Giants on paper, in fairy tales, were a fun fantasy. Giants in real life were petrifying.

Before she could move, the Rolls swerved. It tore straight at her and Aurora as they held the frame between them—not slowing, not even a little.

Elspeth shut her eyes. Her hair was blown roughly back, the frame ripped from her hands. But no impact. Just the sound of an engine roaring louder and louder.

She opened her eyes. The Bentley was zooming toward her like a missile.

Again, she flinched. But again, no impact. Just a whoosh.

And now the giant was bearing down so fast it couldn't stop, its expression every bit as shocked as Elspeth felt. But before either of them could react, it stumbled forward and—with that same mighty whoosh—was gone.

Elspeth staggered back. She turned to see Aurora, windblown and shaken, just a few feet away. Georgie cowered nearby. No roaring engines. No earth-shattering footfalls. Nothing.

She glanced down the drive toward the village. The Rolls, the Bentley, the giant—all gone.

But between the girls, wobbling upright on the drive, was the frame.

It teetered for a moment, then fell back against the pavement.

Empty.

Chapter

23

Darkness hit like a wall.

One moment, Jack was gripping the back of Paxton's seat as the Bentley tore after the Rolls. The next moment, nothing.

The drive, the daylight, the hedgerows—all vanished. For three long seconds, Jack felt suspended in midair like an astronaut, no sense of up or down. Then the car lurched forward, like they'd driven off a cliff, and down they went, down and down, till they crash-landed on something solid.

Breathless, he peered out the window. They were on a dirt road in the middle of a dark forest. Ahead of them, through the cracked windscreen, he could see the Rolls, dented and smoking, still rocking from impact.

But just then, both cars shook. A deafening boom echoed through the forest. Then another. And another. Behind them, farther down the road, trees began to sway.

The giant.

It'd been close on their tail, after all. Whatever magic had dragged the vehicles here had done the same to Stonefist.

The Rolls took off ahead of them, spraying dirt everywhere. Then Paxton, too, mashed his foot on the gas. Jack was thrown back as both cars tore away.

It was all he could do to hang on. The road was so rutted that every jolt sent him flying. As the cars careened around one narrow bend after another, bouncing with every dip and swell, he caught glimpses of huge moss-covered trees in every direction. Thickets and underbrush flashed past. Overhead, the canopy was so thick it felt like they were underwater.

The road narrowed. Then, through a break in the underbrush, Jack spotted something, deep in the woods.

Silvery, glowing. Some kind of creature.

But he didn't get a better look. Without warning, the car ahead of them swerved. Something blocked its way. A pile of what looked like barrels lay strewn across the road. The Rolls clipped one of the casks and then spun into the whole pile, barrels cascading everywhere. Just in time, Paxton cranked the wheel and the Bentley veered, flew for a half second, and plowed into the underbrush.

In the silence that followed, Jack could hear the ominous hiss of the overheated engine. He'd bumped his chin—he could taste blood—but was otherwise unharmed. Paxton began to mutter as he attempted to push open the driver's door.

Jack glanced at Arash. The kid still stared blankly ahead, the dog, unconscious, on his lap.

"C'mon, mate," Jack said. But Arash didn't respond.

Jack grabbed his own backpack, shoved open the door, and climbed out.

The acrid smell of burning rubber filled the air. On the road, the battered Rolls sat amid a chaos of barrels, its brake lights blinking: on, off, on, off. Charles and Tilly had already managed to tumble out.

Charles's normally tan face was tinged with gray, his jaw set. Tilly looked on the brink of tears.

"All right, Till?" Jack asked.

She took a shaky breath. "Elspeth, Georgie, Aurora . . . Do you suppose they . . . Did we . . . Are they okay?"

Jack grimaced. "Hard to say. I could see the Rolls bearing down on them, and then it just . . . vanished. The kids were still standing there, though. I remember the shocked look on Elspeth's face. But then I felt this mighty tug, like we'd entered some sort of black hole, and the Bentley tore straight at them."

Tilly nodded. "That's what it felt like in the Rolls too. But there was no impact. So, maybe they're fine?"

"Assuming the same thing happened when the giant went through."

"But why were you with Paxton at all? And is Zahra still with you?"

"*Who?*"

Paxton climbed unsteadily onto the road, peering back the way they'd come. Then he held up his hand for silence.

Far behind them, the giant was struggling and cursing. Apparently, the forest was so dense, a monster that size couldn't traverse it. Jack gazed upward. No glimpse of sky, just a thick, endless canopy of green. There wasn't an ancient woodland this vast, this untrammeled, within one hundred miles of Upper Wolvern. Possibly not in all of Britain. No, they'd stumbled into some other place entirely.

They listened for several moments until the giant's footfalls began heading away, in the opposite direction.

"We're safe—for now." Paxton's voice broke the quiet. "But it's not over. We must abandon this place."

"No kidding!" Charles muttered and began shoving barrels away from the Rolls.

"Not by car," Paxton clarified. "On foot."

Charles looked at him like he'd lost his mind. "I don't care what tunnel we've fallen through," Charles announced, "or what drugs you all baked into those pastries. I'm staying with the Rolls." He shoved another barrel.

The old man, unbothered, turned back toward the Bentley.

"But where's Zahra, Paxton?" Tilly asked. "Why isn't she with you?"

"Who is *Zahra*?" Jack repeated.

"Oh, just some lost tourist," Charles replied. "She got hurt, so Tilly and I helped her out."

"'Got hurt,' did she?" Paxton all but growled. Tilly glanced uncomfortably at Charles, who lifted his chin and looked away.

Paxton returned to the Bentley. He pulled aside the branches that crowded the back left-hand door and yanked it open. "Come, lad. Give me the creature." Paxton leaned in and reemerged with the stray in his arms. Arash followed, expression still blank, clutching his backpack.

"What *is* that?" Charles asked with disgust as Paxton returned to the road, arms full of fur.

"A stray dog," Jack replied. "We found it in the valley by the cas—" He stopped himself.

Paxton studied Jack's face but said nothing. Then, gently, he rested his gnarled hand on the dog's head. For a moment, it looked like the old man was simply stroking the soft fur. But Jack realized he was also muttering, low and unintelligible.

The dog stirred. It took full, deep breaths. Finally it opened its eyes—including the bad one, which, unaccountably, now looked perfectly normal. The dog blinked at Paxton and thumped its tail.

Paxton set it down. Immediately it twirled around three times and began racing around the barrels, sniffing excitedly.

"So," said Paxton. "That's done. Now, young Jack. If we're ever going to find our way out of this mess, you'd best tell me everything."

Zahra had witnessed it all.

The chase, the giant—everything.

She'd just retreated back through the hedge to rejoin Paxton when the whole incident unfolded before her eyes. Within seconds, it was over. All that remained on the road were a young boy, two girls, and herself.

But how were the girls still *alive*? They'd been lugging something between them, Zahra recalled, something rectangular. But then both wagons, plus the giant, had plowed straight toward them. Surely they were flattened? And yet there they stood, unharmed.

The boy danced around them. "I *knew* it was giants!" he hollered. His red hair stuck up in every direction. "Wasn't that tops? Wasn't that simply *cracking*? It was like rallycross!"

The girls, for their part, seemed too stunned to speak. They appeared to be about Zahra's age, perhaps a bit younger. One resembled Tilly: dark-haired and pale, except thinner. The other, of much sturdier build and blindingly golden hair, seemed on the verge of tears. Between them, Zahra noticed, the rectangular object lay flat on the roadway, broken glass sprinkled everywhere.

"And then they shot right through!" The boy was skipping round and round. "Like it was the Queensway Tunnel!"

"But . . ." The dark-haired girl found her voice. "Where did they go?"

"To the forest! In Frankie's sketch, of course." The boy bent down and hoisted the rectangular object. It was an open frame, apparently, like a window. "See? They got pulled into the picture. And the picture . . . well, the picture must've gotten pulled into itself."

"I . . . I don't understand." The other girl was definitely crying. "How is that possible?"

"And if it *is* possible," the first girl said in a faint voice, "how will they return?"

"C'mon," Georgie urged. "Let's keep moving. We've got to tell Mrs. Fealston!" He whipped around. But at the sight of Zahra, he stopped short. "Oh, hullo!"

As both girls turned, Zahra felt the usual flutter of panic. More strangers. Strangers upon strangers. She cradled her aching wrist and wished Bem would appear again. Someone—anyone—from home. But at the sight of the girls' alarmed faces, Zahra realized she wasn't half as panicked as they were.

Georgie's face broke into an excited smile. "Saw all that, did you?" He hefted the frame and lugged it toward her. "They ended up in here. Can you believe it? All of them: Paxton and Arash, Charles and Tilly, Jack and the giant, the Rolls and the Bentley. Well, not *in here,* if you know what I mean. Inside the picture that *used* to be here."

"Georgie!" The dark-haired girl came running up and tried to pull him away. "I'm so sorry," she said to Zahra. "He's overexcited."

"But she saw it, too, Ellie," he protested. Then to Zahra: "Didn't you?"

She almost shook her head. Pretending none of this had happened—simply wishing it all away—felt irresistibly tempting. But these three had witnessed the giant. And they seemed acquainted with some of the other people that she'd met here in Tellus. If she couldn't speak the truth with these three, who else was there?

"Aye, young sir," Zahra said faintly. "I saw it all."

"Told you!" Georgie scowled at Elspeth.

The second girl had joined them and was wiping her cheeks with the backs of her hands. Together with Elspeth, she eyed Zahra warily.

"And the giant!" Georgie said to Zahra. "Wasn't he just *ripping*? I've never seen one before. Have you?"

Again, Zahra decided to speak the truth. "Alas, I have."

All three of them stared.

"Really?" Georgie's voice rose to a squeak. "Where?"

"Back home," Zahra replied. "In Ternival."

Arash felt like he'd been run over.

The events of the past hour had unfolded like a rambling nightmare—one illogical, outrageous scene after another. And now he was stuck in an utterly strange world with a handful of people he barely knew.

Well, he knew Tilly, of course, from the tea shop. But the old fellow, Paxton, was some sort of handyman at Carrick Hall, a recluse who almost never visited Upper Wolvern except to stop by the pub sometimes. Whereas Charles Heapworth . . . It was hard to forget the cricket club's star bowler. Especially when you repeatedly missed his deliveries during spring practice—and he teased you relentlessly till you finally quit.

But Arash couldn't think about that now. Grandfather was his chief concern.

As instructed, Jack had begun reciting to Paxton all the outrageous things that had happened with the giant, the castle, and Mindra.

"So those were the noises we heard from the hills!" Tilly exclaimed. "Georgie was right, after all."

"You don't really believe all that rubbish, do you?" Charles's incredulous voice cut in. "Like we're still children?"

Tilly looked away, clearly hurt.

At Charles's tone, Arash felt the familiar stab of fear. Did every entitled guy learn the same script? At the first hint of weakness, of difference, they'd zero in. Mock. Laugh. Make themselves feel brilliant. Just like those university students on the train, when Arash was a child. The ones who'd made his grandmother cry. Instinctively, Arash shifted position so that Jack's body blocked Charles from view.

Paxton, meanwhile, gave Charles the severe stare of a schoolmaster. "Until recently," said the old man, "none of you believed in giants either. Nor portals to other worlds." He returned his gaze to Jack. "Go on, lad."

Jack now described his brother's briefcase, Mindra's necklace, and the box of gems—but when he got to the part about the snare and its captives, Tilly gasped in horror.

"Animals? Frankie and Eva? No. Mindra was lying, right? To scare the professor?"

Jack grimaced. "I wish. But then"—he glanced uneasily at Arash—"we watched her do the same to Professor Rastegar."

The dog, who'd been circling the barrels in frenzied loops, now whimpered and pressed its scrawny body against Arash's legs. Mechanically, Arash reached down and scratched its ears.

Paxton studied the cowering creature. "Those three aren't the only ones she's transformed, I'd wager."

Everyone looked at the stray.

"Well, whoever this is," Jack said, "he's a brave little guy. Tried to attack Mindra, but she threw him aside, knocked him unconscious. Then she snatched up the briefcase and said something about returning to Ternival and leaving the giant behind in our world, as a 'gift.'"

He shuddered. "And that's when she marched into the castle . . . and the whole thing just sort of . . . swirled into the sky and disappeared."

There was a startled pause. Even Charles seemed speechless.

"But . . ." Tilly's voice faltered. "Where did it go?"

"Here, no doubt," Paxton said grimly.

Charles snorted but said nothing.

"Oh, but this is awful!" Tilly exclaimed. "We're *here,* and Zahra is *there.* But how will any of us get home again?"

At the word *home,* Arash felt woozy. Something like homesickness washed over him. But no. It was more like *no-home* sickness. Because where was home, anyway? Not Upper Wolvern, where he felt like a permanent outsider. Not Cambridge, where there were clear distinctions between academics and the rest of society—and not London, his birthplace, which he barely remembered. As for Iran? He'd never been there. And his father wasn't in the picture, so that wasn't an option either.

No. Home was wherever his mum was. Wherever his grandparents were. But now they were literally worlds apart. Grandfather was somewhere out there, transformed, captive. His mum and grandmother were back in Upper Wolvern, probably worried out of their minds. And Arash was here, wherever *here* was. Unable to return.

"Anyway, not much more to the story," Jack concluded. "Arash scooped up the dog. And then the giant came back and chased us down from the hills. And the rest you know." He turned to Arash. "Anything to add, mate?"

"Yeah, mate." Charles smirked at Arash. "Anything to add?"

Arash's mind went blank, just like always. Apparently, the ongoing nightmare wasn't over.

Jack and Tilly glanced uncomfortably at Arash, but Paxton leveled his stern gaze at Charles until the guy shrugged. "Oh, c'mon," he muttered. "He knows it's all in fun."

The dog began to whine again.

"It's almost like it understands us," Jack observed. He seemed relieved to change the subject. "I wonder if it can?" He held out his hand, and the dog came to him, trembling. "Tell us, mate. Are we in Ternival? Is this your home?"

The dog swished its tail.

"And what do you know of Mindra? Is she here? Castle and all?"

The creature shrank back, whimpering, and resumed its nervous loops around the barrels.

"Well," Paxton said. "There's our answer." Knees creaking, the old man knelt all the way down and, like Jack, summoned the dog. It approached reluctantly. "Listen, old boy. We must reach the stronghold before Mindra finds us. There are people who need our help. She won't be expecting us to head *towards* danger, understand? So going there might give us just the cover we need. But we need you to lead us."

The creature padded away from him. Then it whirled and disappeared into the underbrush.

Charles sneered. "Fantastic. You've scared it off."

Curious, Arash went to the spot where the dog had disappeared. There, amid the thicket, was the beginning of a trail. He traced it into the forest a few yards. Ahead of him, the stray paused and glanced back, tail wagging.

"Oh, sure," Charles quipped from the barrels. "Let's all get lost in the woods together. With night falling soon. Not a chance. I'm staying with the Rolls."

But just then, a distant rumble echoed through the forest.

The dog took off down the trail, paws skittering, as Charles shot to his feet, all bravado gone.

"If you wish to stay, young sir, the choice is your own," Paxton said. "But we cannot help you." The old man brushed past Charles toward the trail.

"C'mon, Charles!" Tilly urged.

"Listen, mate," Jack reasoned, "we can always come back for the cars later."

And that was when Arash realized: He didn't care *what* happened to Charles. Or to any of them—except the dog. Thanks to its furry heroics in trying to save Grandfather, the stray had earned Arash's loyalty forever. And meanwhile, Arash didn't have the foggiest clue what Ternival was, nor why the enchantress was so keen on the gems, nor what any of it had to do with his grandfather. All Arash cared about was finding Mindra's prisoners—and setting one particular falcon free.

He shouldered his backpack and took off after the stray.

Chapter

25

"What about the larder?" Aurora whispered.

Elspeth shook her head. "Mum goes in and out of there all day." She tiptoed down the passageway that ran behind the kitchen. "It'll have to be the old scullery instead. There's a stool Zahra can sit on, plus some linens for a sling."

Aurora, lugging the empty picture frame, padded along beside her. Then came Georgie, followed by their unexpected guest.

Zahra. From Ternival.

At first, Elspeth had mistaken the girl for yet another costumed tourist, one of many who ignored Carrick Hall's NO TRESPASSING signs and used the private drive as a shortcut to the hills. And yet this girl was different. Bewildered. Disheveled. Far too thin. Plus, her rumpled ensemble of layered tunics and rough sandals looked nothing like the tourists' usual garb.

But then she'd spoken. And Elspeth's mind, which was already reeling, had been blown wide open.

Softly, in a lilting accent full of archaic phrases, Zahra had answered their questions. Georgie, of course, had pestered her for details like he was trying to win at Cluedo. Details about Ternival. And giants. And the fall of Caristor. About Marisith and Mindra and her terrible enchantments. About Zahra's sudden arrival here—together with a dog named Lepp and a cat called Bem, who was lurking, apparently, somewhere about. And everything that'd transpired since then involving Tilly, Charles, Mrs. Fealston, Elspeth's mum, and Paxton.

"Who *is* the venerable Paxton, anyway?" Zahra had paused to ask. "Where is he from?"

"Here, as far as I know," Elspeth had replied. She'd never really thought about it before. He'd always been at Carrick Hall, like the furniture.

Aurora, who'd been pacing restlessly throughout the whole tale, balled her fists. "If Georgie's correct and Frankie's sketch was some sort of portal to Ternival, then how will the others return without it? And how will we explain any of this to our parents? Or to Arash's family? It's just awful!"

Georgie, however, had resumed bouncing around like a beach ball. "You mean, there's a castle up there?" he hollered to Zahra, pointing at the hills. "With a real live witch and everything? C'mon, then! What are we waiting for? Let's go rescue your grandad!"

Zahra had actually smiled. Two glittery tears slid from her long lashes to the dimples that had appeared in her thin cheeks.

"It's the 'real live witch' part," Elspeth had said to Georgie. "Not sure how to get around that."

Eventually they'd decided to seek Mrs. Fealston's advice, after all, which was what they'd set out to do in the first place. So, after hunting in vain along the darkening hedgerows for the elusive Bem, they'd returned to the Hall.

By the time they'd reached the kitchen garden, the sun had begun to set beyond the Wolverns. A lovely blue twilight would soon envelop the grounds, blurring the hedges and vegetable rows. Festivities at the green were winding down. Overnight campers would return to the hills, and the beacons would twinkle with watch fires till sunrise.

Elspeth had paused at the garden gate. She could think of several plausible excuses that would explain the absence of Tilly, Jack, and Charles to the grown-ups. But Paxton? He was too steady, too trustworthy. He'd never, while driving someone to hospital, simply abandon that person on the side of the road. Mrs. Addison would want to know why Zahra had returned to Carrick Hall but Paxton hadn't, and she'd interrogate her children till Georgie caved.

So, right then and there, Elspeth had hatched a plan. They'd smuggle Zahra into the house and hide her somewhere. And then Elspeth and Georgie would distract their mum while Aurora sneaked the frame into Mrs. Fealston's rooms to gauge her response. After that, they'd reunite Zahra with Mrs. Fealston and figure out the rest.

The plan had worked—so far. The kitchen had been empty when they arrived. Elspeth could hear Mrs. Fealston and Mum chatting in the housekeeper's quarters. Meanwhile, Dad was nowhere about. Probably standing guard at the path that led to Table Mount, behind the Hall, to ward off wandering campers.

Elspeth now entered the dim scullery, the others on her heels.

"This will have to do," she whispered. From a pile of clean linens, she grabbed one and tore off a long strip. "Hold still for a moment, Zahra. Let's see if this works." She fashioned the rag into a makeshift sling and then gently slipped it under Zahra's arm and over her shoulder. Sighing with relief, Zahra thanked her and settled onto the stool.

Aurora looked around. "I wish we could turn the lights on in here. You'll be all right, won't you?"

Zahra nodded. She seemed unfazed by the prospect of waiting in the dark. But then again, it probably felt normal to her. Ternival, by all accounts, wasn't particularly technologically advanced—rather like medieval Europe. No electricity. Oil lamps and candles were luxury items. At sundown, unless you were rich, you probably just went to bed.

A prickle of fear ran up Elspeth's neck. Was it almost nightfall in Ternival too? She hoped fervently that Tilly and the others were okay. Especially Tilly.

Elspeth gave Zahra a wave and closed the scullery door, then returned to the kitchen with Georgie and Aurora. In the housekeeper's quarters, Mrs. Fealston's muffled voice was narrating some meandering tale—interspersed with Mum's noncommittal responses. Mum, no doubt, had resigned herself to a long evening, which meant they needed a plan for getting her out of there. Soon.

Tap-ti-tap*tap*-ti-tap*tap.* Someone was rapping on the back door.

Aurora gasped and nearly dropped the picture frame. "It's my dad!" She gestured frantically for Elspeth and Georgie to drop down, out of sight.

But Georgie—for whom Lord Edward was known to keep a stash of miscellaneous candy in his fashionable pockets—marched to the door and flung it open.

"Well, hullo there, young George! Mind if I pop in to pester your mum?" His lordship strode into the kitchen, peeling off a pair of exquisite leather driving gloves. Tall and tanned, with twinkling blue eyes and a wisp of blond hair, he glanced around jovially. "Ah! At least one of my offspring is accounted for, anyway. Spending the night here, Rora, I take it? And in *such* trendy jimjams." Lord Edward paused, hunted around in his blazer, and then tossed a handful of toffees at Georgie. "There you are, my fine fellow. Straight from Walker's Nonsuch. So. Have any of you spotted Charlie, by chance? He seems to have motored off with my Rolls, blast him."

Elspeth glanced at Aurora, whose face had drained of color.

"Evening, sir!" Mum emerged from Mrs. Fealston's rooms. She

dropped the tiniest of curtsies, to which Lord Edward responded with a warm nod. Then she glanced sharply at her children. "And what, may I ask, are you two doing here? Supposed to be with Jack and Tilly, you are. Back at the cottage."

Lord Edward cleared his throat. "Oh, er, not to barge in and all that, but I just happened to stop by the cottage myself. Took a cab from the station to my own place first, of course. Roads all clogged with tourists and whatnot, so it took longer than usual. But when I couldn't find my offspring—nor the Rolls (which is *entirely* coincidental, I'm sure)—my saintly housekeeper suggested they might be hobnobbing with you fine folk. Cottage was all dark, though. No one home, far as I could tell. So, I tootled on up here in my decrepit Jag, which—remind me later—needs an oil change."

But Mum had stopped listening. "No one home?" She frowned at Elspeth and Georgie. "First, Frankie sends no word, all day. And then you two won't stay put. And now Tilly and Jack—" She stopped abruptly and turned back to Lord Edward. "London, did you say?"

His lordship nodded. "Just run up from Paddington Station. Right on time too."

Mum placed a hand on the table as if to brace herself. The evening train from Paddington was most likely the one that Frankie and Eva would've taken.

Just then, the house phone rang. Before anyone else could respond, Mum dashed over and snatched it from the wall. "Carrick Hall."

Elspeth watched as her mother's expression shifted from worry to confusion to grave concern.

"Arash? And the professor? No, Mrs. Tabari, we haven't seen them, I'm afraid. . . . The boys were together at the tea shop this morning, you say? Now, that *is* curious. Jack hasn't chummed about with Arash before that I recall. But we're in a bit of a state here, too, you see, because . . ." She dropped her voice and murmured something Elspeth couldn't hear.

Lord Edward, who'd been drumming his elegant fingers on the table, suddenly halted. He stared, dumbfounded, at the picture frame in his daughter's hands.

"By Jove!" he exclaimed. "But isn't that the frame from your cottage, Ellie? The one that usually holds that first-rate sketch of Frankie's? It's got the carver's signature and everything. Was going to ask your mum about it, in fact. That's what my business was about in London, wouldn't you know? I'd gotten a tip from an arts dealer regarding the artwork that originally hung inside this thing."

Elspeth blinked at him. Hadn't she heard snippets about this before, from Frankie and Eva?

According to them, three frames had been made by the Addisons' ancestor, the wood-carver. The largest of these frames contained the stag tapestry from Carrick Hall, which now graced Lord Edward's own Wolvern Court. The second frame—also from Carrick Hall and nearly as large as the first—had once boasted a tapestry of dryads. But it'd been sold as a unit, long ago, to an antiques dealer. Eventually that frame had been recovered, and it was now on display at Eva's college in Chicago. But the dryad tapestry was yet to be found.

Finally there was a third much smaller frame. The same one that Aurora now handed to her father. It, too, had once held some kind of picture. And that picture had likewise been lost. When Eva was a teenager, she'd discovered the empty frame hanging in the guest bedroom of her great-great-aunt Bertie's house in Cambridge, but shortly thereafter, the frame itself had vanished. It wasn't till several years later, after Bertie died, that Frankie had found it stashed in the old woman's attic. He'd installed his own sketch inside, given it to his siblings for Christmas, and hung it at the Addisons' cottage. But the artwork it'd once held had remained at large.

"Been trying to track the thing down for *years*," Lord Edward continued. "But it was just where the dealer said it'd be. And what an exquisite piece it is too! Didn't think to bring it with me just now, alas. Left it at home when I stopped there first."

Mum hung up the phone. "Begging your pardon, sir," she said briskly. "But you and I need to talk."

Chapter

26

To Tilly's relief, Charles hadn't required much persuading. Just the thought of being alone in these strange woods, with darkness approaching and the distant giant tromping about, was enough—although he'd insisted that Jack and Tilly help him push the Rolls off the road, out of sight. They'd done so nervously. And then he'd hidden the keys under a small rock by the left front tire.

"In case something happens," he'd said grimly.

All three took off down the trail to catch up with the others. As they approached, Paxton put a finger to his lips. Not that any of them were inclined to speak, by that point. The forest was so immense, so dark under its vast canopy, that it awed them into silence.

And it was lovely. Fresh and untrammeled and pure, it held an ancient kind of beauty such as she'd experienced only once or twice before. In the old grove near Carrick Hall, for instance, where several children holding hands couldn't reach the whole way around a sweet chestnut's trunk. If they hadn't been in such great danger, with night approaching, the forest of Ternival would've been one of the most peaceful places she'd ever been.

After a while, Paxton paused. "Hear that?" he whispered. They all stopped.

"Nope," Charles replied at normal volume. Tilly fought the urge to shush him.

"Aye," Paxton said. "Nothing. But on midsummer's eve, we should be hearing birds, I'd wager. Mindra is back, all right. Even the creatures know that some great evil is abroad in the land. We must hurry."

They walked and walked.

Although the canopy obscured any glimpse of sky, Tilly could tell by the fading light that the sun had begun to set. The forest floor was in shadow now, but the trees weren't gloomy. They were peaceful. Her anxiety began to ebb away.

And the others seemed to feel it too. The dog's tail wagged as it trotted ahead of Paxton. The old man's shoulders relaxed. Arash gazed up at the vast leafy ceiling, while Jack swung his arms freely. And Charles, whose blond hair and tanned skin practically glowed in the dusky light, looked at her and smiled.

His steps began to slow. She slowed with him. Finally, as the others got farther ahead, Charles casually reached out and took her hand.

Her arm tingled. Her heart pumped so loudly, she was sure he could hear it. This was exactly how she'd felt when he cruised past her at the roundabout. Desired. Powerful. Beautiful.

But then her brother glanced back at them. Charles withdrew his hand. And the peaceful mood shattered.

Shame flooded Tilly's body. She wanted to bolt into the woods and disappear. Instead, she forced herself to lift her chin, square her shoulders, and stride ahead of Charles.

Just as she caught up to Jack, something in her peripheral vision caught her attention. Movement in the darkening woods. But when she looked again, nothing. Just the deepening shadows on the ancient trunks.

After a while, the trail began to climb a hill. At the crest, they looked out over a strip of forest, beyond which the sun had begun to set into an expanse of sparkling sea. To the left and right, distant bluffs jutted into the water, a matching pair of peninsulas with a wide bay between them. A dark smudge of smoke billowed from the left-hand peninsula, while the boxy battlements of a tall, cruel-looking tower rose above the wooded headlands on the right.

"There it is!" Jack whispered, pointing at the tower. "The castle from the valley!"

"Aye," murmured Paxton. Under his cap, the handyman's long, sad face looked even longer and sadder. "Marisith-over-the-Sea. Ancient stronghold of Mindra the Enchantress. Abandoned, of course, after her defeat by the Three Queens."

"It doesn't look abandoned now," Tilly whispered nervously. A wisp of smoke coiled from its ramparts.

Paxton nodded. Then he pointed to the thicker, darker smoke on the left. "And we should be able to see a second castle, just there. Caristor. The seat of Ternival's sovereigns."

Tilly and Jack stared at him. "How do you know all this, Paxton?" Jack wondered aloud.

With a start, the old man glanced his way, then turned back to the sea. "Eh? Well, you know how Mrs. Fealston is . . ."

Tilly exchanged a confused look with her brother. On the one hand, it made sense that Paxton's source of knowledge would be the Hall's former housekeeper. The old woman knew even more about Ternival than Frankie or Eva, thanks to decades of proximity to people who'd actually been there. On the other hand, Tilly couldn't recall Mrs. Fealston ever mentioning the land's topography, nor had the handyman himself displayed even the slightest interest in any of it.

They studied the billowing smoke. "If that's where Caristor is supposed to be," Tilly asked, "what happened to it? Why isn't it there now?"

"Destroyed, most likely," Paxton replied. "And recently, by the look of things."

At this, the stray began to whine again.

Paxton looked down at the dog, frowning. "If Mindra has returned," he mused, "and if Ternival's royal castle is no more, then we've arrived at a dark hour indeed. Come. We mustn't tarry."

The dog took off again, trailed by Paxton, Arash, and Jack. Tilly turned to follow, but then she saw movement, high above the sea. A flock of birds, circling and circling. Seagulls, perhaps?

Suddenly something brushed against her back pocket. She whipped around. Charles stood a few feet away, grinning broadly. He held the anonymous note from the tea shop.

"Oi, Charles!" Tilly hissed. "Give that back!" She grabbed at the note, but he held it out of reach.

"Love note, is it? From a secret admirer? Oh, wait. I know. It's from Galahad!"

Tilly jumped, but he held the paper aloft, chuckling. Then, with both hands over his head, he flipped it open and looked upward at its contents.

There was a pause. His eyes traveled briefly over the lines. "A man of few words," he said with a smirk. He lowered his arms, handed her the note, and took off down the trail after the others.

Tilly remained in place, mouth slightly open. What on earth was that about? Hadn't he seen what it said? Being around Charles was like riding a roller coaster. Flattery and affection one minute, teasing and mockery the next. It was exhausting. She shoved the note back into her pocket and caught up with the rest of the group.

Paxton, who'd paused to wait for her, motioned for Tilly to pass by so he could bring up the rear. But also, she suspected, he wanted to keep an eye on Charles.

On they walked in the gloaming. And now, for the first time, they began to hear birds. From the underbrush came drowsy warbles, as if the creatures were singing themselves to sleep.

"A good sign," said Paxton. "We're safe to talk quietly. For now."

"Good," said Jack, who walked near the front, behind Arash. "Because there's something I can't quite figure out. It's the enchantress. She can't be the same Mindra as the one from Frankie's stories, right? I mean, didn't she rule here for something like seventy-five years before the Three Queens came along? And it's been—what—another sixty years in our world since the queens returned to Carrick Hall? So wouldn't that make Mindra *really* old?"

"And time flows differently here, doesn't it?" Tilly said. "Just like in other fairy tales about different worlds. Sometimes faster, sometimes slower."

"Sometimes the same," Paxton interjected.

"And yet, even here in Ternival, Mindra seems to live on and on," Jack argued. "Shouldn't she be dead by now?"

"I fear not, lad," said Paxton. "One such as Mindra cannot be destroyed—at least, not in any of the usual ways."

"Maybe it's the gems that keep her alive," Tilly mused. "The closer she gets to them, the greater her strength."

"Okay, so that begs another question," Jack said. "If Mindra has the gems, how will she be defeated? She's powerful, let me tell you." He shuddered. "I'm not even sure she's human."

"Human?" Paxton repeated. "Oh, she's most certainly not human. No, indeed. She's something else entirely. She has powers of which we mortals know nothing. And yet she is no Magister, no World-Weaver who can create something from nothing. Nay, she can only tear and distort, change and corrupt. But she's powerful nonetheless. She can transform herself into many things."

Tilly peered into the forest. The darker it got, the less peaceful it felt.

And then she saw the face.

Chapter

27

Tilly's scream tore through Jack's skull.

"There!" she gasped. "A face! In the trees. I swear, it looked right at me." She was trembling. "But it's gone now."

Unnerved, everyone remained still, glancing around. The stray had attached itself to Arash's shins and cowered there, whining faintly. Even Charles seemed to have nothing snide to say, for once.

But soon the birds began twittering again. The group was still safe—for the moment.

They continued walking.

"So, anyway," said Jack, picking up where they'd left off, "back to my question. According to how time flows in our world, it's been sixty years since the Three Queens reigned in Ternival, like I said. But we don't really know how much time has passed here, right? Or what's been happening along the way? Who's the current sovereign, for instance? And why was Caristor destroyed?"

From the front of the group, the stray gave a sad little yip that devolved into a whine.

Charles began to laugh incredulously. "You know how batty you lot sound, right? Like my dad's crazy great-aunt. When he was a boy, she used to corner him and blather on about portals between worlds, and tapestries coming to life or whatever. And about the gardener of Carrick Hall, who got put in charge of fairyland. But who ever heard of a gardener who became queen?" He snorted.

"Hang on, mate—" Jack began testily.

"And Aurora still believes every word of it, of course," Charles plowed on. "Keeps hoping that the stag in Dad's tapestry will jump off the wall and lead her to some other world. Or that someone roaming about the hills will discover where the queen supposedly stashed the crown—"

Arash halted so suddenly, Jack nearly plowed into him.

"You all right, mate?" Jack said.

Paxton halted too. "Hear that?"

"Let me guess," Charles said sarcastically. "No birds?"

The old man put his finger to his lips.

And then Jack heard it too. Eerie and piercing, wafting through the trees.

The sound of a distant horn.

Zahra jerked awake. The scullery door stood wide open. Beyond it, the silhouette of a short, excited figure bobbed up and down in the passageway.

"C'mon, Zahra!" Georgie squeaked. "The grown-ups are all gone, except Mrs. Fealston—and you won't *believe* what's happened!"

She'd been sitting for so long in the dark, she'd begun to wonder if the entire day had been a dream. Perhaps, all this time, she'd been merely slumbering at home, her mother's woven blanket soft against her skin, the clean night air wafting through the windows, the gentle push and pull of the waves just audible. She could almost smell her mother's dye jars on the shelf above her mat: rich pigments of woad and safflower, oak apples and indigo, madder and weld.

Soon Mother would gently tap her shoulder. "Wake up, sweet lass. Your grandad says to fetch the nets. Time for night fishing."

But no. Mother was gone. And Grandad was imprisoned. And Zahra herself was hiding in an unfamiliar place. Again. Waiting.

Waiting for a rescue. Waiting till it was safe to move. Waiting for the awful events of the recent past to recede like a bad dream and for ordinary life to flow back in like the tide.

She might be waiting forever.

But now, here was Georgie, skipping ahead of her into the kitchen. He was chattering away like a squirrel—something about how the grown-ups, including his own dad, had all taken off to search for their missing children, while the girls had been told to supervise Mrs. Fealston (and himself, but he didn't need looking after, really). And about how Aurora's father, Lord Edward—who'd been sleuthing for *ages*—had finally managed to track down the original artwork that used to hang in the picture frame, before Frankie's sketch was there. Wasn't it all just *tops*?

Night had fallen, but the kitchen was bright as day, lit from the ceiling by what looked like a series of miniature suns. Zahra halted, entranced. What strange fire could produce a light so steady, so unwavering? But Georgie urged her on, and they entered Mrs. Fealston's rooms, where Aurora and Elspeth had drawn up chairs by the old woman's divan.

"Back again, Zahra, I see," said Mrs. Fealston. She sat propped against several pillows, her eyes clear, expectant.

"And then the phone rang," Georgie continued, hardly pausing for breath, "and it was Arash's mum—"

"Hold up, Georgie," Aurora interrupted. "Does Zahra even know who Arash *is*?"

So they did their best, the three of them, to fill her in—although it was a blur of interruptions and clarifications, zigzags and rabbit trails. She understood barely half of what they said. But in the end, she grasped the key points.

First, Frankie and Eva—about whom Mrs. Fealston had told Zahra earlier—were still missing. Tilly, meanwhile, had disappeared with Charles in his storm wagon when it blasted through the frame. And Jack, the Addisons' middle brother, had vanished with Paxton in the other storm wagon, along with a boy named Arash, from the village. And finally—according to the phone call from Arash's mum—Arash's grandfather was nowhere to be found.

"And we can't forget about Zahra's pet cat, Bem." Georgie jumped in again before Zahra had a chance to ask what a phone call was. "She's missing too."

"Oh, but she's not really my—" Zahra began, but Aurora had already turned to Mrs. Fealston.

"You're *sure* they're all in Ternival, Mrs. Fealston?" Aurora asked.

The housekeeper nodded. "Every last one."

"But some of them are still here, venerable mother," Zahra, perplexed, finally piped up. "In the valley, imprisoned in the castle. With Mindra." She couldn't bring herself to mention Grandad.

Mrs. Fealston shook her head sadly. "Ah, my dear, but I'm afraid the enchantress has spirited Marisith away again. She realized she'd been discovered, you see. No. The valley is empty now. Mindra has returned to Ternival—and taken the captives with her."

Even after so many blows, this was the worst. For Zahra, everything until now had felt somewhat bearable because she and Grandad hadn't remained apart for long. Granted, he wasn't human at the moment. But at least she'd known where he was and how to reach him.

Zahra didn't realize she was gripping Georgie's shoulder to keep from crying till he hiccupped. His freckled face had turned bright red. "Oh . . . oh . . . but it's not *fair!*" He gulped a sob. "They're all together, in Ternival, having grand adventures—probably meeting dry-ads and stags and dwarves and all that—and we're stuck *here,* having no fun at *all.*" He buried his face in the blanket at the foot of the bed.

"I wouldn't call being chased by a giant an adventure," Elspeth countered. "And don't forget that Mindra's there too. Plus, doesn't it all sound rather crowded? As if Ternival is one huge tourist attraction, another Upper Wolvern." Then she snorted. "Jack must be chuffed."

"But how do you know all this, Mrs. Fealston?" Aurora pressed. "Have you been to Ternival yourself? Like the other characters in the old tales?"

Mrs. Fealston's eyes grew misty. "No, alas. I've never gone. I've always been the one to help other people in their comings and go-ings. But I'd love to see it, just once. Before the end."

Zahra felt a pang of sadness. The longing in Mrs. Fealston's voice reminded her of Mother. How Mother had longed to see Caristor's Hall of Tapestries, just once, before the end—but never did.

"I still don't understand how you know about everything that's happening, Mrs. Fealston," Aurora continued eventually. "Can you . . . *see* it somehow? In . . . in . . ." She seemed to hunt for the right expression. "In your mind's eye?"

"That's one way of putting it," Mrs. Fealston replied. "Some peo-ple are said to have that gift, you know. The ability to discern what's happening elsewhere, beyond everyday sight. Normally it's just a vague sense of things for me. Not much detail. But today, for some reason, it's particularly strong." The tired lines deepened on her already-wrinkled face, but she kept her attention fixed on the girls.

"I wonder if that's because we're nearing midsummer," Elspeth mused. "I once read something about how the ancient Britons believed the connection between here and the otherworld grew stronger at the solstice. But I doubt anyone really knows."

"Ley lines!" Georgie shouted abruptly. He began hopping around again. "It's what that uppity fellow in the tea shop said to Arash—remember? Told him he'd best be careful about metal detecting in the hills right now. Something about the ley lines being far too strong, how you don't know what could happen."

Mrs. Fealston straightened, her eyes bright again. "Did he, now? Well, that's not far off, I suppose. The cosmos is like one great loom, after all, each world connected to every other along the Warp of Time. It wouldn't surprise me if the pull of the earth round the sun—the passing of time, if you will—had some effect on the warp's tension, for better or worse. Perhaps the Wolverns is one of those places where the tension, right now, is especially high."

"But what happens *after* midsummer?" Elspeth had begun fidgeting with a long lock of her hair, weaving it through the fingers of one hand, back and forth, back and forth.

Zahra, who'd followed the conversation with increasing bewilderment, suddenly understood what Elspeth was getting at. Once midsummer had passed, would the connection between worlds grow weaker again? Would their window for restoring everyone to their proper homes begin to close?

"That, my dear, is a very concerning question." Mrs. Fealston sank back into the pillows, clearly troubled.

Zahra couldn't let herself collapse into despair again. She wouldn't.

"Bem and Lepp," she blurted. "You said everyone was gone, honorable hostess. But what about them?"

Mrs. Fealston closed her eyes for a moment, as if listening to some inner wisdom, then opened them slowly. "Hard to say. Animals are tricky, you know. Something about their self-protective instincts, their ability to hide. But never fear. I sense that those two still have some part to play."

"Oh, there must be a way to help Zahra get home with the others!" Elspeth cried. "And to rescue our own crew."

"I wonder . . ." Aurora began. "Mightn't we go through the frame too? I mean, if the connection between worlds is especially strong right now, perhaps we could put another sketch of Ternival in the frame, to see if it will—"

"Absolutely not," Mrs. Fealston cut in. "Even grown sentries are no match for Mindra, who is now more powerful than ever. No, children. Time for bed. You can explain the whole situation to your parents in the morning." She looked at each of them in turn. "You must promise me that you won't try to get there on your own. Do you understand?"

There was a mulish silence. Zahra stared at the girls and Georgie, astonished at their resistance to a direct command from an elder.

"I will do as you say, venerable mother," Zahra finally replied.

But would the others?

Chapter

28

Thundering hoofbeats echoed through the woods. As Arash swung around, a great din reached his ears: roaring and hollering, bellows and screeches. Shadows flitted overhead. The sound of flapping wings filled the air. Then something whizzed past his cheek and landed with a thunk in a nearby tree.

"Arrows!" Jack yelled behind him. "Get down!"

It was too late. In a flash, they were surrounded.

But they weren't the target of whatever was going on. Instead, a flock of huge, cruel raptors appeared to be locked in combat with a strange company of warriors, many of whom were dressed in medieval garb like this was a reenactment at the midsummer festival. Men on horseback and on foot fought alongside dwarves in full armor, fierce woodland animals, and fantastical creatures for which Arash had no name.

Then one of the raptors swooped down toward Jack. It grasped his backpack in its terrible claws and began to drag it, Jack and all, down the trail. Incredulous, Arash watched as Jack's feet left the ground. Was the great bird truly big enough and strong enough to fly off with him? The kid was ten feet in the air before he managed to wrench free. Arms pinwheeling, he fell and landed, hard, on his backpack. The raptor screamed, soared into the air, and disappeared over the trees.

Just then, someone grabbed Arash from behind. They yanked off his backpack and tied his hands roughly behind him, while someone else shoved a blindfold over his glasses. Kicking and struggling, he was lifted to his feet and dragged away.

It took him a moment to regain his footing, but eventually he managed. What sounded like a small company of men and creatures was rushing through the forest beside him. Crunching footsteps, clinking armor, the occasional hiss or whinny. The din behind them had ceased altogether.

Moments later, the company stopped.

"Halt," said a deep voice. "Unbind them."

At the first volley of arrows, Tilly had spun around wildly, looking for cover. But chaos had engulfed her so fast, she could hardly tell which way was up. And then she'd spotted Charles, sprinting back up the trail. She'd turned to run after him, gotten tangled in some shrubbery, and fallen headlong into a small ditch. By the time she'd untangled herself, it was over.

She was alone. At dusk. In the vast forest of Ternival.

Her mind began doing that frantic, skittish thing it did whenever she was terrified. Rational thought was usually the first to go. Like that time when she'd found a bat flitting around the cottage and, instead of opening the front door so it could escape, she'd grabbed a lampshade and crammed it on her head. As if—Frankie later teased—that would keep a bat from getting caught in her hair. It'd been five-year-old Georgie who'd let it out.

That was just one example, among many, of why she didn't trust herself. Especially under pressure. Which was the reason she hadn't even tried to get a driving license yet. Even ordinary decisions felt heavy, so she let everyone else make them.

Well, there was no one else to make them now.

Tilly forced herself to stand still for a full minute. One one thousand, two one thousand, three . . . Eventually her mind stopped fluttering. Her range of awareness widened again, and she was able to take stock of her surroundings.

In the fading light, evidence of the skirmish was everywhere. Shattered spears, splintered arrows, the occasional helm or sword hilt. And even the crumpled bodies of numerous massive birds. She shuddered. But no bodies of people, thank goodness. Unconsciously, she'd been bracing herself for finding Jack, prone on the ground. Or Charles. Or Arash and Paxton. But hopefully they'd gotten away unscathed.

The air smelled like leather, horses, and sweat—plus some fouler odors she'd rather not think about. Pinching her nose, she picked her way through trampled shrubs and broken branches till she reached the trail. Dusk was falling swiftly now, but she could still distinguish the trail as it wound through the forest.

Tilly glanced around. The trees now felt like a watchful presence. Not sinister, exactly, but not insentient either. The memory of that face was hard to shake. The slender nose, the shapely mouth, the wide, calm eyes. She hadn't even registered what she was seeing, at first. Just a young beech with delicate sprays of hairlike branches on its smooth trunk. But then the beech had turned. It'd looked straight at her—and blinked.

She shivered just thinking about it.

The good news was that she wasn't lost. She knew exactly where she was, more or less. On a trail that somehow led to Marisith. Which meant that she had only two choices. She could press on toward Mindra's stronghold and face whatever she found there, or she could go back up the trail after Charles. And if she couldn't find him, she could at least locate the keys to the Rolls and take shelter in it for the night.

It was a terrible quandary.

On the one hand, Frankie and Eva were almost certainly at Marisith, with Professor Rastegar. And if Paxton, Jack, and Arash had somehow escaped the skirmish, they would most likely make for Marisith themselves.

On the other hand, if no one else showed up at Marisith, Tilly by herself was no match for the enchantress. Plus, there was Charles, the only one whose whereabouts she might be able to track. He'd run back toward the Rolls, of course, which was the logical thing to do. A car like that was mostly impenetrable, with doors that locked. But also, he'd left the rest of them behind, including her. As if she wasn't worth worrying about. As if a car was way more important.

Tilly took a shaky breath. People did weird things in a crisis. You couldn't blame them for acting on instinct—she herself being exhibit A. Right?

Night was almost here. She could see nothing beyond a few yards in any direction. During the skirmish, she'd glimpsed just enough strange and terrifying creatures to know that her current situation was . . . not great. She needed to move. Now.

Whatever she ended up deciding would most likely be wrong. But she turned her face toward Marisith anyway and began to walk.

Chapter

29

Elspeth looked at Aurora, whose wide eyes had grown even wider. There was no *way* they'd tell their parents this story. Who would believe them? Not Mum, that was for sure. Dad would maybe humor them for a few minutes, then stifle a yawn. Lord Edward had the bad habit of only half listening to his children, which meant that any stories longer than a few sentences tended to fall through his brain like a sieve. And Mrs. Tabari? Not a chance.

The girls looked everywhere but at the housekeeper. Even Georgie stayed mutinously silent.

Finally Elspeth realized they had no choice but to comply, like Zahra. And anyway, couldn't they brainstorm ideas, at least, even if they didn't take any action . . . yet?

"Yes, Mrs. Fealston," she mumbled.

The old woman's shoulders relaxed. "Now. It's far too late, and our visitor is tired. Settle her in the old butler's quarters down the hall, with Aurora, and then you and Georgie can sleep on your father's cot in the empty storage room. Mrs. Addison always sleeps on the trundle bed in here with me, so she won't notice that Zahra has returned. And then you can explain everything to your parents in the morning."

Mrs. Fealston leaned back and closed her eyes again. She seemed to have used up her last ounce of energy for the day.

Elspeth began tucking the covers around the housekeeper's tiny body. As she did so, she noticed a book partially hidden under the blanket: *The Princess and the Djinn*. Wasn't this the book Jack had been reading at lunchtime? She'd take it back to the kitchen. With Aurora's help, she lowered the head of the hospital bed and switched off the lamp on the housekeeper's nightstand. Immediately Mrs. Fealston began a light, rhythmic snoring.

The girls and Georgie returned to the kitchen. Elspeth placed Jack's book on the table, then pulled up a stool while the others joined her. They all stared at the frame in silence.

"We *could* try making a sketch," Aurora finally suggested. She looked at Zahra. "Just to see if it works. We don't actually have to use it or anything."

Georgie shot to his feet. "I'm brilliant at drawing! I'll show you. Mum's got some supplies in the butler's pantry upstairs." He dashed out of the room.

Elspeth rolled her eyes. "He *thinks* he can draw. But if we put any of his sketches in the frame, it might transport us to some world that looks like it was made by Picasso."

Georgie soon returned, his arms loaded with art supplies, and settled himself at the table. After cracking his knuckles as if this was some sort of sketch master's World Cup, he started scribbling furiously.

"Even if we manage to find some sort of picture that takes us to Ternival," Elspeth said, ignoring her brother, "what if it gets destroyed in the process, like Frankie's sketch? How will anyone get back?"

Brooding silence descended. It was nearing eleven, and they didn't know when the adults might return. They *had* to think of something.

Then Zahra reached out and touched the frame. "What I don't understand," she mused, "is why you would put a picture in here."

"Because . . . it's . . . a picture frame?" Aurora looked at her quizzically.

Zahra shook her head. "I suppose it can be. But that's not what it's designed for." She ran a slender finger along its top edge, tracing the notches.

"If it's not a picture frame, then what is it?" Elspeth asked.

Zahra picked up the frame in both hands, then turned it over. "It's a loom."

Jack's blindfold was removed, his hands unbound. He glanced about in the gathering dusk. He was in a small company of the men, dwarves, and creatures who'd fought the raptors. And they were all exhausted. Some were actually wounded.

He noticed, with relief, the presence of Paxton and Arash. Like him, they'd been bound and blindfolded, but now their bonds were being removed. But what about Tilly and Charles? And where was the stray?

An enormous mastiff drew near. Jack liked dogs, for the most part, even the stray. But this one was alarming—not just for its size but for its intelligent gaze. Like it knew what Jack was thinking. It circled him, sniffing, before it loped away to do the same to Arash and Paxton.

Several torches were lit. The company formed a kind of circle. And then into the center of the company strode one of the most impressive, strange, and intimidating creatures Jack had ever seen. From the waist down, it was a glossy draft horse, dapple gray, its huge hooves fringed by feathery white fetlocks. But from the waist up, it was a man, bearded and wild and fierce, holding a gleaming spear. It gave Jack a glance so discerning that he shrank away.

Was it possible? A centaur?

The mastiff now approached the centaur and bowed. "News, milord," it said.

Jack shouldn't have been surprised. Of everything he'd witnessed over the past twelve hours—indeed, over the past twelve *seconds*—talking animals was the least shocking. He'd seen it before, in movies. But it was startling nonetheless. And nothing like the movies. For one, the voice wasn't remotely human. It was wilder: half growl, half bark. And for another, the dog's mouth didn't move like one might expect. The sounds came from deeper, in its throat. Clearly, human speech wasn't the mastiff's first language.

"Speak, Fangard," said the centaur.

"I fear we did not capture them all," Fangard announced. "There were others in the company, including a dog of some sort. Not a strange dog, for it smells of Ternival. But not one of our own company, either, for it smells of elsewhere. Moreover, it smells of *her*."

"Told you!" An older man in battered chain mail limped forward. "They're on *her* side, I say. Valorentian spies. Just look at 'em." He glanced in Arash's direction and scowled.

"Peace, Smithfield," commanded the centaur. "Thou knowest nothing of Valorentians. Hold thy tongue."

"But that woman who was with them," the old warrior protested, "she looked just like Mindra, she did. Disappeared right before me eyes!"

A ripple of fear and anger swept through the company. Jack glanced with alarm at Paxton, who was staring back at him. *Say nothing,* the old man's eyes conveyed. *Nothing at all.*

"Peace, I say," repeated the centaur sternly. "Had Mindra been there, I would have known. Hast thou forgotten that this stretch of woods borders the Fenrunnel? While the Sisters rarely interfere in

Selvedge affairs, they do indeed wander beyond their own borders at times. 'Twas one of them, no doubt."

The word *Sisters* sounded ominous, like something from Shakespeare. Jack pictured three hags cavorting around a sinister fire. *Double, double toil and trouble . . .*

"Hotosho. Leonora. Rushyon." The centaur motioned for three wolfhounds to draw near. He gave them whispered instructions that Jack couldn't catch, and they nodded in unison and shot away into the woods.

The centaur now studied Paxton, Jack, and Arash in turn. His eyes were dark as rain clouds, flecked by occasional flashes of light, his brows like thunderheads. On one side, he was flanked by the mastiff called Fangard; on the other, by a dwarf the height of Georgie—but so broad-shouldered and barrel-chested and burdened with armor that he looked like a walking tank. None of them, Jack guessed, had a sense of humor.

"Speak, strangers," commanded the centaur. "State who you are and your purpose here."

Paxton stepped into the center of the company. Compared with the battle-hardened warriors, the old handyman from Carrick Hall seemed even thinner and paler than usual.

"Be it known that we are enemies of Mindra, the foul enchantress of old." His voice was strong. It rang to the edges of the clearing. "She has transformed our people into creatures and stolen from us great treasure, and we shall be avenged."

Jack blinked at Paxton in surprise.

"And if you are Mindra's servants," the old man added, "know that we shall never bow, never serve, and will gladly die honorable deaths."

Silence met this bold announcement.

Jack couldn't help but be impressed. This was a side of Paxton he hadn't seen before. No one in Upper Wolvern ever talked like this. But part of him inwardly cringed. He wasn't ready to die any kind of death, honorable or otherwise.

"Well spoken, good sir," said the centaur with a pleased gleam in his dark eyes. "Be thou assured: We, too, are enemies of Mindra, and thus, we are thy friends."

"But how do we know you can be trusted?" Paxton asked. Again, the old man's confidence was like a bracing draft.

"Loyal sentries of Ternival, show your arms," commanded the centaur.

Men, dwarves, and creatures stepped forward. Torchlight fell upon the image etched into their battered shields, their helms, their thick leathern breastplates.

A stag.

But not just any stag.

The stag.

Chapter

30

Indeed, the frame was a loom. Exactly like the one on which Zahra had learned to weave.

Her mother had never been able to afford a large floor loom, after all—and their hut was too small, anyway. So, instead, she'd started Zahra on a frame loom, on which they'd woven fine, decorative items like sashes, ribbons, and tapestries for their neighbor to take to market. And then Grandad had built Mother a table loom for more substantial items, such as runners and towels, head wraps and shawls. And she could create blankets and carpets, curtains and bedclothes, too, which she'd weave in sections and piece together. When they weren't busy mending nets or drying fish, Zahra and her mother could be found weaving.

"Of course!" Elspeth exclaimed, staring at the frame in Zahra's hands. "I can't believe I've never noticed before."

Zahra set the frame back down on the table, and the girls leaned forward, studying it.

"It's got notches at the top and bottom for the warp threads and everything," Aurora said. "Even the outside corners are reinforced, to support the tension of the warp—just like the kind we've been learning on with Mrs. Tabari." She turned to Zahra. "But how did you know that's what it was?"

"My mother is"—Zahra's voice caught—"*was* . . . a master weaver. I've been weaving since I was a child."

Aurora pointed to Zahra's sash with its complex pattern of golden pears. "Like this? Did you make this?"

As Zahra nodded, Elspeth peered at it, clearly impressed. "How exquisite! Masterful, actually." She sighed. "That's the kind of work I'd like to do. How long did it take you?"

"A few days, I'd say," Zahra replied.

Elspeth's shoulders drooped. "Oh. That's . . . Wow. Amazing."

The girls were silent for a while.

"Here you go," Georgie announced. He'd been beavering away so intently at his drawing that Zahra had almost forgotten he was here. Now he stood, cleared his throat, and flourished his sketch with an air of victory. She looked at the maze of squiggles and lines. They vaguely resembled a pile of drying seaweed.

Elspeth groaned. "For pity's sake, Georgie, we can't even tell what that is."

He flipped it upside down. "What about now?"

Zahra tilted her head.

"Don't you get it?" he yelled. "It's a map! Of Ternival!" He slammed the paper down on the table and pointed. "Look. Here are all the roads and rivers and stuff. And the ruins of the castle. Oh, and there's the forest. Plus, some wolves. See the teeth?" He pointed to a minuscule blob with a jagged grin. "And here you've got the Patchless Sea, or whatever it's called, with some ships and sea monsters, of course. And here"—he jabbed at a stick figure with straggly hair and angry eyebrows—"is Mindra." A large bubble-like circle floated above the figure's head, scrawled with the words *CURSES! FOILED AGAIN.*

For the first time that day, Zahra felt the urge to laugh. Nothing on Georgie's paper looked remotely like Ternival, of course. But his childlike depiction of the enchantress somehow exposed a truth that, up till now, Zahra had been too terrified to notice. It was the total absurdity of Mindra's self-importance. All at once, her grandiosity was exposed as ridiculous. If the enchantress ever saw Georgie's sketch, she'd be insulted beyond words—which, to Zahra, felt unexpectedly liberating. Mindra could be mocked.

Elspeth groaned again. "Oh, Georgie, this will never do! Even if it works and we end up in that world, we can't deal with wolves and sea monsters along with everything else. Plus, it doesn't even look real."

Georgie's enthusiasm deflated like a sail. He gave his sister a look of pure loathing and stomped out of the room.

"It's a really good picture, Georgie!" Aurora called after him. But he was gone.

The girls sat in moody silence for a while. Zahra found the intensity of these children bewildering. Such high feelings. Such loud speech. She'd never experienced anything like it.

"I know!" Aurora suddenly exclaimed. "What if you *weave* a picture, Zahra? On the frame itself, I mean. A tapestry of a place you know in Ternival!" But then her gaze dropped to the sling on Zahra's arm. Her face fell. "Oh, wait . . ."

Elspeth snapped her fingers. "Or the two of us could weave it, Aurora, while Zahra tells us what to do. She could be our instructor, like Mrs. Tabari."

"That's brilliant, Ellie!" Then Aurora's face fell again. "But we left all our supplies at the cottage. One of us will have to run there in the dark to get it and then run all the way back here. And what happens if our parents return in the meantime?"

To Zahra's surprise, Elspeth grinned. She jumped up, opened a cupboard, and returned, flourishing a small key.

"Oh, but we don't need those supplies. We've got loads. In the attic."

Aurora's eyes widened. "But I didn't think we were allowed in that room."

At that moment, an urgent bell jangled somewhere nearby. Startled, Zahra leaped to her feet. None of her companions seemed alarmed, however. Instead, Elspeth calmly stood up, grabbed what looked like a wide, fat handle from the wall, and pressed it to her ear.

"Hullo?"

"Behold," said the centaur, "the Selvedge remnant of Ternival, sworn enemies of Mindra the Usurper. We have pledged to retake the stronghold of Marisith, release the captives, and defeat her utterly."

Arash looked around the clearing. He knew he was supposed to be impressed by these guys, to feel some sort of relief that this "Selvedge remnant," whatever that meant, wasn't on Mindra's side. But instead, he felt numb.

Once again, he was the odd man out.

Even here. Even in a strange world where *everyone* looked weird. Where the definition of normal included things like talking dogs and blokes who were literally horses from the waist down. No, somehow it was still Arash Tabari who was viewed with suspicion. Who clearly didn't belong. As if he hadn't left the Wolverns at all.

Paxton caught his eye. The old man gave a tiny nod as if to say, *It's okay. We're among friends.* But Arash had received this kind of reassurance before, from well-meaning people. And they were always wrong.

"I am Starwise, counselor to the Chief Sentry of Ternival." The centaur continued his speech. "And this is Vahrberg, chieftain of Nisnagard," he said, gesturing to the dwarf at his right. "And to my left is Fangard, captain of the royal hounds and protector of Caristor—may its memory be eternal."

Paxton gave a dignified bow. "Hail, lords of Ternival. Call me Paxton. And these two are Arash and Jack. Fortunate are we to have fallen amidst such noble company."

Arash wanted to be impressed by Paxton's speech too. After all, the old man's formality reminded him of Grandfather when greeting customers at the bookshop. But again, Arash felt only numbness.

"Fortunate indeed," Starwise replied. "And we would hear more tales from thee, but our people are weary. My lords, we shall rest here," he said, raising his voice to the whole company. "Eat, drink, bind wounds, and hear what our guests would say. But we must tarry not. Set the watch forthwith, and build no fires beyond the occasional torch."

With quiet urgency, the company did as Starwise commanded. It was nearly dark by now, but the dwarves set the torches at intervals in a ring around the clearing. Soon Arash found himself seated next to Paxton and Jack, where they were offered flasks of tart juice and leathern pouches containing some kind of hardtack that was mostly tasteless.

Then, to Arash's relief, one of the younger sentries handed the boys their backpacks. "With apologies from Lord Starwise," he said with a slight bow.

Arash quickly inspected his. As far as he could tell, his metal-detecting headphones and other accessories remained right where he'd stashed them, undisturbed. And the treasure, too, thank goodness—although he didn't dare inspect that in the open. He zipped up the backpack again and strapped it to his shoulders. He wasn't going to let it out of his sight, not if he could help it.

Finally Starwise summoned Paxton to sit beside him in the center of the clearing.

"I divine that thou art from another world," said the centaur. "Dost thou deny it?"

"I do not," Paxton replied. "Indeed, we come from Tellus."

A murmur ran through the company.

"Children of Tellus!" the younger sentry cried. "Then it's true! They've arrived in our darkest hour, just as the oracle foretold!"

"And if Mindra is defeated," yipped a fox, "perhaps the rightful sovereign will appear at last!"

The mood of the company shifted considerably. Some of the sentries now looked at Arash with awe, even fearful admiration.

Children of Tellus. It was what that evil woman had said back in the valley. But what did it mean?

"We know nothing of an oracle," Paxton said. "But the boy can tell you more of how we arrived here." He turned to Jack. "It's all right, lad."

For the second time in as many hours, Jack told his story, summarizing all the events leading up to the arrival of both cars in Ternival. "Oh, yeah," Jack added. "And we brought a dog."

"A dog!" Fangard barked triumphantly. "I knew it!"

"Aye," Paxton said. "As you've discerned, we've lost three of our company."

"Fear not," said Starwise. "My scouts have been sent to find them and bring them safely here. But Fangard hath discerned a fourth scent, which accompanies that of the dog. 'Tis a scent we know, that of a Ternivali girl. Zahra, the Fisher Lass."

"Oh!" Jack exclaimed. "Isn't that the girl Tilly mentioned?"

Paxton nodded. "Indeed. Somehow, milords, Zahra found her way to Tellus. But she remains there, as far as we know. And without the gems—which are the only portals known to us for traveling between worlds—we have no means to return to Tellus ourselves. Nor to bring her home."

Another murmur swept through the company.

"Grim news indeed that Zahra remains in Tellus," Starwise said. "For it was she who alerted us this morning to the presence of giants. We had assumed she'd been transformed and imprisoned by Mindra with the rest of Lord Bayard's company—but now, it seems, she must have escaped. Yet I sense that we shall have need of her here, ere this trouble is over. But go on, young Jack. Finish thy tale."

Jack quickly summed up the rest. Being chased by the giant, here in Ternival. Seeing the smoke from the peninsula where Caristor had been. And the skirmish in the woods. When Jack described how the raptor had tried to fly off with his pack, the old sentry eyed Arash's own backpack warily. "Strange-looking burdens, if ye ask me," he muttered to a companion. "I still don't trust 'em."

Fangard gave a low growl of warning. "And is this how you'd like your own son to be treated, Smithfield? If Lepp fell amongst strangers?"

"Nay, Fangard," the sentry mumbled. He averted his eyes and held his peace.

By now, Arash's numbness had given way to bone-deep exhaustion. He didn't care what the Smithfields of Ternival thought. He just wanted to curl up somewhere, alone.

Fangard, meanwhile, had placed himself between Arash and the old warrior, as if to shield them from each other. And yet Arash had the distinct impression the mastiff was there to protect *him*.

Then suddenly Fangard lunged forward and bounded to the edge of the clearing, where he stood, limbs quivering, ears alert. And that was when Arash heard it too. Something or someone was dashing through the woods toward them.

Chapter

31

Before Jack and the rest of the company could scramble to their feet, into the clearing leaped the three wolfhound scouts. Alone.

"Hail, brave ones," said Starwise, rising. "You have news, I see. But take refreshment first."

The hounds lowered their shaggy heads into the leathern pouches proffered by their fellow Selvedges and slurped water noisily. For all their humanlike intelligence, they were still one hundred percent dog. It was really quite fantastic.

Then the hounds delivered their reports. Namely, that they'd been unsuccessful at finding the girl, the youth, or the dog.

First, Hotosho described how he'd tracked the girl, who'd fled farther down the trail toward Marisith before losing her way in the dark. She'd traced a meandering path till she reached the Fenrunnel, where she'd paused briefly. And then she'd crossed it. But the hound hadn't dared to cross the river himself, for without an invitation from the Sisters . . . He shuddered and his voice trailed off.

A murmur of fear swept through the company, and Jack's heart skipped a few beats. Tilly had survived the skirmish, at least. But now she was lost in this strange, beautiful, terrible world. Somewhere in the realm of the Sisters, whoever they were. He fought the urge to sprint out of the clearing in search of her. But no. It was best to stay with this company. If anyone could help Tilly, the Ternivali could.

Leonora went next. She'd tracked the stray, which must've taken off like a shot. It definitely knew its way around, anyway, for it'd skirted the Fenrunnel, as if it knew not to go near it, and instead followed the banks of the Runnelwilde toward the Pathless. But eventually the scent grew cold. Perhaps the stray realized it was being tracked and somehow doubled back to throw off its pursuer. In any case, it was gone.

Jack felt secretly proud. Attaboy. Smart dog. Or wait—no. Stupid dog. Because now they were separated.

Rushyon stepped forward. He'd tracked the youth, who apparently had gone back up the trail from which they'd come. The scent led to the crest of Oracle Hill, from which one can espy both Marisith and the peninsula of Caristor. But there the trail went utterly cold, as if he'd been borne away into the clouds.

"One of the raptors got 'im!" old Smithfield exclaimed. The others peered nervously into the dark branches overhead, as if great birds might descend at any moment.

Jack caught the concerned glance that passed between Starwise and Paxton. This didn't bode well for Charles. Sure, the guy was an entitled, self-centered toff. And even vaguely dangerous, as if he could turn on you at any moment. In fact, it was a relief he wasn't here scoffing at everything—although even the son of Lord Edward Heapworth might be intimidated into silence by the sheer majestic awesomeness of Starwise. But still. The idea of a mostly ordinary kid, a fellow student from Wolvern, being snatched away by a huge raptor, perhaps never to be seen again . . . Jack wouldn't wish that on anyone.

Starwise thanked the hounds. Then he gazed solemnly at the gathered company, which rose, as one body, to its feet.

"Loyal sentries of Ternival," Starwise announced, "the enchantress hath given us no choice. We must storm Marisith at once and recover the gems. If that can be accomplished, Mindra's power will once again diminish and her captives might be set free."

Silence fell. The sentries, weary though they were, fixed their eyes on the centaur determinedly. They seemed to stand taller, their expressions fierce.

'Tis a fool's mission, I fear. For we are up against the giant, and Mindra's enchantments, and her greater power now that she hath all the gems."

"And yet, milord," said Vahrberg, the dwarves' chieftain, "this company has one advantage. As you no doubt recall, during the long years of Mindra's absence, we dwarves from Nisnagard expanded the tunnels under Marisith, to strengthen its defense should Ternival's enemies return. We've carved new entrances and passages, which are so well-hid that 'tis likely she hasn't found them."

"Thus," another dwarf piped up, "a small underland company could sneak into her castle stronghold without being seen—"

"Whilst the larger overland company provides a distraction at the gates," Starwise finished, his eyes glittering in the torchlight. "'Tis a good plan."

Vahrberg puffed out his substantial chest, which made his neck all but disappear between his helm and breastplate. "'Twould be my honor to lead the underlanders, milord."

The centaur nodded solemnly. "And the rest shall muster with me, in the woods beyond the castle clearing, awaiting thy signal to charge."

"But what of the giant?" Smithfield asked. The old warrior just couldn't help himself. A curmudgeon, like Paxton. But a talkative one.

"Leave that to me." Starwise's stony face looked graver than ever.

"But once the underland company reaches Marisith," said a fox, "how shall they recover the gems? Won't Mindra keep them on her person?"

"Nay," Starwise replied. "For their music is such torment to her—particularly now that the gems are together in one place—that she is unable to bear it. She will have hidden them somewhere, no doubt. Somewhere in her stronghold."

"But where?" Vahrberg pressed. "By my recollection, Marisith consists mainly of the high tower built around a central spiral staircase, off which open many rooms. The gems could be anywhere in that foul hole."

"Not to mention," another dwarf added, "once we begin to ascend that staircase, there's no other way out. Moreover, does anyone know what the gems look like?"

There was a brief pause.

Then Jack stepped forward.

"I do."

At first, Tilly thought it was the moon, glimmering through a break in the trees.

She'd already lost the trail in the dark, of course. It hadn't taken long. She'd been wandering ever since, chastising herself for her lousy sense of direction. But now she paused. She sucked in her breath.

That wasn't the moon. It was some kind of creature. With antlers. Was it . . . Could it be? Was that . . . the stag?

It began moving away from her, and Tilly followed cautiously. After perhaps ten minutes, the creature arrived at a large stream, which it crossed nimbly. Then it paused. It looked back at Tilly with a gaze so wise, so piercing, that she felt she'd never been truly known, truly understood, till now.

Without a doubt, this was the stag.

The stream ran deep and swift, but by the stag's light she could discern a series of rocks that made a kind of natural bridge. She leaped from stone to stone and then landed on the opposite shore.

At that moment, the light vanished.

The stag was gone.

Tilly trembled, trying to get her bearings in the pitch dark. It was impossible to hear anything except the stream rushing over the stones. Was she supposed to follow the water somehow? Was that why the stag had led her here? For it *had* led her here. She was certain. Why else would it have turned and given her such a look?

But then, just as swiftly as the stag's light had vanished, an eerie greenish-blue flame appeared. It floated above the ground several yards away, as if someone held a lantern carved from jadeite.

Fear prickled the back of her neck. Someone *was* holding a lantern. A face hovered above the flame, gazing at her with wide, calm eyes. She recognized it immediately.

The face from the forest.

"Hail, Child of Tellus," said the face. Its voice sounded like leaves rustling in a light wind. "We've been awaiting you."

Chapter

32

"Everything all right, Ellie? Anyone rung the Hall?"

It was Mum on the phone, barely audible over the din of a crowd.

"Oh, hullo, Mum!" Elspeth said brightly—too brightly. She had the sudden urge to hide the frame. Her mother always seemed to know, just from her children's tone, when they were up to something. "Yes, everything's fine here. Mrs. Fealston is sound asleep. But no one's rung, I'm afraid."

"Right." Mum either hadn't noticed or was ignoring her forced cheerfulness. "Well, your dad and I are at the police station in Lower Wolvern with Lord Edward and Mrs. Tabari. But the place is a madhouse. Crawling with tourists who've spent too much time at the pubs, by the smell of things. Or got caught trespassing. It might be hours before we hear anything. But don't wait up for us. You'll be all right, won't you?"

This wasn't great news for Elspeth's parents, of course, but it was good news for the kids at Carrick Hall. They could attempt to weave something on the loom while the grown-ups were occupied.

"Yes! Yes, of course." Elspeth tried to hide the relief in her voice.

"Well, good night, then, love."

They hung up.

"They're all tied up at the police station, for now," Elspeth told the other girls. "C'mon!" She grabbed the loom and headed toward the passageway, Zahra and Aurora behind her.

As they passed Mrs. Fealston's rooms, they paused and peeked in. The old woman was still fast asleep. And there was Georgie, curled up snoring at the foot of her bed. He'd probably snuck in through the other door, the one that led from the hallway. His face was flushed, the hair at his temples damp. With a pang of guilt, Elspeth realized he must've cried himself to sleep.

She now led the girls up the back staircase, switching on lights as she went. At each landing, she studiously ignored the closed doors that led to the rest of the Hall, behind which were long, dark corridors, shrouded furnishings, and endless rooms. Other than when Eva's family came to visit, few of its chambers remained in use. Even the formal rooms on the first and second floors, normally open for public tours every summer, were temporarily closed. Mrs. Fealston's health was simply too fragile.

But, Elspeth hoped, the place wouldn't always be this lifeless and creepy. Last summer, she'd overheard snippets of a conversation between Eva and Frankie, something about grant funding and endowments and a loan from Lord Edward. Unintelligible grown-up stuff, actually. But they'd both sounded excited.

When the girls reached the attic, Elspeth led the way down the narrow passage, then paused and unlocked one of the many doors. Beyond it lay a large, shadowy room. She switched on the lights.

"Ohhhh!" Zahra exclaimed.

It was the old weaving studio.

The studio, with its sloping ceiling and gable windows, contained a long worktable at one end, next to a vintage spinning wheel that

Frankie had picked up at an antique shop. At the other end, comfortable chairs flanked a sofa. And along the walls, built-in shelves were laden with skeins of wool, baskets of fabric, spools of natural and dyed thread—plus numerous wooden bobbins, beaters, pickup sticks, and tapestry needles. A weaver's paradise. The only thing missing was an actual loom.

Zahra stood in the middle of the room, eyes shining, mouth slightly open.

"The Hall's previous owner, Professor Kinchurch, was a weaver," Elspeth explained. "So whenever the Three Queens visited her after their return from Ternival, they'd weave up here together. But later, once the High Queen had inherited the house after the others died, the doorway was bricked over, and the studio was mostly forgotten for fifty years. Not long ago, my brother Frankie rediscovered it. He spent part of last summer knocking down the bricks and cleaning the whole place up."

"And isn't this where Frankie and Eva first tried to use the gems?" Aurora asked. "To travel to other worlds themselves?"

Elspeth nodded. "That's one of the reasons why he put a lock on the door."

"So that no one might get in?" Zahra asked, bewilderment on her face.

"So that no one can come out," Aurora said ominously.

Elspeth set the frame on the table. "Well, shall we get started?"

With Zahra's guidance, the girls began collecting supplies and laying everything on the worktable. But then came the hard part: deciding what picture to weave.

"What do you think, Zahra?" Aurora asked. "If you could return to any place in Ternival, where would you want to go?"

For a moment, the girl's face blazed with an expression so poignant, so fierce and primal, that Elspeth took a step back.

"Home."

Zahra said just the one word, but Elspeth sensed it was the only thing that had held her together all day.

The entire company turned and stared at Jack. It was as if they'd forgotten his existence.

"I know what the box of gems looks like," Jack said. "And so does Arash. We've seen it—along with the bag Mindra was keeping it in."

Vahrberg turned to Starwise. "Then our visitors from Tellus should travel with me, in the underland company. While your contingent holds Mindra's attention, we'll clear the way for the lads to search the castle."

So it was agreed. They would surprise-attack Marisith shortly after moonrise.

With practiced swiftness, the company prepared for battle. Jack watched, fascinated, as they cleaned and sharpened swords, repaired torn clothing, and refilled quivers, all by the dim light of the dwarves' torches. They were so confident in their roles, so focused on the task ahead, that before long nearly all of them had assembled in formation behind Starwise, Vahrberg, and Fangard.

A plan began to form in Jack's mind. He checked his backpack to make sure the items he'd brought from the cottage were still there. Yep. Now it was just a matter of timing. He slipped through the sentries, past Paxton and Arash, till he reached the head of the line, behind the centaur. If his plan was going to work, he needed to be able to move swiftly.

Once the company started moving, Jack was impressed by how quiet they were, even the horses. They barely made a rustle in the underbrush. In fact, *he* was the one whose heavy boots sounded like a vast army of tromping Georgies. He tried to walk more silently, to plant his feet the way the woodland creatures did. Ninja feet. Just like in primary school.

The night was dark. And the forest was darker. Not a single star could be seen through the canopy. Which was a good thing for evading enchantresses, but not so great for marching. If it weren't for the occasional torch carried by the dwarves, Jack wouldn't have been able to see his hand in front of his face.

After about a mile, they reached a wide, chattering stream.

"The Fenrunnel," Starwise said over his shoulder to Jack. "Never cross these waters without permission." But the centaur didn't say from whom or why.

The company now turned left and followed the stream until it emptied into what sounded like a much wider river.

"We have reached the ford at the Runnelwilde," Starwise said. "'Tis now safe to cross." Indeed, by the light of the torches Jack could distinguish a dirt road running through the woods down to the river's edge. They crossed the broad, shallow river single file, Jack's boots filling with water so cold he could only breathe in gasps.

The night wore on. Jack was beginning to think they were taking the long way to Marisith. By this point, the callouses on his feet had become mushy wounds inside his soaking socks, and his backpack felt like it weighed a hundred pounds. He could've eaten a family-sized order of fish and chips by himself. This was probably what soldiers felt like on a long march, he realized. In fact, that's exactly what the Selvedges were. Soldiers. On a long march. And so was he, sorta.

Eventually the overhead canopy didn't seem quite so dark. Jack could now distinguish the faces of his companions. It wasn't sunrise, was it? Had they marched all night? But no. It was the moon.

Starwise sent out the wolfhounds again, this time to scout the peninsula of Marisith and report back. A few minutes later, he signaled a halt.

"Behold," said the centaur, "one of our secret entrances to Marisith."

Ahead loomed a bare rock wall in the side of a wooded hill, huge boulders strewn at its base. Secret entrance? All Jack could see in the moonlight was a massive slab of stratified rock.

"Here is where we part ways," Starwise continued. "The underland company, led by Lord Vahrberg, shall enter here, while the overland company shall continue to the woods on the south side of Marisith. There we shall wait within bowshot of the courtyard walls, not far from the portcullis gate through which we can see the postern door." He turned to the dwarf. "Once thy company is in place, wave a torch in front of the small grate at the base of the postern, to alert us to thy readiness."

Just then, the scouts returned.

"'Tis strange, milords," said Rushyon, panting. "The portcullis to the courtyard stands wide open. The giant is nowhere to be seen. The only sign that anyone's there are the lit torches in the courtyard."

"Not even raptors, milords," added Leonora. "Marisith seems abandoned."

"'Tis a trap." Smithfield's voice rose above the company's muttering. "This is how me own son, Lepp, likely met his doom."

"Thou art in the right, no doubt," Starwise agreed. "But we must face Mindra regardless."

The centaur summoned the dwarf chieftain to his side. Several other dwarves and a handful of creatures stepped forward also. All the animals were the kind that like to burrow underground: badgers and foxes, stoats and rabbits. There was even a large rodent that Jack recognized from nature magazines as a groundhog, sometimes called a whistle-pig.

"Now," said the centaur. "Fare forward, underlanders. We shall meet again. If not today, then in the far country."

Starwise stepped aside as if to let them pass. Jack peered into the gloom. Again, he could see nothing but the rock wall of the hillside.

But then Vahrberg strode forward, as if he meant to march straight into the wall. At the last second, he took a sharp right and disappeared.

Jack could see it now. An optical illusion. What he thought was a dark, ragged vein in the rock was, in fact, the cleverly hidden entrance to a cave.

Other dwarves and creatures now entered, followed by Paxton. And then it was Jack's turn. He took a step. Then another. But as he stared at the vein in the rocks, he felt the familiar clamp on his lungs. The edges of his vision blurred. His ears began to ring.

Behind him, Arash halted.

"Go on ahead, mate," Jack whispered.

But Arash didn't move.

"No, really," Jack said between shallow breaths. "Go on."

There was movement behind them. "Steady, young Jack," the centaur said quietly. "Thou shalt ride with me."

Jack felt a flush of shame. "Nah, I'm good," he said. "Just need a minute."

"This is no time for heroics, lad." The centaur's voice was stern now.

For a moment, Jack thought he could push through. He could enter the tunnel, just like he'd entered the crevasse in the Wolverns, and crawl his way to Marisith. But then his head cleared. Why demoralize himself? And anyway, his plan would work even better if he traveled overland.

Jack nodded. Without looking up, he stepped aside.

"You've got this, mate," Jack said as Arash slid past him. "See you on the other side."

Chapter

33

Slowly Arash's eyes adjusted to the dim light of the tunnel. Ahead of him waited Paxton.

"Jack?" the old man mouthed.

Arash shook his head.

"Ah, the poor overland snoof," said the groundhog, who brought up the rear. "Just couldn't do it. Tunnels give him the hivvermejibs. But it's all right. He's with Starwise." A breathy, high-pitched whistle accompanied the creature's every *s*.

Paxton nodded, then turned and followed the rest of the company. Arash did the same, the groundhog close behind.

All the company's torches must've been extinguished, for Arash could see no firelight flickering on the walls or ceiling. But it wasn't totally dark. A faint greenish-blue light shone ahead. Then, just as the moonlit slash of the tunnel's mouth disappeared around a bend behind them, the light grew closer, stronger. It came from the walls themselves, Arash realized with amazement. Strands of pale green spiderwebbed along either side of the tunnel and up into the ceiling. He'd never seen anything like it.

The walls—carved expertly from dirt and rock—were surprisingly smooth, and so was the floor. The tunnel twisted and turned, rose and fell, but the company moved quickly, silently. Even Paxton, old as he was, kept pace. Arash trotted to keep up.

On and on they advanced. Hours seemed to pass. It was impossible to gauge time underground.

At one point, they edged past an echoing stream, which eventually plunged into a deep chasm. Arash shuddered at its yawning mouth. What was down there? He didn't want to know.

Then the tunnel walls dropped away and the company emerged into a cavernous space. Far overhead, the roof disappeared in darkness. The air had changed. Sounds vanished without an echo. But nearby, something like gentle waves lapped on a shore. And then it struck him. The company was standing at the edge of a massive underground lake.

"What *is* this place?" Paxton asked the groundhog.

"The Felmar," whistled the creature cheerfully. "Eighty yards east of Marisith. But as far as we can tell, the great blitheress has never found it. Instead, during her long reign, she chose to delve straight down into the rock below the stronghold, to the shores of the Pathless." The groundhog shivered. "But the Felmar is treacherous enough on its own, mark my vimpers. The roof isn't stable, for one thing—great sections fall all the time. And it's deep, they say. Deep as the sea. Plus, we don't know what lies on the far shore. Anything might be living down here. But it's a helpful shortcut for us underland snerts."

Paxton shot Arash an amused glance. "We'll need a whistle-pig dictionary to keep up with this fellow," the old man murmured under his breath.

For the first time in what felt like weeks, Arash smiled.

The company resumed their march. They skirted the shore at a fast clip, hands on their weapons, glancing around uneasily as if un-named horrors might leap from the water. But eventually they reen-tered the tunnel system and continued onward.

The route now wound tortuously. Stones and debris littered the floor, and the walls were no longer smooth. Every few yards, huge beams braced the jagged roof—to prevent it, Arash guessed, from col-lapsing upon their heads.

"We're well into the peninsula now," said the groundhog. "Not far to go."

The groundhog pointed out the occasional tunnel that branched off to the left. "Escape hatches," he said. "Just in case anyone gets flupmizzled. That tunnel splits in two, with one fork leading to a se-cret exit in the woods near Marisith, while the other heads down to the shore."

Finally the main tunnel ended in a low-ceilinged cave. Scattered around it were tools, crates, and other supplies. The company halted.

"We rest here," Vahrberg announced in a low voice. "Fortify your-selves. For we are just below the gates of Marisith."

The company lowered their burdens and settled upon whatever they could find.

Paxton plopped onto a pile of rucksacks next to Arash. He was breathing hard and wiping his forehead. How old was the fellow, anyway? He had impressive stamina, in any case. Arash pictured his own grandfather, striding up the path into the Wolverns. Was that only yesterday? It felt like a month ago.

The warriors passed around some of the hardtack they'd eaten earlier, munching while they readied their weapons. Arash again tried some of it, but it was dry as dust. He longed for his grandmother's lamb kabobs, her flatbread and ranginak. Did the Selvedge remnant ever eat actual meals? Hot food. While seated at a table. But war was a different world. It reminded him of the few stories his grandparents would share about their flight from Iran. A proper meal? That was a peacetime luxury. The sort of thing you were fighting for, in fact. Hearth. Home.

Home. There was that word again.

The groundhog offered Paxton and Arash some strips of bark to munch on, but they shook their heads. The creature shrugged. "Well, suit yer own quooples." He commenced chewing contentedly, his enormous teeth flashing in the strange light.

Arash studied the walls. Now that the company had finally paused, he could observe the lights more closely. They seemed almost like very fine electric wires, which somehow glowed. Hairlike strands hung from the ceiling and walls like the root system of some vast, biolumi-nescent forest.

He reached out a hand. The nearest strand felt cold and damp, almost rubbery.

Then it shivered. The light inside it pulsed, like it was alive.

Arash yanked his hand away. Horrified, he watched as the pulse began to travel. It rippled from strand to strand, web to web, up into the ceiling, along the walls, spreading farther down the tunnel behind them. As though he'd thrown a pebble into a pond.

Everyone turned. Arash ducked his head. His heart was racing, as always. Stay perfectly still—say nothing, ever—and maybe they wouldn't stare. But they did. Strangers always did.

"Ye've sounded the alarm, right enough," muttered the ground-hog. "The entire forest knows what we're up to now, I'll be blomped."

Soon the pulses in the walls began to die away.

At the far end of the cave, Vahrberg rose to his feet. He gave Arash a stern look. "We can be glad the trees still despise Mindra as much as we do." Then he turned to the rest of the company. "Remnant of Ternival," he announced, "we begin."

Carefully, the dwarf struck some kind of flint, and his torch hissed into flame. Then he motioned for Arash and Paxton to join him at the head of the company.

Arash stood. His hands were shaking. Rattled was what he was. Shaken by what'd just happened. He'd already screwed up once. What if he screwed up again?

"Ready, lad?" Paxton whispered.

Arash pushed his glasses up his nose and nodded.

But it was a lie.

They could keep their stupid gems. *He* was going to search Marisith for one purpose and one purpose only.

To set his grandfather free.

Chapter

34

The face belonged to a dryad, of course.

"You are the one they call Tilly," the woman said. "I am Goldleaf, thy guide. Come. The Sisters are waiting." Tilly didn't have the chance to ask who the Sisters were before Goldleaf turned and began pacing away.

Tilly hesitated. If the stag had led her here, she could trust this person, right?

She took a deep breath, then followed.

As they walked, the forest grew brighter. A half-moon was rising above the canopy, and now Tilly could see her guide more clearly. Goldleaf was a tall, slender woman with smooth skin like a beech tree and long hair that fell in thick layers like leaves. She walked with a calm, steady gait that reminded Tilly of the opening procession at the church in Upper Wolvern. No rush, no worry. As if they had all the time in the world.

After about fifteen minutes, numerous greenish-blue lights flickered through the trees ahead. Tilly and her guide were approaching some kind of encampment in a clearing. As they drew nearer, she could discern a cluster of domed tentlike structures encircling a bright watch fire so greenish blue, it looked like burning ice. Lanterns twinkled in the branches overhead, and the murmur of voices drifted through the trees. Dryads like Goldleaf, Tilly guessed.

Sure enough, as Goldleaf and Tilly approached, dozens of dryads rose from their spots around the encampment. And they were all curiously different. Tall, short, skinny, stumpy, rough-skinned or smooth—they were as unique as separate species of trees.

Goldleaf led Tilly around the clearing, making introductions. "Allow me to introduce Brambletop, my sister," Goldleaf would say. And then, a moment later, "These are my sisters Willowbud and Oakholm." Tilly's guide, apparently, was related to everyone in the clearing. "Wait. Is this just one huge family, or what?" Tilly finally asked after the fifteenth introduction along these lines.

Goldleaf seemed confused. "Are not humans also one family? Just as trees are connected by their roots underground, we are all sisters."

This made sense, sort of. "How about brothers? I've got lots of those," Tilly said.

"Oh yes, we have brothers. But long ago, they left for their own adventures. Wherever they are, we wish them well."

Tilly halted, amazed. For her entire life, she'd been surrounded by boys. An older brother to admire, two younger brothers to supervise, plus all their stuff: cricket bats and rugby balls, geodes and hiking boots, the occasional beetle or stick or dirty sock. Not to mention an endless supply of random snacks they seemed unable to live without. At mealtimes, she knew to guard her plate and grab seconds as soon as possible—because if she paused to blink, the food would be gone. Brothers took up so much . . . *space*.

But there were positives to having brothers too. When he wasn't teasing her, Frankie was a deep thinker who listened well and offered sound advice. She valued his opinion more than anyone else's, actually. And Jack, for all his annoying independence, could be relied upon to fix your bike or mow the lawn if you really needed him. And Georgie? He was a hugger. The loudest hugger ever, but still, you could count on him for a cuddle when you were sad.

In fact, for better or worse, boys had dominated Tilly's life for as long as she could remember. And not just brothers either.

Charles.

She pictured him huddled in the driver's seat of the Rolls, doors locked, holding vigil as the night wore on. He'd do his best to stay awake. But eventually his eyelids would droop and his tousled head would nod. He'd drift into an uneasy slumber, jolting awake periodically before exhaustion dragged him back to sleep. Did he wonder where she was and if she was safe? After the incident with the note and his flight from the skirmish, she wasn't sure what to think anymore.

Around the clearing, the dryads were preparing some kind of feast. Each tent had its own cooking fire, which burned a bright, greenish white, while several long stone slabs were laid with baskets of fruit, nuts, seeds, and flatbread.

While they waited for the feast to start, Goldleaf took Tilly on a tour of the encampment. It'd been set up within a wide oxbow of a river called the Runnelwilde, which, Goldleaf said, formed the northern border of the Sister Land. The smaller stream called the Fenrunnel—which Tilly had crossed in pursuit of the stag—formed the southern border. And further downriver, where the Fenrunnel emptied into the Runnelwilde, the Sister Land ended. From there, the Runnelwilde cut through the Great Forest of Ternival all the way to the Pathless.

Here along the riverbank a fleet of odd, flat-bottomed, oval-shaped boats lay overturned, one against the other.

"Curraghs," Goldleaf told her. "Each dryad has her own, for plying the river. 'Tis how we move quickly through the forest, including down to the Pathless."

By the time they returned to the clearing, the feast was well underway. More dryads had arrived, and Tilly found herself surrounded by laughing, eating, singing revelers accompanied by a quintet of flutes and harps. Best of all, the dryads were dancing. In fact, it was one great party, a midsummer festival, dryad-style.

"Children of Tellus have similar revelries at midsummer, do you not?" Goldleaf asked as they seated themselves at one of the long tables.

"Oh, sure. Eating and drinking and watch fires and all that. Plus, dancing, sort of. Although if everyone danced like dryads, it would make our festival a thousand times better."

Tilly took a bite of the flatbread, which reminded her of Mrs. Rastegar's sangak. When was the last time she'd eaten, anyway? She couldn't remember. And now, for the first time, she was able to turn her mind toward Jack and the others. Were they okay? Had they found themselves among friends, or had they fallen into the hands of the enchantress? Either way, they were probably hungry too.

She set the bread down and gazed at the dancers. "But how *can* they dance right now?" Tilly asked her hostess. "Don't they know that Mindra has returned?"

"Oh yes," Goldleaf replied. The serene expression never seemed to leave her face. "The trees told us everything. About the coming of the giants this morning, and the fall of Caristor, and about the many Ternivali who were transformed and imprisoned. Yes, we know it."

"Even so, the Sisters dance?"

"'Tis our tradition, the way we welcome the world's longest day. Do not forget: The sun has burst forth every morning since the first dawn, long before Mindra ever stepped foot in this world. And it will continue to do so long after she is gone. Why should we give her more power than she already thinks she has? No, dear Child of Tellus. We dance *because* Mindra has returned."

As Tilly looked on, she was more and more mesmerized by the sheer, radiant joy of the dancers. It wasn't anything like glib happiness or tepid pleasure. It was fierce, defiant, wild. A dance of rebellion against Mindra's hold on Ternival, a dance that made Tilly want to leap from her seat, take up a spear, and march against Marisith.

"Come!" called Goldleaf, rising. "Dance with us!"

"Oh, but I'm really, really bad at it," Tilly protested. "Two left feet and all that."

"Nonsense," Goldleaf replied. "I shall show you."

Tilly would never forget the hour that followed. The rising moon. The whirling dryads. The complex steps that her feet began to master as soon as she stopped thinking about them. And the more she danced, the greater her confidence grew. She no longer worried about the next step, or the next. She wasn't thinking about whether it would be the wrong or right choice. She simply trusted her instincts. She'd become part of a great unfolding pattern—in which she had a unique role to play—and instead of paralyzing her, it felt freeing.

Eventually the dancers grew weary. But it was a good kind of tired. Everyone sat down around the watch fire and simply rested.

Fascinated, Tilly stared into the flames. What kept the fire going? The dryads didn't seem to burn wood nor use any kindling. Indeed, it seemed to be a product of spontaneous combustion.

Then one of the Sisters began to play a strange sort of lute carved from a gourd strung with taut vines. As the moon rose higher, the musician began to sing. The other Sisters answered, back and forth, back and forth, a beautiful call-and-response.

Comfortable and well-fed, Tilly began to drift off to sleep.

But just as her eyes were closing, the watch fire's light pulsed. It flashed again and again, almost like Morse code. As the pulse rippled out to the lanterns and cooking fires, the singer stopped abruptly. The other dryads went silent, too, watching.

Eventually the pulses died away. But the atmosphere had shifted. The dryads began murmuring to one another, their faces solemn in the moonlight.

"What was that?" Tilly asked Goldleaf. "What happened?"

"News from near Marisith," the dryad replied. "The trees have sent warning. A company of Mindra's sworn enemies, the Selvedges, have entered their secret tunnels and are headed her way. They mean to attack the stronghold."

She gave Tilly a look so poignant that her heart dropped.

"Among them, it seems, are Children of Tellus."

Chapter

35

ome wouldn't be the same without Grandad there.

Zahra knew this, of course. But the hut was their abode nonetheless. And hopefully Mindra wouldn't have any use for a structure so lowly and unimportant. Which meant that if, by some miracle, the frame's magic actually worked, they might have a chance of arriving in Ternival undetected.

"Can you describe it for us?" Elspeth asked her. "Your home, I mean. I can picture what a fisherman's hut looks like, but it might not resemble yours."

So, Zahra described the stone walls and slate roof, built to withstand a tempest. The sturdy wooden door Grandad had designed and lathed himself. The open windows, which the family covered with heavy woven curtains during foul weather. The racks of drying nets, the overturned boat, all set against a backdrop of sky and shore.

"Oh, that should be easy!" Aurora said when Zahra finished. "Mostly just blue on blue, right? With some puffy white stuff for clouds. And then a brownish square in one corner."

"But it will need to be precise if it's going to work," Elspeth cut in, fidgeting with her long hair again. "Basically perfect. Maybe I should do it."

Aurora looked miffed. "But you'll take forever, Ellie! Why don't *you* weave the hut, and I'll do the other stuff?"

It was Elspeth's turn to look miffed. "Fine. Clouds and water are constantly moving, anyway, so they don't need to be exact."

Aurora's eyes flashed, but she said nothing more.

Zahra could feel the tension in the air. Instinctively, she rested her good hand on Aurora's arm, then on Elspeth's. "It will first need to be warped, in any case," she said gently. "And then you can take turns weaving."

Both girls seemed to snap out of it. Elspeth's fingers stopped fidgeting. Aurora's fists, which she'd balled at her sides, opened again. They eyed each other sheepishly.

"Right," Elspeth said, shifting focus back to the task at hand. "Taking turns sounds like a good plan. While one of us works here in the studio with Zahra, the other can hang out in the kitchen, listening for the phone. Oh, and from the kitchen, we can keep an eye on Mrs. Fealston and Georgie too. Maybe switch every forty-five minutes or so?"

"Great!" Aurora agreed. "I'm happy to weave first." Her previous excitement had returned.

Elspeth hesitated, her lips pressed together.

Again, Zahra placed her good hand lightly on Elspeth's arm. "Perhaps Elspeth should begin," Zahra suggested to Aurora, "since you're not as familiar with the contents of the studio. Elspeth can warp the loom, then return downstairs to fetch you."

"Oh! Right. Makes sense to me," Aurora said. "See you in a bit."

As Aurora's footsteps died away, Elspeth sat down at the table, where they'd propped the loom on a stand.

"Ready?" Zahra asked.

The girl gave a determined nod. "Ready."

While Jack regained his composure at the mouth of the tunnel, Starwise gazed solemnly at the remaining company.

"Fellow Selvedges," he announced, "now we sally forth. To what doom or victory, I cannot say. Whatever happens, we must distract Mindra, at all costs."

By the light of the moon, Jack tried to make out some of the facial expressions of those around him. Were they afraid? Were they worried for the friends and family they'd left behind? He again thought of Tilly, lost somewhere in the woods. And Frankie and Eva, trapped in the stronghold ahead. And Charles, wherever he was. He hoped against hope they were okay.

The noble centaur now turned to Jack and lowered his forelegs.

"No time to waste, young sir," Starwise said. "Thou shalt ride with me."

Whispers rippled through the company. With as much dignity as he could muster, Jack scrambled astride the centaur's back and held on tightly. Starwise sighed, as if transporting an untried rider was one of his pet peeves. But he said nothing.

They moved at a terrific pace, the night air cool on Jack's face, moonlight dappling the forest floor, stars visible through breaks in the dark canopy overhead. In the bracing chill, Jack's wooziness abated. Every creature within the overland company was the sort that loved to run. Wolfhounds, of course, but also deer and antelope and brush wolves and horses, often in a joyous gallop.

Eventually the trees began to thin, and Jack caught occasional glimpses of the distant sea. Dark and vast and . . . pathless. Unlike the coast of England, this shore was empty of all light. No twinkling streetlamps, no lit cottage windows, no piers or wharfs or shipping channels. Farther down the coast, inky black against the stars, was the left-hand peninsula they'd seen from the hilltop. Between that far point and this one, nothing but high bluffs, steep wooded hillsides, and a thin sweep of shingle.

Dead ahead, a clearing came into view: an open field of waving grasses, dotted with rock outcroppings. And now Jack spied the castle at the far end, perched atop the last lonely cliff above the Pathless. A solitary flame winked in a high window, and beyond the highest battlement, nothing but stars.

But instead of continuing straight, across the clearing, Starwise veered left, sticking to the trees.

"Isn't that a more direct route?" Jack leaned forward and pointed toward the clearing.

Starwise nodded. "'Tis indeed. But far more dangerous. It traverses the roof of the Felmar, which might not hold the weight of all our company. Plus, we daren't be seen from the battlements. Nay, the woods are best."

As the company crossed a dirt road and skirted the clearing, drawing nearer and nearer to Marisith, there was still no sign of the giant—not even the smell of him. Nonetheless, Starwise proceeded more cautiously now. The centaur slipped from shadow to shadow, hoof-beats muffled by leaves and pine needles, the company nearly silent behind him. Then he halted.

"Should we be forced to retreat," Starwise whispered to Jack, "meet at that stand of spruces." He pointed to a cluster of pines deeper in the woods. "'Tis the hidden mouth of yet another secret tunnel, an escape route from the main Selvedge passageway under Marisith. One of its forks leads down to the shore."

They'd halted roughly thirty yards from the courtyard walls. As the hounds had reported, torchlight flickered at the base of the central tower, which was clearly visible through the open portcullis. Jack could discern the familiar outline of the postern door set in the castle wall—and below that, close to the ground, a small rectangular smudge.

"The ventilation grate," Starwise whispered. "We shall await the signal here. And now, lad, if thou hast recovered, 'tis time for thee to dismount."

Jack slid awkwardly from the centaur's back onto the carpet of leaves.

Suddenly a clamor of cascading rocks and debris came from the bluff on their left. Cresting the rim of it—massive against the stars—was the giant. The company drew back into the shadows, and Jack held his breath. But the giant couldn't see them. And they were downwind, so he couldn't smell them either—although now they could most certainly smell *him*. Stonefist proceeded to tromp toward the courtyard wall and plop down just in front of the open portcullis, muttering about not having eaten all day and no fishies to be found either.

Jack's heart constricted with excitement. Stonefist couldn't have sat in a more perfect spot.

Jack shouldered his backpack. This was the moment.

Silent as a shadow, he began to creep away.

Chapter

36

It was taking Elspeth far too long to warp the loom.

Not because of Zahra, who sat nearby, quietly advising her. But because Elspeth was Elspeth. Fastidious. Precise. Leery of messing up. Especially when the stakes were so high.

Next to her, Zahra occasionally sighed. Elspeth hoped it was from exhaustion rather than annoyance, which would've made her feel even more flustered. The last thing she wanted was to be another Georgie, driving people bonkers with his personality quirks.

Finally, after numerous false starts and tangled threads, Elspeth finished the warping. She leaned back, releasing the breath she must've been holding.

"Well done, Elspeth," Zahra said, peering at her work. "Shall we give Aurora a turn?"

It was time to switch, of course. But even so, as Elspeth descended the back staircase, she felt a bit deflated. Her emotions were all over the place right now. And how late was it, anyway?

She found Aurora seated at the kitchen table, sipping tea, her nose buried in Jack's book. She looked up as Elspeth entered.

"Have you read any of this?" Aurora asked. "I swear, the djinn sounds just like our giant."

"Not yet," Elspeth replied. "Any word from the parents?"

Aurora shook her head. "Georgie and Mrs. Fealston are having a first-rate snooze, though. That's probably what he needed, poor little guy."

There it was again: the pang of guilt.

"And the tapestry? How's that going?" Aurora asked.

Elspeth shrugged. "Took a while to warp the thing, so I haven't even started yet. But Zahra is great—she'll tell you *exactly* what you need to do."

Elspeth had put rather too much emphasis on the word *exactly*. But Aurora needed to understand how high the stakes were, right? She couldn't just spear feathers through the whole thing and call it good. Then again, Elspeth was no master weaver. Recalling Zahra's seemingly limitless patience with a fastidious slow coach like herself, she gave Aurora what she hoped was an apologetic grin.

"You'll do just fine," she said. "We make a great team, right?"

Aurora smiled back. "Right. Well, I'm off."

Elspeth put the kettle on and began flipping through Jack's book. It was a simple collection of fairy tales, apparently—not Jack's usual fare at all. But the stories had intriguing titles like "The Weaver's Magic Runes" and "How the Jewels Were Found." Before long, she was immersed.

When drowsiness threatened to overtake her, she got up and stepped outside. The night air felt fresh and cool. A half-moon bathed everything in a faint glow, and watch fires twinkled along the ridgeline of the Wolverns. If she squinted, the whole thing looked like a dragon constellation, one long thread beaded with fire.

Her mind turned to Tilly and Jack. Were they and the others

okay? And what had happened to Professor Rastegar? She pictured her parents down at the crowded police station, with Mrs. Tabari and Lord Edward, of all people. Was a more unlikely team of comrades even possible? No. Definitely not.

Elspeth went back inside. She tried not to think about whatever Aurora might be doing to the work they'd started. Sprinkling the shore with glitter, no doubt. Gluing on actual pebbles. But no. Zahra wouldn't let her do that, would she?

Finally Elspeth couldn't bear the suspense any longer. It was probably her turn again, anyway. She left the kitchen and vaulted up the stairs.

Jack slipped away from Starwise and Fangard, away from the company's front line. Then, when the path was clear, he took off at a crouching run toward the courtyard wall.

It took several heartbeats before someone gasped from the tree line behind him. He'd been spotted. But none of the company would dare follow, right? For fear of alerting the giant? Jack hoped they'd stay put, anyway. This was a one-man job.

He reached the courtyard wall. It was an ancient surface, battered and pocked, with plenty of handholds. Not much different from the rock faces he regularly climbed in the Wolverns, actually. He paused to unzip his backpack and pull out the length of rope. After looping it several times around his waist, he tucked the end securely in his belt and began to climb.

Compared with the crevasse, this was a breeze. As he scrambled upward, he imagined the company's dismay turning to admiration. Yes, good people of Ternival. He was Jack the Giant Killer. He was the Child of Tellus, about whom the oracle spoke. Not that he believed in oracles, but it helped to know that *they* did.

Quickly Jack scaled the wall. At some point in its history, the top must've been crenellated, but it had worn away until the surface was merely uneven. Using a kind of commando crawl, he slithered along it toward the portcullis. Just a few more feet, and the back of the giant's head was nearly at eye level. The monster's great ugly neck, visible in the moonlight, was covered with warts the size of footballs and bristling with spikes of hair.

For the first time, Jack hesitated. The giant's neck was much, much thicker than he'd anticipated. But there was no time to rethink things. Either he went through with his plan, or . . .

Slowly, silently, he unwound the rope from around his waist. He twisted it into a coil and hefted the loops over his shoulder, then inched forward again. But just when the giant was almost within reach, its stench hit Jack like a boulder. A wave of nausea swept over him, leaving him cold and shivering, drenched in sweat.

And that was when Stonefist sniffed.

The monster straightened and sniffed again, just like in the valley. Then it leaned forward, peering into the darkness beyond the torchlight. "Fee, fi, fo, fum," Stonefist chanted. "I smell the blood of . . . the blood of . . ."

Then, with a swiftness that nearly sent Jack flying, the giant swiveled its great head. It looked him dead in the eye. A horrible smile spread across its face.

"Supper," said the giant.

What happened next would live in Jack's nightmares forever.

For all its bumbling clumsiness, the giant, when it came to food, moved quick as lightning. It snatched Jack up in its meaty fist and peered at him in the moonlight—as if to confirm that he was indeed edible. And then Stonefist began to squeeze.

Jack knew this feeling, of course. The pressure on his lungs, his breath getting shallower and shallower. His ears buzzed with that familiar high-pitched whine as his vision tunneled, tunneled, to one glimpse of a star above the giant's massive forehead. Except, this time, the feeling wasn't a flashback. It wasn't the London Underground at rush hour, when a small child on holiday with his family could be swept into the crush of bodies, unable to move, unable to breathe.

And this time, his dad wasn't here to grasp him by the collar and lift him out.

Stone. Fist.

Of course.

Jack's last thought, before darkness took him, was that the centaur—somewhere far below him—should really stop yelling if he wanted to live.

Chapter

37

Arash joined Vahrberg at the head of the company, Paxton and the groundhog close behind.

"Don't ye worry," said the groundhog as he hopped into position next to Arash. His cheerful tone had returned. "I'll stick with ye. The cranky old blitheress can't turn *me* into a creature, now, can she?"

Arash gave the groundhog a faint smile, his second that day. Under different circumstances, the creature's words and whistles would've been hilarious. They *were* hilarious. And somehow calming. Arash's knees no longer shook.

The grim dwarf signaled for the company to follow him. He slipped through a slit in the rock. Arash went next and emerged into a much-wider passageway from behind a stack of carefully positioned crates. This was no rough-hewn tunnel. It was an actual hallway. Made of cut stones.

They were in the bowels of Marisith.

Vahrberg pressed onward through the passage, the rest of the company close behind. And then the dwarf rounded a bend and halted.

Ahead of them rose a narrow flight of stone steps. Fresh, cool air, smelling of the sea, made the torch gutter in the dwarf's hand.

"There's the grate!" Vahrberg said. Sure enough, high in the left-hand wall, the metal ventilation grill covered a small opening in the stones.

"Do we know if that great lump of a giant has returned?" asked the groundhog.

An excitable little stoat began dashing about in a frenzy. "I can find out for us!" it squeaked. "Lift me up so I can slip through."

But just then, a massive boom rocked the roof.

Then another and another. Dust rained down everywhere.

Footfalls. Overhead.

The demon was back.

"What do you think, so far?" Aurora asked Zahra.

Cradling her aching arm with its makeshift sling, Zahra peered at the loom. Under normal circumstances, the girls would've woven the tapestry from the back—or the "wrong"—side of the image instead of the front. That way, grubby fingers and dangling threads wouldn't mar the finished project. But these weren't normal circumstances. The girls had decided to weave from the front—or outward-facing—side, as quickly as possible.

Zahra inspected Aurora's work. What the girl had accomplished was impressive, actually—especially considering her propensity to deviate from any kind of plan. Zahra had intended for her to use a skein of finely spun blue wool for the sea, which the girl had dutifully threaded into the tapestry needle. But after the first three passes didn't add more than a sliver of color to the weft, Aurora had hunted around in the storage baskets and found a fat roll of wide gray-blue ribbon.

"Here," she'd said brightly. "This will go much faster, don't you think?"

It'd taken all of Zahra's self-control to let her give it a try.

But the girl had been right. Looping the ribbon through by hand, Aurora had quickly managed to complete a passable swath of undulating sea. And then she'd done the same for the shore, for which she'd selected a grainy burlap-style twine. True, her work hadn't been very precise—she'd skipped a warp thread here and there, sometimes several in a row—but then again, as Elspeth had unhelpfully pointed out, none of Aurora's subject matter needed to be exact.

Now footsteps sounded on the staircase, and Elspeth herself appeared. Zahra's heart sank. She could tell from the girl's face that she'd gotten all wound up with worry again.

But Aurora glanced up with a grin, seemingly oblivious. "Look, Ellie! It's coming along brilliantly, don't you think?"

Elspeth stood next to her friend, arms akimbo. Her expression was guarded. "It's really coming along," she said in a careful monotone.

"I'm happy to keep going, if you like," Aurora offered.

A frustrated look crossed Elspeth's face.

"Very kind of you, Aurora," Zahra intervened. "But we don't want to get too far ahead with the sea and sky, or there won't be room for the hut."

"Oh, right. Well, I'm off again!" Aurora trotted out the door.

Elspeth resumed her spot at the loom, flexing her fingers and windmilling her arms like she was warming up for a competition. Zahra handed her one of the skeins of brown-and-gray wool she'd selected for the hut.

"See that section of shoreline, where Aurora left off? That's where the hut will go."

"About how big, would you say?" Elspeth asked. Squinting, she picked up a needle and attempted to thread it.

"We can keep the place fairly small," Zahra replied. "I mean, it *is* small, in real life. Two of them would fit in this studio."

Elspeth glanced up. "Gosh! And I thought my family's cottage was tiny."

"Well, we don't need much room," Zahra said. "After all, there's only three of us. Two, I mean. Two."

After several attempts, Elspeth finally threaded the needle and got to work. But it didn't take long before frustration set in. First, she accidentally skipped one of the warp threads and decided to start over. Then she pulled the weft too tight—which made the hut look uneven—so she tore it all out again. Things deteriorated from there till Elspeth was nearly in tears.

Zahra knew the feeling. When she was learning to weave, she'd once gotten so wound up about being perfect that she'd ruined a ribbon her mother had started for her.

"You need to loosen up, dear one," Mother had said. "You're like a thread that's too taut. If you're not careful, you'll snap. Instead, sense the joy as it hums down the warp—do you feel it? The wool was made for creating something beautiful, and so were you. And anyway, you're thinking too much. Have I told you the tale of the princess and the djinn?"

At this, Zahra had laughed. It was one of Grandad's many tales from the land known as Valorenta, of course, which she could recite backward and forward. But Mother had told it again anyway. And sure enough, the calming cadence of her mother's voice had provided just the distraction she needed.

After that, storytelling had become their tradition. Whenever they sat down to weave, Mother would glance up and say, "Have I told you the tale of the prince who found six magical jewels?" Or, "Have I told you about the king who was cursed by a terrible witch?"

Now it was Zahra's turn to help an anxious weaver.

"Shall I tell you the tale of the weaver by the sea," she began, "who once wove a tapestry so exquisite, all the princes of the world wished to possess it?"

Elspeth looked up, frowning. "The weaver by the sea? Like the one from Jack's book?"

Now it was Zahra's turn to be confused. "From . . . a book?"

"Jack got it today, at the Rastegars' shop." Elspeth worked the needle swiftly as she talked. "A djinn came and demanded that the weaver sell the tapestry to him, for the djinn's boss, a witch. But the weaver wouldn't. So the djinn threatened to destroy the weaver and his family if he didn't deliver it to the witch's palace by dawn."

Zahra felt suddenly lightheaded. Her wrist had begun to throb again. But . . . how was this possible? How had Grandad's tales ended up here, in Tellus? As far as she knew, the only people who'd ever heard them were Grandad, Mother, and herself.

Shakily, she lowered herself onto the sofa. "Yes, the very same," she managed to say. "Pray, continue."

"Well, the weaver wouldn't budge, of course," Elspeth continued. "So, after the djinn left, he and his wife and son packed up the tapestry and fled into a nearby cave, along the shore. But they got lost in the dark and suddenly found themselves in another world."

By now, sharp pain was shooting from Zahra's wrist to her shoulder. Her head ached, and she wanted nothing more than to lie down. But at the same time, the distraction of storytelling seemed to be working. Elspeth had already completed the bottom part of the hut. Interruptions were the last thing she needed.

Gingerly, Zahra leaned back against the soft cushions.

"Do go on, Elspeth," she said. "And then what happened?"

Chapter

38

As soon as he hit the ground, Jack snapped back to consciousness.

Pain, apparently, worked more efficiently than box breathing or whatever other coping strategies the school nurse had tried to teach him. Pain and fear.

He rolled to his side, ears ringing. Stonefist must've dropped him right by the open portcullis. And there was the centaur thundering past, just outside the courtyard walls. The giant's massive feet stumbled after Starwise, its great legs like tree trunks, every footfall an earthquake.

Shouting reached Jack's ears: Starwise, hurling taunts, and the giant, growing more and more enraged. And then Starwise lunged. He slashed at the giant's thigh with his spear and galloped away, out into the clearing. Howling, the giant limped after him.

But what was the centaur doing now? He wasn't leading the giant away from Marisith, like one would expect. Instead, he was luring it around and around the clearing in ever-tightening circles. And the angrier Stonefist grew, the harder the ground shook beneath them both. Was the centaur mad?

And then, with a cataclysmic roar that echoed out over the sea, the clearing imploded. It collapsed into the earth, thousands of tons of rock and dirt pouring down and down. A plume of dust rose into the moonlight, obscuring Jack's vision. But when the dust settled, the truth of what'd happened hit him like a train.

Starwise and the giant were gone.

They'd fallen into the huge chasm that now severed Marisith from the rest of the peninsula.

Jack struggled to his feet under the archway. His torso felt like one enormous bruise, as if his backpack had fused with his vertebrae. He was almost certain he'd broken a rib or two. But worst of all, his eyes wouldn't work. The moonlit woods looked smeared; the torchlight bled to the edges of his vision.

Oh, wait, no. He was crying.

Tears for the fall of Starwise. Tears for his own spectacular stupidity. If only the earth would swallow him too. But the night wasn't over. Not by a long shot.

Behind him came a loud crash from the courtyard. The postern door, he guessed, had just been thrown open. Grief instantly turned to dread.

"Ah! And here's our hero, the great Child of Tellus." It was the voice he'd hoped never to hear again. "Thought to vanquish my giant, no doubt, but murdered thine only guide and helper instead."

Jack turned slowly, his ribs on fire. Mindra, of course. Stalking out of the postern toward him like a harbinger of death. It was almost comical, really, how well she mimicked every bad guy in the books: So, *so* serious. So convinced of her singular importance. And was she drenched in *blood*? No. She'd merely changed from street clothes into a crimson cloak and black dress that matched her sinister gloves. Like she'd just marched into Lower Wolvern's community theater for try-outs, convinced she'd snag lead villain, but was trying a *bit* too hard.

Jack couldn't help it. As the enchantress approached, red cloak billowing, he began to laugh.

He laughed and laughed and laughed. It hurt too. Holding his ribs, tears pouring down his face, Jack released all the conflicting emotions he'd bottled up since his primal howl in the valley. He'd ruined everything, anyway, so what did he have to lose? Starwise was dead. Mindra was unbeatable. And Jack the Failed Giant Killer had zero chance of surviving whatever happened next.

Mindra halted. Confusion and outrage warred on her face.

But just then, a horn sounded from the woods. Beyond the courtyard, the overland company poured forth from the trees like a flood, Fangard leading the charge. Within moments, they'd read the portcullis and breached the walls.

The Battle of Marisith had begun.

Coughing and sputtering, Arash picked himself up off the floor. Debris crunched underfoot, and he could tell by the grit on his face that a cloud of fine dust filled the air.

"What the blinklevopping whiffenburf was that?" the groundhog said somewhere nearby. Arash could hear him shaking himself like a wet dog.

Arash peered into the darkened passageway. What little light remained now came from the other side of a huge pile of rubble that blocked the tunnel. Part of the ceiling must've collapsed. It was just him and the groundhog on this side of the mound. But to his relief, muffled conversation reached him from the other side.

"Is that the whistle-pig?" came Paxton's voice. "Everything all right, sir? Is the boy with you?"

"Aye, sir!" called the groundhog cheerfully. "Both here, and fit as two fandoodles. And yerselves?"

"All well and accounted for." There was a note of relief in the old man's voice.

Then came a different sound. Quite near, just beyond the grate, the high, taunting voice of the enchantress. Then a distant horn, followed by the thunderous din of a small army advancing upon Marisith.

"Did you hear that, milord?" cried a dwarf from beyond the rubble. "Mindra's voice, that was. And a Selvedge horn too. The overland company is attacking Marisith!"

"But . . . the signal!" Vahrberg's voice shook with rage. "Why didn't they wait for our signal?"

"Perhaps they were discovered, sir!" It was the excitable little stoat.

"Maybe the earthquake had something to do with it," a sentry suggested.

"But if they were discovered," yipped the fox, "why not double back to the forest, where they've got the advantage? Why sally forth to the gates?"

"What does it matter?" Paxton's voice had drawn closer to the rubble that stood between them. "Arash, can you hear me, lad? Mindra is preoccupied, just as we'd hoped. If you've got a clear shot up those steps, I'm afraid it's now or never."

"But who will guard the main staircase whilst he searches the tower?" argued Vahrberg. "We're sending the boy to his doom."

The groundhog—who'd been pawing through the rubble, probably in search of an opening—straightened on his haunches. "Nay, milord!" he called. "He's got ole Barkwhistler here. I'll not let that vile pilferer anywhere near the boy, mark my vimpers." The groundhog peered up at Arash. "Think ye can do it, lad?"

Arash knew better than to hesitate. If he froze, he would never unfreeze.

He nodded. Then he turned and vaulted up the steps two at a time.

At first, Tilly wondered if the giant was back. A distant rumble, like a thunderstorm, echoed from somewhere across the Runnelwilde, beyond the Sisters' encampment. But the rumble intensified. It was much louder than anything she'd heard in the Wolverns. Beneath her, the earth trembled, while lanterns in the overhead branches swayed, ever so slightly. Then the noise died away.

Tilly looked at Goldleaf, who was gazing, perplexed, at her sister dryads.

"What . . . what was that?" Tilly whispered.

But before her guide could respond, the watch fire began pulsing again—this time in a halting manner, with long pauses in between, as if the distant trees were struggling to find sufficient words. Then the pulses, too, died away.

Tilly looked around the circle. The Sisters had grown so still and silent, they might have slipped into a trance.

"A great one has fallen," came Goldleaf's somber voice at last.

Slowly several dryads got to their feet. They began a solemn, stately dance, passing around and between one another, touching hands, lifting their arms to the moon, then bowing low, as if bent with grief. More dryads joined in, and soon even the nearby trees seemed to sway, their branches drooping. Sadness had become a living thing, here in the encampment, and tears slid down Tilly's cheeks. It was as though the threads of her soul had rooted and become entangled with the forest's vast underground lifeline.

Tilly had no idea who'd fallen, nor how, but as the dryads grieved, she grieved.

She was reminded of when her grandfather Stokes had died. It'd been comforting, as a young girl, to stand at the graveside amid family and friends. Her brother Frankie had been a stalwart presence, and she'd buried her face in his shoulder and wept. But she'd also felt strangely isolated. Everyone expressed their grief so very differently—and, in some cases, not at all. Indeed, Tilly's most vivid memory of that loss was loneliness.

But the Sisters were different. At some point in their lives, they'd been taught the steps of grief. And they knew how to dance the steps together, rather than cutting themselves off from one another. Their shared loss made them stronger.

Tilly couldn't imagine doing something like this with Frankie. Nor with Jack and Georgie. And certainly not with other boys, like Charles. But with Elspeth? Yes. Perhaps that's why she and Elspeth had been close for so long. They could team up and define their space, their preferences, their way of doing things. A small sisterhood in a vast fraternal sea. Until recently.

She felt a wave of regret. Lately she'd taken Elspeth for granted. But now, suddenly, she missed having a sister. Even more, she missed *Elspeth*. The girl's thin elfin face. Her intelligent gaze. Her fierce loyalty, wit, forthrightness. Would they ever see each other again? Would their most recent exchange really be their last?

Watching the dryads dance, she realized that Charles—or a boy like him—wasn't the only thing she longed for. And not *Charles,* per se, but romantic love itself. It was nice, albeit complicated. But it didn't fill every empty spot in her heart. Other loves were also important. Family. Friendship. Sisterhood. If Tilly ever saw Elspeth again, she'd do whatever it took to reclaim their bond. After all, boys like Charles might come and go, but Elspeth would always be her sister.

Eventually the dryads returned to the watch fire. They sat themselves in a great circle around it, legs folded, arms loosely at their sides. No one spoke. No one moved. Their faces gleamed with tears, which they didn't wipe away. They sat in utter stillness for a long, long time.

Tilly herself had no more tears left. Exhaustion took her, and she fell asleep.

Chapter

39

The Selvedges fought valiantly. But Mindra was stronger. She felled them right and left, turning sentries into animals, flinging dwarves and creatures aside with ease. No one could touch her. And now Jack counted at least two of her massive raptors swooping around, diving at the Selvedge army with their vicious beaks and razor-sharp claws. No one could touch them either.

Jack himself was no help whatsoever. The best he could do was stay out of the Selvedges' way and hope he didn't get crushed. Shielding his ribs, he dodged, ducked, and sprinted helplessly from one part of the courtyard to another. And then, just as he spun to avoid colliding with one of the brush wolves, she was there.

Mindra herself. Face-to-face. But it wasn't his face she was staring at. It was his backpack.

"Thwarted me once, fool," she said, eyes glittering, "but never again."

Nothing seemed funny now. She raised her arms—those terrible white arms—and Jack found himself shrinking.

Down and down, growing smaller and smaller, while everything around him expanded outrageously. His heart rate accelerated—his breath too—while his ears became like sonar transducers, overwhelmed by the tiniest noise. Even the dirt beneath him seemed full of noises, every footfall like a gunshot. And the dirt was close, almost in front of his nose—along with a vast curtain of crimson that fell from somewhere high above and stretched as far as he could see, blocking his way.

He looked up. Mindra's simply enormous face peered down at him from a great height, sneering hideously.

Jack yelled—or tried to yell. But the only noise he made was a mousy squeak.

She leaned forward, her terrible gloved hand reaching down. Then she grabbed the strap of his backpack, which was now the size of his family's cottage, and swung it onto her shoulder.

"Much obliged," she said, her voice disturbingly deep. She straightened, smiling.

And that was when he saw it. From above her head, swiftly descending, came a raptor the size of a school bus.

"Were I a repugnant rodent like thyself," said Mindra, her teeth glinting like lances, "I'd run."

"Spiffety-ho!" shouted the groundhog and charged up the steps into Marisith after Arash.

At the top, another passageway led to a kind of foyer, where Arash could see the open postern door—from the inside, this time, instead of the outside. Beyond it was a terrible scene.

Tall, pale, impossibly beautiful, Mindra stood amid an advancing tide of warriors, flicking them away like flies. But her features, in the torchlight, were now twisted with agony. She seemed agitated, irritated by her opponents, as if her real trouble lay elsewhere.

"Over here!" Barkwhistler stood near the bottom step of the central stairwell. "I'll stand guard by the door. Don't ye worry. Up ye go, now!"

Again, Arash didn't hesitate, didn't wait for the familiar paralysis to set in. He launched himself up the staircase. Before he turned out of sight, he glanced back at the groundhog. Barkwhistler looked so small. So powerless. What could he do against a might like Mindra's? But Arash couldn't think about that now.

He ran. Up and up the torchlit staircase he sprinted till he reached a landing with a heavy wooden door. Locked, of course. He kept going. Another landing, another locked door. Landing upon landing, door upon door, all locked.

Panting, Arash paused by an arrow slit cut into the outer wall. From there he could see the dim, moonlit outline of the coast, stretching away. So calm and beautiful. He could barely hear the din from the courtyard now.

He pressed on. Soon he couldn't hear the battle below at all. Only his breath, coming in gasps. His legs had begun to feel wobbly.

Then he arrived at a landing where the door stood wide open.

Cautiously, he peered inside. It was some kind of furnished, torchlit chamber. A surprisingly cozy fire crackled in a stone fireplace. Thick velvety curtains covered what he guessed was a deep window well. Candles burned low on a long table, which was strewn with papers and cutlery and the remains of an unfinished meal.

Mindra's headquarters. He was sure of it. If the gems were anywhere in Marisith, they were here. But he could come back for them later. Right now, he needed to find his grandfather.

He turned to leave, but then a sound sent his heart racing. Slow footsteps approached. From somewhere beyond the curtains.

He froze. There was nowhere to hide.

The curtains swished open.

"Tabari, of course," said a familiar sardonic voice. "Was this your plan all along? To betray us at last?"

There, in the curtained doorway to a side chamber, stood Charles Heapworth.

It took Arash a panicked beat to realize that Charles wasn't well. Blood trickled from a gash on his forehead. His clothes were torn and filthy. His left arm hung limply while the other gripped some kind of crutch.

But no. It wasn't a crutch. It was Arash's own Garrett Infinium.

"What are you doing here, mate?" Charles asked angrily. "How'd you get into this lousy place? I've been stuck here for hours, ever since that hideous bird snatched me up. Dislocated my shoulder, too, I think. But there's no way out, far as I can tell."

Charles's blue eyes bored into him. Sharp, accusing.

"Nothing to say for yourself, as usual. But you've been on Mindra's side all along, no doubt. How else would this piece of junk have gotten here?"

He tried lifting Arash's Infinium but grimaced.

"And where's Tilly?" Charles continued in a fainter voice. "And the others? You've abandoned them, haven't you? Left them to fend for themselves or—worse yet—betrayed them. A traitor who can't be trusted, Tabari. That's what you are."

Arash's shoes felt stuck to the floor. His body was unable to flee or protest or obey anything his brain screamed for it to do.

But what about you, *Heapworth?* he wanted to yell back. *How are you even here, free and fully human instead of transformed or chained or dead?*

"Come on. Speak up!" Charles taunted him. "Do you deny it? No, of course not. Your silence says everything."

The guy took a step forward, then winced. Clutching the Infinium, he sank to his knees. Arash reached out. It was instinct, drilled into him from infancy. To express concern for your host. Even if the host was your worst enemy.

But Charles flinched and pulled away. "That's right," he said. "Hit a man when he's down. I'd expect nothing less."

For a moment, Arash imagined doing exactly that. Raw power coursing through his hands. Knuckles connecting with flesh. Charles's face snapping to the side . . .

But before he could become the person Charles already thought he was, Arash bolted to the stairwell. Forget Charles. Forget the gems. It was Grandfather he was looking for.

"She's coming, lad!" Barkwhistler's distant voice came from below, calling up the stairwell. "Flee the tower while you can!"

For a moment, Arash hesitated. He couldn't just leave Grandfather up there. But he'd be no help to anyone if Mindra transformed him too.

Arash had no choice. He dashed back down the stairs.

Chapter

40

At first, Jack's brain shut down. He became pure mouse instinct, running as he'd never run in his life—and he'd already run plenty today. He was fleetingly aware of how crazy fast his little feet could move, how he dashed and zigzagged through a nightmarish maze of moving objects without concern for what came next. Dodge, weave, find somewhere to hide—but there was nothing that stayed still long enough. With the relentless drum of wingbeats behind him, he aimed for the shadows, the darkness, the shelter of the castle wall, the ventilation grate he knew was there somewhere.

Then his logical mind kicked in again. He scanned the base of the wall for the grate. There. Dead ahead. He put on a frantic burst of speed, his lungs and heart ready to explode. Mighty wingbeats descended. A blast of air ruffled his fur and kicked up grit in his little face. But just as he heard the raptor's claws extend, he was through.

He'd imagined, for some reason, that he'd emerge into some sort of room, inside Marisith, where the grate was flush with the floor. But it wasn't. Before he knew it, all four paws had left the ground, and he sailed into dark nothingness as if he was back in the Bentley.

If human Jack had experienced a proportional drop, the landing would've killed him. Instead—miraculously—he landed on his feet, shaken but unharmed. Without pausing for breath, he kept running.

Darkness surrounded him. Darkness, weirdly, that didn't seem so dark. It was like he'd been given extra senses beyond the usual five. Whiskers, for one thing. They were a never-ending source of data. And his sight had become a superpower—just like his hearing, which picked up every pounding footfall from the battle overhead. He was running along the floor of a huge underground passage toward what looked like a mountain made of massive glacial deposits. It was a great pile of rubble that must've dislodged from the ceiling at some point. Just the sort of place where a mouse could hide.

But the mound of rubble wasn't stable. Nothing was. With every overhead boom, debris fell from the high ceiling or clattered down the side of the mound, which shifted treacherously. If he was going to survive, he needed to get out of this passage, away from Marisith, away from the battle that raged above.

A light draft wafted across the stone floor, tickling his whiskers. Yes, now he could see it. An opening, no bigger than a mousehole, at the bottom of the opposite wall. The draft smelled of earth and roots and damp stones—and something else, something that he didn't often encounter but that always thrilled him when he did.

Faintly, Jack could smell the sea.

He dashed across the open floor and through the hole into a mouse-sized tunnel. It was, if possible, darker than the passageway he'd just left. It seemed to twist and turn forever, winding down, up, sideways, and down again, occasionally branching into multiple side tunnels. Either his rodent predecessors had been terrible at underground navigation, or they'd bumped into numerous sections of unyielding rock that forced a constant change of direction.

None of his predecessors was still around, however. His new sensory superpowers told him that no living creature had been this way for a long, long time. He could hear nothing up ahead nor behind, and no overhead tremors either. He was completely alone, deep underground.

And that was when his lungs began to constrict. It was such a tight squeeze in here, with so many tons of earth pressing down. Would he ever get out? What if he became lost forever? Or—worse—what if he suddenly changed back into a human again, right here?

But by now his lungs had stopped working properly. With almost-scientific detachment, he wondered if mice could hyperventilate, like humans. And then he blacked out.

Arash whirled down the spiral staircase, backpack bouncing, till he reached the final turn. Below him, on the bottom step, stood Barkwhistler.

The groundhog gestured frantically. "Hurry, lad! The overlanders have kept her busy outside, but she's headed this way. Did ye find them? The gems?" But at Arash's downcast expression, his furry face fell. "Well, ye did your briffiest, I'm sure. No matter. We'll give her what for! C'mon!" Brandishing a dagger the size of a butter knife, Barkwhistler charged through the postern into the fray.

But Arash paused at the threshold.

The scene outside was utter madness. Terrified animals ran wild in the courtyard. A crowd of men and dwarves and creatures surged, first in one direction, then another. At least two of Mindra's raptors screamed overhead, swooping and diving. They snatched up the smaller creatures and flung them over the walls. The giant was nowhere to be seen, but there, in the middle of everything, stood the enchantress.

In her hands she held what Arash recognized as Jack's backpack. As the raptors fended off her attackers, she ripped the backpack open and dug through it frantically, tossing its contents aside. Then she slammed it to the ground. Whatever she'd been looking for, it wasn't in there.

"Retreat!" came the voice of Fangard, somewhere in the fray. "Fall back!" The Selvedge army began fleeing the courtyard, back through the portcullis.

Mindra's head snapped up like she'd heard a siren. Her eyes began scanning the courtyard, hungrily searching, searching. And then, finally, they locked on Arash.

It was over. He knew it.

She'd found him, and no one could do anything to stop her.

Unblinking, Mindra began advancing toward him like a siege tower. He willed his legs to move. Nothing. Sentries charged her, but she flung them away until, at last, there was no one between her and Arash.

Except one.

"Come at me first, ye ole blitheress!"

Barkwhistler, flourishing his dagger, blocked her way.

In the split second that Mindra blinked, Arash started sprinting toward the open portcullis. And he almost made it. The groundhog kept her busy for a moment, feinting and dodging and blocking. But then Arash heard a thwack, and Barkwhistler came sliding past him through the gate. Something caught the hood of Arash's pullover, which tightened around his neck, and he was yanked backward onto the ground.

From a distance, the enchantress had been terrifying. Up close, towering over him, she was a living nightmare. Sickly white skin, eyes like murky wells, dark hair that might've been luxurious if it weren't so obviously . . . dead. And yet her features—despite their tormented grimace—were as perfectly sculpted as a supermodel's.

She glared at him, taking in his floppy dark hair, his battered glasses, his backpack.

Especially his backpack.

"Fool!" she said. "Didst thou hope to claim it for thyself? And without my knowing? Nay. Thou canst not hide it from me. Louder has been its call, for three days—and louder still, now that it hath entered my own house. Surrender it at once, or thou shalt meet thy doom."

Arash was too petrified to move. She lifted her white arms, just as she'd done with his grandfather. "Pity that the other traitors are not here to watch."

But before Arash could flinch, a ball of fur barreled into Mindra's torso. Snarling, snapping, lunging at her face, the creature attacked the enchantress till she, too, fell back upon the ground.

It was the stray. Out of nowhere. For the second time in twelve hours.

Startled into boldness, Arash sprang to his feet, ready to charge. Mindra could come at him, Charles could accuse him, but *no one* would mess with that dog. Not a second time. Not on his watch.

But strong arms held Arash back, just as they had when his grandfather was transformed. A trio of Selvedges was dragging him away—to save him, he knew—but he fought them all the same.

They wrestled him through the gateway and out of the courtyard seconds before the portcullis slid down with a crash.

Chapter

41

Elspeth lifted her head from the table.

Had she fallen asleep? Her neck felt stiff, and her right cheekbone ached. Jack's book lay open in front of her, and next to that, a cold cup of tea.

She remembered switching with Aurora, at some point, and coming back downstairs. Then, just as she'd put the kettle on, the phone had rung again. It'd been Mum, ringing from the cottage. The grown-ups had made their reports at the police station and then driven around the countryside in separate vehicles, combing the area. Eventually they'd decided that Mrs. Tabari and Mum would keep vigil at their respective homes in case anyone rang either place, while the fathers would hike the Wolverns with torches, Lord Edward's mobile phone at the ready. Regional authorities had been informed.

Regional authorities? Elspeth had felt slightly panicked. That was the moment she should've told her mother everything. But then she'd imagined the incredulity in her mother's voice—the anger, even. This was no time for childish pranks, Mum would say, her voice shaking with rage. So, Elspeth had said nothing.

"Don't wait up for us," Mum had continued. "Why don't you

camp out in the guest rooms off the kitchen? I'm sure you'll hear the phone if anyone rings the Hall—and then let me know right away, won't you?"

Elspeth had promised she would, and they'd hung up.

She'd poured herself a cup and sat down with Jack's book. And then . . .

And then . . .

She'd been running for her life up a steep mountain pass. Wind tearing at her hair, snow in her lashes, long cloak whipping around her feet, she fled the djinn that had already killed her family. And then a Valani sentinel with intense dark eyes had stepped from behind a boulder, wielding a scimitar. But before she could scream, he'd slain the djinn in the snow. They'd run together, she and the sentinel, over the high pass, across the desert, and into the vast plain of Valan. There, far away on the edge of the sea, glimmered a beautiful city. And then . . .

And then . . .

All a dream, of course. Based on the last story she'd been reading in Jack's book. She looked down at the open page. The sentinel was the prince of Valan in disguise, of course. And the refugee girl was a princess from a distant realm that'd been overrun by its enemies. The two had gotten married, and lived in the palace in the golden city, and had many descendants. And that's where Elspeth had left off.

She rubbed her eyes, then glanced at the clock on the range. She shot to her feet. Why hadn't Aurora wakened her when it was time to switch?

Elspeth bolted from the kitchen and dashed up the stairs to the studio. There was Aurora, working diligently at the loom. She glanced up with a smile, put a finger to her lips, and nodded in the direction of the sofa, where Zahra was crashed out asleep, cradling her arm.

"Both of you were sleeping so soundly, I hated to wake you," Aurora whispered cheerfully. "So I just kept going. But I think it's done! How does it look? Shall we wake Zahra and see if it works?"

There was no *way* Aurora could have completed the tapestry by now. Elspeth herself hadn't even finished the hut's roof—and what had Zahra ultimately decided for the sky, anyway? Night or day? With a feeling of dread, Elspeth joined her friend by the loom.

It was worse than she'd imagined. The top half looked as though Aurora had torn open a pillow and crammed the filling randomly into the warp. White fuzz was everywhere, nearly obscuring the hut and shoreline. The weft edges were uneven, the weave too thick in some places, too thin in others—the sort of work that Mrs. Tabari hated. Elspeth too.

The tapestry was ruined.

"Aurora!" Elspeth groaned. "What on earth were you thinking? The white stuff: It's . . . it's . . ." She waved her hands in front of the frame helplessly.

"Clouds. See?" Aurora pointed to the fluff that hid the top of the hut. "Clouds on a windy day in Ternival."

"But . . . but . . . it doesn't look anything like Zahra described!"

Aurora stepped back and crossed her arms, scowling. "Well, let's wake her and ask what *she* thinks."

Elspeth was too tired and frustrated to hold back any longer. "There's no point in waking Zahra now. It will never work. She'll never get home. You know that, right? This isn't a tapestry. It's a mess!"

Aurora's face turned pink. She glared at Elspeth the way she glared at Charles when he was being cruel. "Okay, Ms. *Perfect*. Tear it all out and start over. But good luck finishing it while the ley lines are strongest or whatever. Good luck finishing *at all*."

Instantly Elspeth regretted everything. She regretted not holding her tongue. She regretted not letting Aurora simply be her own person. In fact, she felt terrible that her perfectionism had inserted itself—over and over, all day long—driving a wedge between her and everyone else. She'd expected Tilly to be the model older sister who ignored boys like Charles in favor of spending time with her. And she'd failed to be kind to Georgie about his drawing, when the poor kid was simply trying to help. And now she'd hurt her best friend.

Over on the sofa, Zahra began to stir.

"Shh!" Elspeth hissed. She desperately wished she had more time to settle things with Aurora before anyone else got involved. "Let's not wake her. I'm sure we'll figure something out."

"Too late now," Aurora snarled. She stomped toward the door. "You can do whatever you want. I'm going to bed." Without looking back, she left.

Chapter

42

"Let 'im go, lads." Barkwhistler was picking himself up from the shadows by the closed portcullis, looking none the worse for his encounter with Mindra.

Arash, on the other hand, felt like a crossbow ready to fire. His Selvedge rescuers released him, and he pushed away, blinking furiously. The stray was probably dead, and his grandfather was still trapped inside Marisith, and it was all these guys' fault. Well, maybe his fault too.

Nearby, a group of rats were cheering like they'd just won a rugby match.

"That'll teach her not to secure the gate with mere rope next time!" one of them whooped. He rubbed his huge incisors appreciatively.

Suddenly a horrible scream rent the air. From over the top of the wall, Mindra's last two raptors swooped down, heading straight for Arash.

"Run for the trees!" yelled the groundhog.

But before Arash could turn and flee, both birds listed and tumbled to the ground—struck by a volley of arrows that'd come whizzing from the woods.

"It's Vahrberg!" Barkwhistler cried. "With the rest of the remnant. Spiffety-ho!"

The groundhog took off for the trees. As Arash ran with the retreating Selvedges, moonlight and shadow played tricks on his mind. He could've sworn that to his left—roughly a cricket pitch from the courtyard walls—a huge chasm yawned in the earth, big enough to swallow Marisith itself. Dust rose in the air above it, as if the whole thing had collapsed recently. And it had, Arash realized. That was the earthquake they'd felt beneath Marisith. But what had happened?

They raced toward a clump of spruce deeper in the woods, where a ragtag ensemble of both overland and underland survivors had begun to gather. Among them were Vahrberg and several dwarves, a smattering of woodland animals and miscellaneous creatures, plus a handful of sentries like Smithfield, many of whom were wounded. In the middle were Fangard, the wolfhounds, and—to Arash's relief—Paxton.

The old man's face, under the shadow of his cap, looked like he'd aged another seventy years.

"Hail, milord!" Fangard bounded up to the dwarf captain. "What a sight for sore eyes you were, emerging unscathed from Marisith!"

"Indeed," replied Vahrberg gruffly. "We were cut off, for a moment, down in the tunnels. But we dwarves are nothing if not handy with a spade. Now, tell us, Fangard. What happened up here? Do my eyes deceive me, or has the Felmar collapsed? And why didn't Lord Starwise wait for our signal?"

"Yes, where *is* our leader, best of centaurs?" asked one of the horses, hobbling forward.

"Plus," Paxton interjected, "has anyone seen Jack?"

"Alas, milords," said Fangard, "we dare not tarry. To the shore, every one of us, and swiftly. But not overland—those routes are blocked forever, I fear. This tunnel is our only chance. I'll explain as we go."

Quickly Vahrberg and his dwarves pushed aside some branches and entered the mouth of a hidden tunnel. Fangard and the wolf-hounds followed, with Paxton, Arash, Barkwhistler, and the rest of the company on their heels.

As Arash stumbled along the narrow passage, no glowing roots hung from these rough-hewn walls. The only light was a flickering torch carried by one of the dwarves up ahead. Arash hurried to keep pace.

After a few moments, Fangard began his story. Of Jack's failed attempt to kill Stonefist. And of the centaur's intervention and the chase around the clearing. And finally, of the sudden implosion that'd left the overland routes blocked, the Selvedges without a leader, and Jack alone in the courtyard, face-to-face with Mindra.

A horrified silence followed. Arash could picture every detail, down to Jack's last glimpse of Starwise vanishing into the earth. If blood could run cold, that's how Arash felt.

"And Jack?" Paxton insisted. "What of the lad?"

"Transformed, we think," the mastiff replied. "But no one knows for certain."

Just then, a cascade of debris rained upon their heads, dislodged by their noise and movement. They paused, coughing.

"Not another sound," Vahrberg announced in a raspy whisper once the dust had settled. "From now on, we tread lightly and say nothing, or none shall reach the shore alive."

It was a terrifying ten minutes. The roof, clearly unstable, continued to rain dust and debris. But eventually the company emerged onto a wide shingle under a steep wooded bluff. Once again, moonlight shimmered on the water, and for a moment, Arash was mesmerized by the unexpected beauty of it all. How *could* the sea be so lovely when their circumstances were so disastrous?

"Follow me!" Fangard headed deeper into the shadowed woods to their left. The rest of the remnant staggered behind. When he finally signaled a halt, they collapsed in various states of exhaustion under the trees.

But before Arash could catch his breath, Paxton wheeled around.

"And when were you planning to tell us?" the old man bellowed. His expression was so uncharacteristically animated that Arash began backing away, hands up.

"When?" Paxton hollered. "Once she'd ripped the treasure from your powerless hands? Once she'd restored the gems to their settings and become the foulest tyrant in a thousand worlds?"

The rest of the company stared.

"You *heard* young Heapworth speak of it, lad," Paxton raged, "and yet you said nothing! Nothing! Even without words, you could've *shown* us."

It was true. Arash knew it. He should've revealed it hours ago.

He felt the sting of tears. But he wouldn't cry in front of everyone. He wouldn't. Blinking furiously, he swung his backpack to the ground, knelt beside it, and yanked the zipper open. Then he reached inside and pulled out the T-shirt-wrapped object he'd been keeping secret for three whole days.

Even though he knew what the shirt contained, he paused. Maybe somehow he'd left the treasure under his bed, after all. Or perhaps his mother had found it, thought it was junk, and replaced it with a bunch of pastries. Pistachio cookies, ideally. The kind with drizzle on top. Perhaps the shirt held enough cookies for everyone. That way, they'd turn their attention from Arash and—like the tea shop customers—focus on pastries instead.

But no. He could tell by the weight of the object and the hard points under the cloth. It was still the treasure. His treasure. And not just any treasure, either: the most spectacular find in the history of the Wolverns.

Slowly he set the bundle on the ground. Slowly he unwrapped it.

There, in the moonlit woods, lay the ancient crown of Ternival.

The company now drew near, murmuring with amazement.

"Is it . . ." Vahrberg's voice was hushed with awe.

"It is," said Fangard solemnly.

"But . . . how did the lad come to possess it?"

"Found it by accident, no doubt," Paxton said, his voice now more controlled. "He had no idea what it was, either—not at first. But if you don't mind a long story, milords, I think I can explain."

"Continue, pray," said the mastiff. "For I suspect this discovery will change everything."

So Paxton did.

He told of how Mindra's great enemies, the Three Queens, hadn't disappeared into nothingness when they'd vanished from Ternival, as its citizens supposed. Rather, the queens had stumbled back into Tellus, with the ancient crown of Ternival and its six magical gems. The queens knew not how to return to their beloved realm, but they feared little would stop Mindra from traversing worlds to find them.

So they'd sundered the gems and crown and buried both, lest their music and magnetism lead Mindra to Tellus. The gems they'd locked in a carved wooden box, which was later found by one of the High Queen's descendants. The crown, meanwhile, the High Queen herself had stashed somewhere in the hills behind the great house where all their adventures had begun. Indeed, she'd kept its location a secret to the day she died, and there might it have languished forever, had Arash not found it.

"Just a few days ago, by my guess," Paxton said. "And not on purpose. Rather, I suspect he was hunting for ancient artifacts specific to

that region of Tellus. Because he wanted to earn recognition. To become part of the story of that land, of that people."

Arash stared at the ground, willing the old man to stop talking.

"Look at me, lad," Paxton said.

Reluctantly, Arash looked up. What he saw gave him a jolt of surprise. The old man's eyes glittered with tears. Paxton's anger had
given way to sadness—or compassion. Possibly both.

"You are part of a very great story," Paxton said in a low voice. "A
story that no one can take from you. Never forget this. Understand?"

For a moment, Arash thought he was joking. How did Paxton
know? Had he overheard one of Grandfather's speeches? They were
nearly verbatim. The only thing missing was some kind of Shakespearian proverb.

"This above all," Paxton whispered. "To thine own self be true.
And it must follow, as the night the day . . ."

Arash was no longer listening. He knew what came next: some of
the most famous lines from *Hamlet*, which he'd heard a hundred
times. As the old man removed his cap, Arash stared at him, transfixed. Moonlight fell upon the handyman's balding head, his craggy
brows, the unique shape of his ears.

"Thou canst not then be false to any man."

If Arash hadn't known better, he would've thought Paxton was
Grandfather himself.

Chapter

43

When Jack came to, he was still in the tunnel, still a mouse. But up ahead was the mouth of a larger passageway. The first two facts weren't great; the third was fantastic. He leaped to his feet and crept to the opening. Even in the murky darkness, he could tell this new tunnel was much bigger, designed for human children or even dwarves. It was littered with rubble, as if it hadn't been used in decades. And from somewhere farther down came the faint scent of seawater.

For a while, anyway. Within a few yards, the new tunnel made a sharp turn, branched into three, and then twisted and turned so relentlessly that he lost all sense of direction. Lifting his quivering nose, he smelled nothing but dirt and the mineral tanginess of dripping groundwater. He was now completely, utterly lost.

Again, the panic.

Again, he blacked out.

And again, he awoke in total darkness, alone.

This time, he lay still for what felt like hours, staring blankly into the gloom. What was the point of going on? He'd messed up. Big time. No—scratch that. He'd ruined *everything*. For everyone.

Because of him, the attack on Marisith had failed. Most of the overlanders were probably wounded or transformed or even . . . gone, never to return home to their loved ones. And what of the underlanders? Crushed, most likely, in the collapse of the Felmar.

Arash. Paxton. Vahrberg and the other dwarves. It made him sick just thinking about it.

And then there was Starwise.

The scene would remain emblazoned on his memory forever: The valiant centaur, galloping through the tall grasses of the clearing in the moonlight, the furious giant lumbering after him. Starwise circling, circling, making sure the giant grew so enraged that its footfalls turned to stomping. Stomp, stomp, stomp, the earth trembling, the grasses undulating.

The centaur had known exactly what he was doing, of course. He'd known the roof would collapse under them. But he'd done it anyway.

To save Jack. To save them all.

Mrs. Fealston had been right. The most outrageous thing about those fairy tales wasn't the magic. It wasn't that witches like Mindra could turn humans into animals. It wasn't that ordinary people like Jack could somehow crash through portals into other worlds. Rather, it was the notion that someone could single-handedly take down the enemy—and not only live to tell about it, but also win the crown and the kingdom and return home a hero.

No. Starwise had fallen because of him. Because he'd tried to go it alone, to vanquish evil by himself.

Sprawled full length on the dank tunnel floor, he wondered if mice could cry. He'd never felt more alone. If something or someone didn't intervene, he'd be lost forever underground, never to return.

For the first time in his life, Jack wished someone would interfere.

Then another memory flashed through his mind: that brief glimpse from the Bentley of the glowing creature, deep in the woods. It'd been the stag, of course. He hadn't imagined it. And the creature's appearance hadn't been accidental. It'd shown itself to him on purpose, giving him a glimpse of what was possible, of what could be. Of the true hope and help of Ternival—or of anywhere. Not from *inside* himself, weak and foolish mortal that he was. No, it would have to be from outside himself entirely.

But who could help him now?

Zahra was dreaming again. She was strolling along the ramparts of a glittering palace by the sea, her long, glossy hair wafting in the wind, her embroidered gown rustling around her sandaled feet. Ahead of her ran the children. Her three young princes, in matching kurtas, raced to the farthest parapet and back. They were laughing, and she was laughing, and the wind and waves were laughing.

But then her middle son tripped. Down he went on the colorful tiles, smacking his little hands as he fell. Sweet Navid, the gentle-hearted one. She hurried to his side as he began to wail and scooped him up.

"Maman," called the eldest. He was gazing upward, shielding his eyes. "What is that great, terrible bird?"

She looked up, squinting, Navid's warm body in her arms. At first glance, the bird seemed no bigger than a gull. But when she grasped how high it flew, she realized what a truly enormous creature it had to be. And it was circling the palace in slow, sinister arcs, descending all the while.

Her breath caught. "Come, my children," she called, trying to keep her voice calm. "Time for lessons."

As her eldest and youngest raced back to the mosaic-filled archway that led to the inner courtyard, she tried to follow. But for some reason, Navid had grown terribly heavy. The arm that supported him had begun to throb, and her feet would not move as she commanded. And though she tried to set the boy down, he clung still tighter, sending pain shooting from her wrist to her shoulder.

Then Navid screamed. "It's coming, Maman!" Great wingbeats flapped behind them as she tried and failed to run. Then Navid twisted in her arms, the pain slammed through her whole body, and Zahra woke with a gasp.

She was lying on the sofa in the studio at Carrick Hall. Her wrist, which she'd unconsciously slipped from the sling to support the cushion under her head, felt like it was on fire. She stifled a moan and tried to sit up.

Across the way, Elspeth was sitting at the worktable. She stared mournfully at the loom, her eyes puffy, her nose red. As Zahra stirred, the girl took a shuddering breath and brushed tears from her cheeks.

"My apologies," Zahra said, wincing. She attempted to slip the sling back into position. "Have I slept long? Is everything all right?"

Elspeth shrugged, her expression glum. "It's not great." Her voice wobbled. "But that's not your fault. It's mine."

Between sniffles, she went on to describe what had transpired. From falling asleep at the kitchen table to first laying eyes on the finished tapestry—and the bitter argument that followed with Aurora. Now Elspeth lifted the loom for Zahra to see.

"Ohhh . . ." Zahra said, her voice trailing to a whisper. The tapestry was every bit as wild as Elspeth had said. No wonder the girl couldn't stop weeping.

At that moment, Zahra's pain grew so great that it obliterated every other thought. Squeezing her eyes shut, she rocked in place.

Elspeth leaped to her feet. "Zahra?"

But Zahra couldn't respond.

Elspeth ran to the sofa and gently placed a hand on her knee. "Do you think you can stand? I hate to make you move, but I've got medicine downstairs, and then you can lie down in a proper bed. We can leave the tapestry here for now."

Zahra nodded wearily. With Elspeth at her good elbow, she carefully made the torturous descent to the kitchen, where the girl gave her a strange, awful-tasting pill. Then Elspeth helped her slip some kind of small pillow into the sling and around her wrist. It was magically cold, frozen, as if it'd been filled with snow or ice. She felt instant relief. Elspeth then led her down the hallway to the guest bedroom.

Aurora had already climbed into one of the beds, her back to the door. Zahra couldn't tell if the girl was asleep or merely ignoring them, but either way, she made no sound as they entered. Elspeth pointed to the other bed, and Zahra gingerly climbed underneath the covers.

"If you need anything, I'll be in the room next door," Elspeth whispered. Her voice sounded thick again, like she was trying not to burst into fresh tears. Then she left, closing the door behind her.

Luxuriously comfortable, in the softest bedding she'd ever lain upon, Zahra should've fallen asleep right away. But by now she felt flushed, like she'd spiked a fever. As she lay there, she wished she could help with the tapestry somehow. They didn't need to tear out everything, most likely, just the fluffy white material. And the hut's roof needed finishing. But what could she do? Nothing.

The familiar despair descended. At this rate, she'd never get through the frame back to Ternival. But Grandad needed her. How was he holding up in that awful cage? Did his illness continue to affect him? Would she ever see him again?

She just wanted their old life back. Their safe, quiet, invisible life. Whenever they got involved with other people, bad things happened. At the same time, worse things might happen if they didn't. What if they hadn't alerted Starwise about the giants, for instance? It wasn't fair that having a conscience required action, and action required courage, and both hurt so, so much.

Eventually the medicine began to work. Her pain became a dull ache, and she drifted into a restless slumber.

Chapter

44

"But why doesn't the lad speak for himself?"

It was old Smithfield, of course. Surly, suspicious. Arash stared numbly at the ground. Why did people have to speak as though he wasn't here?

"It's the quiet ones you have to watch," Smithfield continued with a growl. "Mark my words. Can't be trusted."

"At least the quiet ones keep their own counsel," Barkwhistler retorted.

"Indeed," Fangard said. "Silence can be wisdom, for the world is cruel." The great mastiff had placed his body in front of Arash again, as if to guard him.

"But what of his quest at Marisith?" the old sentry pressed. "Did he find the gems? Or is he hiding those too? Wouldn't surprise me, a'course. Valorentians were the ones who stole the gems from the crown in the first place, some say, and hid them in the moun—"

Barkwhistler sprang to his feet, the fur on his back bristling. "Enough of that whimbypoddled nonsense! Not a word of truth in it, neither. And anyway, after all yer wamby-grousing, who could blame the lad for keeping quiet?"

"Peace, both of you. This is exactly what Mindra wants," Vahrberg warned. "For us to blame each other and argue amongst ourselves instead of focusing on the true enemy: the witch herself."

"Well spoken, good dwarf," Fangard said. "Our greatest concern is the enchantress. But we can't face her in such a state, not with our diminished numbers. We need reinforcements, and soon. For if Mindra can hear the crown calling, she will surely follow us—sooner rather than later, by my guess. Nay, we must flee to a safe place, where the enchantress will think twice about attacking us."

"What of our great fastness at Nisnagard?" Vahrberg suggested, a touch of pride in his voice. He puffed out his chest. "She'd think twice about that."

"Aye," Fangard agreed, "but 'tis a long journey, and I doubt we can outrun her. Nay, there's another place, quite close."

The rest of the company eyed one another uneasily. Even sturdy Vahrberg looked unnerved. "You don't mean," he began in a hushed voice. "Surely not . . . the *Sisters*?"

"But it's said they allow none to enter their land uninvited," Smithfield protested. The others glanced around at the shadowed trees.

Arash shivered. Whoever the Sisters were, seeking their help didn't sound like a good idea. Not at all.

"It is also said that the Sisters come to the aid of all who seek refuge—especially from a shared enemy." Fangard was undeterred. "You forget how deep and ancient is their hatred for Mindra, how she felled the orchards at the death of Kador and allowed wicked thornbushes to overtake the forest. The pear trees from Inspiria are now almost extinct because of her, and the Sisters have never forgotten. Come. I know the way from here."

Eventually the others had no choice. Vahrberg and Smithfield bowed their assent, and Fangard took charge as the undisputed guide.

"Before we leave," said the mastiff, "we must decide who will carry the crown."

"It mustn't stay with the boy," Paxton said, "or Mindra will destroy him, for certain. And I don't wish for any of you to take that risk upon yourselves. Nay, I shall carry it."

"A noble offer, good sir," Fangard said. "I suggest you wrap it up, as it was, and carry the boy's pack yourself."

Paxton looked down at Arash. "Come, lad," the old man said gruffly. "There's nothing else for it but to do as the fellow says."

By this point, Arash was beyond thinking, beyond feeling. Robotically, he handed his backpack to Paxton, who rewrapped the crown and returned it to the pack.

"Now," said Fangard, "follow me."

They set off.

For a mile or so, Fangard led them along the wooded trail at the base of the bluff, its steep side on their left, the shore on their right. Occasionally, through the trees, Arash caught glimpses of moonlight shimmering on the water.

Finally Fangard halted. "The main road from Marisith to Caristor runs atop the bluff," he said. "But we shall continue along the shore till we reach the mouth of the Runnelwilde. Then we'll follow the river into the forest as far as possible. The Sisters will find us before we find them, I wager."

The company struggled onward, some pressing ahead near Fangard, others straggling behind, exhausted. As they spread out along the trail, Arash found himself among the weariest of the sentries, their heads bowed, their arms limp at their sides. Even when they reached a break in the woods beneath a breathtaking sky—full of constellations Arash had never seen before—they didn't seem to notice.

But for Arash, it was the strangeness of the stars that finally broke something inside him. He no longer cared about the tears or snot running down his face. He no longer cared about being admired, about belonging, about anything at all.

He'd failed.

He hadn't found the gems. And everyone was furious about the crown. Plus, Charles had accused him of treachery. Oh, and the stray had probably died while trying to save him. And Starwise had certainly died trying to save Jack. And—worst of all—Arash's grandfather was still back in Marisith, trapped. Where Arash had abandoned him.

He couldn't bear it. He couldn't simply traipse along with everyone, knowing he'd let them all down. Even with the crown in hand, they had little chance of success.

And it was all his fault.

Eventually they reached a river whose wide mouth emptied into the sea. Though a bridge was faintly visible upriver in the moonlight, Fangard leaped across a series of stones to the other side, the rest of the company in his wake.

In the darkness, as they began following the river inland, no one noticed when Arash stepped silently off the trail. No one saw him wait, motionless, under the trees till they were out of earshot.

No one realized that the Rastegars' grandson had slipped away, alone, back toward the shore.

That's where Arash had intended to go, anyway. But in his exhaustion and numbness, he missed a turn somewhere and only noticed when the ground beneath his feet began to feel mushy. He looked around. Whatever trail he'd been following had vanished. The woods had been replaced by reeds so tall, there was no seeing over them. And the air smelled stagnant and briny, with whiffs of rotting foliage.

Great. Somehow he'd stumbled into a marsh between the bluffs and the shore. And he had no idea how to get out.

Weariness gripped him. All he wanted was to lie down. And yet everywhere he placed his feet, the terrain felt like one enormous oversaturated sponge. He kept going.

The night wore on. The half-moon blazed overhead, obscuring the strange stars. But its light did nothing to help him. Occasionally he'd follow what he thought was a trail, only to end up stuck in a snarl of sedge grass or blocked by a wide pool of standing water. Several times, he could've sworn he heard a light patter of footsteps not far behind him, but when he turned, there was nothing.

Finally, just when he'd decided there was no point in going on, he saw something up ahead, glowing through a break in the reeds. It was a huge deerlike creature. But before he could get a better look, it moved away, beyond his line of sight. Quietly Arash followed. If the thing had gotten into the marsh, odds were pretty good it could also get out.

Sure enough, the animal was following some sort of winding, nearly invisible trail. What *was* that creature, anyway? Arash craned his neck but couldn't get a clearer glimpse.

And then, to his surprise, he found himself stumbling out of the marsh onto a moonlit beach. Ahead of him was the wide sweep of bay, framed by the distant peninsulas, that he'd seen from the hilltop with Paxton. But the glowing creature was gone.

To Arash's left were a couple of dark smudges farther down the shingle. One of them seemed to be a house of some kind—and by now, he was so exhausted that he didn't care who lived there. All he wanted was a place to lie down.

He stumbled in that direction. It was a longer trek than he'd anticipated, but eventually he could tell that one of the smudges was an overturned boat. And indeed, the other smudge was a tiny hut. As he drew closer, he realized the place was surrounded by racks of drying nets, the occasional barrel and crate, and a hodgepodge of poles and oars and other tools. But no light came from inside. No smoke rose from the stone chimney. Whoever lived here was either asleep or gone.

He reached the rustic wooden door and knocked. No answer. He knocked louder. Still no answer. The place seemed deserted.

But then he heard it. Again. Light footsteps, skittering behind him on the shingle. A rush of panic gripped him, and without glancing back, he lifted the latch, shoved the door open, and slipped inside, then latched the door firmly closed.

Arash paused, listening for noises on the other side. Nothing. Whatever was tracking him had either been stymied or wandered off.

As suddenly as it had come, the adrenaline left his body. The weariness he'd been fighting for hours finally took over. He was vaguely aware that he'd entered a one-room dwelling, humbly furnished, with moonlight slanting through several uncovered windows. It all smelled pleasantly of woodsmoke—and of another familiar combination of scents that he couldn't quite place, something that reminded him, oddly, of his mother.

But he was too exhausted to care. The only thing that mattered was that no one seemed to be home. Stumbling across the room, he tumbled into a bunk in the corner, closed its heavy drapes, and fell instantly asleep.

PART THREE

Since all the world is but a story, it were well for thee to buy the more enduring story, rather than the story that is less enduring.
—Attributed to COLUMBA OF IONA, sixth century

What you seek is seeking you.
—Attributed to RŪMĪ, thirteenth century

Chapter

45

"Wake up, Ellie! You won't believe it!"

Elspeth opened her eyes to find a face roughly four inches from her nose. Georgie, of course.

"Gah!" she shrieked and swatted him away.

He seemed unfazed, as always. "C'mon! It's in the kitchen. I already woke Aurora, and Zahra is coming too."

Groaning, Elspeth stumbled out of bed and followed him to the kitchen. Aurora was already standing at the table, peering down at the frame loom. The tapestry looked even more chaotic in the overhead lighting, the white fuzz like a cloud obscuring almost everything. And then Elspeth stopped short.

"Is it . . ." She couldn't finish. It was too incredible.

Cautiously, she approached the table. Yes, it was just as she'd thought.

The white stuff wasn't fuzz.

It was actual clouds. And they were moving. Elspeth held her breath. Was this truly happening? Was the magic working?

"See?" Georgie bounded to the table. "When I woke up, Mrs. Fealston was still asleep, but no one else was about. So, I went upstairs to see if you were in the studio. And that's when I saw it! I brought it down here. Look, Zahra!"

The girl from Ternival had appeared in the doorway, swaying slightly. Immediately Elspeth could tell something wasn't right. Zahra's eyes glittered the way Georgie's used to, back when he was a toddler with near-constant ear infections. She seemed only partially awake, blinking in confusion at the bright lights and excited company.

"Everything all right?" Aurora asked her.

Zahra nodded faintly and wandered over to a stool at the table. Then she looked down at the frame. She suddenly sat up straight, wide awake. "It *is* working!" she gasped.

The scene in the tapestry had now grown quite dark, as if night had fallen. The water and shore were now barely visible beneath the shifting clouds, which had deepened to a murky gray, and the hut had vanished completely. In fact, it didn't look like the same scene at all.

"What's happening, Zahra?" Elspeth asked. "Do you suppose this is Ternival?"

But Zahra wasn't listening. She was running the trembling fingers of her good hand around the edges of the frame, mesmerized, as if the image inside was a long-lost friend.

"What are we waiting for?" Georgie said impatiently. "We need to jump in before Mrs. Fealston wakes up, or the grown-ups return, or the ley lines get weaker or whatever!"

"But how?" Aurora asked. "Do we just run at it, like the giant did?"

"Maybe we should drive into it, like Charles and Paxton!" Georgie said.

"The cars are all gone with the grown-ups," Elspeth said.

"I can go get the lawn mower!" Georgie suggested.

Elspeth rolled her eyes. "What, and blast through the frame at one mile per hour? We can *run* faster than that, Georgie. Plus, none of us knows how to drive."

"I do," said Aurora. She shrugged, fiddling with a loose thread on her orange pullover. "Charles taught me this spring. In Dad's old Jag."

"Cool!" Georgie squeaked, eyes wide. "That's a manual transmission too."

Aurora shrugged again.

"Well, that's grand and everything," Elspeth sniped, "but we don't have a Jag handy at the moment. And anyway, we don't even know where this picture leads—"

"Shh!" Zahra interrupted. She'd been ignoring the whole exchange and now leaned toward the frame, tense and alert. "Listen. Do you hear it?"

The girls and Georgie leaned forward too. Yes, Elspeth heard something. She bent even closer. It was the faint sound of waves lapping on a shore.

Just then, she felt a tug, like a huge magnet had locked onto her whole body. The others must've felt it, too, for Zahra gasped, Aurora braced her hands on the table, and Georgie slid forward into Elspeth.

"Wh—" Elspeth began. But by now she was being pulled by some inexorable, invisible force toward the frame. Hands flailing, unable to keep her balance, she slammed into the table as though the room was listing like a ship in high seas.

And then, before she could grasp what was happening, the frame seemed to expand like the maw of a monster. The table, lights, kitchen—everything—vanished, and she found herself tumbling headfirst into nothing.

He almost didn't hear it. Jack's isolation was so complete, his own heartbeat was the only audible thing in that tunnel for what felt like hours. Along with the blood rushing in his enormous ears. And his own ragged breathing: in, out, in, out. Loneliness was very loud.

But then, from somewhere in the tunnel behind him, he heard it. A faint snuffling. His overactive ears caught the slight hiss, the breath, and then the near-silent padding of feet. Some kind of creature was sniffing the dirt, the air, the walls. And it was coming his way.

Quivering, he leaped up. It smelled like a predator, although its name escaped him. Maybe mice found it too terrifying for words? Instinct told him to run—and, if he couldn't run fast enough, to hide. But there was nowhere to hide. And even if he were to run, his skittering footsteps would attract the attention of whatever it was. If a mouse could tiptoe, that was what he did now, as silently and quickly as possible, farther down the dwarf-sized tunnel.

The padding of feet continued. After a few yards, the tunnel again branched into three. Jack wished he still had opposable thumbs. If he could chuck a rock down one tunnel and scurry silently up another, he might have a chance. Or maybe at the fork he could lose his horrible companion anyway.

But no. At the fork, there it was again: the faintest of snuffles behind him. On and on he went, speeding up, slowing down, taking one fork after another. And always the footsteps followed. What *was* this thing? Probably some awful creature of Mindra's, guarding the tunnels down here in the dark. Stalking him.

And now the walls were getting narrower, the ceiling lower, the floor in places slick with some sort of putrid slime. Eventually the tunnel narrowed so that anything bigger than a dog would have to scoot on its belly. At yet another split, he wished he could go some direction other than down, for once. Because down meant many more tons of earth above him, more pounds of pressure on his tiny lungs . . .

No. Stop. You're a rodent. You're at home here.

Somehow he took a deep breath and kept going.

Chapter

46

If Zahra had been wide awake before, she was even wider awake now.

For a heartbeat, she'd been tumbling through a terrifying abyss of nothingness. But then she'd plunged into cold, dark seawater.

Her training kicked in. Just like Grandad had taught her. She calmed herself, found purchase beneath her feet, and pushed her head above the surface. She gulped air, found purchase again, and realized she could stand.

She was up to her waist in the sandy shallows of some large body of water. At night. In a dense fog. And despite the darkness, she knew by the gentle tug and sigh of waves that she was just a few yards from shore.

A sudden splashing and spluttering told her that the others had landed nearby. One of them was flailing about in a panic. She could hear the terrified gasps. She waded swiftly in that direction till she could grasp hold of an arm with her good hand and drag the person to their feet.

"It's all right," Zahra said. "You can stand here. And we're close to shore."

Whoever it was started coughing violently.

"Wow, it's cold!" came the voice of Aurora, somewhere to their left. "And dark. I can't see a thing. Ellie? Zahra? Georgie? Anyone?"

"I'm here," Zahra said. Her wrist throbbed, but once she adjusted the sling, the pain subsided, for the moment.

"And me," her companion wheezed. It was Elspeth.

"We did it!" crowed Georgie from their right. "It worked! Didn't it, Zahra? Is this Ternival?"

"It feels like no place at all," Aurora said.

"I'm not sure," Zahra said. "But wherever we are, the shore is close. Follow my voice." She splashed forward, leading Elspeth with a light grip on the girl's elbow. "This way."

They reached land without incident, their feet crunching onto a mixture of sand and pebbles. The shore smelled faintly of fish, and Zahra's heart began to race. It was all too familiar. Was this her own stretch of Writbard Bay? In the darkness and fog, she couldn't be sure.

Georgie was hopping around, too excited and cold to stand still. "This is the Patchless, right, Zahra? Just like in the picture? So, your hut should be somewhere about!"

"The *Pathless*," Elspeth corrected him. The girl's teeth were chattering. All their teeth were chattering.

"Feels like we're inside a cloud," said Aurora.

"We are," Zahra confirmed. It was the kind of dense fog that made navigation almost impossible.

"What do we do now?" Elspeth asked.

At that moment, the gloom shifted, and a ragged glimpse of a half-moon appeared overhead. It disappeared just as quickly, but in the fleeting light Zahra had seen something, farther up the shore. A long, dark smudge on the ground. Again, her heart raced.

"This way," she said. "Hold hands and follow me."

She gave Elspeth her good hand, and the others joined them in a line. As she led them across the shingle, her damaged wrist throbbed again—worse, this time. Her heart skipped, pounded, double-skipped, and raced again. She felt slightly woozy, and there was a faint buzzing in her ears. This wasn't mere excitement. Her fever was back.

Zahra stumbled on and soon drew near the object she'd glimpsed in the moonlight. Yes, it was! Grandad's overturned fishing boat. She let go of Elspeth's hand and ran her fingers along the smoothly planed hull, smelling the tar he'd used to seal the seams, inhaling the scent of brine and nets and all the other familiar things of home.

"I smell fish-and-chips," Georgie's voice said from the darkness.

"And a campfire, I think," said Aurora.

"Oh!" Elspeth cried. "I see something!"

A few yards away, through the shifting gloom, Zahra could make out the corner of her family's hut. Her heart exploded into a gallop. The buzzing in her ears swelled to high-pitched ringing, and patchy gray swirls began clouding what little she could see. She lurched in the hut's direction, no longer bothering to grasp Elspeth's hand. She just wanted to cross that beautiful threshold, to collapse on her own mat under her mother's blanket and sleep forever.

But before she'd taken three steps, the sound of paws skittered across the pebbles in front of her. A low, half-hearted growl reached her ears, followed by an apologetic whine.

"Don't be silly," Zahra heard herself saying. "It's just me and some friends. And how did you get here, anyway, Lepp?"

And then the darkness took her.

When Tilly awoke, it was still nighttime. She was lying on a soft mat of pine needles inside one of the domed tents, where someone must've gently carried her. And standing in the tent's doorway, holding a lantern, was Goldleaf.

"We've received news from the trees at the shore," Goldleaf said in a low voice. "A remnant of Selvedges from Marisith have reached the Runnelwilde and are headed this way. Among them is a Child of Tellus. And meanwhile, other Children of Tellus have converged at a small house by Writbard Bay, just south of the river, below the bluffs. And one of them has fallen gravely ill."

Tilly threw off the blanket of leaves. "It's Jack! Or Arash. Or maybe Charles. Oh, but this is awful!" She stood and quickly fixed her top-knot. "Okay. I'm ready to go."

Goldleaf's normally calm brow wrinkled with confusion. "Go? Go where?"

Tilly blinked at her. "To the shore. Isn't that why you woke me?"

The dryad still seemed baffled. "Nay. We have been summoned to the fire. To watch and listen."

Tilly stared. "To *what*? You mean, we're not taking the curraghs down the Runnelwilde? To help?"

It was Goldleaf's turn to stare. "And how should we help, sister? We dryads only know the ways of tree and root, sunlight and starshine, of creatures that travel by day and creatures that travel by night. But of humans we know little. You have your own brokenness and, thus, your own ways of healing. Nay, there is no aid we can render."

"But weren't there dryads with the original Selvedges, back when the Three Queens battled Mindra? You aided everyone then."

Goldleaf hesitated. "That was a different age," she replied, as if by rote.

"So, why did you wake me?"

The dryad tilted her head. "To watch and listen with us. That is what we do. We keep vigil. And by our vigilance, the land knows peace."

"Well, the land doesn't know peace anymore," Tilly blurted, exasperated. "Mindra has returned, and she is cruel. She has harmed many people—humans and animals and other creatures too. Plus, that could be my brother who has fallen ill. He needs our help. And yet you do nothing." She wasn't sure where this new boldness came from.

Goldleaf's eyes flashed with a bright emerald light. Dryads, apparently, could get angry. "Watch, listen—these are not nothing. And these brothers of yours: They have brought trouble upon themselves, have they not? The eldest lost the gems. The middle one caused the fall of a great and noble soul. All because they failed to watch, failed to listen. And because of them, Ternival no longer knows peace."

"No, sister." Tilly startled herself. She felt a hundred times more confident than she'd been even one minute ago. What was happening? "It's because of *Mindra* that Ternival no longer knows peace. These are choices that *she* made. Sure, my brothers have messed up. But I've messed up too. Lots. And right now, I think you and the Sisters are messing up, just like the rest of us."

Tilly brushed past the dryad and stepped from the tent into the clearing. The night was darker than before. A few lanterns remained lit around the encampment. Otherwise, the only light came from the dim and dying watch fire, its greenish flame burning so low it looked almost coppery. Around the fire, a handful of dryads had gathered.

At the sight of their calm, confident faces, Tilly felt her first twinge of uncertainty. It was one thing to argue with a lone dryad. It was quite another to plead one's case before a whole company of them. But was it necessary? She knew where the curraghs were kept. She knew that the dryads regularly paddled downriver to where the Runnelwilde emptied into the Pathless. How hard could it be to find her way there? She was looking for a small house on a bay, south of the river, at the base of some bluffs. All she needed was a paddle.

She slipped away from the clearing and headed down the path toward the river. She wasn't sure where this new decisiveness came from—maybe from dancing with the Sisters? And while the feeling was unfamiliar, it wasn't strange or scary. Rather, it was like being given a new pair of shoes that actually fit.

A pale green light traced the path's edge, like she was backstage somewhere, and she followed it closely. Soon she could hear the burbling river ahead. As before, the boats were resting upside down on the riverbank, their hulls glowing dimly. Which boat should she take? They all looked alike in the gloom.

"That one is mine," came a quiet voice behind her. Startled, Tilly turned to see Goldleaf approaching, the strange flame of her lantern guttering as she walked. Just like when they'd first met, mere hours before. Hours? It felt like days.

The dryad stepped past Tilly, her expression serene, and set her lantern on the riverbank. Then she effortlessly righted one of the curraghs, hung the lantern in the bow, and, from the branches of a nearby tree, pulled down a paddle nearly as tall as Tilly, its handle gleaming as if it was made from mother-of-pearl.

"Climb aboard, sister," said Goldleaf. "I shall take you."

Chapter

47

Arash stumbled through the rocky valley toward the shore, holding tightly to his mother's hand.

Except . . . this woman looked nothing like his mother. Instead, she was tall and slender and wore a beautiful embroidered gown that whispered around her sandaled feet.

And he wasn't a teenager. He was a little boy, maybe five years old, wearing a long kurta his mother had made for his birthday. Ahead of them ran his father and middle brother, while the oldest brought up the rear behind them.

"*Hurry, Shahin,*" she said to him in the language of their hearts. "*To the caves with Baba.*"

"*But what happened, Maman joon?*" he asked. "*Why must we run?*"

"*No time, little prince. We must be swift and silent, like the falcon.*"

He tried to keep up, his little feet pumping. Finally they reached the shadowed overhang where his father and middle brother waited, breathing heavily from their mad dash through the valley below the palace. His oldest brother joined them. The sound of waves crashing against rocks told him the sea was near, just around the next bend. But they weren't going to the shore.

Under the overhang, the dark mouths of three caves yawned. And now his father—a slight, gentle man with warm eyes and beautiful hands—knelt on the stony ground. He withdrew a long, rolled-up object from inside his kurta. Then he slowly unfurled it and laid it flat upon the stones.

Shahin recognized it at once. It was his father's greatest treasure, the oldest and most intricate of all the tapestries that hung in the palace. Centuries ago, it had been woven with finely spun wool dyed all the colors of the world, along with threads of gold and silver. The image of a fairylike castle rose atop a high bluff overlooking a turquoise sea, with flocks of birds circling in the blue, blue sky overhead.

Woven into the sky, the bluff, and the sea were three sets of swirling letters that Shahin wasn't yet old enough to read. Runes of great power, his mother had told him, woven generations ago to protect their family, their kingdom, and their hearts. Each of the three princes had been taught to say one of the runes, his own rune, over and over till he knew it backward and forward.

Their father motioned for them to kneel. He gazed at each of them in turn, his jaw working, his eyes sad.

"*What is wrong, Baba?*" asked Pejman, the oldest. "*Why are we here? Who was that terrible bird?*"

"*Hush, child,*" said their father. "*Listen closely.*" He drew a sharp knife from his kurta. "*You are in great danger, all of you. You must flee at once, each into a different cave. For the evil witch who once conquered the land of my great-grandmother now seeks revenge for my betrayal of the gems to her enemies.*"

"*But they aren't the witch's gems,*" said Navid, the middle prince. He was always wanting to settle disputes justly, to bring a good turn to bad events. "*They belonged to her enemies in the first place. She is the queen of liars, bent on destroying everything.*"

"*You and I know this,*" said their father. "*But over many long years she has grown more corrupt than ever. She can no longer recognize good from evil. So now you are in danger. Your mother and I must send you away, far away, where the witch and her creatures can never find you. And where you are going, you must tell no one who you are. Do you understand? No one."*

Shahin's lower lip trembled. *"But you and Maman are coming, too, yes, Baba?"* he whispered.

His mother placed a warm hand on his shoulder, while his father looked at him with an expression so sorrowful that Shahin's own tears began to fall.

"You are safer if we do not," Baba said simply. Then he lifted the tapestry and—to Shahin's utter shock—cut it with the knife.

"Baba!" cried Pejman. The three boys watched, horrified, as their father carefully sliced through the warp, sundering the sea with its rune from the rest of the picture. Then he held up the sections to Shahin's mother, who swiftly lit a taper with a flint she'd drawn from her gown and scorched all the cut edges so they wouldn't unravel. Shahin could smell the gold and silver melting together.

All three boys were crying now, not bothering to wipe their cheeks. Even their mother wept. Without hesitation, Baba cut the warp a second time, sundering the castle and bluffs from the sky with its flocks of birds, each section with its distinctive rune intact. Again, their mother scorched the edges.

Now their father picked up one of the fragments and held it out to Pejman. *"You, my son, are part of a very great story,"* he said in a low voice. *"A story that no one can take from you. Never forget this. This rune is your birthright, your protection, wherever your travels take you. Tell no one of its meaning or power. And only speak it aloud when there is no hope left. Do you promise me, Pejman?"*

Pejman could only nod, take his fragment of the tapestry, and stand. Their mother gathered him into her arms, then led him to the middle cave.

"*Speak the rune with me as you leave, Pejman,*" she said softly. "*Now go till you can no longer hear my voice.*"

She and Pejman began speaking, Pejman's words barely audible, their mother's nearly incoherent with grief. As Pejman entered the cave, Maman stood at the mouth of it till Pejman's faint voice could no longer be heard.

Next it was Navid's turn. Baba and Maman repeated their instructions and sent Navid, with his fragment of the tapestry, into the right-hand cave. Again, Maman stood at the cave's mouth until Navid's trembling voice vanished into nothingness.

And finally it was time for Shahin. His mother drew near, but he clung to her leg, unwilling to move. Gently, she detached him, and his father placed the remaining fragment in his grubby little hands.

"*Look at me, Shahin,*" Baba said. Shahin did. There were tears in Baba's eyes that Shahin would remember to the end of his days. His father repeated everything he'd told the older two, and then he and Maman helped Shahin to his feet and led him to the mouth of the left-hand cave.

"*Now go, child,*" said his mother.

Shahin took a step into the darkness of the cave, even though everything inside him resisted. But he couldn't do it. He turned back, reached for his maman. And yet all was dark now. He felt himself sliding away from his parents, as if drawn by the tide.

"*Speak the rune with me, Navid!*" came his mother's voice. She began repeating words from the tapestry. *But I am not Navid,* he wanted to call to her. *And this is not the rune you taught me.*

Shahin tried to tell her this, to explain that she'd gotten it wrong, but his voice wouldn't work. His mouth moved, but no sounds emerged. He was sliding away faster and faster, down and down and down . . .

And then Arash woke up.

He was lying on his back in the dark curtained bunk of the hut in Ternival. Beyond the curtains, three people were talking in low, worried tones. And a fourth was mumbling in that lilting language he knew so well.

A girl. Speaking a rune he didn't know. In the language of his grandfather.

Chapter

48

"I'm pretty sure it was a seizure," Aurora whispered.

Elspeth wiped the tears from her face and looked down at Zahra, who lay restlessly on a mat inside the hut. In the flickering candlelight, the girl's eyes were squeezed shut in pain. Her wispy hair clung to the sweat on her forehead, along with sand and pebbles from when she'd fallen at the threshold. Her mumbling voice wandered incoherently, sometimes in English and sometimes in another language that Elspeth didn't know. The dog paced between her and some sort of curtained bunk in the corner, whining.

Georgie looked up from where he was lighting another candle. "Is that why Zahra was thrashing about? I couldn't really see . . ."

Elspeth hadn't been able to see a whole lot, either, in the dark. But the memory of Zahra's collapse would haunt her forever. The girl's stiff body. Her twitching arms and legs. And, most terrifying of all, the glimpse of her eyes rolled all the way back as the moon shone briefly through the fog.

Aurora, it turned out, was incredibly levelheaded in a crisis. She'd quickly stripped down to her T-shirt and shorts and placed her damp

pullover under Zahra's head, to cushion it. She'd moved a nearby
crate aside so that Zahra didn't hurt herself as she flailed about. And
then, when Zahra had stopped thrashing, Aurora calmly told Georgie
to enter the hut and see if he could find some sort of light while she
and Elspeth helped get Zahra inside.

Lepp, meanwhile, had dashed into the hut with Georgie, sniffing
the place up and down. At the curtained bunk in the corner, Lepp
had pawed at the drapes, whining, but then continued sniffing around
the hut till they located a tinderbox and candle. With a couple of
quick taps, Georgie had sparked a flame and lit the wick—something
he'd learned from Tilly, who'd learned it from scouting when she was
younger. Then Lepp had begun pacing, back and forth, back and
forth, as if holding vigil was his one and only job.

Which made three out of four conscious persons, including the
dog, who could actually do something useful at the moment. Elspeth,
by contrast, wasn't one of them. After helping get Zahra onto the
mat, she'd stood to the side, unable to do anything except cry.

Zahra now gave a miserable moan and muttered something Elspeth couldn't understand.

"Unfortunately," Aurora said, "what Zahra needs is a hospital."

"But there's no way of returning to the Wolverns now," Elspeth
said, her nose stuffy from weeping. "I wish I'd given her more medicine before we left. If only we knew someone in Ternival who could
help!"

Lepp stopped short. With a yip, he raced to the door, pulled the
latch with his teeth, slipped outside, and vanished into the fog.

"What was that about?" Elspeth whispered. "Did he hear something?"

Aurora stood, opened the door wider, and peered into the night.
"No idea," she said after a moment. She closed the door and latched

it firmly. "He'll scratch if he wants back in, I suppose. Georgie, keep an ear open, would you? And, Ellie, let's see if we can find Zahra something dry to wear. Might help her feel more comfortable."

Elspeth joined Aurora in a quick tour of the one-room abode, which was a combination of kitchen, living quarters, and tidy workspace. Tools filled bins near the door, while, under the largest window, a large shelf held a table loom and other weaving supplies. In the corner by Zahra's mat, beautifully woven bed curtains had been pulled aside and tied to the wall with embroidered ribbons. Weavings covered every inch of available wall space—but in the dim light, their details were hard to see.

Aurora rifled through a wooden chest next to Zahra's mat. "Ah! Here we go." She pulled out a plain tunic with long sleeves. "The only problem is how to move her without bumping that arm."

The girls did their best. They gently removed Zahra's woven sash and outer tunic while the girl continued to mumble her incoherent story. But as they tried to shift the next layer, the thin, damp fabric stuck to her clammy skin. Her limbs began to grow restless again.

"Pejman!" Zahra called sorrowfully. Tears squeezed from the corners of her fluttering eyelids. "Navid! Shahin joon!"

Elspeth thought her own heart would break.

"We need to stop," Aurora said. "If she gets too upset, the fever might spike again and cause another seizure." She pulled a blanket from the foot of the mat and draped it softly over the girl's body.

Immediately Zahra calmed down. She continued to mumble, but her limbs relaxed.

Again, Elspeth berated herself for not thinking to give Zahra more medicine. They should've brought the whole bottle along, for that matter. This was something the fairy tales never talked about: how it's all fun and games in a medieval realm till someone has a medical emergency. Hadn't Elspeth known, the moment Zahra stepped into the kitchen, that something wasn't right? So, why hadn't she done anything about it? Yet another person to whom she owed an apology . . .

Well, she could try to make things right with at least one of them, anyway.

Elspeth looked at Aurora, whose white-blond braid was finally a disaster, all matted and damp from the plunge in the Pathless. Her Wolvern Cricket Club T-shirt looked about six sizes too big, probably a hand-me-down from Charles, and for the first time Elspeth noticed that Aurora had secured the baggy shorts around her waist with a length of twine.

This was Elspeth's best friend. The one she'd unnecessarily insulted about the tapestry. The one who'd taken charge so effortlessly, making decisions under pressure as if she did this sort of thing every day. In fact, Aurora's unconcern for perfection was a kind of superpower. It had saved them more than once so far.

Elspeth took a deep breath, ready to voice her apology. But just then, a noise came from the bunk in the opposite corner. The curtains swished aside, and someone drew in a sharp breath.

"Oh!" Georgie exclaimed from his spot near the tinderbox. "Hullo, Arash!"

Jack tried to ignore the footsteps behind him. Instead, he focused on breathing.

Inhale through the quivering, whiskered nose. Hold. Then exhale from the toothy mouth. It was kind of amazing, when he remembered to breathe, how his mind stopped going all fuzzy and his body started functioning again. The school nurse had been right, after all.

As his feet kept moving and his head cleared, he thought more and more of Starwise. About the centaur's incredible bravery. His willingness to sacrifice everything. His trust that what he was doing would give the company a fighting chance. How he hadn't really thought of himself at all.

In fact, Starwise was the opposite of a fairy tale hero. It was almost as though the fairy tales had gotten it all wrong—that Starwise's version was the *real* story.

Jack nearly stopped in his tracks.

What if it was? What if all the shame he felt was entirely misplaced? What if he hadn't flunked at being a hero, after all? Instead, what if the whole concept of the lofty, self-sufficient action man was stupid to begin with?

His sudden exhilaration was like a thousand tons of earth flying off his back. He zoomed down the tunnel. He'd been foolish and selfish, yes. He'd bought into some bizarre ideal that didn't exist. But he wasn't buying into it now. He could still do something meaningful, however minor. Not because he was a hero, but because this whole thing wasn't about him at all.

Then he smelled something up ahead. It was the sea. He continued racing down the tunnel. Was it truly . . . Yes! He was hearing waves now. A bit farther, and faint daylight came from around the next bend. His tunnel was about to join a much larger passageway, one with actual stone walls, which led, at long last, down to the shore.

He could finally escape.

But then he heard a voice. The sound was so startling, after his many hours alone, that he nearly jumped out of his skin. And now he could see it: a bent figure, backlit against the mouth of the passageway, shuffling toward him from the sea. It was muttering to itself and hissing with pain, as though every movement was torturous.

An embroidered bag was slung over the person's shoulder.

It was the enchantress herself.

Chapter

49

etween the dense fog, the vanished moon, the rocketing white water, and the curragh's spin, Tilly would've perished had she gone alone. She could just imagine what the epitaph would've said:

> HERE LIES MATILDE ADDISON,
> AGED 16, OF UPPER WOLVERN.
> DIED AT MIDSUMMER
> ON THE BANKS OF THE RUNNELWILDE.
> "HOW HARD COULD IT BE TO STEER A CURRAGH?"

Freakishly hard, it turned out. But Goldleaf ran the white water like an Olympian. A massive boulder would suddenly appear in the lantern light, and at the last second, they'd cannon away, unharmed. One riverbend after another, the banks of the Runnelwilde grew steeper. Eventually they were barreling through a gorge so dark, Tilly could no longer discern anything ahead.

And then, with a suddenness that sent her lurching into the curragh's footwell, they were clear. The rapids ceased, and the river seemed to have widened.

"Ah, the bridge," Goldleaf said. "Almost to the Pathless now."

Tilly pulled herself up. She could see nothing in any direction except dense fog, as if they floated through a cloud. But then a dark line appeared up ahead, closer than she expected, and soon they swept under a stone bridge to the calm waters on the other side.

The air seemed to lighten. They drew near the left-hand bank, which wasn't quite as steep as the gorge they'd plunged through. And it had fewer trees. Then the woods ceased altogether, and the curragh was swirling past what she guessed were tall grasses. She smelled the briny tang of seawater, and the stale, almost-sulfurous odor of marshes. Finally, at an open spit of land, Goldleaf guided the curragh to shore, where it scraped to a stop on a sweep of shingle.

"The fog will hide us from prying eyes," said the dryad. "But we'll quench the light and stash the curragh, all the same."

With shaky legs, Tilly disembarked while the dryad blew out the lantern. Together they pulled the boat—which was surprisingly light—into the tall reeds. In the utter stillness, Tilly could hear distant waves sliding into shore and pulling away. Otherwise, all was dark and still.

"Not far to go now," Goldleaf whispered. "Follow me."

Unlit lantern in hand, the dryad set out across the shingle, keeping the waves to their right and a dark smudge of what might've been wooded bluffs to their left. But they hadn't gone more than a few yards when something brought them up short.

A whispered, whistling "Hsst!" followed, and human footsteps stopped abruptly.

Somehow Tilly managed not to scream.

Goldleaf motioned for Tilly to stay hidden behind her. Then she drew herself up to her impressive height. "Speak, strangers," she said sternly. "For we are Sisters of the Wood, and we have no fear of you."

Don't we? It was all Tilly could do not to sprint back down the shingle.

But a happy whine burst from the throat of the creature that had growled.

"Thought we were about to get our whompers betoodled, I did," the whistling voice whispered with relief.

"Well met, madam," a sheepish voice said aloud. "There's nothing to fear from us, anyway."

"Paxton!" Tilly cried.

In the candlelight, Arash was only vaguely aware that yet another set of Addisons must've somehow arrived in Ternival. Along with that blond girl from school—Charles's sister—who took weaving lessons from Mum. But he didn't bother to wonder how or when they'd arrived. All he cared about was the voice in the corner.

Because that was where the words were coming from. The beautiful, secret words of a rune he'd never heard before.

"*Each son only ever learnt his own rune, you see,*" Grandfather had always said, "*the one written on his own fragment of tapestry. Like this.*" The old man would point to the oldest weaving that hung in Mum's studio, the one with a circular pattern of birds and the scorched threads along its bottom edge. "*This one speaks the words of deliverance.*"

"*But it's all just a story,*" Arash would say.

Grandfather would close his eyes and shake his head. "*I know that is what my dear daughter tells you. But she is wrong. Someday, my boy. Someday you will know. And so will your mother.*"

"*Know what?*"

"*That the words are true. And they have power. Someday—when you hear another voice speaking words like this—you will know.*"

Well, Arash was hearing another voice now. The words weren't the exact ones Grandfather had taught him, but they were a similar rune, in the same language, with the same lilting cadence. And likewise, the voice had said names he knew from Grandfather's stories: Pejman. Navid. Shahin. As if his grandfather hadn't invented the stories at all. As if the voice in the corner came from the three princes' own mother.

"How did you get here, to Zahra's hut?"

"Where are the others?"

"What happened?"

Arash walked toward the mat, ignoring the questions that everyone else fired his way.

At the moment, none of that mattered.

He looked down. The person lying on the mat wasn't the mother from the stories, of course. She was merely a girl. Maybe his own age, maybe a bit older. Zahra, apparently. The one from Ternival, whom Tilly and Paxton and Starwise had been talking about. Her eyes were squeezed shut with anguish. Evidently, this hut belonged to her—and to whoever had taught her to speak the language of his grandfather. But how was that possible?

"Arash," said Charles's sister. Her name was Aurora, he remembered now. She spoke with quiet firmness, like his grandmother did whenever she had something important to say.

He finally looked up.

The Addisons and Aurora were standing nearby, watching. He shrank back. He should've stayed in the bunk and observed everything from behind the curtains. But he'd been so surprised by Zahra's words that he'd acted without thinking. In any case, it was too late now. Aurora—who looked disconcertingly like Charles—was studying him with concern.

"I know it's hard for you to . . . explain things," she continued gently. "But if you know anything about how we can find help for this girl, she is very, very ill."

Just then, a candle flame leaped in a light draft, and the room brightened. Behind Aurora's head, something caught Arash's eye. It was one of the hut's many wall hangings, a tapestry roughly the size of the one in his mother's studio, swirled with the same kind of looping script. But this one was different. Instead of depicting flocks of circling birds, it featured rolling waves of gentian blue and turquoise, with silvery whitecaps that shimmered in the flickering light.

And now he had a name for the familiar scents he'd noticed when he'd entered the hut. Woad and safflower. Indigo and weld. Dyes his mother used on the wool she bought and carded and spun.

Someone in this house was a weaver too. And they had a tapestry like his family's.

Arash shifted his gaze to Aurora. He'd heard the words she'd said. He wished he could respond. If he knew where to find Paxton, for instance, maybe the old man could do whatever weird thing he'd done for the stray. But they were all pretty much doomed, anyway— unless Arash's grandfather had been right about the runes. If Aurora would only move two steps to the left, he could get a closer look at that tapestry . . .

Zahra spoke again. More clearly this time. Arash turned and looked down at her. She'd opened her glittering, feverish eyes and was staring at him, transfixed.

"*Hurry!*" she whispered in the language he knew so well. "*Speak the rune, Shahin. For only you have the words of deliverance. Only you can unbind them.*"

And that was when the door crashed open.

Chapter

50

Elspeth screamed, long and loud.

"Ellie, it's me!"

Tilly's voice was so unexpected, so out of context, that at first Elspeth didn't recognize her. But then slim arms wrapped around Elspeth in a tight hug, and Tilly's wet strands of hair were sticking to Elspeth's neck, and both girls were crying and crying and crying.

Elspeth pulled away. "Where's Jack?" she asked.

"How did you get here?" Tilly said at the same time.

"Long story," they both said—and started laughing.

"But where is Charlie?" Aurora asked.

Tilly's face fell. "Oh, er . . ."

"It's a dryad!" Georgie hollered.

Elspeth now noticed the other arrivals. Lepp was back. And there was Paxton, carrying some sort of backpack. And with him, to her astonishment, was a large rodent whose front teeth flashed in the candlelight. And finally, the strangest woman Elspeth had ever seen. She was tall and slender, with smooth silvery skin, layers of choppy golden hair that resembled leaves, and a tunic that might've been woven of thin, pliable branches. A dryad, of course. Just like Georgie had said.

"Oi, there ye are, lad!" said the rodent to Arash. "We feared ye'd gotten flupmizzled."

Elspeth shrieked. "It talks!"

"It talks!" Georgie echoed in an excited squeak.

"It?" said the rodent, clearly offended. "*It* has a name, thank ye very much. Barkwhistler the groundhog, at yer service."

"Talk some more!" Georgie cried.

Paxton brushed past Georgie and lifted his cap to the girls. Even in the dim light, his face looked haggard with exhaustion. "Pardon the intrusion," he said. "But where is she?"

He didn't need an answer, however. Lepp was already whining at Zahra's feet.

Paxton strode swiftly to the mat in the corner. Sliding the backpack from his shoulders, he knelt, rested a hand on the girl's brow, and murmured something unintelligible. Then he took hold of Zahra's injured wrist in one hand and massaged it carefully with the other, muttering all the while.

Elspeth watched, awestruck, as Zahra's grimace of pain smoothed into an expression of relief. The girl's body relaxed. Then she opened her eyes, lifted her injured arm from Paxton's light grasp, and rotated her hand—first in one direction, then the other. Finally she looked at Paxton in wonder.

Arash, who'd been hovering nearby, gave a strangled yelp. It was the first verbal sound Elspeth had ever heard him make.

"Glad to see you safe and sound, lad," Paxton growled. He helped Zahra to a sitting position and then rose stiffly to his feet, shouldering the backpack again. He glanced at Elspeth and Aurora. "We've no time for formal introductions, I'm afraid. But you'd best tell us how you got here. And keep it brief." He shot a meaningful look at Georgie, who opened his mouth and shut it again.

"You tell it, Aurora," Elspeth managed to say. After everything she'd seen in the past few minutes, she wasn't sure she could find words to express much of anything. "You were the one who got us here, after all."

So, while the others listened, enrapt, Aurora summarized all that had happened in Upper Wolvern, from Georgie's discovery about the picture frame to their unexpected tumble into Ternival.

"And then, just as we arrived at the hut, Lepp appeared—"

"Ye mean Smithfield's son?" Barkwhistler interrupted. "But we all thought he was lost at Marisith!" The groundhog glanced around the room, as if expecting to see someone he'd overlooked. "Where is the lad?"

The dog approached him, tail wagging. Elspeth's brain seemed to freeze. Wait . . . Lepp wasn't actually a dog?

The groundhog seemed equally astonished. "Well, I'll be blomped."

"But . . . I thought he was Zahra's pet," Georgie said.

"Nay, Georgie. Didn't I tell you?" Zahra spoke up from her seated position on the mat. "I was there at Marisith when Mindra transformed him." Elspeth noticed how much stronger the girl looked, how refreshed and calm and alert.

Arash plopped down suddenly in the corner near the far bunk. He was staring at the dog, his expression shifting from astonishment to alarm to confusion.

Paxton waved an impatient hand at Aurora. "Go on, lass."

As Aurora continued her story, Elspeth observed that Arash remained in the shadows, staring blankly at the floor. She had the impression he wished he was far, far away. Back in Upper Wolvern, maybe. Or farther away than that. Lepp had settled at Arash's feet with a sigh, but the kid shifted position to avoid any contact, as if the dog's presence added to his misery.

Elspeth then glanced at Zahra. The girl could hardly tear her eyes from Arash's face. She studied him intently, as if he seemed familiar, but she couldn't quite place him.

Soon, Aurora wrapped up her tale. The groundhog whistled. "Well, twimp my whiskers. Never heard of a weaver who could conjure mist from naught. Clever, that is."

"Just an accident, really," Aurora said with a shrug.

"A lucky one," Barkwhistler added.

"Aye," said Paxton from where he was pacing distractedly by the door. "We can be grateful for it too. Fog is likely the reason Mindra hasn't yet descended upon this place. Now, Matilde. A quick summary from our side, if you please."

Tilly obliged. With occasional interruptions and clarifications from Paxton and the groundhog, their story unfolded. Of what they'd learned from Jack about the boys' discovery of the castle and the giant. And about the bizarre showdown between Mindra and Professor Rastegar. When Tilly got to the part about Frankie's briefcase, she looked at Elspeth and Georgie sorrowfully.

"Mindra must've intercepted Frankie and Eva at Paddington somehow," Tilly told them. "Because, according to Jack, when the professor asked Mindra what she'd done to them, she held up a mouse and a mole."

Elspeth gaped at her sister, fighting a shriek of disbelief. "But . . . what was she after?" she eventually choked out. "*The Writ of Queens* or something?"

"Apparently, Mindra was also holding that locked wooden box of Frankie's—you know, the one he takes everywhere? She stuffed it into some kind of embroidered bag, gloating about how she finally had all the gems."

"The gems!" Zahra exclaimed.

"Aye," said Paxton grimly. "The lost gems of Mesterra. Hidden in

Tellus and kept safe, all these years. Till now. But I fear the lass must continue. We've no time."

Tilly then described the cars' arrival in Ternival, the skirmish in the woods, and her own encounter with the stag and the dryads. "But all that time, I had no idea what had happened to Paxton or the boys. *None* of us knows what happened to Charles, actually."

"Oh, Charlie," Aurora said in a small voice. "Whatever will I tell Dad?"

Paxton now filled in more details, narrating how he and the boys fell in with the Selvedges, then marched with them to Marisith. As he told of the underground cavern's collapse, the giant's demise, and how Jack had been captured or transformed or worse, he spoke in a near monotone, as if expressing emotion was simply too exhausting.

Again, a shriek rose in Elspeth's throat. First Frankie and Eva. And now Jack. How many more of Elspeth's loved ones would Mindra harm? And how would the remaining siblings explain any of this to their parents? Assuming they ever managed to get home, of course . . .

The old man's already-grim expression had become—if possible—even grimmer. "The overland routes to the stronghold are all cut off now." He looked at Zahra. "And I hate to tell you, lass, but the centaur fell too."

"Lord Starwise?" Zahra gasped. She bowed her head, covered her face with her hands, and didn't move for a long, long time.

"Ohhh," Tilly whispered. "So, *that's* why the Sisters danced."

"That's when the Selvedge remnant retreated to the shore," Barkwhistler said. "But then we learned what young Arash here had found—"

Paxton cut him off. "All in good time, my friend."

Barkwhistler glanced at Arash, who'd pulled back even farther into the shadows. "Anyway," the groundhog said, "our brave Lord Paxton here—as soon as he realized Arash was missing from the Selvedge company—decided to slip away on his own. But he learnt quick enough that he can't outsneak an underland snert."

Elspeth looked at the handyman from Carrick Hall. He didn't seem to have noticed the extraordinary title the groundhog had just given him. Instead, he'd gone stock-still, peering at one of the tapestries on the wall by the door. Lepp got to his feet and padded over to him.

"I'd finally caught up to our good fellow," Barkwhistler continued, "when this lad found us." He pointed to the dog. "Seemed in a bit of a fliffle-me-doo. Whined enough to get our attention, anyway, till we decided to follow him."

"And that's when we ran into you," Tilly said.

"Righty-ho!" said Barkwhistler cheerfully.

"But . . . back to your part of the story." Tilly turned to Aurora and Elspeth. "What I don't understand is why the figures in Frankie's sketch have never moved before. I mean, all these years it's hung in the cottage, and we've never had an inkling that it could be some kind of portal."

"Ley lines!" Georgie blurted for the second time that night. "Do you remember, Arash? What that fellow said to you in the tea shop?"

Arash looked up briefly, as if he'd been nudged awake.

"Ley lines?" said the groundhog.

"Invisible strands of power," Aurora explained, "which some people believe run between landmarks or whatever. And they're supposedly stronger at the solstices. Mrs. Fealston thinks the tourist might've been onto something, actually—except *she* thinks the lines connect more than just landmarks. They're like warp threads that run through multiple weavings on the same loom. Connecting worlds."

"I've heard of such things." Goldleaf spoke for the first time. She had the calmest voice Elspeth had ever heard. "It's similar to the roots of our trees. What happens to one affects the others. But in this case, it's like roots between worlds."

"Oh!" Tilly's eyes grew wide. "But what happens when it's no longer midsummer? Does the magic, or whatever it is, stop working?"

"Even if it does, I'm not sure there's anything we can do about it now," Aurora said ruefully. "The frame is probably still in the kitchen, back at the Hall."

"And the gems are still at Marisith, with Mindra," said Elspeth.

"So . . . we're stuck in Ternival?" Georgie said hopefully.

"Well, we don't want to leave without the others, in any case," Tilly said.

Zahra finally lowered her hands and lifted her head. "Also, if the honorable Paxton could attend to my ill grandad before anyone leaves, I'd be most grateful."

"Oh yes!" Elspeth said. "Couldn't you, Paxton?"

"Paxton?" echoed Georgie, hopping to his feet.

Everyone looked around in bewilderment.

Barkwhistler smacked his paws together in frustration. "And where has that minkle-headed oofengop gone *now*?"

"Not to mention," said Aurora, "where's Lepp?"

Chapter

51

Paxton was gone, and Zahra hadn't even thanked him.

She stood in the doorway with the others, rubbing her miraculously restored wrist and peering into the fog. The air to the east, above the bluffs, had begun to brighten. Midsummer sunrise was almost here. And if it hadn't been for Paxton, she might not have survived to see it.

"Where'd they *go*?" Tilly wailed.

Barkwhistler, who was sniffing the ground nearby, suddenly straightened. "Footprints! Headed towards the bluff. Hold yer whompers. I'll be right back."

"Me too," Georgie said, but Elspeth grabbed his arm.

After several tense minutes, the groundhog returned. He breathlessly motioned for everyone to follow him back inside, then shut the door.

"Well, I'm blomped," he wheezed. "Looks like they've headed up the bluff. There's a steep footpath behind the hut."

It was, in fact, the same footpath that Zahra had climbed to warn Lord Starwise about the giants. And which Grandad had taken, with the other fisherfolk, to join the refugees fleeing from Caristor. Other than the bridge over the mouth of the Runnelwilde, at the north end of Writbard Bay, the footpath was the only way to reach the blufftop from shore.

"Ah," said Goldleaf, nodding. "They seek the main road, no doubt, that runs between Caristor and Marisith."

"Oh!" Tilly exclaimed. "I wonder if that's the same road we landed on when we first arrived. We drove on it for a bit before we crashed into a pile of barrels."

Of course. Goody Pearblossom's barrels, from the wagon. "I know right where that is," Zahra said. "You were only a mile or two from this bay—as the crow flies."

"So, does that mean both cars are still up there, on the main road?" Aurora asked. She'd begun to pace in circles, frowning with concentration.

Tilly nodded. "Unless they've gotten moved somehow."

"Then I wonder if that's where Paxton is going," Aurora mused. "I mean, if he's trying to get away quickly, driving is a lot faster than walking."

"But it's just a dirt wagon track," Tilly said. "No offense to our hosts, but it's not made for motorcars."

Georgie's eyes were shining. "Like off-road racing!" he breathed. "It sounds *amazing*."

"In any case," the groundhog added, "me snozzwhiffler tells me Lord Paxton has had a mighty head start, and we'll not catch him easily, if at all."

"But where will he go once he reaches the road?" Elspeth wondered.

"I'll ask the trees," said the dryad serenely. She'd returned to her stool at the table.

"You can *do* that?" Georgie squeaked.

"Shush," Tilly said. "Watch."

Everyone crowded around Goldleaf. Even the one they called Arash—whose features seemed so eerily familiar to Zahra—rose from his shadowed corner to hover behind the rest.

Goldleaf opened her lantern and snapped two long fingers several times over the wick. Her smooth skin made a dry whooshing sound. Suddenly chartreuse sparks jumped from her fingers, and the wick caught, guttered, then began to burn with a steady ice-green flame.

"Cool!" Georgie hollered.

Goldleaf closed the lantern, stared intently at the flame—and waited.

"What's happening?" Elspeth whispered.

"They grow a bit sluggish in the warmer season," the dryad murmured. "It can take a while to wake them."

"Sounds like the rest of us on summer hols," Aurora said.

"So . . . that's it?" Georgie's shoulders drooped. "Now we just . . . wait?"

"Yep," Tilly said with a sigh. "Watch. Listen. And wait."

Restless, the group dispersed and settled wherever they could find a spot.

Outside, the dawn light steadily increased. The fog now swirled in ragged strands. Through the windows, Zahra could discern more of the shoreline in both directions. A sense of dread began to bubble in her stomach. Once the sun had risen over the bluffs, it might burn away the fog altogether, and they'd be exposed to Mindra's spying gaze from Marisith.

But Zahra couldn't worry about that now. Her immediate duty was right here, to these people. She could imagine just how appalled Grandad would be that she'd offered her guests no food, no drink, no clean linens with which to wash their weary faces or dry their damp hair. Her recent brush with death was no excuse. Hospitality came first.

Swiftly, Zahra distributed her family's modest provisions. Smoked fish. Dried pears. Pickled beets. A few hard-boiled eggs. The last wheel of hard cheese and loaf of bread. The treasured jars of mulberry juice from Goody Pearblossom, plus pouches of fresh water from the spring behind the hut. All gone within minutes.

Arash, in particular, devoured what she gave him as if he hadn't eaten in days. She handed him a chunk of bread, trying not to stare. With his long face, mournful eyes, and mop of dark hair, he looked nothing like the other Children of Tellus that she'd met so far. He could almost be an older version of Shahin, the boy from Grandad's stories—the youngest of the princes who'd appeared in her fever dreams. Her initial astonishment at seeing him had shifted to curiosity and wonder. Who *was* he? Where had he come from?

Arash, still chewing, now made a beeline for the weavings on the wall by the door. He halted in front of her family's most prized possession, the ancient tapestry of ocean waves in various shades of blue, into which had been woven the flowing script she'd learned by heart.

He reached up a slender hand. Unlike the hut's other wall hangings, this tapestry's upper warp threads hadn't been tied off in a neat fringe. Rather, they'd been cut close to the weft, as if they'd once been part of a larger weaving. And then, to prevent unraveling, they'd been scorched. But in the hut's dim light, the scorching wasn't obvious until you touched it.

Zahra held her breath as Arash ran a trembling finger along the tapestry's topmost edge. Then he whipped around. His wide eyes found Zahra's. They stared at each other, a thousand unsaid things floating in the air between them.

"News from the trees!" Goldleaf announced just then.

The others raced to the table.

"What do they say?" Aurora asked.

"The Selvedge remnant has sought refuge at the encampment of the Sisters, who have met them with welcome. And Lord Paxton is indeed on the road to Caristor. He's being followed by a dog, but the trees are uncertain if the old man is aware of it. Beyond this, I do not know."

"Oh, *why* did Paxton leave us?" Elspeth lamented.

"For yer own safety, is my guess," said the groundhog. "He'll get as far away as possible so Mindra can't track the call of the High Queen's crown here, to this house—oh!" He clapped his paws over his whiskered mouth.

"The call of the *what*?" Tilly gasped.

For a moment, Zahra felt as though her fever had returned. Her knees grew wobbly.

The groundhog dropped his paws and looked apologetically at Arash. "Well, lad. Ole Barkwhistler is a minkle-headed oofengop."

Arash's face had gone blank again. He stared at the floor, not moving, not responding.

"I . . . I don't understand," Elspeth said in a shaky voice. "Are you saying . . . that the crown of Ternival, which once held the gems, has been found?"

"But I thought it'd returned to Tellus, with Eva's grandmother," said Aurora. "And that no one knows where she hid it."

Barkwhistler heaved a sigh of regret. "Aye, lass. And then the lad found it. Didn't have the slightest zinkling what it was, of course. Been carrying it in that stashbag of his. But now Lord Paxton has it— and soon that great blitheress will track his lordship down."

There was an appalled silence.

"But if the crown is finally back here, in Ternival, mightn't that be a good thing?" Aurora said after a moment. "I mean, if we can some-how get the gems back, and restore them to the crown—and maybe even find the rightful sovereign, whoever that is—then won't the crown's protective power become stronger than ever? Won't Mindra be utterly defeated?"

"The oracle hints at this," Goldleaf agreed. "And if ever there was a moment when its promise could be fulfilled, that time is now."

Zahra's heart began to gallop again—and not from fever, this time. She tried to catch Arash's gaze, but he'd withdrawn into the shadows again. If only Grandad were here!

"And yet . . . if Mindra gets her hands on the crown while she's still in possession of the gems," Elspeth countered, "all is lost."

Another silence.

"More news!" Goldleaf announced. "The trees say Lord Paxton has reached the pile of barrels on the main road. He hasn't noticed the dog, who's staying out of sight. Now the old man has pushed one of the strange wagons from Tellus out of the underbrush."

"The Bentley!" said Tilly.

Goldleaf continued to stare intently into the pulsing flame. "He has climbed inside the wagon. The trees say it rumbles like a black-smith's furnace—which is strange, for it produces no smoke."

"Clean as a whistle, that old exhaust system," Georgie commented smugly. "Good ole Paxton!"

"And now the wagon has begun to move. Faster and faster. The trees have never seen its equal for speed—except, perhaps, the Run-nelwilde in flood."

"Oh no!" said Elspeth. "He's left Lepp behind!"

"Which direction is he headed?" Barkwhistler asked.

"North."

"North?" Aurora echoed. "Which way is north?"

Zahra's breath left her lungs. "Toward Marisith," she said faintly.

"But I thought he was trying to get *away*!" Tilly exclaimed. "To put as much distance between himself and Mindra as possible."

"Why would he go there?" Elspeth cried. "It doesn't make sense!"

And that was when Zahra knew.

She understood everything.

Her grandfather's warning in the courtyard at Marisith: *Whatever befalls, say nothing of the tapestry. Not to her, not to anyone.* And Paxton's words as she left the Bentley: *Wait. Let me help you.* And Arash's reaction to her family's woven heirloom. Even the oracle—which had always seemed so obscure, so much a part of Ternivali lore that it felt like a fairy tale—she understood that now too. The quiet life she'd lived with her family on the shores of the Pathless was over. Forever. It was time to act.

She went to Arash, who finally looked her in the eye.

"Alas, kind friends," Zahra announced to the whole company. She kept her gaze locked on Arash's face. "The venerable Paxton does not flee. Instead, he intends to offer ransom."

Then she lowered her voice so only Arash could hear.

"And *we* must stop him."

Chapter

52

At the sight of Mindra's tortured gait, Jack pulled deeper into the shadows. A startled hiss came from the tunnel behind him. His stalker had halted too. Apparently, the creature didn't wish to be spotted by the enchantress any more than Jack did.

"Dare they wage a new war, these Children of Tellus?" Mindra muttered in that weird Shakespearian way of hers. "Tried to forge an alliance with the Sisters, no doubt, but found themselves turned away." The enchantress chuckled mirthlessly. "And now mine enemies dare return to my very house—and with the treasure too. They cannot resist the chance to unseat me whilst they think me absent. But the treasure calls, stronger than ever. 'Tis right above me now, within these castle walls. And I shall show *them* the power of the gems!"

She patted the bag. Muffled squeaks reached Jack's ears. Frankie and Eva! They were still in there—along with the box of gems.

"Quiet, wretches!" Mindra shrieked. Her voice bounced around the stone walls.

As the enchantress passed Jack's hiding spot and continued up the passageway, he suddenly realized what he had to do. Even though everything inside him screamed in protest—even though he was mere steps from freedom—he knew.

Behind him, his pursuer resumed its approach. If he didn't act now, the creature would pounce.

Summoning a courage he didn't feel, Jack silently bolted into the passageway after the retreating enchantress. He jumped, undetected, onto the rustling hem of her cape and scaled its swishing folds till he could leap onto the bag. Then he scrambled to the opening at the top, where he paused, trembling.

You're a mouse. You were made for this.

After taking a deep breath, he plunged into the suffocating darkness.

"Let's try to cut Paxton off at the top!" Aurora was yelling. "He'll drive right past us on his way to Marisith."

Tilly raced with the others toward the footpath that ran up the wooded bluff behind the hut. But they hadn't climbed far before they heard a roaring above them. The sound was so foreign, so out of place in Ternival, that at first Tilly couldn't tell what it was. Then it drew near, zoomed along the bluff past where their path intersected with the road, and faded northward.

"What the blinklevopping whiffenburf was *that*?" The groundhog was quivering from head to toe.

"The Bentley!" Georgie wailed and burst into tears.

Elspeth groaned. "We're too late."

"If only we had the keys to the Rolls!" Aurora said from the front of the line. "We could try catching up to him."

"Actually, Charles hid them near the car," Tilly said, "in case something happened to him . . ." Her voice trailed off. Something *had* happened. And they might never know what. "But I don't know how to drive," she added.

"I do!" Georgie said, wiping his tears with grubby fists.

"You do not," Elspeth said irritably. "But Aurora does."

"Then let's keep going," said the groundhog, "before we get flupmizzled."

"But is there room in the car for all eight of us?" Tilly asked.

Aurora shrugged. "Some can ride on the outside, I suppose. On the bonnet. Or the boot."

Georgie squealed with delight.

"But what if our plan doesn't work?" Tilly continued. "What if I can't find the keys? Or the car won't start?" Her newfound decisiveness had fled, for the moment, and her anxiety brain was back. "Or we run out of petrol? We'll be farther from Marisith than when we started."

"What if no one stops Paxton?" Elspeth shot back.

"Aye!" Barkwhistler agreed. "No need for us to get all whimbypoddled, now."

"Although, Tilly has a point," Aurora countered. "Perhaps we should split up in case something goes wrong or any of us gets caught."

From the back of the line, Zahra's quiet voice cut through the chatter. "Some can travel by sea."

Everyone turned.

"Grandad's fishing boat can only hold a few of us," she clarified. "But I know the way. And it's still the most direct route to Marisith."

"Could we take the curragh too?" Tilly asked Goldleaf.

The dryad smiled. "Alas, sister. A river curragh isn't made for open water."

So, there on the bluffside, it was decided. They'd split into two groups. Tilly, Aurora, and Georgie would continue up the path with

Barkwhistler to the Rolls. If they could get the car started, they'd head to Marisith. Otherwise, they'd return to the hut and wait for word from the others. Meanwhile, Zahra, Elspeth, and Arash would climb back down to shore and row across the bay to the tip of the peninsula. If all went as planned, the two groups would meet in the tunnels directly under the watchtower.

"What about you?" Tilly turned to Goldleaf again.

"Do not trouble yourself, sister," the dryad replied. "I shall help Zahra launch the boat, and then there's something I must do. But never fear: The trees will guard you. And they will send word to the Sisters of all that befalls you, for good or ill. We shall meet again."

Farther down the path, Elspeth was already following Zahra toward the shore.

"Ellie!" Tilly called. "Els!" But the younger girl couldn't seem to hear her. Tilly stood, watching, till the fog hid her sister from view. Reluctantly, she resumed climbing and joined the others at the top.

As they reached the road and headed south, the fog created a gray gloom under the trees like never-ending dusk. But it was, in fact, midsummer morning. The longest day of the year. Had she really watched the sun set, near this very bluff, less than eight hours ago? And now it was rising somewhere beyond the veil of cloud.

What was happening in the Wolverns right about now? Sunrise was always the main event of the festival. The crowds on Table Mount—functioning on maybe two hours of sleep, if any—would cheer the golden disc as it rose above the pasturelands beyond the hills. Then they'd douse their watch fires, pack up their tents, and create legendary traffic jams from Worcester to the Cotswolds. And her parents were probably worried out of their minds. Every single one of their children had now vanished, and who knew if they'd ever return?

Tilly began to lag behind, feeling more and more overwhelmed by the impossibility of defeating Mindra, or of returning home, or both. But then she noticed the trees. Even in the fog, they seemed more beautiful than before—and not even remotely spooky. She'd rarely felt safer, in fact, knowing they'd send word to the Sisters if anything happened. Plus, ahead of her scampered Barkwhistler, who seemed to know the topography of Ternival like the back of his paw.

They'd be okay. Somehow.

Wouldn't they?

Chapter

53

The fog was thick as stew.

To Arash, it felt like the boat was going in circles. But somewhere ahead was their destination: the tip of the northern peninsula. Somewhere behind lay the ruins of Caristor. To the right, Arash caught occasional glimpses of the distant shore from which they'd come. And to their left, beyond a thick curtain of mist, the gray Pathless rolled on and on into the unknown.

It was a good thing Zahra knew these waters so well, or they might never see land again.

After the two groups had parted company on the footpath, Arash, Elspeth, and the dryad had helped Zahra right her grandfather's fishing boat and push it across the sand into the water. Everyone had climbed aboard except the dryad, who'd waded with the boat against the tide to push them farther out.

The dryad had handed Elspeth the lantern with its eerie green flame.

"Take this, sister," Goldleaf had said. "You will need it for the tunnels under the castle. For the trees' glowing roots do not extend that far—they dislike the very earth under Marisith. Let this be your light, and along the way, the Sisters can track your journey."

Then the dryad had turned to Zahra. "Do not hug the shore," she'd warned, her normally serene tone urgent. "Instead, steer a course straight across the open water to Marisith. Swift and silent, understand? Let the fog be your shield."

Nodding, Zahra had set the oars. And then, between one incoming breaker and the next, the dryad had given them a mighty shove into the bay.

Arash now watched as Zahra rowed. With her back to the bow and her sandaled feet braced against the footwell, the fisherman's granddaughter pulled both oars with steady strokes. Up and pull, down and push, up and pull, down and push, cutting smoothly through the waves. She made it look easy, but he could tell it was hard work. Despite the oars having been designed for someone twice her size, she managed to power the boat with a skilled unselfconsciousness that made him envious.

Every so often, Zahra glanced at him, as if wanting to say something. And he'd look away as if he hadn't seen, as if everything that'd happened in the hut didn't mean anything.

But it did.

Everything was different now. Because of the tapestry, of course. But also because of an unrelated detail that mattered more than Arash wanted to admit.

The dog wasn't really a dog.

Instead of being one hundred percent canine—loyal, trusting, protective, single-minded—the stray was actually some guy named Lepp with a xenophobe for a dad. It was like being told the creature had died.

Arash kept his eyes averted from Zahra, not wanting her to see the tears that annoyingly hovered in his lashes. He stared over the gray waves. The light continued to grow. A gentle breeze kicked up, and the fog seemed to be thinning.

"What if the fog blows away altogether?" Elspeth asked, knuckles white as she clutched the bench. "Mindra will be sure to see us."

"She might," Zahra replied, pulling on the oars. "Or she might not. I don't imagine she expects any threat from sea."

"How did you learn to steer in the fog, anyway?" Elspeth continued. "I'd be worried I'd overshoot and end up miles from my goal."

Zahra took another stroke. "Grandad taught me, for night fishing. When the sky is overcast, you learn to read the waves, the tides, the currents."

"Have you steered like this to Marisith before?"

Zahra nodded and rested the oars for a moment. "Sometimes, in the very early morning before sunrise, we fish below the watchtower. But not often. The entrance to Mindra's tunnels is there, of course. Which is not pleasant to contemplate on a dark night." She shuddered. "Plus, you can only fish that close to the end of the peninsula at high tide. Otherwise, it's far too hazardous."

"How high will the tide be once we arrive?" Arash could hear the anxiety in Elspeth's voice.

"Not quite at its fullest," Zahra reassured her. "We'll have the tide in our favor." She resumed rowing and they lapsed back into silence.

Arash noticed that Zahra's thin face had begun to look haggard again. Had she eaten anything at the hut, or had she given it all away to her guests? It was the sort of thing his grandmother would do, actually: pastries for everyone except the chef. And meanwhile, would the girl's wrist hold up under such treatment, or was she risking another injury?

Knowing what his mum would say if she was here, Arash rose from his seat and carefully clambered toward the rowing bench. He motioned for Zahra to move aside. She hesitated, at first. But eventually she nodded and slid over so he could take the oars.

As she moved to the other bench, he heard her murmur something that almost made him lose his grip.

"*Thank you,*" she said.

In the language of his grandfather.

Traveling in Mindra's bag was the nightmare Jack didn't know he'd been dreading all his life.

It was crowded and airless, like the London Underground—except the floor and walls never stopped moving. Jostled relentlessly, he lost his footing in the shifting fabric every five seconds. *Breathe. Rodents love places like this. It makes them feel safe, protected. No,* his brain protested. *Rodents are stupid.*

But he kept breathing.

He lost his footing again and fell. He collided with a nasty, spiny thing that turned out to be the large seashell Mindra had put to her lips, like a horn, back in the valley. She hadn't blown it, but he could imagine, just by the feel of its spines, how disturbing its call must sound.

Then he was knocked slithering along a flat wooden surface with extensive indentations. He realized they were carvings and grabbed on with his toes. He crawled around its surface till he reached one of its edges. Yes, it was the box of gems. He could feel the slash across the lid and trace the carver's signature, the tree encircled by a coronet.

Beneath the box he sensed movement. Some thing or things were wiggling and squirming down there. He sniffed. One was a mouse, he guessed. And the other was a mole. Frankie and Eva, of course.

He clambered closer and began to feel his way around in the dark.

They were still trapped in the mesh snare. If he could just untie it at the top somehow, they could escape. But then the creatures became aware of his presence. They started scrambling frantically, trying to reach him—no, trying to get away from him. Maybe both things at once. They jostled and shoved and clawed till he lost his grip and almost fell to the bottom of the bag. Rodents were *definitely* stupid.

"Frankie, Eva, if you don't stop shoving," he found himself saying, "I'll bite your noses off." It came out as a series of tiny squeaks.

The squirming stopped. One of them, the mouse, put two paws on the snare and sniffed in his direction, its whiskers quivering.

"Wait. Is that you, Jack?" it squeaked.

Chapter

54

Everything looked just as Tilly remembered.

Barrels still littered the road. The Bentley was gone, of course, but the Silver Shadow was there, tucked into the underbrush. And the keys were right where Charles had hidden them, too, under the rock near the front left tire.

Quickly Aurora unlocked the door, climbed into the driver's seat, and put the car in neutral. She steered as Georgie and Tilly pushed it out of the shrubbery.

"Do you suppose Lepp is still somewhere about?" Georgie grunted, shoving with all his nine-year-old might.

"Hopefully he'd appear if he was," Tilly replied. Steadily they angled the car onto the road.

"Well, twimp my whiskers!" the groundhog whistled as the shiny chrome bumpers came into view.

"Right?" Georgie said, dancing on the balls of his feet. "Isn't it simply *ripping*?"

For the first time ever, he had an appreciative audience for his fountain of motorcar trivia. As he blathered on about gearboxes and chassis, disc brakes and rear suspension, Barkwhistler peppered him with questions till Aurora honked the horn.

"Next stop, Marisith," she called. "Mind the gap." She turned the key in the ignition. For a heart-stopping moment, nothing happened. Then the Rolls coughed to life. The groundhog gave a startled yelp and clapped as if this was a magic show. Finally everyone jumped in: Georgie and Barkwhistler in the front seat next to Aurora, and Tilly alone in the back. Then Aurora floored it.

The youngest of Lord Edward's children, it turned out, was a terrible motorist. Or rather, she had the fearlessness of a rallycross racer who would've gotten pulled over for reckless driving if this had been the Wolverns. She blasted around blind corners, barreled up steep inclines, and bottomed out on deep ruts, Georgie and Barkwhistler whooping all the while. Clearly, this was a person who'd never colored between the lines. Tilly, clutching the back of Aurora's seat, could just imagine Charles's reaction.

As they descended like a roller-coaster train toward the bridge over the Runnelwilde, a thought flashed through Tilly's mind.

"Wait!" she shouted. "Didn't Paxton say the peninsula is cut off? So hasn't the road been cut off too?"

"Don't ye worry, lass!" Barkwhistler called over his shoulder. He looked like a pirate captain at the helm of a schooner, back paws balanced on the seat and front paws on the dash. "Just after the bridge, we'll take the spur that runs down to the beach. And then we'll bombdozzle across the shingle to the Selvedges' secret entrance at the base of the bluff."

"You mean," Georgie bellowed, "we'll drive on the beach? Like the racers at Bridlington?" He whooped again as the car bounced so hard, both he and Barkwhistler bumped their heads on the windscreen. *Good thing it's already cracked.*

Aurora followed Barkwhistler's directions from the bridge to the beach, then gunned the engine on the open straightaway. Maybe it was a good thing you couldn't see much from the windows except fog, or there'd be a lot more screaming—at least from the back seat. So much for arriving at Marisith with any kind of stealth.

Soon the dark wall of the northern peninsula became visible straight ahead, through the fog. The beach now swept westward in a wide arc. As they rounded the bend, Tilly spied a jagged gorge cutting through the bluff on their right, full of downed trees and other debris that looked recently dislodged. Was that where it had been severed from the mainland?

"Tide's coming in," barked the groundhog. "Stick close to the trees at the base of the bluffs, lass, or we'll sink like plopmarkles."

"Look!" Georgie hollered. "There's the Bentley!"

"My turn," Elspeth said to Arash. "You need a break."

The kid had been rowing for a long time, but like Zahra, he resisted the offer of help—at first, anyway. Elspeth didn't relent, however. She had three brothers and knew how to plant herself squarely in their line of vision till they gave up and did what she wanted. Soon Arash nodded and let her take his place at the oars.

"I have no idea what I'm doing," she admitted aloud. It was a confession she resisted with every cell in her body. But then again, if she'd learned anything through her friendship with Aurora, it was that nothing meaningful would ever get accomplished if you waited till you were an expert.

Which was a lovely notion—in theory. In practice? It was an exercise in mortification. Elspeth was so bad at rowing, it was almost comical. And yet she didn't give up. With the others' help, she tried and tried again till her arms finally got the hang of it.

Up and pull, down and push. Up and pull, down and push.

She was rowing them to Marisith.

Her back and shoulders began to ache. She was thirstier than she ever remembered being in her life. The boat had slowed to a crawl. No doubt, her hands would be blistered and bloody when it was all over. But they were closer to Marisith than they'd been before, and she'd given her companions a break.

She kept rowing. The sheer monotony was almost mind-numbing. She found herself staring at Goldleaf's strange, flickering lantern flame in the stern. "Sister," the dryad had called her. And Elspeth had felt flattered. But when Goldleaf had called Tilly "sister" on the footpath, Elspeth had felt a flash of envy. *I'm Tilly's sister,* she'd felt like saying. *You've known her for what—six hours?* Which was why Elspeth had headed down the path so quickly. She'd heard Tilly calling her name, but she'd ignored her.

Elspeth regretted that now.

Zahra clambered toward her. "Once we see the farthest point," the girl said over the rising wind, "we'll aim for three large rocks that form a triangle, roughly a hundred yards from the beach below the tower. We call them the Three Queens. At low tide, they're connected to the mainland by a natural bridge of sand. But right now, they're more like islands."

Elspeth could no longer feel her hands, but she didn't stop rowing.

"There!" Zahra announced after a while. "Marisith."

Elspeth rested the oars and looked over her shoulder. Sure enough, a sheer rock cliff rose from a narrow shelf of beach to a high bluff. And at the top, mostly hidden by mist, a boxy, crenelated tower jutted over the water.

"See those three rocks? At the base of the cliff?" Zahra pointed. "We need to run between the two on the right. But it will be tricky.

We'll have to turn towards shore immediately after we pass the first one, or we'll miss the only safe place to beach the boat."

Elspeth resumed rowing. She could feel her hands again but wished she couldn't. They were like lumps of burning coal.

A few minutes later, Zahra approached the rowing bench.

"I'll take it from here," she said with a grateful smile. "I need you in the bow, to keep watch."

Relieved, Elspeth took Zahra's spot in the bow. But she didn't have time to relax. Soon they were within yards of the first rock, which loomed ahead like a small mountain. They powered toward it rapidly.

"Tell me when," Zahra called through gritted teeth.

"Almost there," Elspeth called back. "Three, two, one—now!"

Zahra cranked the shoreward oar. The boat turned slightly, but not enough. Elspeth clung to the gunwales as a tall wave broadsided them. They were listing perilously. Water slipped over the rail.

Then suddenly the nose swung toward shore. The boat righted. Elspeth looked back. Arash had grasped the seaward oar and was cranking it opposite of Zahra's strokes.

And then they were through. They'd cleared the rocks. The boat now surfed the breakers effortlessly toward the strip of beach beneath the towering cliff. One last wave deposited the boat high on the sand, then receded.

They'd done it. They'd arrived at Marisith.

And right in front of them was the dark mouth of a cave.

Chapter

55

"Hold on," Jack squeaked to Eva, his whiskers quivering with excitement. "You can understand me? Are we *talking animals*?"

"Well, the two of us seem to be," Eva said. "But not Frankie. I can't comprehend a thing he says—and vice versa, as far as I can tell."

"I wonder if it's because you and I are the same species?" Jack said. "Maybe we're fluent in Mouse or whatever. And he's fluent in Mole."

"Oh!" Eva said. "That makes sense. But tell me, Jack, how on earth did you get here? We've been stuck in this thing for what feels like days—without food or water or anything. And I can't reach the knot at the top of the snare to chew through it. Can you?"

"With these?" he said, baring his incisors. "Absolutely. Why don't you tell your side of things first while I get the knot sorted?"

He clambered to the top of the snare and set to work on the twine. And as he gnawed, Eva quietly caught him up to speed on all that had transpired since Mindra intercepted her and Frankie at Paddington Station.

When Eva got to Mindra's standoff with the professor, Jack spat out a mouthful of twine. "I was there, actually. Me and Arash. Long story. But go on."

"Well, once the enchantress entered the castle, she stashed this awful bag—with us and the box of gems inside—somewhere in an upper chamber. But every once in a while, she'd come back to the chamber, sort of muttering to herself and hissing, like she was in terrible pain. Probably from the gems, I'm guessing. She never stayed long. But from the things she's said, I've pieced together a bit of what's been going on."

When Eva finished talking, Jack filled in the gaps of the time line as best he could with his own details. "Oh, Jack," she murmured sympathetically when he described the fall of Starwise. "You couldn't have known he'd risk his life like that. But I know the feeling . . . like you've let everyone down."

Embarrassed by her kindness, Jack concentrated on chewing through another strand. "At least the giant is dead," he added. "Not much else to tell you, actually. Mindra turned me into a mouse. I somehow dodged one of her raptors. And then I spent all night lost in the tunnels. Some sort of creature began following me, but I somehow managed to dodge that too. In fact, I'd almost reached the shore when I spotted Mindra in the passageway. And then I heard you two squeaking—"

"You mean, you climbed in here to help us," Eva interrupted, "when you could've escaped from the tunnels entirely? Jack, that's amazing! And I know how much you hate enclosed spaces too."

"Any idea why Mindra came down here?" He quickly changed the subject.

"I think she was on the hunt for something—something that was calling to her, she said. She kept bragging to herself about the 'brilliant' tunnel system she'd built, all those years ago, below Marisith. And eventually I could smell the sea and hear waves up ahead. But then she seemed to change her mind. She'd just turned back around, in fact, when you appeared."

As Jack applied his incisors to another strand in the knot, the whole thing snapped clean through. The opening at the top un-cinched, and Eva and Frankie scrambled excitedly out of the snare. Mouse teeth were *fantastic.*

All three of them now climbed onto the lid of the box, where Frankie snuffled blindly around the edges, his enormous whiskers like a radar antenna. Jack watched with a kind of appalled fascination. Moles were their dad's least favorite mammal of all time, and here was his eldest son—complete with ridiculously long claws—sniffing like he was born this way. And he seemed completely unaware of who Jack was.

"I wonder what Mindra was after?" Jack mused, still staring at Frankie. "There's a lot I don't know, actually. Where Tilly and Charles ended up, for instance. And what happened to the Selvedges after the raid on Marisith. And why everyone in Ternival seems to be counting on the Children of Tellus to show up and save the day, just like in the old stories. And how the true sovereign is supposed to appear, at long last—not that anyone seems to know who that is."

They were silent for a moment.

"Who *would* the rightful sovereign be?" Eva wondered aloud.

"Could it be your mum?" Jack mused. "I mean, Ternival hasn't had a sovereign since the Three Queens. And your grandmother was the only one of the three to have a child. So, that would put your mum next in line, right?"

Eva shook her head. "There must be a reason why the stag led my grandmother back to Carrick Hall after her time as queen. I don't think she was meant to stay in Ternival forever—to marry and have a family here. And anyway, even if Mum were the rightful sovereign, she'd abdicate in a heartbeat."

"But if your mum abdicates, then *you* would be queen, right?"

Eva was silent again. "No," she finally said in a small voice. "That chapter of my family's story is over." Jack could tell this was difficult for her to say, like she was relinquishing a long-held secret dream.

Frankie had begun scratching at the lock of the box. It was frighteningly easy for Jack to forget that his brother wasn't actually a mole. Is this what would happen if they never changed back? Would they eventually lose their humanness? Would their lifespan shrink to whatever a small animal's lifespan was? Would—

"Oh!" Eva's tiny squeak broke through Jack's spiraling thoughts. "What if we trace back to the beginning, to the First Queen of Mesterra? She had no children, but she did have a nephew. Your grandfather Stokes! Which would make *your* mum her nearest kin, right?"

It'd never crossed Jack's mind. He couldn't imagine his mum here in Ternival at *all*, much less ruling over the whole thing. She'd always said that taking care of five children—plus Carrick Hall—was quite enough responsibility for her, thank you very much.

"Nah," he said. "She'd abdicate too."

"So, if Mrs. Addison abdicates, then the heir would be . . ."

They looked at Frankie. He was still happily scratching at the lock like he was trying to file his ridiculous nails. Jack couldn't imagine a *less* likely candidate for kingship, actually. So, if Frankie was off the roster, that meant Tilly was next in line—if anyone knew her whereabouts. And if not Tilly, then . . .

Jack himself.

Grand visions of ruling as king of Ternival filled his imagination. Maybe he *was* the Child of Tellus about whom the oracle had spoken! Maybe his failure with the giant was part of his training or something, the next step in his journey to greatness.

But then he snapped out of it. The likelihood of any Addison ruling Ternival was less than zero percent—especially if Mindra's power continued to grow. Especially if she kept turning humans into animals. Plus, if Frankie seemed like an unlikely prospect in his current condition, that disqualified Jack too.

"No," he concluded, "I imagine the stag had his reasons for sending the First Queen of Mesterra back to Carrick Hall, same as he did for your family. That chapter of our story is over too."

There was a sudden jolt as the bag began bouncing.

"Mindra is on the tower stairs again," Eva said. "I can tell by the way her footsteps echo, like they did when we arrived at Marisith. She's climbing back up."

"Then we should get out of here," Jack said, attempting to scramble upward, "now that we're out of those tunnels!" But the bag was bouncing so violently, there was no way they'd make it to freedom without falling to their deaths or alerting their captor.

He tried to ignore the feeling of dread that made him want to jump right out of here. Once Mindra arrived wherever she was headed, what then?

"I wonder about the people who ruled Mesterra, after the First Queen," Eva continued. She seemed determined not to worry about Mindra's next move. "The stories say that they, too, were Children of Tellus. That they somehow stumbled into Mesterra from our world through portals unknown. But we don't really know anything else about them. Their descendants ruled for generations and generations, though. Queen Ternivia, for instance. And her son Prince Wefan, who eventually founded Ternival. He married Andella the Archeress, and *their* descendants also ruled for a long, long time."

Jack now dredged up another vague detail from somewhere in his brain. "Didn't their royal line end when Mindra murdered that one king—that guy she married? And then she took control of Ternival."

Eva nodded solemnly. "Kador. Whom she'd deceived into matrimony. The stories say that at his death 'the heirs of Wefan and Andella perished or were lost.'"

"I wonder what *lost* means, exactly," Jack mused. "*Lost,* as in, no one could find them? Or *lost,* as in, they couldn't find their way to wherever they were going?"

"Or maybe not lost at all. Merely hidden."

Just then, the lock burst apart with a loud crack.

The bag stopped moving. For one terrifying moment, Jack thought the game was up. Mindra would look inside the bag and discover the busted snare, the liberated prisoners, the broken lock, and the extra mouse. But instead, she started climbing again—faster, this time.

"The fool!" the enchantress muttered. "He thought to unseat me. But the time has come to end it all, at last."

"Did you hear that?" Eva whispered after a moment. "Another set of footsteps, farther up the stairs. Oh, I wish we could warn whoever it is that she's coming!"

Frankie, meanwhile, had returned to the lock. He nudged aside the broken pieces till they fell off the box altogether.

And that gave Jack an idea.

By the time Mindra reached the top of the tower, he knew exactly what they needed to do.

Chapter

56

When Arash finally emerged with Elspeth and Zahra into the damaged passageway under Marisith, he felt like a blob of marmalade.

Cricket had been an enjoyable physical challenge, one that he'd begun to miss since he quit in May. But twenty-four hours of running, hiking, rowing, and climbing for his life—on a mostly empty stomach, in the company of relative strangers—was enough to make him forswear athletics forever.

As they rounded the bend where part of the ceiling had collapsed into a pile of rubble, he could hear muffled whispers on the other side. A small opening had been dug through the pile—thanks to Vahrberg's dwarves—and beyond it a small battery-powered torch flickered.

The whispers ceased as they drew near. The torch clicked off. The only light now came from the dryad's lantern, which Elspeth had carried through Mindra's tunnels. It'd glowed strangely down here— pulsing pink and ice-blue and yellow—as if some kind of urgent communication was happening that they couldn't understand. But now it blazed with its usual greenish light.

"That you, Ellie?" came Tilly's whisper.

"Yep. We made it." Elspeth's voice sounded as exhausted as Arash felt. He and Zahra followed her through the opening in the rubble, where the crew that had traveled by car was waiting. "How long have you been here?"

"Just arrived ourselves," Aurora replied.

"And Paxton's here too!" Georgie whispered excitedly. "We saw the Bentley parked at the base of the bluff. So that's where Aurora left the Rolls. She grabbed a torch from under the seat, and we were here in two shakes."

"If he's here, then we must hurry!" Zahra exclaimed. She rushed toward the steps that led up into the castle.

Arash and the others followed.

"But is there some kind of plan?" Tilly called from behind.

"How about, stop Paxton from giving Mindra the crown?" Elspeth called back.

Within seconds, they'd entered the foyer where the staircase spiraled up and away. But just as they reached the bottom step, Zahra halted.

"Charlie!" Aurora cried.

"Roar? What are you doing here?"

It was Heapworth, of course. Arash had forgotten all about the guy.

Charles stood in the stairwell, his face haggard, his clothes dirty and torn. But the gash on his forehead had somehow closed to a bluish scar, and his shoulder no longer drooped. In fact, he looked a thousand percent better than the last time Arash had seen him.

But then Charles spotted Arash. His face clouded, and he flung his arms across the stairwell to block it.

"Don't let that traitor move! He'll let his witchy boss know we're here, and then she'll be upon us in a moment."

Barkwhistler lunged forward, reaching for his tiny dagger. "Say that again, ye villainous smurd!" Georgie held him back.

"Charles!" Tilly sounded shocked. "It's Arash."

"Yeah, I know," Charles snapped. "We're best mates. We've hung out recently."

Zahra was trying to edge past Charles up the stairs. "Please, good sir, there's not a moment to lose. We must—"

"And I suppose you're in on it too." Charles glared at her.

"Charlie," Aurora said sternly, "don't be an idiot. Let them go. They're trying to stop Paxton from doing something stupid."

Charles hesitated. "Paxton?" He frowned, as if trying to remember something. "Maybe *that's* who it was. Someone came into the room where the witch kept me imprisoned, anyway. Found me on the floor and put his hand on my forehead . . . my shoulder . . ."

"Paxton healed you!" Georgie exclaimed. "Just like he did to Zahra."

Zahra, meanwhile, had grabbed Arash's arm and was bravely attempting to sidle by Charles a second time. But he spun around and blocked their way again.

"Come, now," Zahra said to him in a low voice. "To the winning side. Before 'tis too late."

"It's already too late," Charles growled. "You traitors aren't going anywhere except out of here. We're leaving, and you're coming with us."

The familiar rage gripped Arash's body. *Here we go again. I might actually hit the guy.* Then he felt a strange warmth where Zahra's hand touched his arm. The rage ebbed away as quickly as it had come.

"Stop calling them that!" Elspeth's own rage, apparently, was just getting started.

"Why should I?" Charles fired back. "I found the kid's metal detector in the witch's rooms. And then he—"

"Of *course* Mindra has Arash's metal detector," Tilly interrupted. "Because she took it from the valley, back home."

"You just don't like him, because he's different, because he's not from the Wolverns." Elspeth cut in again. "Well, guess what? Neither are you. You were born in London, for pity's sake." Then her eyebrows shot up. "I know! *You're* the one who's been sending those awful anonymous notes to the Rastegars!"

"What? What notes?" Aurora looked back and forth between them.

At that moment, Georgie—who'd let go of the groundhog and was bouncing around impatiently—seemed to lose all reason. He came plowing up the stairs toward Charles.

"Run, Zahra!" Georgie yelled. And then he bowled Charles right over.

"Spiffety-ho!" roared the groundhog. He launched himself onto the pile of arms and legs like it was a rugby match.

Amid the chaos, Zahra let go of Arash's arm and dashed up the stairwell. Arash followed. He could hear Elspeth and Aurora racing behind—and then, after a beat, Georgie's excited, "Wait for me!"

Above them, a growing din sounded like a stadium full of zoo animals. The noise grew louder and louder, until he and Zahra finally burst onto the topmost landing into a room of cages.

But Charles had been right. It was already too late.

"Give it a rest, Barkwhistler!" Tilly cried, pulling on the groundhog's furry arm. "Go help Zahra."

The rodent finally jumped off Charles, who was sprawled across the steps on his back, hands up in surrender.

"Move from this here spot while I'm gone," the groundhog snarled

at him, "and I'll betoodle yer poddynoggin." Then the creature scampered up the stairs.

Slowly Charles sat up, scowling.

Tilly observed him warily. Other than the fresh scar and the sad
state of his clothes, he looked no worse than if he'd fallen asleep on
the couch fully dressed. Even his mussed hair seemed calculated to
melt the hardest, least romantic of hearts.

But this time, Tilly wasn't swayed. She'd seen real ugliness in him.
Apparently, someone could be really gorgeous but capable of cruelty
and unreason. Sure, Tilly was no saint herself. But at least she knew
it and was willing to change.

Charles brushed himself off, still scowling, then got to his feet and
began to head back up the stairs. "C'mon. The kids are up there."

But now it was Tilly's turn to block the way. She pulled the anonymous note from her pocket and held it up. "Is it true?" She kept her
tone as neutral as possible.

Charles averted his eyes. "No."

And that was when it hit her. Of course! "It couldn't have been
you!" she exclaimed. "Because—"

He glanced at her with alarm.

"Oh, Charles . . ." Tilly wanted to shake him. "Why didn't you tell
me? Why haven't you told anyone?"

He grimaced. "Really? You can't imagine why? Look at me. Son
of Lord Edward Heapworth. Wolvern's star cricketer."

She threw her hands in the air. "Well, yes. It makes perfect sense,
of course. But you know I wouldn't blab to everyone, right? It's not
like you're the first person who struggles—"

"Struggles?" He gave a caustic laugh. "That's a good one. Can't *at
all,* more like."

"Aurora doesn't know?"

He shrugged. "Maybe, maybe not. Between boarding school and our parents' divorce, we've rarely lived in the same house for more than a few weeks at a time."

"And your dad?"

"He thinks I don't take academics seriously, that I don't try. That I'm set on embarrassing him. And he's right, I suppose . . ."

Tilly finally understood it all. Charles's outrageous confidence. His teasing and taunting—and, yes, bullying. It was all smoke and mirrors, designed to deflect attention from the shame he felt. To make others feel as badly as he did. But he needed to admit the truth. He needed to stop taking his feelings of worthlessness out on other people. And apologize to Arash. To everyone.

Tilly looked him full in the face.

"This can't continue," she said firmly. "You need to trust me. You need to trust everyone. And apologize—to Arash, especially. Shall I tell them, or will you?"

Chapter

57

By the time Zahra arrived at the top of the tower, she knew what she'd find.

Mindra, of course.

Twirling slowly among the stacked cages, her arms raised, somehow more awful and more fascinating than Zahra remembered. The enchantress's skin had taken on a sickly pall, as if her blood ran with venom. Her features no longer looked like those of a living, breathing human but of something else entirely, something from a nightmare. In the surrounding cages, the captive animals squawked or brayed or squealed with agitation, but the enchantress ignored them all.

At Mindra's feet lay a large embroidered bag. The same one, according to Paxton, that held the box of gems. The source of her disfiguring agony.

But that wasn't the only source. There was another.

The crown.

There it was, gleaming from atop the balding head of the thin, elderly man. He faced off with the enchantress, arms spread wide, hands open, just like Zahra's grandad. Strapped to his shoulders was the pack he'd been carrying at the hut.

Someone gripped Zahra's elbow. Elspeth. She'd arrived with Arash, Aurora, and Georgie and was now staring in horror at the drama unfolding in the center of the room.

"'Twas *thou,* all along!" Mindra hissed. Her horrible glare never left the old man's face. "Thy brethren were mere decoys. 'Twas thy plan, of course. Thou wert too cowardly to wrest it from the High Queen whilst she lived. But once she was dead . . ."

The old man, for his part, didn't flinch. Instead, to Zahra's surprise, he began advancing slowly.

"It's what you would've done in my stead, no doubt," he said. "For you have allowed your heart to become bent and your mind twisted, Mindra of Old. You cannot fathom anything but your own will. And yet the High Queen was chosen to wear the crown. And it was my choice to watch over them both, queen and crown alike."

"But mortals were never meant to wear it!" Mindra screeched. Her eyes bulged with fury. "You are but beasts, all of you. 'Tis *ours,* by rights. We, the Engela of Magister's own house. His first children and truest heirs. But once Magister grew soft—once he'd given away his power to such weak and foolish creatures—that's when I knew. His wisdom was not sound. He could no longer be trusted."

The old man seemed almost amused. "And who are you to question the work of the World-Weaver? There is a pattern of which you know nothing. It began before the first thread was ever shot through the warp of Time and will not end till the last weft of Worlds is finished." He continued to advance with a steadiness that was almost horrifying.

"I shall transform thee!" Mindra warned. But her voice wobbled.

"Ah, but this trinket shall do far worse to you, I fear," he said. His demeanor was so deadly calm that Zahra shivered. "It shall strip the false flesh from your false bones. It shall flay your twisted spirit into a thousand tiny shreds. That which you desire shall destroy you utterly, till there's naught left of you to wear it."

With every phrase, the old man advanced. The enchantress trembled, fear and outrage and torment on her face.

But then Mindra caught sight of the terrified group in the doorway. Her thin lips lifted in a cruel sneer. "'Tis thine own choice, traitor. Give me the crown, and the heirs go free. Or refuse and meet thy doom—and seal theirs as well."

The old man flicked a glance at the doorway, then turned back to Mindra.

"Set them all free," he bargained matter-of-factly. "Ternivali and Children of Tellus alike. Free them from their cages and enchanted bodies. And guarantee their safe passage to Tellus without condition. Do all this, Mindra of Old, and you shall have it."

"*No, uncle!*"

It was a boy's voice. Hoarse, unfamiliar.

Arash.

Speaking words that Zahra had learned from her grandad. And that Arash had learned from his. Speaking the mother tongue of Valan, the land beyond the mountains—which the people of Ternival called Valorenta.

Speaking to Paxton, the old man from Carrick Hall.

Whose real name was Pejman.

Arash couldn't recall the exact moment when he'd figured it out.

Maybe it was at the bottom of the stairs, just now, when he felt the calming peace of Zahra's hand. Or maybe it was when he saw the rune in her family's tapestry and ran his finger along the charred border. Or possibly earlier, when she spoke in Valanish from the depths of her fever dream—and called him by his grandfather's name.

Or it could've been when Paxton healed her. Or when the old man quoted Grandfather, in the moonlit woods, and their physical resemblance struck Arash like a blow. Or even further back, when Paxton had healed the dog . . .

Regardless, by the time Arash reached the top of the stairs, he'd put all the pieces together.

His grandfather's stories were true.

The three lost princes of Valan were real. And they were right here, in Ternival. In this very room.

Paxton was the eldest, of course, otherwise known as Pejman. And Zahra's grandad, the second brother, was Navid. And Grandfather, the youngest, was Shahin. Three brothers, separated in childhood. Sent away, for their own safety, to where Mindra could never find them.

And it had worked, for the most part. Pejman had ended up in England, near Carrick Hall, where he must've been raised by a local family. And Navid had found himself near Caristor, on the shores of the Pathless, where a fisherman had taken him in. And Shahin, Arash's grandfather, had stumbled into the land of their forebears, in the village on the Caspian Sea where all their stories had begun.

Each prince had preserved his fragment of the ancient tapestry from their father's palace. Each had learned one of the three runes of power that their ancestor, the weaver, had woven into the pattern. Each prince had hung his tapestry in his adopted land so he would never forget: He was part of a very great story, which no one could take away.

But Mindra had found them, at last.

She'd tracked the brothers down, determined to punish them for what their late father, the king, had done.

For it was he whose great-grandmother had been the only surviving heir of Wefan and Andella when the royal house of Ternival was destroyed. It was he who'd listened as a child, enrapt, to her tales about the crown and the long-lost gems, the slaughter of her family, and her flight over the mountains. And it was he who'd unexpectedly rediscovered the gems themselves and given them to the Selvedges, that Mindra might be overthrown and the slaughter of his ancestors redressed.

Thus, the three princes were Mindra's greatest enemies. And now Pejman—heir to both royal houses—was about to undo it all.

"*No, uncle!*" Arash called. But immediately he wished he hadn't.

Startled, Paxton glanced his way. And that was when Mindra moved.

Quick as an arrow, she threw her arms outward. The old man began to shrink and grow thinner, if that was possible. His long face elongated even more, while Arash's backpack fell from his shoulders with a thud. He arched his neck and flapped his arms awkwardly, as if ready to take flight, then rose a few feet into the air and molted into a long-legged gray heron.

The crown, which had slipped sideways on his avian head, began to fall. But before Mindra could snatch it, the heron stabbed at her with his substantial beak. Barkwhistler—who'd appeared from nowhere—charged, followed by a very excited, very unprepared Georgie.

Instinctively, Arash darted forward and dove for the crown. Two seasons of fielding for cricket hadn't gone to waste, apparently, for he caught it easily, then sprang to his feet and scrambled away. Not to the exit, but to the piles of cages stacked against the western wall. He vaulted upward, grasping for handholds like this was just another crevasse in the Wolverns, till he reached the large window that overlooked the Pathless.

Behind him, he could hear the enchantress fending off her attackers, shrieking with rage. He glanced over the sill. Mist swirled in thick patches, but straight down, the three large rocks, far below, were almost submerged by high tide. He shuddered. He'd better not lose his balance. Marisith was indeed over the sea.

Summoning all his willpower, he thrust the crown out the window and held it there.

"Not one more move, murderess," Arash croaked above the din, "or I shall drop it."

Everything stopped.

All eyes fixed on him. The animals froze in their cages, paralyzed with suspense. The heron and the groundhog halted in surprise. He couldn't see Georgie anywhere, but Zahra, Elspeth, and Aurora stood in the doorway, mouths open. And behind them, on the landing, were Tilly and Charles.

Arash's mouth went dry. Silence had fallen so completely, he could hear the galloping of his own heart and the distant breakers rolling toward shore.

"If thou shouldst drop it," came Mindra's voice, low and hateful, from the center of the room, "thy family's power shall be destroyed forever."

"*It is not true, cousin!*" Zahra called in Valanish, her voice shaking. "*Do not believe her.*"

Mindra ignored the girl. "Thy future shall cease. Thy past shall be erased. Thou shalt be known as the heir of destruction, the gravedigger who buried the hope of thy grandfather's grandfathers."

"*She is the queen of nothing but lies,*" Zahra insisted.

Mindra flinched, as if tempted to spin around and silence the girl for good. Instead, the enchantress kept her eyes fixed on Arash. "For thou art a wanderer with no home, whose story shall be taken from thee—"

But that was Mindra's mistake.

Because Arash knew better. He understood now what his grand-father had been trying to tell him.

"Taken?" Arash echoed hoarsely. "My story? Nah." He cleared his throat. "I've been silenced before, but it won't work on me now. It won't work on any of us."

He looked at the faces staring up at him. The heron cocked one eye as if to say, *That's it, lad.* Barkwhistler held his tiny dagger aloft as if awaiting Arash's signal. Somewhere in this maze of cages were Grandfather and Zahra's grandad. And countless other people whose worth couldn't be measured merely by the functions and instincts of their animal bodies. They, too, had stories to tell.

Arash looked at Zahra. Her eyes held a light of hope so strong, it would take a flood to quench it. He looked at Elspeth, Aurora, and Tilly, whose lives were now so intertwined with his that you couldn't narrate one tale without the others. Even Charles, whose expression had shifted from petulance to amazement—he had a part to play.

So, here in the castle of Marisith, on midsummer morning, Arash began to speak.

And once he started, it was as though a dam had burst. Words tumbled out. Beautiful, powerful, magical words. Poetry in the language of his heart, the language he'd whispered in secret for so long. And as he spoke, his voice grew stronger, his pronunciation more precise, the glad waterfall of Valanish like laughter on his tongue.

Here in the room of cages, he spoke the words of Shahin, the youngest prince of Valan, who'd been given the rune of deliverance.

And when the final word was spoken, Arash pulled the crown in toward his chest, then threw it with electric precision into the fog.

Chapter

58

Elspeth would remember what happened next to the end of her days.

The cages erupted. Animals burst forth with a din so thunderous, Elspeth couldn't hear Mindra screaming—which the enchantress was most certainly doing, for her eyes bulged, and her mouth had widened to a hideous red O. The cages not only broke open but also melted away, like mist. Soon nothing stood between the former captives and their captor. They were upon her in an instant.

Elspeth ducked and ran with the lantern toward the wall near the doorway. From the corner of her eye, she glimpsed Charles and Tilly bolting back down the stairs from the landing. Elspeth felt a flash of anger. How could Tilly stick with *that guy* instead of staying with her own family? Elspeth herself wasn't about to leave without Georgie. The kid was nowhere to be seen, however—although Barkwhistler was expertly dodging feet while chasing a tiny striped rodent with enormous cheeks.

Elspeth slid against the wall. Aurora was already crouched there. But Zahra, apparently, had leaped into the mob.

Despite Mindra's diminished power, she was still incredibly strong.

Creatures attacked, but she threw them off, fighting her way outward. And she must've snatched up the embroidered bag again, at some point, for it was strapped across her chest. Shielding it with one gloved hand, she fought bitterly with the other, her aim focused, forceful. She wasn't about to lose this treasure too.

Then Aurora gripped Elspeth's arm. She pointed to the high window, where Arash was clinging desperately to the sill. Without cages to stand upon, there was nothing but air between his feet and the distant floor. Then a pair of birds swooped up. A banded falcon and the long-legged heron grasped Arash's pullover with their toes and talons, beating their wings furiously to stay aloft. They weren't powerful enough to carry him, but they managed to break his fall. He landed like a parachutist with a bump.

Someone slid against the wall next to her. Zahra was back, holding what looked like a shapeless pile of white and black feathers in her arms. Yet another bird of some kind. Elspeth couldn't tell if it was lifeless or merely limp—but tears streaked Zahra's face. She was speaking rapidly, something about Grandad, his illness, and needing Paxton's help.

At that moment, Mindra broke free. Mere yards away, she sent creatures spinning, left and right, till there was nothing between her and the doorway—nothing except three terrified girls huddled against the wall.

Never before had Elspeth been this close to an actual predator. Mindra's face lacked any hint of compassion or empathy, any sign of humanity at all, and Elspeth felt a horror so primal, it rooted her to the spot.

Zahra, by contrast, seemed to have finally overcome it. She thrust the bird at Elspeth, then stood and blocked the doorway. Arms out, hands open, just like Paxton. But before she could say a word, hooves clattered across the flagstones. Some kind of boar with huge tusks was hurtling through the crowd. He bumped Zahra briskly to the side and then, with a satisfied grunt, knocked Mindra clean off her feet, across the landing, and down the stairs.

At first, no one moved. It was as though they'd been enchanted all over again. But then the entire mob rose with a roar like a tidal wave and stampeded down the stairwell after the enchantress. Soon the room was almost empty.

The girls picked themselves up off the floor.

"Gosh, that was brave of you, Zahra!" Aurora said.

The fisherman's granddaughter, clearly shaken, reached out to Elspeth, who handed her the bird. The creature was alive. Elspeth had felt the flutter of its heartbeat, the warmth of its body. But how long could it last?

Arash ran up. He was toting his backpack, the one that had fallen from Paxton's shoulders, his face flushed with excitement. Overhead, the falcon and the heron circled in one big arc, then flew out of the high window.

"C'mon!" Arash said in that raspy, unfamiliar voice. "We can't let her get away!"

Elspeth grabbed the dryad's lantern, and the four friends dashed down the stairs. At the bottom, a flood of figures was swirling through the foyer toward the open postern door. In addition to the throng from the tower, humans in medieval armor were now surging up from the tunnels, along with what Elspeth realized were dwarves in battle gear—dwarves! They were accompanied by an unfamiliar band of creatures led by a large mastiff.

"To the shore!" the mastiff bellowed. "She survived the stairs and has fled over the cliff, but she must be stopped."

"'Tis Fangard!" Zahra gasped.

"The Selvedge remnant is here!" said Arash.

The four of them joined the flood. It swept them out the door, through the courtyard, and under an open archway, where the portcullis had been battered to bits. But as the rest of the crowd raced toward the woods, Zahra and Arash halted in amazement.

"What's the matter?" Elspeth shouted over the chaos.

"The trees," Arash shouted back hoarsely. "They weren't like this before."

Surrounding the castle, growing right up to the courtyard walls, was the densest forest Elspeth had ever seen. The trees stood almost trunk to trunk, covering every inch of the peninsula like some vast, immovable army. But it wasn't immovable, she realized. The trees were actually moving. And not just waving in a breeze either. They were advancing steadily, their roots trailing in great strands while their branches swung like mighty arms. And slipping between the trunks came a host of dryads.

Arash began to run toward a break in the woods, where the trees had parted for the Selvedges to pass. "C'mon! There's another secret tunnel down to the shore."

Within minutes, they were trailing the last of the Selvedges through a narrow underground passage. In the dim light, the dryad's lantern pulsed with an angry blood-red flame. The trees were *not* playing, apparently. This was war.

Soon Elspeth and her companions burst onto the fogbound beach. The entire company of Selvedges was rushing toward the peninsula's distant point, which had disappeared into swirling mist. She craned her neck. Georgie, Tilly, and Charles were nowhere to be seen. But a pack of hounds was racing back along the beach toward them. And above the pack soared a flock of Ternivali birds.

"There's Hotosho!" a voice called from the crowd. "The hounds are returning."

Moments later, two magpies landed on the beach.

"Bad news," one of them announced. "Mindra fled by boat to sea. And she eluded our birds in the fog."

"Alas, friends," said the other. "The enchantress has escaped."

Cries of dismay echoed along the bluffs. Mindra had found Zahra's rowboat, of course. Without realizing it, the group from the hut had provided the enchantress with her means of escape.

Elspeth's heart sank. The gems were now gone for good—along with their only hope of ever returning home.

But even worse, Frankie and Eva were gone too.

And she'd probably never see them again.

Jack limped along in the shadows of what had been the room of cages.

Even if he made it to the landing, how would he manage the steps? They were steep and made of unforgiving stone, and his leg was bad. *Really* bad.

Which was his own fault. When the cages had burst open, Jack, Frankie, and Eva had attempted to exit the bag. But Jack hadn't moved fast enough. He'd zigged away from Mindra's bag, but he hadn't zagged—and then someone had trampled him underfoot.

Gingerly, he reached the landing and paused at the top of the stairs.

And that was when he heard it.

The familiar snuffling behind him. The soft padding of feet.

But this time, before he could react, the thing pounced. It grabbed him between its teeth with a happy little yowl and immediately took off down the stairs.

Jack didn't even bother to fight. The harder he struggled, the tighter those sharp teeth would clamp—and so far, they hadn't punctured his skin. He lay still, amazed that he hadn't passed out. Amazed that he'd evaded this thing for so long. Amazed that he wasn't dead.

Soon they reentered the underground tunnel system. So, this was where it would end, after all. The thing would drag him down to its awful lair, and then . . . the final sentence of Jack's story.

But at a certain point, the downward slope of the tunnel evened out. Daylight came from somewhere up ahead. And before long, the creature emerged onto a gray beach in the open air. It trotted through a crowd of animals and people, then stopped.

"Bem!" a girl's voice exclaimed. "Wherever did you come from? And drop that poor mouse, you naughty thing."

A rash jumped back as the ginger cat dropped a small gray mouse at Zahra's feet.

It was one thing for a normal cat to show off its hunting prowess, but it was appalling if the feline was actually a human. Like Bem, apparently, who now twined around Zahra's ankles, purring with pride.

The mouse, by contrast, seemed to have collapsed from shock. But it wasn't injured, as far as Arash could tell. It just lay there, eyes closed, tiny chest heaving.

"Poor fellow," said Aurora. She reached down.

"Ew!" Elspeth said. "Don't touch it. Probably has fleas."

"But how on earth did Bem get here?" Aurora asked the fisherman's granddaughter.

Zahra shook her head, clearly baffled.

"Oh!" Elspeth said. "Do you think she hopped into one of the cars on the drive near Carrick Hall? Before they crashed through the frame?"

The cat meowed in confirmation.

At that moment, a small striped rodent with the biggest cheeks

Arash had ever seen came skittering up. It was a chipmunk. Not native to England but still recognizable. And oblivious to the presence of a fanged predator. It zipped around the group excitedly, like it was trying to tell them something, then took off again into the throng.

"Get back here, ye bitty snert!" Barkwhistler's chunky body swerved around a flock of hens as he gave chase. "Or I'll tromp yer poddynoggin!"

"Any sign of Georgie?" Aurora asked. "Or Charlie and Tilly?"

"I thought I saw—" Elspeth began, but she was interrupted by a loud cry.

Zahra had collapsed to her knees. She was bent over the bundle of pied feathers she'd been carrying and now rocked back and forth, her voice like a lone gull on a desolate shore. Quickly Arash knelt beside her. He had no idea why the rune of deliverance began pouring from his mouth again. But out it flowed, louder and louder, till it echoed from the bluffs like a call to arms. And as Arash spoke, the falcon and the heron descended swiftly, as if to lend him their silent, invisible strength.

When the last words died away, a tremor like an earthquake passed through the company. And then, to Arash's astonishment, the animals began to change. Not all of them, of course. But those that had once been human expanded, lost their fur and feathers, and stood upright in human garments. Before he could even grasp what was happening, Arash and his grandfather were embracing and weeping and laughing, there on the shores of the Pathless Sea.

"O, wonder!" cried the old man, gazing at the company on the beach. "How many goodly creatures are there here! How beauteous mankind is! O brave new world, that has such people in't!"

Arash grinned. Grandfather was back. Quoting Shakespeare, as usual.

"Jack!" Elspeth dropped to the sand, her middle brother sprawled awkwardly where the mouse had been. The kid seemed to be having trouble getting up, but Arash couldn't tell if it was because Elspeth wouldn't stop hugging him or because something was wrong with his leg.

"Where's Georgie?" Jack kept asking. "Did he make it out with the others?"

"If Mindra turned him into that batty chipmunk, I think he's around here somewhere," Aurora said.

The ginger cat had vanished, and now a red-haired girl in a rustic tunic stood in its place. "Mum!" the girl cried. She ran toward a middle-aged woman who wore a rough kirtle and headscarf. "Oh, my Bem!" The woman wrapped her arms around the girl, weeping and laughing. "My brave, sweet lass!"

All around them, the sounds of joyful reunion filled the air. Mindra may have escaped, but her enchantments were broken.

Yet not all was well.

An old man whom Arash didn't recognize lay crumpled on the nearby shingle. Eyes closed, utterly still, he wore a lightweight kurta over loose trousers, and Zahra was gripping his hand anxiously. Paxton, no longer a heron, knelt swiftly and rested his palm on the man's chest, while Arash's grandfather drew near and knelt at the man's feet.

Then Paxton began to speak. In the same lilting cadence as Arash, he uttered the rune of restoration, the prayer for healing—but this time, his voice grew louder and stronger till it boomed along the bluffs and out to sea.

As the last words left Paxton's lips, the old man on the sand took a great breath and let it out slowly, color returning to his skin. He opened his eyes. At the sight of Zahra, a slow smile spread across his face. Then he noticed Paxton and the professor. His expression became pure wonder.

"*Is it you?*" he whispered in Valanish. "*You at last?*"

"*It is I, your own Shahin,*" said Arash's grandfather. His eyes twinkled behind their smudged spectacles, and Arash could tell he was very, very happy.

"*And I am, Pejman,*" said Paxton. For the first time possibly ever, the handyman from Carrick Hall cracked a smile that wasn't immediately eclipsed by grim stoicism. "*And you are our brother Navid, of course. For you still have that scar on your palm from when you tripped and fell on the ramparts.*"

Zahra's grandad grinned slyly. "*I did not trip. I was pushed. And you, elder brother, I would know anywhere by that long, melancholy face.*"

Paxton chuckled.

"*And you, younger brother,*" continued the fisherman to Arash's grandfather, "*you always had your nose buried in a book.*"

"'*Tis still the case,*" said Grandfather, smiling.

Paxton shuddered. "*I never was one for book learning. Otherwise, I might've visited your shop, Shahin, long before now.*"

"*Such a small village too,*" Grandfather observed, studying his oldest brother keenly.

Paxton shrugged. "*I've kept to myself. Attended to those at Carrick Hall, all these years. Probably shouldn't have. Missed out on a lot.*" He glanced at Arash. "*Meeting this grandnephew of mine, for one.*"

"*Take heart, elder brother,*" said Grandfather. "*For though time seems out of joint, we bear no spite. Grace abounds to make things right. And look at what great things your rune has done!*"

Nearby, Jack now stood up with ease. Indeed, any humans or creatures that had sustained wounds were healed.

Suddenly sunlight broke through the mist. The fog, which remained dense and dark over deeper water, obscuring the horizon, had begun to clear from the bay.

"Look!" cried one of the magpies. "To the south. Do you see it?"

Everyone turned. Arash expected to see the empty ridge of the southern peninsula where once a castle had stood. But there, shimmering in the midsummer sunlight, were the elegant towers of Ternival's royal house.

Paxton's rune hadn't merely restored the bodies of living creatures. It had also healed Caristor.

Chapter

60

As the crowd of Selvedges took off joyfully toward the southern peninsula, Elspeth found herself standing on the beach below Marisith, surrounded by people from home.

Aurora, Paxton, Arash, Jack, and Professor Rastegar were here—plus, some of their new friends from Ternival, including Zahra and her grandad. Meanwhile, red-haired Bem and a kind-looking woman, whom Elspeth took to be Bem's mother, also hovered nearby, observing the strangers from Tellus with shy fascination.

"Georgie?" Jack kept saying. He shielded his eyes and gazed up and down the beach. "Where'd the kid go?"

Aurora pointed. "There's Charlie! And Tilly!"

Sure enough, their older siblings were approaching across the sand. But what was Charles carrying? Some kind of long-handled instrument that reminded her of Dad's weed cutters. But no. It was Arash's metal detector.

Elspeth clenched her teeth, ready to light into Charles again. But one look at her sister's pleading eyes, and she pressed her lips together. Whatever was going on, it was up to Charles to make things right.

"Jack!" Tilly cried and grabbed her brother in a fierce hug.

Jack reciprocated distractedly. "Seen Georgie?"

Tilly shook her head.

"We keep telling you," Elspeth cut in, "he's around here some-where."

Charles now held out the detector to Arash, his expression concil-iatory.

"That was a brilliant bit of fielding up there, mate," Charles said. There was a hint of an apology in his tone.

Time seemed to stop. Arash didn't move. Lord Edward's son con-tinued awkwardly holding out the instrument, his jaw working, like he wanted to say more but couldn't find the courage.

Finally, without a word, Arash accepted the detector and turned away. Professor Rastegar gave his grandson a concerned glance, but he, too, said nothing.

"Oi, there you are, Georgie!" Jack suddenly yelled.

The youngest Addison came running up, his mouth closed, for once. He was dancing around like he was ready to burst. Barkwhistler came puffing after him.

"Chased the errant oofengop all over the blasted beach!" the groundhog said irritably.

"C'mon, Georgie," Jack urged. "Spit it out."

But just then, Tilly gasped. Elspeth followed her gaze farther down the shore. Could it be? Was that Frankie and Eva? Coming toward them across the shingle? But how . . .

"They made it out after all!" Jack exclaimed.

And that was when Georgie gobbed something out of his mouth.

At first, Elspeth thought it was one of those small plush pouches from a jewelry shop. Except it wasn't cinched at the top. So, as it landed on the sand, the jagged square of black velvet fell open to re-veal what looked like tiny stars. Glorious music, like distant bells, burst into the air.

Elspeth caught her breath.

The gems! From the crown of Ternival. All six of them, rescued somehow from the velvet-lined box in Mindra's bag.

"You did it, Georgie!" Eva cried as she and Frankie came running up.

Both looked exhausted and disheveled—especially Eva, whose fashionable wrap skirt was a crumpled mess and whose ginger-blond curls stuck out in every direction. And no wonder: She'd endured an overnight flight before any of this had even started.

Frankie, meanwhile, wore that gaunt, annoyed expression their mother called hangry. His freckles stood out on his pale face, and he blinked in the sunlight like it pained him. But Elspeth didn't care. She threw herself at her brother and Eva, wrapping her arms around both their necks at once. The rest of the siblings soon joined in a sweaty, awkward group hug.

"But what on earth happened?" Elspeth asked as they finally pulled away. "How did Georgie get the gems? And how did you all escape?"

Everyone began talking at once.

"And then Arash made that brilliant catch." Georgie's voice soon drowned out the rest. "And Mindra turned me into a chipmunk— which was the best thing *ever*. The place went bonkers, of course, but I was a lot closer to the ground than usual, so I could see how Mindra's bag was sort of squirming, like something was in there. So, I wriggled inside, and there they all were—"

"We couldn't really talk to him," Eva cut in. "But we knew it was Georgie, because we'd had front row seats from the mouth of the bag to everything Mindra was doing—including Georgie's transformation."

"You and Jack did," Frankie clarified. "I might as well have been blind. Weirdest twenty-four hours of my life . . ."

"Anyway, somehow they'd broken the lock on the box," Georgie

plunged on, "and chewed away a section of velvet lining from inside
it. And they were trying to wrap up the gems in the velvet without
touching them."

"Which was tricky," Jack added. "Because the bag kept getting
bumped—plus, at any moment we might've been squashed by all the
feet tromping about."

"Georgie ended up stuffing the whole bundle into one of his huge
cheek pouches," Eva said, "and all four of us escaped unnoticed before Mindra picked up the bag again."

"Oh!" Tilly exclaimed. "Now that we have the gems, can we try
to go home?"

There was a startled pause.

"But won't we need to find someplace with a closer connection to
Carrick Hall?" Aurora asked. "Some kind of landmark?"

"Ley lines!" Georgie shouted for what felt like the umpteenth
time.

"Caristor, most likely," Paxton surmised.

"That'd be *brilliant*," Frankie said, beaming. "I've always wanted to
see the place."

Eva looked as though she might burst into happy tears. "Me too."

"If only Mother were here . . ." Zahra said softly. She took her
grandad's hand. "She'd finally get to see the Hall of Tapestries."

"You should proceed to the castle anyway," the fisherman said to
Paxton. "It's your rightful—"

"Enough chatting," Paxton interrupted gruffly. "Time to go."

"Oh, please, please. Can we take the cars?" Georgie begged. "We'll
get there faster."

Charles's eyebrows shot up. He glanced around in bewilderment.
"Wait. The cars are *here*?"

Aurora ignored him. "Makes sense to me. I can take six if we
smush together."

"*You?*" Charles said.

Paxton made a quick tally. "Sixteen of us, with the whistle-pig. I'll take another six, and the rest can ride on the outside."

Barkwhistler chuckled. "Me gran used to call us that. Whistle-pigs."

"You mean, on the boot? The bonnet? The *bumpers?*" Georgie's eyes were so big, Elspeth thought they'd pop right out of his head.

The whole crew now headed to where the cars were parked at the base of the bluff.

"What the——" Charles stared at the Silver Shadow, aghast. The little scratch he'd put on the bonnet was nothing to what Aurora had done to Lord Edward's beloved car.

"It'll be all right," Aurora reassured her brother. "If we ever see Dad again, he won't care about the Rolls. What he cares about is us." Before Charles could respond, she retrieved the keys from under a rock by the front tire and hopped into the driver's seat. "Next stop, Caristor!" she called.

But a sudden rumble from the bluff stopped everyone in their tracks. They looked up.

"Please tell me that's not the giant," Jack said faintly.

"Nay," said Paxton, shielding his eyes. "D'you see the trees? They're moving."

"Look!" Georgie cried.

And now Elspeth could see it too. The army of trees and dryads was dismantling the courtyard walls of Marisith. The watchtower was coming undone.

Everyone began cheering.

"But——Frankie's briefcase!" Tilly gasped. "I didn't get the chance to search for it. When Charles and I ran down to Mindra's chambers, we were so focused on finding Arash's metal detector."

Eva looked at Frankie sorrowfully. "*The Writ of Queens.* Your lovely illustrations."

Frankie shrugged. "Losing them is worth it if Mindra can't ever rule from Marisith again. Plus, I made copies."

"Still . . ." Eva took his hand.

"Pardon the rush," Paxton said, "but we really must be going."

Within minutes, they were all piled in—and on—the cars, racing to Caristor.

It was the wildest ride of Elspeth's life. Aurora and Paxton hurtled along the sand like rallycross drivers, their passengers shrieking with either terror or delight. Georgie, Barkwhistler, and Frankie rode, whooping, on the Rolls's bumpers, while Jack and Arash clung to the boot of the Bentley.

Soon the cars reached the mouth of a river and careened up a dirt track that joined the main road. As they crossed a stone bridge and climbed the wooded bluffs on the other side, they began to pass groups of Selvedges that were headed to the castle. The foot travelers stepped aside, astonished, when the cars roared past—although some of the Ternivali cheered and waved. A trio of hounds ran alongside them for a while, then abandoned chase, tongues lolling.

As the cars wound along the bluffs and passed a scattered pile of barrels, Elspeth wondered, with a pang, if she'd ever return to Ternival. She'd been here hardly more than a few hours, and already they were preparing to leave. Would she revisit this forest, this bay of the Pathless? Would she ever see these creatures again?

Before long, they pulled up to the open, welcoming gates of Caristor.

And there, lounging against the archway—as if awaiting the ten-fifty to Paddington Station—was a tall, lean figure in a fashionable blazer.

Chapter

61

"Dad!" Aurora shrieked and launched herself from the car into her father's arms.

Tilly stared blankly at Lord Edward. He was here? In Ternival? But—

The cars emptied in an instant, and soon Lord Edward was surrounded by the whole chattering company—all except Charles, who hung back apprehensively. But the gentleman strode through the crowd and embraced his son.

"Arms, Charlie," said Lord Edward as his son froze. "They go round your dear old dad, like so." He didn't let go till Charles responded in kind.

Lord Edward then turned to Tilly. "And *very* good to see you, too, Matilde. Not sure how you managed to preserve that glorious topknot all night, but it'll set the Ternivali fashion trends for years, no doubt." Tilly sensed by his twinkling eyes that both she and Charles were forgiven. She smiled sheepishly.

Aurora's dad now glanced at the Rolls, then over at his grubby daughter. "And you, Rora, have developed a fine taste for motorsport, I see," he said with a wry grin. "Watched you and the Bentley bomb across the beach, in fact—fairly certain it was a tie, too, although I'd say Paxton is a *bit* more experienced. I happened to be having a lovely chat with a pair of magpies, at the time, who regaled me with the tales of your dazzling exploits. Bit startling to be addressed by feathered persons, to be honest. But considering I'd just been chasing the stag up and down the Wolverns—and hurtling through the space-time continuum, or whatever your frame does to a person, Ellie—I'd say I handled it rather well."

"The stag?" Aurora asked, her eyes wide. "From our tapestry? And you got here through the Addisons' frame? What *happened,* Dad?"

He waved a hand. "Details, details. The point is, you're all accounted for—with limbs intact, no less—and the portal thingy will stay open at least till midnight, according to jolly Mrs. F. She's out on the front porch, by the way, having a lovely snooze."

"Wait—Mrs. Fealston is *here*?" Eva cried.

"Wouldn't have stayed behind if I'd chained her," he replied breezily. "She'll be relieved to see you lot, that's for sure."

"Let's go inside!" Georgie shouted.

But Aurora planted herself in front of her father, arms crossed. "Dad, stop blathering and tell us how you got here. And more importantly, do you know how we can get back?"

"Ah, one can always count on one's offspring to name one's flaws in spectacularly public ways," Lord Edward said with an exaggerated sigh. "But, yes, my child. I shall oblige with the shortest long story possible. Walk with me, and I'll show you. This place is a first-rate pile, by the way. And just wait till you see the gallery . . ."

Then, as if conducting a tour of his own Wolvern Court, Lord Edward led the way through the courtyard, up the sweeping front steps, and into the Great Hall of Caristor.

Tilly paused on the threshold. Ternival's royal house was just as glorious as Frankie's stories had described. Carven stone pillars rose to the vaulted ceiling, where numerous birds flitted around excitedly, and the walls were hung with shining shields. Banqueting boards lined the perimeter, while a large open space in the middle housed a massive wrought-iron fire ring.

But Lord Edward breezed through the Great Hall without stopping. Beyond it was a long, bright gallery. Light flooded the large room from tall windows that overlooked the Pathless, while the floor sparkled with beautiful marble flagstones. Best of all, between the windows, magnificent weavings hung from floor to ceiling. It was the famous Hall of Tapestries.

Lord Edward slowed, inhaled luxuriously, and spread wide his arms. "Behold!" he announced, "the finest collection of tapestries in this—and any other—world."

Next to Tilly, Zahra and the fisherman halted. They gazed around the gallery in awe, their eyes shining with delight or sorrow—Tilly wasn't sure which. As the rest of the group fanned out, Elspeth and Aurora joined Zahra and her grandad in a slow, wonder-filled tour. Professor Rastegar followed, accompanied by Arash and Jack, while Frankie and Eva stood in the center of the room, simply drinking it all in. Only Charles, of all the company, seemed uninterested. He stuck close to Tilly, as if wanting to tell her something.

"Sister!"

She turned to see Goldleaf approaching with a broad smile, arms extended. Behind her was a small company of dryads.

"What on earth are *those*?" Charles exclaimed under his breath.

Tilly ignored him and instead reached for Goldleaf's hands. "Was that you?" she asked. "Were you the one who convinced the dryads and trees to join the Selvedges against Marisith?"

Goldleaf smiled at her. "Aye. But 'twas your persuasive speech I used to change their hearts."

Across the room, Elspeth glanced at them, then looked away again.

Georgie, meanwhile, was darting every which way, exclaiming over the tapestries. "Oooh, this one's got ships in it!" he hollered. And, "D'you suppose this island is Islagard?" Or, "That queen's got a longbow!" But then his excitement changed to confusion. "Hang on!" he said. "Isn't this Carrick Hall?"

Everyone rushed over. Sure enough, a small framed tapestry on the wall featured the unmistakable manor house set against the familiar backdrop of the Wolvern Hills.

Tilly peered closer. "The smoke from the chimney," she said, incredulous. "Is it *moving*?"

Frankie joined her. "And I recognize this as the frame from our house, if I'm not mistaken."

"Marvelous, eh?" Lord Edward said, beaming. "Mrs. F. is the genius who figured it all out, of course. When I showed up at the Hall again, early this morning—after following the stag, you see, who'd apparently gotten bored with *our* tapestry at the Court, for he'd vanished right out of it and begun cavorting about the hills—the intrepid old lady answered the door, spry as a spring chicken. And she wasn't the least bit surprised when I asked, 'You wouldn't happen to have seen a rather large stag wandering about, would you?'"

"Dad," Aurora warned, "cut to the chase."

"Right you are, m'dear. So. Good ole Mrs. F. showed me Frankie's frame on the table and explained everything. And then she insisted we hop through it ourselves, at once, before midsummer was over, using some sort of picture."

"Oh! Did you find one of Frankie's old sketches?" Elspeth interrupted. "He used to keep a bunch at the Hall, up in the studio."

"They're all at Cambridge now, though," Frankie countered.

"A fine suggestion," Lord Edward replied, "and one that works brilliantly, I'm told. But as it happened, I was already in possession of the very thing we needed. You see, the frame was the original home of the castle tapestry I'd finally tracked down in London—"

"Begging your pardon," said a raspy voice. It was still so unusual for Arash to speak that everyone turned. "A tapestry of a castle, you say?"

Next to Tilly, Zahra gasped. "The third rune!" She looked at Paxton. Some unspoken communication seemed to pass between them, for she clammed up again.

But Lord Edward apparently hadn't heard her. "Righto," he said to Arash. "Exquisite piece of work it is too. Anyway, as soon as I framed the thing, the standards on the battlements began rippling in the breeze, and we felt ourselves tugged forward. And then—voilà! Popped out here, in the gallery. And the rest you know."

"So, that's how you got *here*," Aurora said. "But how will everyone get *back*?"

"Oh, did I forget that part?" Lord Edward replied cheerfully. "Turns out, jolly Mrs. F. is a positive expert on such things. And she would've explained it to you sweet urchins, as well, if you'd bothered to stick around." He gave his daughter a look of mild reprimand. "I'm sure she'd be happy to explain. She's just through those doors."

"C'mon, Ellie, Rora," said Georgie. "I think he means we should apologize."

Lord Edward tapped his forehead with a knowing smile. "Genius, that one," he said. "Come, Charlie. Whilst they make amends, so shall we."

Charles glanced at Tilly with raised eyebrows, then turned reluctantly and followed his father.

And that was when they heard it. Again.

The sound of a hunting horn.

Chapter

62

When the Selvedge army strode through the open castle doors, banners aloft, Jack fought a sinking feeling in his chest.

The last time he'd seen most of these guys, he'd just committed the worst mistake of his life. He'd endangered every single one of them, including their fearless leader—who hadn't survived. What must they think of him now?

But the first Selvedge who entered the castle wasn't someone who Jack knew. This was an impressive, stern-faced warrior in full armor, sitting astride a chestnut warhorse that looked ready for another skirmish.

"It's Lord Bayard!" Zahra exclaimed next to Jack. "Ternival's Chief Sentry! Mindra had transformed him at Marisith, but he's been restored."

The fellow was flanked on one side by Vahrberg and the dwarves, and on the other by Fangard and the wolfhounds. Dozens upon dozens of sentries followed—some on horseback, some on foot—accompanied by flocks of excited birds and hordes of cheering

Ternivali. Despite their bedraggled appearance, the remnant held their heads high in triumph.

The warhorse cantered to the center of the room, and Bayard swiftly dismounted.

"Friends and fellow Selvedges!" the Chief Sentry called, his powerful voice echoing around the Great Hall. "Honored guests from Tellus." He bowed in the direction of Paxton and Professor Rastegar, who bowed in return. "In the long, desperate hours since Mindra's giants appeared, it has been mine honor to bear witness to your great deeds of bravery. Because of you, the fell enchantress has fled this realm, the crown's gems have been recovered, and the crown itself has been cast into the depths of the sea."

As the room erupted in cheers, Bayard gave Arash an approving nod.

"And now," the Chief Sentry continued, "because we, the Selvedge remnant, can finally lay down our arms, I propose a feast to celebrate our deliverance and restoration!"

Immediately the hall filled with laughter and singing and the clinking of weapons being thrown aside. One of the dwarves lit a fire in the center ring, and in short order, the boards were set with a bountiful feast, raided from the stores that had remained intact down in the castle's larders and dairies.

Everyone was starving, apparently, from the smallest stoat to Bayard's mighty horse. Jack soon found himself seated on a bench near the head table, surrounded by the company from Tellus, all of whom were digging in with gusto. Nevertheless, there seemed to be plenty for everyone, including seconds, thirds, and even—for Georgie—fourths.

Then, partway through the meal, Lord Bayard climbed upon a chair and hefted a stone chalice above his head. The hall grew quiet.

"A toast," the Chief Sentry announced. His bold tenor had grown solemn. "To the memory of our fallen counselor, best of centaurs. We remember Lord Starwise, son of Stormrunner, son of Moongazer, whose ancestors long dreamt of this day. May he know rest eternal!"

Mugs and cups were lifted around the hall. "We remember Lord Starwise!"

This was supposed to be the moment.

This was when Starwise himself would reappear.

Just like in the fairy tales. The castle doors would crash open, and the fallen mentor would march in—preferably in a white garment with sunlight blazing behind him—not dead, after all. Death would prove to be a boringly uncreative narrative device that wouldn't get the last word. There were so many cooler ways to end a story.

But this wasn't one of those moments.

During the ensuing silence, which seemed to go on and on and on, Jack wanted to crawl under the bench. All of this was his fault. And everyone knew it. He felt as worthless and unlikable as a mouse.

But then the dryads began to dance.

First, they moved in a slow, funereal procession. *Such is the way of things,* their movements seemed to say. *Life and death, hurting others and being hurt, messing up and trying again. In this world—same as any other—you will have trouble. You'll* make *trouble—and not in a good way. But take heart. Trouble won't last forever. You aren't alone.*

Jack began to feel slightly better. But only slightly.

Then a dryad with a strange sort of lute began to play. The treelike women now shifted into a circular folk dance that grew faster and livelier as the music continued. In and out the dryads wove, their faces alight with joy. And soon they were joined by others—including, to Jack's surprise, Tilly, who flung herself into the swirling circles as if she'd been dancing with dryads all her life.

Eventually, for reasons Jack never could explain, the clasped hands and laughing faces began to stir a longing inside him. He wanted, more than anything, to make things right.

And he wasn't the only one. A tall, awkward youth, whose right eye sported a fading yellow bruise, passed behind Jack's bench. The youth was accompanied by a familiar figure: old Smithfield, the sentry who'd expressed such paranoia about traitors—and whose son, Lepp, was presumed lost at Marisith. But of course! The youth *was* Lepp. Who'd once been the stray dog.

"C'mon, Dad," Lepp was saying. "I want ye to meet the fellow that saved me life."

At the next trestle over, Arash was sitting near Zahra with their grandfathers between them. As Lepp and his father approached, the kid glanced up, then quickly averted his eyes. Smithfield, for his part, ground to a halt. But Professor Rastegar rose, grasped Lepp by both shoulders, and gave him a hearty embrace.

Zahra's grandad likewise rose, and so did she. Introductions followed—not that Jack could hear them over the general din. Smithfield continued to keep his distance, armed crossed, while Lepp made some sort of halting speech. But he hadn't even finished before Zahra gave him a fierce, spontaneous hug. And then even Arash finally stood, took Lepp's hand, and shook it with a cautious smile.

The sudden relief in Lepp's demeanor was like a bolt of lightning through Jack's brain.

It was now his turn. He had his own apologies to make.

Gathering his courage, he got to his feet and approached the boards where Vahrberg, Fangard, and the other dwarves and hounds were seated, heartily devouring what looked a ten-year supply of beef jerky. A stony silence fell.

"Er, sorry to interrupt," Jack began. This was much harder than Lepp had made it look. "I . . . er . . . want to apologize. What I did at Marisith was stupid. Worse than stupid. I had no business trying to take down that giant. My behavior endangered all of you, but especially Starwise." Jack gulped. "I can't bring him back. But I'll try to live a life worthy of his sacrifice. And I hope someday you can forgive me."

Silence continued for another beat. "You are forgiven, Child of Tellus," Fangard said in his loud voice—louder than was necessary, really.

The Great Hall grew quiet as every eye turned their way.

"We grieve our fallen leader. But 'tis clear that you grieve him, too, and are ready to change your ways."

"I am," Jack replied. His voice sounded small compared with Fangard's.

"Then go in peace, lad. You are free."

For a moment, Jack thought he'd actually rocket upward with relief. It felt like the ceiling of the Felmar had been lifted from his back. And suddenly he didn't care that everyone was watching. They'd witnessed him make a public spectacle of himself, after all. So why not witness him attempt to make things right?

Speechless with gratitude, Jack nodded his thanks and turned away—but found himself face-to-face with the girl called Bem. The Ternivali with carroty hair even redder than his own, who'd formerly been the cat that'd stalked him in the bowels of Marisith.

"Oi, Jack," she said, planting herself in front of him. "I just wanted to tell ye . . . that was an impressive thing ye tried to do. To Stonefist."

He felt a flush of embarrassment. Great. She'd been there. She'd watched the whole epic disaster. "I wouldn't call it impressive, personally," he admitted. "More like stupid."

She shrugged. "How d'ye think I became a cat? I tried to attack Mindra all by meself. Had I been in yer shoes, facin' the giant, I woulda done the same thing."

Just in time, Jack stopped himself from gaping.

"And I'm sorry for giving ye such a fright," she added with a half grin.

"Oh, er . . . right," he managed to reply. "I should be *thanking* you, really. For . . . er . . . not letting me stay lost on my own under Marisith. Or at least, in retrospect, I think that's what you were doing. Keeping me company or something. And of course, thanks especially for rescuing me. Up there in the room of cages. Well, in the room that used to have cages . . ."

It was one of the longest—and most terrible—speeches of his life, made worse by the fact that Bem had bright green eyes and dimples that were . . . Okay, so they were really cute. He couldn't think of a more abysmal way to meet a girl.

Bem shrugged again. "Yer welcome, a'course. Well, cheers!"

Then she bounded away.

As Jack returned to his seat, he could've sworn he was floating.

Chapter

63

Earlier, while the Selvedge army was preparing the banquet, Elspeth had headed through the gallery's double doors with Frankie, Eva, Aurora, and Georgie.

They'd found themselves on a broad rampart overlooking the wide mouth of the River Ter, where it emptied into the Pathless. Warm sunlight had fallen upon their faces, and the glad cry of gulls filled the air. And not far away, just as Lord Edward had said, a tiny bundled figure was seated on a carven chair facing the water.

"So good to see you, Mrs. Fealston!" Eva had said, taking the old woman's hand. The retired housekeeper smiled up at her, then glanced at Aurora and each of the Addisons in turn. Finally her gaze stopped at Elspeth.

"You have something to say, I imagine," the old woman had observed acerbically.

Elspeth had hesitated, then stepped forward. "I do. I mean, we all do: Aurora, Georgie, and me. We're sorry for disobeying you. It wasn't right. Can you forgive us?"

Mrs. Fealston's expression had softened. "Of course, my dears.

Although you're very lucky things didn't turn out for the worse. In any case, everyone is here now. All is well."

"And you've finally gotten to see Ternival!" Georgie had exclaimed. "Like you'd always hoped!"

The old woman had turned her face toward the midsummer sun. "Yes, I most certainly have. Just once, before the end."

Frankie then leaned down and offered his arm. "They're setting the boards for a great feast, Mrs. Fealston," he'd said. "Shall we?"

So, in short order, they'd seated the old housekeeper at one of the trestles and settled themselves around her. The feast had begun.

Partway through, Aurora had turned to Mrs. Fealston. "So . . . about the frame," she'd said. "Can we use it to return to Carrick Hall? My dad insists *you're* the expert on how it all works."

The old woman had chuckled. "Expert, am I? Very kind of him, I'm sure. But I'm afraid it's all quite mysterious. Somehow, if you grasp hold of the frame as you pass through—instead of plunging willy-nilly into whatever picture it contains—the portal will stay open. And the frame will remain accessible from both worlds. Meanwhile, the picture itself will stay intact, but the reverse side will depict the world you've just come from. None of this is guaranteed, however—although, apparently, it's more reliable at the solstices."

"How did you learn all this, Mrs. Fealston?" Frankie had asked.

"From the person to whom the frame originally belonged, of course. But that," she'd added cryptically, "is not my story to tell."

And that was when Lord Bayard had climbed upon the chair near the head table. The company had toasted the memory of Starwise, the dryads had begun their promenade, and the lute's lively melody had filled the hall.

Now Elspeth stood off to the side, watching her only sister dance. Somehow Tilly had abandoned her habitual indecisiveness and was twirling confidently, weaving in and out of the Sisters like she was one of them. But instead of feeling jealous and resentful, Elspeth found herself longing, more than anything, to be reconciled—and not just with Tilly.

Quickly Elspeth set off in search of Georgie, whom she found at one of the trestles, devouring what was probably his sixth piece of mulberry pie. He glanced up, his nose and cheeks and chin stained a dark reddish purple.

"I'm sorry for saying such unkind things about your sketch," Elspeth said in a rush. "The map was really creative, and a lot of hard work. And I'm proud of you for trying."

Georgie swallowed. Then he gave her a smile so wide, with such disturbingly purple teeth, that for a moment he looked like a deranged vampire. "You're the *best,* Ellie," he declared.

Barkwhistler, who'd been loudly regaling a nearby group of rats with stories from the Battle of Marisith, now scampered up to Georgie. "Got any more of that frimlicious pie, lad?" the groundhog asked. "Me snozzwhiffler says it's time to fill the ole wamby again."

Georgie shoved a plate toward the rodent, then grinned again at Elspeth.

Taking this to mean she was forgiven, Elspeth spun around to find Aurora running toward her.

"There you are, Els!" said her friend. She halted, looking uncertain. "I just wanted to say I'm sorr—"

"Please, don't apologize." Elspeth cut her off. "It's all my fault. For being so cruel about the tapestry. What you wove was simply brilliant, but I was so caught up in being perfect that I hurt my best friend. I'm really, really sorry."

Aurora opened her mouth, then closed it and threw her arms around Elspeth in a bear hug.

"C'mon, Ellie!" a voice called. From the center of the dancing

Sisters came Tilly, breathless and sweating, her eyes bright. The music had switched to a rollicking reel, and before Elspeth knew what was happening, Tilly had grabbed her hands and swung her into the middle of the floor.

"But I don't know the steps!" Elspeth cried.

Tilly giggled. "Neither do I!" She linked elbows with a dryad, skipped around in a full three-sixty, then did the same with Elspeth.

"But what if I mess it up for everyone?" Elspeth gasped as they switched arms and skipped in the other direction.

Tilly pulled up short. She placed both hands on Elspeth's shoulders. "What if the keys hadn't been where Charles left them? Or the Rolls wouldn't start? Or we'd run out of petrol? What if Paxton had succeeded in ransoming himself and the crown?"

Tilly was repeating their argument from the footpath behind Zahra's hut.

Elspeth began to grin. "You'd still be my only sister," she replied. "And I'd still be yours."

"Always," Tilly agreed firmly. "For keeps. Now. Shall we ruin this dance together?"

Laughing, Elspeth looped her elbow through Tilly's and began to spin.

Eventually the two sisters—perspiring, exhausted, happy—headed to where Zahra and Arash were sitting with Jack and Aurora. Not far away, the fisherman rested on a bench against the wall, Paxton and Professor Rastegar by his side. The fellow looked weak and pale again, like he wasn't fully recovered.

"Is there nothing further you can do for him?" Elspeth overheard the professor say as she walked by. "No means to heal him for good?"

Paxton sighed in his melancholy way. "I'm no World-Weaver, alas. The rune of healing can only do so much for a permanent condition. I'm afraid what he really needs is modern medicine."

The sisters glanced at each other with concern and took their seats. Zahra was gazing happily at the dancers, oblivious. The old men, apparently, didn't want her to worry.

As the girls joined their friends, Arash looked over and then blanched at something beyond Elspeth's right shoulder.

"Oh no," he said faintly and ducked his head.

Elspeth swiveled around. Striding their way, his expression grim, resolute, came the son of Lord Edward Heapworth.

As Charles approached, everyone—including Tilly—froze.

"Hullo, Charlie," Aurora said after a beat.

Charles gave his sister a distracted nod. Then he turned to Arash.

"I don't expect you to forgive me, mate," he said in a stilted manner, as if reciting a formal pledge. "But I shouldn't have teased you about your batting. About anything, really. You're a first-rate fielder, and anyone would be lucky to have you on their team." Then Charles turned to Zahra. "And it was wrong of me to accuse you both of being traitors. People who look like—"

He stopped abruptly. Tilly had the impression he was calibrating some sort of internal compass, one that'd pointed off course for so long, he'd forgotten which way was north.

"I made assumptions based on appearances," Charles said, "and I'm realizing what a load of nonsense that is. And, worse, how much damage . . ." He paused again, his neck turning pink. "I've been a fool, and I'm sorry."

There was a long, awkward silence. Arash stared blankly at the wall, while Zahra fidgeted with the edge of her kurta. Their faces revealed very little.

But eventually Arash looked Charles in the eye.

"Thank you," the girl from Ternival murmured.

Charles nodded. Then he turned to Elspeth. "And I know it sounds dodgy, but I didn't write those notes. It wasn't me, because . . ." He gulped and glanced at Tilly. "Because I can't."

Elspeth frowned in confusion. "Can't *what?*"

"Oh, Charlie," Aurora whispered, as if she knew what was coming.

"You guessed, Roar?" He grimaced. "I suppose I shouldn't be surprised." He turned back to Elspeth. "You see, I've got no business attending Wolvern—or anywhere, for that matter. I only get to stay because of who my father is. Well, and because the school likes having a star cricketer on its rolls, for donor support and all that. The truth is . . . The fact is . . ."

His face grew bright red. Tilly had never seen Charles look so vulnerable.

"I can't read."

Elspeth's mouth fell open. "What?" Of the many things Tilly's sister thought Charles might say, this probably wasn't even on the list.

But Tilly had figured it out. Somehow her unconscious mind had stitched together all his odd behavior—from driving in circles around the Wolverns to merely smirking at the anonymous note from the tea shop—until the full picture had come into focus.

"Dyslexia, I think," Charles bumbled on, his neck flushing deeper by the second. "I mean, if I work really, really hard, I can figure out enough words to understand what something says. But not when I'm in a rush. Not under pressure. And I'm not much of a writer, obviously—but I've always been able to hide it, thanks to loads of tutors. Well, and the occasional classmate who isn't above bribery."

He looked apologetically at Arash.

"Anyway, that's no excuse for how I've treated you. But at least you know the notes aren't mine."

Again, Arash said nothing. There were no quick fixes here, Tilly realized. He might forgive Charles, eventually. Or he might not. And even if he did, the Rastegars' grandson wasn't about to get all chummy or anything. Rather like if someone has pushed you down the stairs, Tilly supposed. The person might apologize, but your limp will never go away. And meanwhile, you're not obligated to stand with them at the top of the stairs again, that's for sure.

"So, if *you* haven't been writing the notes," Elspeth asked Charles, "who has?"

"One of the tourists?" Aurora suggested.

"But it must be someone who lives in the Wolverns," Tilly countered. "It's been going on for weeks."

Another pause.

"Maybe we'll never find out," Elspeth said, scowling. "I *hate* that."

"Sometimes evil goes underground, you know," Jack said out of the blue. The group looked at him in surprise. "That's what Mrs. Fealston told me, anyway. Evil hides itself, from one generation to the next, before emerging again later, in some new form." He turned to Arash. "It's like something I heard your grandfather say, back at the bookshop. Some sort of Shakespeare quote."

"Which one?" Arash said.

Tilly swallowed a grin. She didn't know if Arash was the kind to deadpan a joke, since she'd never heard the kid speak before today. But then she noticed the crinkles at the corners of his eyes. After years of saying nothing at all, he'd mastered the art of the poker face.

"Danger deviseth shifts," Jack quipped. "Wit waits on fear."

"Because what evil hates most is to be exposed," came a quavering old voice from a nearby chair.

It was Mrs. Fealston, who was observing them from beneath drowsy lids. "The more we can stay vigilant," the old woman murmured, as if to herself, "and the more we can remind each other of what evil has done in the past—then the better chance we have of recognizing it when it returns. For it *will* return."

Everyone waited. Then, with a contented sigh, the retired housekeeper closed her eyes and began to snore.

At that moment, Lord Bayard stepped to the middle of the hall. The room fell silent.

"Alas, I must interrupt our revelry. The future of Ternival—and of our guests from Tellus—is, as yet, uncertain. Therefore, I request the presence of all captains, chieftains, and esteemed elders, from both worlds, in the council chambers."

Vahrberg, Fangard, and numerous other Ternivali followed Lord Bayard from the hall, along with Goldleaf and several other dryads.

"Are we 'esteemed elders'?" Tilly heard Frankie ask as he and Eva joined the exodus.

"I'm feeling rather youthful, personally," Lord Edward declared, coming up behind them. "Something about Ternival's unpolluted air, no doubt. Too bad we can't bottle it up and sell it, like mineral water. We'd make a fortune, by Jove! But, alas, elders we must be, because there's jolly ole Paxton and the professor, and that plucky fisherman fellow, waving us forward."

As the grown-ups left the room, Tilly realized that Charles was now standing beside her.

"Er, might we step away for a bit of a chat?" he said in a low voice.

She turned. His transformation from confident romancer to chastened, disheveled mess was total. But his eyes hadn't changed. They were still a startling bright blue, and they now studied her with a mixture of embarrassment and nervousness.

Tilly nodded and moved with him toward one of the deep windows that overlooked the courtyard.

"So . . ." he began, his neck flushing pink again. "When you called me insufferable, back in the tea shop . . . you had no idea, really. But you were right. That's what I am, and what I've been. And I know I've got a long road ahead to change all that. But at some point, along the way, I hope we might try again."

Out of habit, she was getting all melty. Those eyes . . . But she pulled herself together and kept her expression noncommittal. "What you said to Arash and Zahra," she told him. "I know that was really difficult. But important. And a good start."

The pink flush reached his cheeks. "Well, Dad *is* rather persuasive," he admitted. "I've got to work off the damage to the Rolls, of course. But I must do so by volunteering at the Rastegars' shops and coaching the junior cricketers. Oh, and he said he'll clear up everything with your parents, by the way. Put their minds at ease about why we all went missing. His usual vague ramble, I imagine, which neglects to mention literally anything of importance."

She bit her lip to hide a grin. Like her mother had said, Lord Edward had a way of sorting things out.

Just then, Georgie came bounding up. He'd given his face a scrub and looked slightly less deranged. "Any idea where Jack and Elspeth went?"

"Come to think of it," Charles said, looking around the hall, "I don't see my sister either."

"Nor Arash," Tilly added.

And that was when they heard it. The sound of a car engine, roaring away from Caristor.

Chapter

64

"How much time do you think we've got?" Aurora hollered to Arash.

"Maybe twenty minutes?" Arash yelled back. "Not sure."

The moment Aurora had fired up the Rolls and peeled away from Caristor—with Arash in the front seat and Jack and Elspeth in the back—the damage to Lord Edward's beloved car had become obvious. Its suspension was completely shot, and something near the front tires was grinding ominously. Aurora had to fight the steering wheel to keep it from cranking left, while every warning light on the dashboard blazed. There was no way to talk without shouting.

As they crossed the bridge and careened toward the beach, Elspeth pointed from the back seat at the fuel gauge. "Brilliant," Jack said with flat sarcasm.

Apparently, they'd be lucky to get there at all.

Arash held on to the seat as they turned right and raced along the beach. Far out to sea, a curtain of fog still blurred the horizon, but the air near shore was perfectly clear. Dead ahead, the army of trees was working on the chasm from the collapse of the Felmar. They didn't seem interested in repair, however. If anything, they were dredging it even deeper.

Then the Rolls banked left, onto what had been the strip of sand at the base of the peninsula's bluffs. But the beach was wider now. Low tide had opened up the shoreline, creating a broad straightaway toward the cliff on which Marisith stood. Aurora gunned it, and soon Arash could see the narrow bridge of sand that connected the mainland to the three rock islands. But the Three Queens weren't islands, at the moment—though that wouldn't last long.

As the Rolls drew closer to the base of the cliff, Arash caught his breath. The sand bridge was definitely getting narrower.

"Tide's coming in!" he yelled. "Just go ahead and park right up against the cliff, and I'll jump out and make a run for it."

But Aurora didn't stop. She didn't even slow. She just kept her foot mashed down on the gas as if the beach continued for miles. Out onto the sand bridge they roared, tires sloshing, spray zinging through the windows. Arash gripped the dash and glanced at Aurora, who wore the same smug expression as Charles whenever he bowled a fast yorker.

"Aurora!" Elspeth shrieked from the back seat. Even Jack looked shocked.

"You'll ruin it forever!" Arash shouted. The tires were beginning to bog down in the saturated sand.

Aurora stared at him in mock alarm. "By Jove, so I will!" she shouted back. It was such a pitch-perfect imitation of her father that Arash began to laugh.

And once he started, he couldn't stop.

It'd been so long since he'd used his voice like this that his larynx actually ached. But he wasn't laughing because of Aurora. Rather, he was making up for all the hundreds of times he wished he could've joked with peers, or cracked up in class, or even scoffed at guys like those drunk university students on the train—the ones whom Charles so resembled—who'd poured beer on Mum's weaving bag and mocked Grandfather's English and made Grandmother cry. The ones who'd humiliated Arash's family so completely that he hadn't spoken a word to non-family ever since.

Until today. Until he'd finally broken his silence in a room full of strangers and the spell had shattered.

The overwhelming freedom of it, the sheer power of that deliverance and restoration, made him laugh till he cried. By the time Lord Edward's doomed car ran out of petrol, sluggishly burbled past the first rock, and coughed to a stop in a foot of water, Arash could barely breathe.

But there was no time to dwell on the absurdity of it all. As his companions kicked off their shoes and waded into the shallows, Arash opened his backpack and retrieved the waterproof headphones his mum had bought him. Then he stuffed his socks, shoes, pullover, and glasses into the pack, rolled up his trousers, opened the door, and waded out to retrieve the Infinium from the boot. Within minutes, everything was hooked up and ready to go.

The others were already sloshing toward the center of the triangle made by the three rocks.

"Right about here, you think?" Aurora called. She peered into the chilly water, probing the sea bottom with her bare feet. "You said you aimed for dead center between them, but of course, the tide going out probably buried it a bit."

Arash nodded as he put on the headphones. Then he inspected the dials on the control housing. This was the moment of truth. Had the Infinium survived its rough handling? Was the battery still charged? Would he figure out how to adjust the controls for a saltwater environment?

There was only one way to find out.

Arash lowered the search coil into the knee-high water, then turned the dials. With a slow grin, he began waving the coil back and forth over the sea bottom.

Charles had been right. That'd been a brilliant bit of fielding, up there in the tower. And it was about to pay off.

Zahra looked around the hut one last time.

It seemed bereft and lonely without her mother's weavings. They were carefully layered inside the wooden chest, with other household items, or piled atop the large basket full of weaving supplies—both of which now waited by the door. Paxton would be here any minute to help haul her family's meager possessions up the footpath to the bluff, where his fire wagon would be waiting. But for the moment, she had the place to herself.

To bid farewell.

Roughly an hour ago, when they'd heard the other storm wagon leaving Caristor, Bem had been the one to pound on the doors to the council chamber. The Rolls was gone, Tilly had told the startled grown-ups, and so were Aurora, Jack, Arash, and Elspeth.

"Any idea where they've toddled off to?" Lord Edward had asked.

"Georgie thinks he spotted the Rolls way, way out there, on the beach below Marisith," Tilly had explained. "But we can't be sure."

"I'll track them with the Bentley shortly," Paxton had interjected. "But first, Lord Bayard has an announcement."

As the rest of Caristor's guests gathered round, the Chief Sentry had laid out the council's plans. The company from Tellus would return through the frame back to their world, taking the gems with them. And then the portal between worlds would be closed and carefully guarded—because Mindra, they believed, had fled to Islagard, only thirty miles offshore, to nurse her wounded pride and recover what little power she had left. She might even attempt to follow the call of both the gems and the crown. But without either, her power was weakened, if not utterly broken.

"But won't she still pose a danger to Ternival?" Zahra had heard Tilly whisper to Paxton.

"She might," he'd replied. "But Ternivali birds will keep watch on Islagard. And the sentries themselves will guard the shore. Might even attempt a siege of the island, to capture her at last. But in any case, if she tries to return and salvage the crown from the shallows, they'll be there to stop her."

Lord Bayard had then gestured toward Zahra's grandad. "Meanwhile, this noble fisherman—whose livelihood was destroyed when the enchantress stole his boat and whose health requires greater care than Ternival can provide—he shall join the company of Tellus, together with his granddaughter, to whom many of us owe our lives."

Zahra had turned to Grandad in confusion. "You mean, leave Ternival?" she'd whispered. "Leave our home?"

"Leave our temporary home for another," he'd replied gently. "At least in Tellus, we shall be among family."

So, while Grandad rested at Caristor to preserve his strength, Paxton had driven Zahra in his storm wagon to the footpath at the top of the bluff. From there she'd descended to the hut to pack her family's belongings as Paxton continued toward Marisith in search of the Rolls and its passengers. Eventually he would return to help Zahra lug everything up the bluff and take her back to Caristor.

Now Zahra waited on the hut's threshold. She was loath to leave. But did anything remain that was worth staying for? Mother was gone. Their boat too. Every ounce of their small stores had been shared with hungry guests. And if Grandad didn't receive help soon, Zahra might spend the rest of her days alone on the shores of the Pathless.

Voices were coming from the footpath. It was Paxton, bringing Arash, Aurora, Jack, and Elspeth with him. When they arrived at the hut, they all seemed twitchy with excitement, like they'd found a secret gift they couldn't wait to share with everyone. Something had happened to the Rolls, but they didn't say what. Cheerfully, they grabbed Zahra's wooden chest and the overflowing basket and began hauling them up the bluff to Paxton's fire wagon.

Zahra didn't follow. Paxton paused with her on the threshold, studying her face. His mournful expression was even more grieved than usual.

"*We were happy here, uncle,*" she whispered in Valanish. "*The three of us. Until Mother died. That was hard, but we were still happy, Grandad and me. And then the giants came.*"

Paxton nodded. "*Aye, lass. The three of us brothers were happy in Valan too.*"

"*And you never saw your mother, nor your home, again. Like me.*"

"*Nay, lass. Nor our father.*"

For a long moment Zahra couldn't speak. "*Must we always leave what we love?*" she whispered.

"*Not always. But neither can we hide away from the world in our own protective shell. That's what I've done, for far too long.*"

In the silence, she could hear the familiar waves whispering along the shore like the sound of her mother's fading heartbeat.

She knew it was time.

"*I am ready, uncle.*"

Paxton followed her down to the water's edge. There, on the shingle, she unfurled her family's most treasured tapestry of all, the ancient fragment with its shorn topmost edge, its shimmering turquoise waves, its undulating script.

The rune of peace.

Indeed, Grandad's rune had been the source of Ternival's tranquility for all the long years that he and his daughter and grandchild had dwelt on that shore. While the royal house had remained without a sovereign, the realm had known peace. Even after the enchantress had recovered one gem in the Night Wood and her power had begun to return, the combined strength of the rune in the mouths of Grandad, Mother, and Zahra had held Mindra back.

Then, one year ago, Mother had died. The rune had weakened. The enchantress managed to escape from the Night Wood and build her small army of giants and raptors on the abandoned island of Islagard. And eventually, at long last, she'd surprised Ternival by sea.

Now, however, Mindra's power was broken. She possessed no gems at all. No giants, no raptors. Not even the crown. And Ternival might yet remain untroubled, even without Zahra's family here. But just in case, Zahra would offer the only gift she had, the strength of her family's ancient blessing, before she left her home forever.

Here, on the shores of the Pathless, over the waters from which Mindra might dare to appear again, Zahra lifted her hands and spoke the rune of peace. Her grandad's language tumbled over her tongue like a sparkling brook, the words echoing along the bluffs, Paxton's eyes glittering with unfallen tears. And when she was done, she rolled up the tapestry and tucked it into her kurta, then climbed the footpath with Paxton to join the others. It was time to return to Caristor.

The Great Hall was a cacophonous din of farewells when they arrived. Bem and Goody Pearblossom gave Zahra and her grandad fierce hugs. Nearby, Goldleaf received her lantern back from Elspeth, followed by a swift embrace from Tilly. Arash, Paxton, and Jack were bidding farewell to the Selvedge remnant, and Lepp shook their hands, blinking rapidly. Off to the side, Charles stood by his father, looking chastened, while Aurora hugged everybody.

Georgie, meanwhile, was trying to convince Barkwhistler to come too. "You won't believe the motorcars!" the boy urged. "And the green lawns. So much great digging . . ."

"Much obliged by the invitation," the groundhog replied, "but I'm needed here, ye see. To keep watch on the ole blitheress with the other briffy sentries."

"Honored guests of Tellus"—Lord Bayard's voice now rose above the din—"the time has come."

In slow procession, the Ternivali lined up on either side of the long, bright gallery. The company from Tellus, together with Zahra and her grandad, gathered in a clump by the doors, while one of the dryads began to play a slow march on her lute. And then, at a signal from Lord Bayard, the company from Tellus passed through the saluting Ternivali toward the framed tapestry of Carrick Hall.

As they stood before the tapestry, Zahra clutched her grandad's arm. Jack, Elspeth, Arash, and Aurora hovered nearby, carrying her family's things. If all went as planned, Zahra would soon find herself, together with everything she held dear, in the kitchen at Carrick Hall. But would everything turn out as they hoped?

Mrs. Fealston, who was tottering along on the arm of Lord Edward, glanced up in sleepy confusion at the gathered company. Then she spotted the tapestry. Her eyes cleared, and her expression became stern.

"Everyone bound for Tellus must hold hands," she warned crisply. "We must return together, or the portal won't close properly."

Next to Zahra, Tilly swiveled round. "Wait. Where are Frankie and Eva?"

Georgie dashed to one of the windows overlooking the ramparts. "I see them!" he shouted, jumping up and down. "By the parapet. Ooooh, Frankie's holding her hands! And Eva is crying."

Zahra joined the crush of onlookers at the windows.

"Happy tears, I hope?" asked Aurora.

"Well, she's laughing," Jack said. "So I'm guessing that's a yes."

"Aw!" Tilly squealed. "She can't stop hugging him!"

"Do you suppose he finally popped the question?" Georgie asked.

Elspeth groaned. "Gah, Georgie . . . What else would he be doing?"

Just then, Zahra heard a distant rumble. It came from the peninsula of Marisith, where a green mass was moving slowly, like a lava flow, back to the mainland. The trees were finally retreating.

And then the jagged gash in the bluffs began to widen. The northern peninsula was breaking away. The entire thing was sliding, like a great glacier, out into the Pathless.

Finally the castle of Marisith, with its hideous tower and terrible tunnels—along with the ruined Rolls and all the other things they'd left behind—sank beneath the waves.

Epilogue

Jack handed Arash the geode he'd just found in the scree at the base of the crevasse.

"How about this for the last stone?" Jack said. He adjusted the straps of his new backpack and squinted at the clifftops. Morning sunlight had nearly reached the valley floor, which meant it was almost time for the funeral.

Arash carefully placed the geode atop the second of two cairns they'd built that morning: one in memory of Starwise and the other in memory of Mrs. Fealston. On the spot where once a castle had stood.

A distant bell began to toll.

"Well, I suppose we should be going," Jack said. "My family's probably at the church already. Meet you there? And then back here tomorrow, right? I wager you'll find loads of great stuff in the lake."

Arash nodded. "Although it'll have to be after cricket practice."

"Oh! Right."

Arash picked up his metal detector, and the boys skirted the lake toward the path that led out of the valley. At the crest of the ridge, they looked back.

Once, not long ago, a castle had appeared. A watchtower from another world. But now it was gone forever. And the portal was closed, and no one knew if they'd ever see that world again. If it weren't for the crown, wrapped in Arash's old T-shirt and returned to the niche in the Wolverns where the High Queen had stashed it, they might question whether any of their adventures had happened at all.

But Jack would never forget.

Because the stories were true. He believed them, every word.

And they were his stories now.

The
Princess
and the
Djinn

Selected Tales of Valan
Second Edition

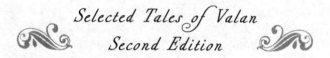

COMPILED AND TRANSLATED
BY S. RASTEGAR

ILLUSTRATED BY F. ADDISON

Carrick Hall Press | *Upper Wolvern*

The Weaver's Magic Runes

Long, long ago, there lived a humble weaver by the shores of the Caspian Sea. Known far and wide for his exquisite tapestries, he—with the help of his wife and young son—was kept busy day and night, spinning and weaving for all the noblemen of the land.

Then one day, the weaver began making the most beautiful tapestry in the world. Shot through with threads of silver and gold, it depicted an intricate pattern of birds circling above a mighty castle that overlooked the sea. And into its pattern he wove three powerful runes that would protect its owner with peace, healing, and deliverance.

While the tapestry was still incomplete, many a rich prince offered a fortune to own it. But the weaver would not sell. "I have worked all my life for other men," said he, "but this treasure is for my son."

Not long before the last thread was woven, an evil djinn arrived on horseback, pretending to be a wealthy nobleman who wished to buy the unfinished tapestry. But in truth, the djinn was enslaved to a cruel witch who desired the beautiful weaving above all things.

As usual, the weaver refused. Raging and cursing, the djinn stormed out of the hut. But before he rode away, he threatened to return and kill the whole family if the weaver did not deliver the finished tapestry to the witch's palace by sunrise.

That night, the weaver and his family swiftly finished the tapestry, cut it from the loom, and then fled with it by moonlight toward the caves behind their hut. Into one of these caves they ran, wandering deeper than they had ever gone. Soon they were lost in the dark.

Suddenly, they felt themselves sliding—not down but up—as if drawn by a powerful draft. Before long, their feet found solid ground, and they were standing in broad daylight on a strange shore in another world altogether.

They climbed up into the wooded hills above the shore, amazed by the beauty of the lush land. Even though they could hear birds singing amidst the cedars and small animals rustling in the underbrush, not a human soul or structure could be seen in any direction.

Then, as they traversed a marshy area, they heard some sort of creature struggling in a nearby bog. They drew closer. It was a huge silver hart, with antlers like great branches, up to its neck in mud.

Quickly, the weaver's son found a long, stout branch. Grasping his father's hand, he leaned over the mud and extended the branch to the hart, which grabbed hold of it with its jaws. The boy and his parents pulled, and the hart clambered out of the bog to safety.

"Thou hast rescued me," said the hart to the boy. "Therefore art thou granted sovereignty over all this land—thou and thine heirs forever."

Then, spying the tapestry they carried, the hart added, "And these runes I imbue with my powers of restoration, deliverance, and peace, which shall flow from thine hands and tongue to the hearts of all who art near thee. And wherever thou art, the land in which thou dwellest shall retain these powers too."

And so it was. The boy became king of that land and married a dryad, and their heirs were known for many generations as bringers of healing, liberation, and serenity.

In time, the language of the runes became the language of all that great people. And the land in which they dwelt was called Valan.

ERYLIESSA AND THE DJINN

Beyond the mountains, on the shores of the western sea, lies the land of Tarani.

Long ago, its isolated valley was peaceful and prosperous, protected by mountains to the south, the sea to the west, a great forest to the east, and barren lands to the north. Most of all, it was protected by an ancient crown that had been given to Tarani's first sovereign.

The crown had once held six magical jewels that sang with their own music and glowed with their own light. But at some point in the crown's long history, the jewels had been sundered from it and lost deep in the mountains. Even so, the crown by itself retained enough strength to sustain Tarani's peace for many a long year.

One fateful day, there came an evil witch disguised as a great lady to the court of Tarani. She wormed her way into the heart of the king, who eventually married her—but all the while, she secretly hungered for the crown and its power. And likewise did she crave the restoration of the jewels to their ancient settings, that the crown's power might increase a hundredfold.

Thus, into the king's ear did she whisper all manner of lies, that she might weaken his household, fray Tarani's borders, and disrupt its peace.

For when the time came, she wanted none to stand between herself and the crown.

By his wife's wicked counsel, the king accused his only sibling, a sister, of plotting to overthrow him. He set guards at her great house in the foothills of the mountains to ensure that none from her household could venture abroad without his knowledge. The sister—who was a gentle, loyal soul—grieved for her brother and feared for the safety of her loved ones. But things grew far worse than she could have dreamt.

One day in deep winter, news reached the sister's household that the witch-queen had slain the king and taken up his crown. Furthermore, a company of ogres and djinns had been dispatched to do the very same to all who remained of the royal line.

Weeping, she sent her only child, Eryliessa, into the mountains disguised as a servant. The young princess carried nothing but a bow, a full quiver, and enough food for a week. And indeed, the girl fled just in time. Her mother's household was soon overrun, and all that line was presumed to have perished.

And Eryliessa might have perished also, for one of the witch's djinns tracked her high above the tree line. The monster attacked, gloating of how it had killed her kin, while Eryliessa in fury sank all her arrows into its hide—but to no avail. Then, just when she thought all hope was lost, a young Valani sentinel emerged from behind a boulder and slew the djinn in the snow.

The sentinel was none other than the prince of Valan in disguise. He had been hunting alone on horseback in search of a huge silvery hart that was rumored to wander the far side of the mountains. But it was a fearsome journey. That very morning, the prince had been waylaid by a pack of wolves, which he had beheaded, one by one. Shortly thereafter, he had glimpsed the hart itself.

Marveling, he had followed the hart until it vanished. Then the refugee princess had appeared, and he had slain the djinn. Upon hearing Eryliessa's tale of woe, he abandoned his quest for the hart, that he might escort the princess over the mountains, away from Tarani, to safety. But he said nothing of his true identity.

On horseback they traversed the high passes down to the great desert that bordered his father's realm. But it would be a dangerous crossing. Earlier on his journey, the prince had slain two lions that had attacked his horse in the sands. So, as the prince and his guest crossed the desert by night, he kept vigil whilst she slept. By dawn they reached the fertile plain of Valan unharmed.

The sentinel took Eryliessa to the palace of the king on the shores of the southern sea, where it was revealed that he was, in fact, the Valani king's only child. By that point, he and the princess had fallen in love, and they were soon married. Upon the king's death, they ruled that noble land together.

Thus, the last living heir of Tarani's royal house also became queen of Valan. And both royal lines were intertwined from that day forward—though none in Tarani knew it.

Eryliessa kept her identity secret from all save her beloved husband and their heirs. But ever did she grieve her homeland beyond the mountains, and she told its tales to her children, and their children, and their children's children. Tales of the crown and its jewels. Tales of the witch and her overthrow of Eryliessa's family. Tales, especially, of an ancient prophecy to which the Tarani people had clung with hope. One day, it was said, the chosen sovereigns would appear, the lost jewels would be found, and the crown would be restored. And the witch, at last, would meet her doom.

Above all, Eryliessa taught her heirs to put their hope in the great hart, whose presence brought deliverance, restoration, and peace. She urged them also to search far and wide for the jewels. For in finding them might her heirs be protected from the witch's endless hunger, lest it destroy them all.

How the Jewels Were Found

The witch-queen reigned in Tarani for seventy-five years, never changing or growing old or lessening in strength. Indeed, she only grew stronger and sought to stamp out any subjects loyal to the murdered king.

And meanwhile, heavy snows fell in the high mountains year after year, and no news passed between the lands of Valan and Tarani.

Then, one autumn, another prince of Valan—Mirza, the great-grandson of Eryliessa—ascended into the mountains with a small company. He sought the lost jewels of which his great-grandmother had spoken. Yet if his quest failed, he hoped at least to cross the mountains and gaze upon her homeland. He longed to breathe its air and perhaps espy the hart, should the creature deign to appear.

But a great snowstorm overtook Mirza and his company in the highest pass, and they fled into nearby caves. There they were cut off from the lands below for three days.

Whilst the company from Valan waited out the storm, they explored the caves—one of which proved to be the entrance to an ancient mine. They followed its treacherous tunnels as far as they dared. But soon the prince became separated from the others. Wandering in the dark, Mirza fell into a crevasse. Though unharmed, he could discern no way out. All hope seemed lost.

Just then, he heard a lovely sound, like the singing of distant stars. Light shone from a fissure in the rock wall beside him. With his gloved hand, he reached in, grasped hold of the glowing thing, and drew it out. It was a clear crystal box, within which were six gleaming jewels.

The prince knew at once they were the lost jewels of Tarani. They gave off enough light that he was able to climb out of the crevasse and find his way back to the main tunnel, where he was reunited with his company. He told no one of his discovery, however. Instead, he wrapped the crystal box in a heavy woven cloak to muffle the jewels' light and music, then tucked it inside his satchel.

After the storm had passed, when the Valani company finally ventured from the caves, they came upon a dwarf from Tarani. He had likewise ridden out the storm and was returning to a secret rebel outpost in the mountains. From the dwarf, Mirza learned of the rebels' desire to overthrow the witch, if only they had the means to defeat her. And the prince's heart leapt within him.

At that very moment, one of Mirza's guards spotted a large raptor circling overhead. Fearing it was a spy sent by the witch-queen, the guard nocked an arrow and made ready to bring it down. But the dwarf stopped him. It was a loyal rebel from Tarani, the dwarf insisted. A messenger, by the look of it.

The falcon descended and delivered its news. Three maidens from another world had appeared in the Wilderlands. They were thought to be the hart's chosen sovereigns who would fulfill the prophecy and cast the witch from her throne at last. Indeed, the rebels were to muster on the northern downs in five days' time to storm her stronghold.

The prince hailed the falcon and its news with joy. Then did he offer the greatest gift in his possession for the rescuing of Tarani.

The six magical jewels.

The dwarf was amazed. He urged the whole company to join him at the rebel fortress, that they might be received with honor. But Mirza had further aid to offer. He pledged the strength of himself and his company against the witch. There was just one condition: that the prince's identity would not be revealed, nor would anyone speak of how the jewels were recovered or of Valan's role in the battle.

Disguising themselves as members of the mountain outpost, the Valani joined the dwarf's company and traveled with them to the mustering place. And then, with the rebel armies, they attacked the witch's fastness.

So great was her power, however, that they might have failed, were it not for three important things.

First, the eldest of the three maidens found the crown in the witch's hall, restored the jewels to their settings, and placed the crown upon her own head. Instantly the witch's spells were undone.

Second, the great hart, which had not been seen for many years, once again appeared. He banished the witch to the farthest reaches of the Wilderlands, where the distant song of the jewels would ever be a torment to her—and yet her hunger to possess them and the crown would never cease.

Finally, the three maidens were established by the hart as Tarani's royal sovereigns. And thus was that great land saved.

The young prince of Valan never revealed his true identity, despite having a fair claim to the throne himself. For Mirza deeply respected the prophecy and the hart's choosing of the three maidens. So he departed with his company.

But before he left, he bid a fond farewell to one of the rebels. It was a young fellow from a family of fishmongers who dwelt near Tarani's ruined royal house. Unaware of the prince's identity, this fellow had nonetheless saved his life in battle. Now that the witch was defeated, the fishmonger sought to return home, build his own hut on the shore, and help restore the castle to its former glory.

So Mirza returned the way he had come—first to the rebel outpost in the mountains and then, after many long weeks, back to his wife, Ziba, and three young sons at their palace by the southern sea.

THE THREE LOST PRINCES

A few years after the witch-queen was banished from Tarani, she somehow learnt of the Valani prince's role in her defeat. By this time, Mirza's father had died and the prince had become king. So to the palace the witch dispatched a huge, cruel raptor. Laughing wickedly, it delivered her message:

For thy role in my undoing—and for thy betrayal of the jewels—thou art cursed, as are thy children and thy children's children. Forever shall they fear me. And once my power is restored, they shall perish in fire and agony, and thine heirs shall be stamped out for all ages.

Mirza's counselors tried to persuade him to kill the bird for its insolence. But he was an honorable man and did not fault the bird for its tidings nor its temperament. He let it go.

But his wife, Ziba, was distraught. The queen feared that the raptor would tell the witch about their household, especially about their three young sons. What if the witch someday became strong enough to make good on her threat?

Nothing the king said could persuade his wife that they were in little danger. And she was right to fear. For the raptor indeed returned to the wilderlands and told the witch of all that he had seen. And thus, the witch cursed each of the king's sons in turn and renewed her pledge to destroy them all.

Rumors of the witch's fury soon reached the court of Valan. Deeply grieved, the king and queen realized they had no choice but to send their young sons far, far away. The three princes would be sundered from one another, for their own safety, and raised in distant lands by those who could be trusted to keep their heritage a secret.

So, that very day, the family fled the palace to the caves along the shore where their ancestors had arrived, centuries earlier, from another world. Each cave contained a portal to a distant land—whether the land be in their own world or another—and by these would the princes be transported to safety.

But before the boys left, their parents gathered them into their arms. They embraced each child and gave him this warning: "Tell no one who thou art. Tell no one these tales unless they be friends of Valan or Tarani. And even then, be wary. For though many worlds may lie between the witch and thee, yet she might grow in strength and find thee still."

Then each son was given a fragment of the ancient tapestry from their ancestor, the weaver, into which was woven one of the three runes of power. To the youngest prince, Shahin, they gave the topmost portion, which depicted a flock of circling birds intertwined with the rune of deliverance. To the middle prince, Navid, they gave the bottom portion, which depicted undulating waves inscribed with the rune of peace. And to the eldest, Pejman—heir of both Valan and Tarani—they gave the middle portion, which depicted a castle interwoven with the rune of restoration.

The eldest son they sent to the kingdom in another world from which all the Tarani sovereigns thus far had come. There he was raised by an older childless couple who understood his incurable melancholy.

For they, too, had once fled the witch-queen's power and grieved all that was lost.

The middle son they sent to Tarani, near its newly restored castle, where he was raised by the fishmonger and his family. By this son's vigilance, Tarani knew many decades of peace, despite the absence of a sovereign to grace its royal house.

And the youngest they sent away by the same portal that had brought their ancestor, the weaver, thither. This prince was raised by a doctor and his family in a humble village near the Caspian Sea. In time, the prince married the doctor's incomparable daughter, became a brilliant scholar, and skillfully recorded these tales in the language of all their hearts.

None of the brothers knew where the others had been sent. And thus might they have lived in loneliness and exile to the end of their days, were it not for the bravery of their grandchildren.

Acknowledgments

If the first book in this series, *Once a Queen,* took longer to write than anything should, *Once a Castle* was a delirious blur of a roller coaster. That I survived at all is thanks to the following heroes.

My editor and friend, Sarah Rubio (and the whole WaterBrook/ Penguin Random House team!), who is as worthy a candidate for sainthood as anyone I've ever met.

My literary agents, Alice Fugate Brown and Henry Thayer, who somehow managed a mid-series Olympic-relay handoff with barely a pause. I'm ridiculously lucky!

My fantastic crew of beta readers, who were given mere days to blitz through the manuscript but managed to deliver thoughtful, helpful, reputation-saving feedback anyway: Alice (again), Nicole Mazzarella, Keiko Nakamura, Allison Spooner, and Aleta Watton, among others. A special thank-you to Cyrus McGoldrick, whose insight and encouragement brought me to (happy) tears.

My local teen launch team for *Once a Queen,* who came out in force to kick off this series and are eagerly awaiting book 2. Crowns for everyone!

Sarah Mackenzie and the amazing community at Read-Aloud Revival, who selected *Once a Queen* for their summer book club.

Book 2 is for all your lovely families, especially those awkward preteen-teen sibling relationships.

Daniel Nayeri, who has so kindly cheered me on behind the scenes. I couldn't have asked for a better instructor in the art and craft of YA lit, including how not to waste the "prime real estate" of the opening sentence.

David Bates, who weighed in on authentic Britishisms and dialogue. (Any errors are entirely my own).

My parents, Bob and Peg Faulman, who were my first patrons of the arts. This vocation wouldn't be possible without you!

My preteen/teen sons, Micah and Sam, who listened at bedtime as I read material I'd written that day. Your feedback and enthusiasm were more delightful, heartening, and validating than you'll ever know.

My husband, Tom, whose love and support mean all the world(s).

I'm amazed and humbled. May all our words deliver joy, courage, and hope!

Sarah Arthur is a fun-loving speaker and the author of over a dozen books for teens and adults, including the bestselling *Once a Queen* and *Walking with Frodo: A Devotional Journey Through The Lord of the Rings*. After decades working with teens, she plays a wicked game of four square, but don't ask her to eat cold pizza from a box, ever. Among other nerdy adventures, she has served as preliminary fiction judge for *Christianity Today*'s Book Awards, was a founding board member of the annual Northern Michigan C. S. Lewis Festival, and co-directs the Madeleine L'Engle Writing Retreats. Her preteen/teen sons have Very Important Things to Say About Books, and so far, *Once a Castle* is their favorite Carrick Hall novel.

SNEAK PREVIEW OF BOOK 3,

ONCE A CROWN

"There's a prince in the toolshed," Georgie announced.

Elspeth's youngest brother tromped into the kitchen at Carrick Hall and slammed the door behind him.

Elspeth didn't bother looking up from her book. Georgie was always saying things like that. *There's a dryad in the old grove.* Or, *Giants are playing at ninepins again.* And just yesterday, *There's a footballer at Wolvern who can play on air. No, like, really on air. He can fly.*

While such things were certainly possible, as Elspeth well knew, the likelihood of an *actual* prince in the toolshed was slim. Especially if the news came from Georgie.

"Shut it, mate," said their middle brother, Jack. The freckled redhead sat nearby, poring over a topographic map of the Wolvern Hills.

Elspeth glared at Jack. "Must you be so unkind?"

"I've got a mum already, thanks," he retorted. Of all the Addison siblings, Jack had the least amount of patience for Georgie's tales.

"I'm serious. There's a prince in the toolshed," Georgie repeated, "and he's talking to Frankie."

"Frankie's back?" Elspeth threw down the book. "Why didn't he tell us?" She launched to her feet and dashed out the door.

The July sun had set. A blue-gray gloaming lingered in the kitchen garden, blurring the walls and hedges. But sure enough, there in the doorway of the lamplit toolshed stood their oldest brother, Frankie. And he was definitely talking to someone. After spending two weeks in Chicago visiting Eva, his American fiancée, Frankie couldn't have called to tell them he was coming home?

Georgie stumped along behind Elspeth. He never simply walked normally—he marched like a stocky foot soldier. "I told you," he insisted. "There's a prince. It's the footballer who can play on air. He can fly."

Elspeth rolled her eyes. "C'mon. You're old enough—"

She'd almost said "to know better" but stopped herself. After the wild adventures they'd had with their siblings and friends—during which they'd tumbled through magic portals into the fairy-tale land of Ternival—she'd learned not to second-guess her siblings. Not even Georgie.

And anyway, it was impossible to embarrass the kid. When he was convinced he was right, nothing could sway him. Dryads, giants, magic footballers—he believed all of it. And now princes. Princes who were magic footballers.

As Elspeth threaded her way through the dark, voices came to her from the toolshed.

"Not to worry," Frankie was saying in that alarmingly grown-up way he had now. "The window was already cracked and needed replacing. No harm done."

"I—I can clean it up," came an anxious voice with a lilting accent. It sounded like a youngish guy.

"It's too dark right now," Frankie reassured him. "One of us here can do it in the morning."

"I'm . . . Well, thanks," the guy replied.

"Oh," Frankie added, "and here's the ball—soccer ball, as my fiancée would say. That must've been quite a kick. More than eighty yards from the trees, eh?" He sounded just a touch skeptical, like he knew more than he was saying.

The other speaker gave a short laugh. "Something like that," he said with pride in his voice.

"Well, good luck."

The guy emerged from the toolshed, holding a football. Lithe and alert, dressed in a Wolvern Summer Camp shirt from the boarding school on the adjoining property, he walked with his dark head held high. Like the son of a sultan. Exactly as Georgie had said.

Elspeth paused. She'd seen this student before.

It'd been this afternoon, when she'd taken a walk by the wall along the back of the school property. At the time, she'd thought it odd that while the other campers were kicking a ball around the pitch, this guy was digging up a vine instead. Like he wasn't a camper at all. And yet he'd been wearing the requisite school shirt, like everyone else.

Then the ball had flown out of bounds in his direction. He'd turned, locked eyes on it, and one-touch-kicked it expertly—no, *miraculously*—into the goal.

There'd been an awed silence.

Finally, a snide voice had said, "Back to work, Bijan." It was an older girl whose shining black hair rippled in the sunlight. The other players had laughed, the coach had blown a whistle, and the pitch had emptied out—all except for the guy named Bijan. He'd gone back to the vine. As he pulled it up viciously, Elspeth had felt the sudden urge to help him, questioned the awkwardness of that gesture, and then hurried along the trail before he could see her.

Now, coming upon the two siblings in the garden, the guy halted.

"Did you kick it from the treetops?" Georgie blurted. "Like you did last night? I don't know how you can fly, but you're brilliant!"

Bijan's panicked glance darted from Georgie to Elspeth and back again.

"Georgie!" Elspeth whispered.

Her brother tipped forward in a clumsy bow. "Oh, I mean, *Your Highness.*"

The guy's face calcified into a wounded sneer, giving his cheekbones angry, hollowed-out edges. Like he'd been denied proper food for a year. It was then that Elspeth noticed how skinny he looked, how actually hungry.

"Begging your pardon," Bijan said, his lips barely moving. "Must get back." He pivoted off the path and strode down a vegetable row till he reached the exit to the circle drive. Then he vanished like a gaunt ghost in the deepening dark.

Elspeth rounded on Georgie. "Why did you say that? He thought you were mocking him."

Georgie's shoulders slumped. "I didn't mean it that way," he said. "Really, I didn't."

Frankie sauntered toward them from the toolshed, hands in his pockets. "Hullo there, littles. Miss me?"

"Why didn't you tell us you were coming back tonight?" Elspeth demanded. "Mum would've waited on you for supper."

"Happy to see you too."

"Well?"

"Estate business, if you must know. I was able to catch a flight last-minute and didn't have time to call."

"You should get a mobile, like Eva," Georgie declared.

Frankie looked at him in mock horror. "And chain myself to *you* lot? I've got enough on my plate already, thank you very much."

Elspeth hadn't yet adjusted to the idea that her oldest brother was now a man. Gone was the cautious, earnest boy who'd worked the gardens with their father and grandfather. Gone was the teenager who'd drawn elaborate pictures by firelight to entertain his younger siblings, the kid whose fervent belief in fairy tales had actually proved true. In that boy's place was the grown-up Frankie, who—by virtue of his upcoming wedding to Eva Joyce, heiress to Carrick Hall— would eventually be responsible for all the land they could see.

"I wish Eva could've come back with you," Georgie said wistfully.

"Ah, little man," Frankie said with a sigh. "You're not the only one."

"*Must* you wait so long to get married?" Georgie continued as they began to make their way back toward the kitchen.

"I'm afraid so. Her internship at the Art Institute lasts through August, and then we'll need time to get the Hall in order."

"But won't you be lonely here without her?" Everyone knew that Georgie had a crush on his future sister-in-law. And who could blame him? With her ginger-blond curls and breezy summer fashion, Eva was a bright contrast to her family's grim, lifeless estate.

Frankie chuckled. "Well, I'll have Kinchurch's papers to keep me company. It'll take me at least till the end of summer hols to catalog everything." As part of his doctoral research, he was sorting through trunks of materials that'd once belonged to the Hall's former owner, Professor Augusta Kinchurch. She'd penned a collection of fairy tales about Ternival, long ago, under the alias A.H.W. Clifton. Most people assumed the stories were fictional. But Eva and the Addison siblings knew otherwise.

"That guy in the toolshed," Elspeth interrupted. "I've seen him at the school. Who is he? Why was he here?"

"He can fly, you know," Georgie added.

Frankie raised an eyebrow. "Oh?"

"Well?" Elspeth pressed.

"An accident. That's all," Frankie explained. "I was walking up the drive when I saw the football sail over the gardens. Heard the crash. Toolshed window broken, of course. The kid showed up a minute later, full of apologies. No harm done, though. The old window was ready to break."

"But who is he?"

"No idea."

"A prince," Georgie said sadly. "And I ruined everything."

The three siblings approached the kitchen stoop.

"C'mon," Elspeth said. "There's pork pie in the larder."

"I wish he could eat some too," Georgie said. "He was the hungriest prince I've ever seen."

Read the first book in the series

ONCE A QUEEN

by SARAH ARTHUR

 WATERBROOK